Lincolnshire
COUNTY COUNCIL

D0785619

JM

This bo ~~ok should be returned~~ **r before** ~~the due date.~~

NA1

w.deloresfossen.com.

James, a *New York Times* bestselling author, started
ing when her sister challenged her to write a romance
She has managed a full-time job and raised three
erful children, and she and her husband even tried
ing exotic birds (ostriches, emus and rheas). Ask
nd she'll tell you what it's like to go toe-to-toe
an angry three-hundred-and-fifty-pound bird! Elle
to hear from fans at ellejames@earthlink.net or
ames.com.

To re

05205191

Discover more at millsandboon.co.uk

Court ignored the call, and the ding of the voice mail that followed, and went up the steps to the front door. This wasn't his first time here. Once, he'd made many trips to Rayna's door—before she'd chosen another man over him. Once, he'd had feelings for her. He had feelings now, too, but they had nothing to do with the old attraction he'd once felt.

He steeled himself and put his hand over his firearm in case Rayna wasn't finished with her shooting spree today.

"Open up," Court said, knocking on the door. Of course, he knocked a lot louder than necessary, but he wanted to make sure she heard him.

If she did hear him, she darn sure didn't answer. He knocked again, his anger rising even more, and Court finally tested the knob. Unlocked. So, he threw open the door.

And he found a gun pointed right in his face.

Rayna's finger was on the trigger.

Court cursed and automatically drew his own weapon. Obviously, it was too late because she could have fired before he'd even had a chance to do that. She didn't though. Maybe because Rayna felt she'd already fulfilled her quota of shooting McCalls today.

"Put down your gun," he snarled.

"No." Rayna shook her head, and that was when he noticed there was blood in her blond hair. Blood on the side of her face, too. Added to that, he could see bruises and cuts on her knuckles and wrists. "I'm not going to let you try to kill me again."

"Again?" Court was certain he looked very con-

fused. Because he was. "What the devil are you talking about? I came here to arrest you for shooting my father."

If that news surprised her in the least, she didn't show it. She didn't lower her gun, either. Rayna stood there, glaring at him.

What the hell had happened here?

Court looked behind her to see if the person who'd given her those injuries was still around. There was no sign of anyone else, but the furniture in the living room had been tossed around. There was a broken lamp on the floor. More blood, too. All indications of a struggle.

"Start talking," Court demanded, making sure he sounded like the lawman that he was.

"I will. When Egan gets here."

Court cursed again. Egan definitely wasn't going to approve of Court storming out here to see her, but his brother also couldn't ignore the evidence that Rayna had shot their father. There was definitely something else going on though.

"My father's alive," Court told her. "You didn't manage to kill him after all."

She looked down at his shirt. At the blood. And Rayna glanced away as if the sight of it sickened her. Court took advantage of her glance and knocked the gun from her hand.

At least that was what he tried to do, but Rayna held on. She pushed him, and in the same motion, she turned to run. That was when Court tackled her. Her gun went flying, skittering all the way into the living room, and both Court and she landed hard on the floor.

Rayna groaned in pain. It wasn't a soft groan, and while holding her side, she scrambled away from him.

Court was about to dive at her again, but he saw yet more blood. This time on the side that she was holding.

That stopped him.

"What's wrong with you? What happened?" Court snapped.

She looked around as if considering another run for it, but then her shoulders sagged as if she was surrendering.

Rayna sat up, putting her weight, and the back of her head, against the wall. She opened her mouth as if to start with that explanation, but she had to pause when her breath shuddered. She waved that off as if embarrassed by it and then hiked up her chin. It seemed to him as if she was trying to look strong.

She failed.

"When I came in from the barn about an hour ago, there was someone in my house," Rayna said, her voice still a little unsteady. "I didn't see who it was because he immediately clubbed me on the head and grabbed me from behind." She winced again when she rubbed her left side. "I think he cracked my ribs when he hit me with something."

Well, hell. Court certainly hadn't expected any of this. And reminded himself that maybe it was all a lie, to cover up for the fact that she'd committed a crime. But those wounds weren't lies. They were the real deal. That didn't mean that they weren't self-inflicted.

"I got away from him," she continued a moment later. "After he hit me a few more times. And I pulled my gun, which I had in a slide holster in the back of my jeans. That's when he left. I'm not sure where he went."

That didn't make sense. "If someone really broke

in an hour ago, why didn't you call the sheriff's office right away?"

Rayna lifted her head a little and raised her eyebrow. For a simple gesture, it said loads. She didn't trust the cops. Didn't trust *him*.

Well, the feeling was mutual.

"I passed out for a while," she added. She shook her head as if even she was confused by that, and she lifted the side of her shirt that had the blood. There was a bruise there, too, and what appeared to be a puncture wound. One that had likely caused the bleeding. "Or maybe the guy drugged me."

"Great," he muttered. This was getting more far-fetched with each passing moment. "FYI, I'm not buying this. And as for not calling the cops when you were attacked, you called Egan when you saw me," Court pointed out.

"Because I didn't want things to escalate to this." She motioned to their positions on the floor. "Obviously, it didn't work."

He huffed. "And neither is this story you're telling." Court got to his feet and took out his phone. "Only a couple of minutes before my father was gunned down, a waitress in the diner across the street from the sheriff's office spotted you in the parking lot. There's no way you could have been here in your house during this so-called attack because you were in town."

She quit wincing so she could glare at him. "I was here." Her tone said *I don't care if you believe me or not.*

He didn't believe her. "You must have known my father had been shot because you didn't react when I told you."

"I did know. Whitney called me when I was walking back from the barn. I'd just gotten off the phone with her when that goon clubbed me."

Whitney Goble, her best friend. And it was entirely possible that Whitney had either seen his father get shot or heard about it shortly thereafter because she worked part-time as a dispatcher for the sheriff's office. It would be easy enough to check to see if Whitney had indeed called her, and using her cell phone records, they could possibly figure out Rayna's location when she'd talked to her friend. Court was betting it hadn't been on Rayna's walk back from the barn. It had been while she was escaping from the scene of the shooting.

"This waitress claims she saw me shoot your father?" Rayna asked.

He hated that he couldn't answer yes to that, but Court couldn't. "She was in the kitchen when the actual shot was fired. But the bullet came from the park directly behind the sheriff's office parking lot. The very parking lot where you were right before the attack."

Judging from her repeated flat look, Rayna was about to deny that, so Court took out his phone and opened the photo. "The waitress took that picture of you."

Court didn't go closer to her with the phone, but Rayna stood. Not easily. She continued to clutch her side and blew out some short, rough breaths. However, she shook her head the moment her attention landed on the grainy shot of the woman in a red dress. A woman with hair the same color blond as Rayna's.

"That's not me," she insisted. "I don't have a dress that color. And besides, I wasn't there."

This was a very frustrating conversation, but thankfully he had more. He tapped the car that was just up the street from the woman in the photo. "That's your car, your license plate."

With her forehead bunched up, Rayna snatched the phone from him and had a closer look. "That's not my car. I've been home all morning." Her gaze flew to his, and now there was some venom in her eyes. "You're trying to set me up." She groaned and practically threw his phone at him. "Haven't you McCalls already done enough to me without adding this?"

Court caught his phone, but he had to answer her through clenched teeth. "We haven't done anything."

She laughed, but there wasn't a trace of humor in it. "Right. Remember Bobby Joe?" she spat out. "Or did you forget about him?"

Bobby Joe Hawley. No, Court hadn't forgotten. Obviously, neither had Rayna.

"Three years ago, your father tried to pin Bobby Joe's murder on me," Rayna continued. "It didn't work. A jury acquitted me."

He couldn't deny the acquittal. "Being found not guilty isn't the same as being innocent."

Something that ate away at him. Because the evidence had been there. Bobby Joe's blood in Rayna's house. Blood that she'd tried to clean up. There'd also been the knife found in her barn. It'd had Bobby Joe's blood on it, too. What was missing were Rayna's prints. Ditto for the body. They'd never found it, but Rayna could have hidden it along with wiping her prints from the murder weapon.

The jury hadn't seen it that way though.

Possibly because they hadn't been able to look past one other piece of evidence. Bobby Joe had assaulted

Rayna on several occasions, both while they'd been together and after their breakup when she'd gotten a restraining order against him. In her mind, she probably thought that was justification to kill him. And equal justification to now go after Court's father, who'd been sheriff at the time. Warren had been the one to press for Rayna's arrest and trial. After that, his father had retired. But Rayna could have been holding a serious grudge against him all this time.

She'd certainly held one against Court.

He heard the sound of a vehicle pulling up in front of Rayna's house and knew it was Egan before he glanced out the still-open door. He also knew Egan wouldn't be pleased. And he was right. His brother was sporting a scowl when he got out of the cruiser and started for the door.

Egan was only two years older than Court, but he definitely had that "big brother, I'm in charge" air about him. Egan had somehow managed to have that even when he'd still been a deputy. Folks liked to joke that he could kick your butt even before you'd known it was kicked.

"If you think Egan is going to let you walk, think again," Court warned her.

"I won't let him railroad me," she insisted, aiming another scowl at Court. "I won't let you do it, either. It doesn't matter that we have a history together. That history gives you no right to pull some stunt like this."

They had a history all right. Filled with both good and bad memories. They'd been high school sweethearts, but that "young love" was significantly overshadowed by the bad blood that was between them now.

Egan stepped into the house, putting his hands on

his hips, and made a sweeping glance around the room before his attention landed on Court. "Please tell me you're not responsible for any of this."

"I'm not." At least Court hoped he wasn't, but it was possible he'd added some to the damage when he tackled her. "Rayna said someone broke in."

Court figured his brother was also going to have a hard time believing that. It did seem too much of a coincidence that his father would be shot and Rayna would have a break-in around the same time.

"You shouldn't have come," Egan said to him in a rough whisper.

Court was certain he'd hear more of that later, but he had a darn good reason for being here. "I didn't want her to escape."

"And I thought he'd come here to kill me," Rayna countered. "I pulled a gun on him." She swallowed hard. "Things didn't go well after that."

Egan huffed and grumbled something that Court didn't catch before he took out his phone and texted someone.

"Court didn't do any of the damage in this room," Rayna added. "It happened when an intruder attacked me."

That only tightened Egan's mouth even more before he shifted his gaze to Rayna. "An ambulance is on the way. How bad are you hurt?" he asked and put his phone back in his pocket.

She waved it off, wincing again while she did that. Yeah, she was hurt. But Court thought Egan was missing what was really important here.

"She shot Dad," Court reminded Egan. "We have the picture, remember?" Though he knew there was no way his brother could have forgotten that. "It's proof she was there. Proof that she shot him."

"No, it's not." Egan groaned, scrubbed his hand over his face. "I think someone tried to set Rayna up."

Court opened his mouth to say that wasn't true. But then Egan took out his own phone and showed him a picture.

"A few minutes after you stormed out of the hospital," Egan continued, "Eldon Cooper, the clerk at the hardware store, found this."

"This" was a blond-haired woman wearing a red dress. An identical dress to the one in the photo the waitress had taken. But this one had one big difference from the first picture.

In this one, the woman was dead.

Chapter Two

Rayna slowly walked toward Egan so she could see the photograph that had caused Court to go stiff. It had caused him to mumble some profanity, too, and Rayna soon knew why.

The woman in the photograph had been shot in the head.

There was blood. Her body was limp, and her lifeless eyes were fixed in a permanent blank stare at the sky.

Rayna dropped back a step, an icy chill going through her. Because Court had been right. The woman did look like her. The one in the first picture did, anyway. The second photo was much clearer, and while it wasn't a perfect match, the dead woman looked enough like her to be a relative. But Rayna knew she didn't have any living relatives.

"Someone killed her because of me?" she whispered.

Neither Court nor Egan denied it.

She felt the tears threaten. The panic, too. But Rayna forced herself not to give in to either of them. Not in front of Court, anyway. Later, she could have a cry, tend to her wounds and try to figure out what the heck was going on.

"Who is she?" Rayna asked.

"We don't have an ID on her yet, but we will soon. After the medical examiner's had a look at her, then we'll search for any ID. If there isn't any on her body or in the car, we'll run her prints."

It was so hard for Rayna to think with her head hurting, but she forced herself to try to figure this out. "Why would someone go to all the trouble of having a look-alike and then leave a car behind with bogus plates?"

Egan shrugged again. "It goes back to someone setting you up." He sounded a little skeptical about that though. "Unless you hired the woman in that photo to pose as you. You could have gotten spooked when something went wrong and left the car."

Even though she'd braced herself to have more accusations tossed at her, that still stung. It always did. Because this accusation went beyond just hiring an impostor. He was almost certainly implying that she had something to do with the woman's death, too.

"No. I didn't hire her," Rayna managed to say, though her throat had clamped shut. "And I didn't shoot your father. I haven't been in town in weeks, and that wasn't my car parked near the sheriff's office."

Egan nodded, glanced at Court. "She's right about the car. The plates are fake. I had one of the deputies go out and take a look at it. It's still parked up the street from the office. Someone painted over the numbers so that it matched the plates on Rayna's vehicle."

Again, Egan was making it sound as if she had something to do with that. Good grief. Why was she always having to defend herself when it came to the McCalls?

Of course, she knew the answer.

She'd made her own bed when it'd come to Bobby Joe. She had stayed with him even after he'd hit her and called her every name in the book. She had let him rob her of her confidence. Her dignity.

And nearly her life.

But Egan and Court—and their father—hadn't seen things that way. Bobby Joe had kept the abuse hidden. A wolf in sheep's clothing, and very few people in town had been on her side when Warren McCall had arrested her for Bobby Joe's murder.

"You're barking up the wrong tree—again," Rayna added. "I didn't have anything to do with this. And why would I? If I were going to shoot anyone, why would I send in a look-alike? Why would I pick a spot like Main Street, which is practically on the doorstep of a building filled with cowboy cops?"

Egan shrugged. "Maybe to make us believe you're innocent and knew nothing about it."

"I am innocent," she practically yelled. Rayna stopped though and peered at the mess in the living room. "But maybe my intruder is behind what happened in town and what happened to that woman, as well. He could have arranged to have your father shot, killed her, and then he could have come out here to attack me. His prints could be on the lamp. It's what he used to bash me over the head."

Court looked at her, and for a split second, she thought she saw some sympathy in his intense gray eyes. It was gone as quickly as it'd come, and he stood there, waiting. Maybe for an explanation that would cause all of this to make sense. But she couldn't give him that.

Rayna huffed. "If I was going to do something to fake an assault, I wouldn't have hit myself that hard on my head or cracked my ribs. And I wouldn't have broken my grandmother's lamp."

It sickened her to see it shattered like that. In the grand scheme of things, it wasn't a huge deal, but it felt like one to her. It was one of the few things she had left of her gran. And now it was gone—much like what little peace of mind she'd managed to regain over the past year.

"Who do you think would have done something like this?" Court asked, tipping his head toward the living room.

"Bobby Joe," she answered without thinking. She knew it would get huffs and eye rolls from them, and it did. "You think he's dead, that I killed him. But I know I didn't. So, that means he could still be out there."

Court didn't repeat his huff, but she could tell he wanted to. "So, you think Bobby Joe set you up for my father's shooting and then came out here and attacked you? If he's really alive, why would he wait three years to do that?"

Rayna gave it some thought and didn't have an answer. However, she wouldn't put it past Bobby Joe. At the end of their relationship, he'd threatened to kill her. Maybe this was his way of doing that. Bobby Joe could be toying with her while also getting back at Warren McCall, who hadn't managed to get her convicted of murder.

But there was something else. A piece that didn't seem to fit.

"Tell me about the waitress," Rayna insisted. "Who was she, and why did she take the picture of the woman in the parking lot?"

"Her name is Janet Bolin," Court answered. "She said she took the photo because she thought you…or rather the woman…was acting strange."

Egan groaned. Probably because he was agreeing with her theory of an ill-fitting puzzle piece. "I'll get a CSI team out here to process the place." He pressed a button on his phone and went onto the porch to make the call.

"You know this waitress?" Rayna asked Court.

He shook his head. "She's new, has only been working there a week or so, but I've seen her around. We'll bring her in for questioning."

Good. Because it meant Rayna was finally making some headway in convincing Court that she hadn't fired that shot or had anything to do with that woman's death.

She hesitated before asking her next question. "How's your father?" Warren was a touchy subject for both of them.

A muscle flickered in Court's jaw. "He's out of surgery but still unconscious. We don't know just how bad the damage is yet."

He might have added more, might, but a sound outside stopped him. Sirens. They were from the ambulance that was coming up the road. Since her house was the only one out here, they were here for her.

"I don't want an ambulance," she insisted. "I'll go to the hospital on my own." And it wouldn't be to the one in McCall Canyon. She would drive into nearby San Antonio.

"That's not a very smart thing to do." No pause for Court that time. "We're not sure what's going on here. Plus, your ribs could be broken. You don't need to be driving if they are."

She couldn't help it. Rayna gave him a snarky smile before she could stop herself. "Worried about me?"

That earned her another glare, but this one didn't last. And for a moment she saw something else. Not the sympathy this time, either. But the old attraction. Even now, it tugged at her. Apparently, it tugged at Court because he cursed again and looked away.

"I just wanted to make sure I didn't hurt you when we fell on the floor," Court said.

"You didn't." That was probably a lie, but Rayna was hurting in so many places that it was hard to tell who was responsible for the bruises and cuts.

Court's gaze came back to her. "Was there anything…sexual about the assault after you got hit on the head?"

"No." Thank God. That was something at least. "In fact, I'm not even sure he intended to kill me. I mean, he could have shot me the moment I walked into my house—"

"Maybe he didn't have a gun. He could have been robbing the place and got spooked when you came in."

True. But that didn't feel right. Neither did the spot on her ribs, and Rayna had another look. Too bad that meant pulling up her top again, and this time Court examined it, too. He leaned in, so close that she could feel his breath hitting her skin.

"It looks like a needle mark," he said. "And you mentioned something about passing out?"

She nodded. "But the man was gone by the time

that happened." Of course, he could have come back. Heck, he could still come back.

That made her stomach tighten, and she gave an uneasy glance around the front and side yards. There were plenty of places on her land for someone to hide.

"You're sure it was a man?" Court asked. He was using his lawman's tone again. Good. That was easier to deal with than the old attraction. "You said you didn't get a look at the person, so how do you know it was a man?"

"I've had a man's hands on me before, so yes, I'm sure he was male." She immediately hated that she'd blurted that out, even if it was true. But Rayna didn't like reminding anyone, especially Court, of just how wrong she'd been about Bobby Joe. After all, she'd let Court go to be with him.

"After he clubbed me with the lamp," Rayna added, "he hooked his arm around my throat. My back landed against his chest, so I know it was a man."

Court took a moment, obviously processing that, and he looked at the lock on the front door. "There's no sign of forced entry. Was it locked, and did you have on your security system?"

Everything inside her went still. With all the chaos that had gone on, it hadn't occurred to Rayna to ask herself those questions. "Yes, it would have been locked, and the security system was on. I never leave the house without doing that."

"Even if you were just going to the barn?" Court immediately asked.

"Even then." She gathered her breath, which had suddenly gone thin again. It always did when she thought of the woman she'd become. "I honestly believe Bobby Joe is alive and that he could come after me."

Court looked ready to grumble out some profanity, but Rayna wasn't sure if that was because he felt sorry for her or because he thought she was crazy for being so wary about a man he believed was dead.

"The front door was unlocked when I got here," Court continued several moments later. "Is it possible your intruder had a key?"

"No. And I don't keep a spare one lying around, either." She kept her attention on the ambulance that stopped behind the cruiser. "Plus, he would have had to disarm the security system. It's tamperproof, so he couldn't have simply cut a wire or something. He would have had to know the code."

With each word, that knot in her stomach got tighter and tighter. She had taken all the necessary precautions, and it hadn't been enough. That hurt. Because she might never feel safe here again in this house that she loved. Her gran's house. That didn't mean she would leave. No. She wouldn't give Bobby Joe the satisfaction of seeing her run, but Rayna figured there'd be a lot more sleepless nights in her future.

Egan was still on the phone when the medics got out of the ambulance and started for the porch. Rayna went out to tell them they could leave, but she spotted another vehicle. A familiar one.

Whitney's red Mustang.

"You called her?" Court asked.

Rayna shook her head, but it didn't surprise her that Whitney had heard about what happened and then had driven out to see her. They'd been friends since third grade, and even though that friendship had cooled a little after Rayna had gotten involved with Bobby Joe, Whitney had usually been there for her. Whitney was also one of the few people who'd stood by her when Rayna had been on trial.

Her friend bolted from the car and ran past the medics to get to Rayna. Whitney immediately pulled her into her arms for a hug. An uncomfortable one because Rayna felt the pain from her ribs, and she backed away.

"I came as fast as I could get someone to cover for me at work." Whitney's words rushed together. "My God, you're hurt." She reached out as if to touch the wound on Rayna's hand, but she stopped. "It must be bad if the ambulance came."

"No. They were just leaving." Rayna made sure she said that loud enough for the medics to hear.

"They're not leaving," Court snapped, and he motioned for them to wait. No doubt so he could try to talk Rayna into going with them.

Whitney volleyed puzzled looks between Court and her. "Is, uh, anything going on between you two? I mean, you're not back together, are you?"

"No," Court and Rayna answered in unison, but it did make Rayna wonder what Whitney had picked up on to make her think that.

Whitney released her breath as if relieved. Maybe because she knew Rayna wasn't ready for a relationship. Especially one with Court McCall.

"What happened here?" Whitney asked, glancing inside.

"Someone broke in," Rayna settled for saying. She planned to give Whitney more information later, but her friend filled in the blanks.

"And you think it was Bobby Joe," Whitney concluded. But she immediately shook her head after saying that. "It seems to be more than that going on. I mean, what with Warren being shot."

Court made a sound of agreement. "Do you have a key to Rayna's house? And no, I'm not accusing her of anything," Court quickly added to Rayna. "I'm just trying to figure out how the intruder got in."

"No key," Whitney answered. "Bobby Joe wouldn't have one, either. Rayna changed all the locks after she was acquitted. She had the windows and doors wired for security, too. Did she tell you that she has guns stashed all around the house?"

Rayna gave Whitney a sharp look to get her to hush. But it was too late. After hearing that, Court was probably even more convinced that she was about to go off the deep end.

"So, are you coming with us?" one of the medics called out. He sounded, and looked, impatient.

Rayna knew him. His name was Dustin Mendoza. A friend of Bobby Joe's. Of course, pretty much every man in McCall Canyon in their midthirties fell into that particular category.

"No," Rayna repeated.

She figured Court was about to do some repeating as well and insist that she go. He didn't. "I'll drive Rayna to the hospital. I need to ask her some more questions about the break-in."

Dustin didn't wait around to see if that was okay with her. He motioned for his partner to leave, and they started back for the ambulance.

"I also think you should consider protective custody," Court said to her. "The intruder obviously knows how to get in your house, and he could come back."

That had already occurred to Rayna, but it chilled her to the bone to hear someone say it.

"You can stay with me," Whitney suggested. "In fact, I can take you to the hospital."

It was generous of Whitney, and Rayna was about to consider accepting, but Court spoke before she could say anything. "That could be dangerous. For Whitney. If this intruder is still after you, he could go to her place while looking for you."

That drained some of the color from Whitney's face. Obviously, it wasn't something she'd considered when she'd made the offer.

"It's okay," Rayna assured her. "I can make other plans."

She didn't know what exactly those plans would be, but she might have to hire a bodyguard. And put some distance between her and the McCalls. Whatever was going on seemed to be connected to them. Rayna didn't think it was a coincidence about the timing of Warren's attack, the break-in and the dead woman.

Egan finally finished his call, and the moment he turned to walk toward them, Rayna knew something was wrong.

"Is it Dad?" Court immediately asked.

Egan shook his head. "It's the waitress. Janet Bolin. She's dead. Someone murdered her."

Chapter Three

Another murder. Two women killed only hours apart. There was no way Court could dismiss them as not being connected.

But connected to what?

Rayna. His father. Or maybe both.

He put on a clean shirt that he took from his locker and thought about that possible connection while he made his way back into the squad room, where Rayna was waiting. Or rather where she was pacing. He nearly reminded her that she should probably be sitting down. That was what the doctor had wanted anyway when he'd come to the sheriff's office to examine her. Rayna wasn't having any part of that though. And he couldn't blame her. It was hard to sit still with all this restless energy bubbling up inside him.

"Anything?" she asked the moment she saw him.

Court took a deep breath that sounded as weary as he felt. "There's no gunshot residue on your hands." He'd swabbed her hands as soon as they'd gotten to the sheriff's office but hadn't been able to run the test right away because of all the other calls.

And changing his shirt.

Court had figured he'd worn his father's blood long enough and no longer wanted it in his sight.

Rayna didn't huff, but it was close. "Tell me something I don't know. Of course there wasn't gunshot residue on my hands, because I didn't fire a gun."

He almost pointed out that she could have cleaned up afterward, but plain and simple, that probably hadn't happened. And it wouldn't explain how she'd gotten all those wounds. So, Court did as Rayna asked and gave her something she almost certainly didn't know.

"Janet was killed with a single shot to the head at point-blank range. Her body was in the alley behind the diner, and it doesn't appear as if she was moved after she was shot. No ID yet on the other woman."

But the two had something in common. There'd been no defensive wounds, which meant their killer had gotten close enough to deliver the fatal shots without alarming the women.

"No one in or around the diner heard the shot?" she pressed.

"No. But she had her purse, and Pete, the cook, said she had three more hours on her shift. She didn't have a cell phone on her, but maybe she'd made arrangements to meet someone."

And that *someone* had killed her.

That could mean Janet was in on his father's shooting. Or maybe she'd just been duped into taking the photo that had almost certainly been meant to frame Rayna.

"There aren't any surveillance cameras back there," Court added. That pretty much applied to most of the town. Simply put, there hadn't been much need for them.

Until now, that was.

There'd been only two murders in the past ten years. A drunken brawl at the local bar and Bobby Joe's. But now they had two unsolved homicides, an attempted murder, breaking and entering, and an assault. It was no wonder Egan had been tied up in the past three hours. His brother was at the first murder scene, and that was why Court had been manning the phones along with keeping an eye on Rayna.

Court hadn't mentioned it yet, but she was now a key witness, since she might be able to recall something about the man who'd attacked her. She was almost certainly in grave danger, as well.

"It doesn't make sense," Rayna mumbled.

It was something she'd said multiple times after Court had insisted that she come to the sheriff's office. Well, first he'd tried to talk her into going to the hospital, and when he'd failed at that, he'd brought her here instead. It was far better than her being at Whitney's, and both Rayna and she had finally agreed on that. Rayna had also agreed on the doctor seeing her.

"How are your ribs and your head?" Court asked.

"Fine," she answered, practically waving off his concern.

But he knew there had to be some pain. The doctor didn't think her ribs were broken, but there was a deep bruise, and a second one on her head where the intruder had hit her.

"The doctor drew blood," she added, rubbing the inside of her arm. "Whatever the thug slammed into me might still be in my system."

Yeah, but it might not give them any new info to catch him. Still, it was something they needed to know so they could make sure it didn't have any serious side effects.

He tipped his head toward Egan's office, which was just off the squad room. "There's a semicomfortable chair in there. Some bottled water, too. You could sit and wait while I call the lab and push them to get an ID on the first woman."

Rayna stopped pacing and made eye contact with him. "You're being nice to me."

Was he? Court lifted his shoulder. "I just figured we could call a truce and try to get through this hellish day."

Rayna kept staring at him a moment before she nodded and headed for the office. Court was right behind her, but he glanced around the squad room first to make sure all was well. There was only one other deputy, Thea Morris, who was taking a statement from another waitress who worked at the diner. The other four deputies were out at their three crime scenes.

"If you want to go to the hospital to see your dad," Rayna said, "please do. I know you'd rather be with him."

He would. But his father was still unconscious, so there was nothing Court could do. Plus, his mom, Helen, and his sister, Rachel, were there. Along with a Texas Ranger, Griff Morris, who Warren had practically raised. He was like family, and he'd call Court if there were any changes in his father's condition. Or if any more trouble surfaced. Right now, Court would do his dad more good by trying to figure out who'd put that bullet in him.

"You don't have to babysit me," Rayna added.

He did indeed have to do just that, and Court didn't bother to pull any punches when he looked at her.

"Oh," she said, and Rayna looked even more unsteady when she sank into the chair across from the desk.

"It's not personal," he added because he thought that might help. Help who exactly, Court didn't know. It certainly felt personal. And it couldn't. He couldn't let their past—either the good or the bad parts—play into this.

He made the call to the lab, promptly got put on hold, so while he was waiting, Court took a copy of her statement that he'd printed out and passed it to her.

"Look this over and try to fill in any gaps in details," he instructed. "For instance, do you remember hearing the sound of a vehicle when your attacker fled?"

"No." Rayna sounded steady enough when she said that, but when Court gave her a closer look, he saw that she was blinking back tears. Waving them off, too, when she realized he'd noticed.

"I hate this," she said. "I've spent three years rebuilding my life, and now it feels as if it's falling apart again."

Court had no idea how to respond to that, so he stayed quiet, fished out a box of tissues from the bottom drawer and passed them to her.

"I took self-defense classes," she went on. "Firearms training. I installed a security system and don't go anywhere without a gun. Except here, of course."

He would have liked to have told her there was no need for one here, that she was under the roof with two deputies, but since his father had been shot just yards from here, he doubted his words would give her much assurance. Plus, there was the part about her not trusting him.

"You did all of that because you were afraid of Bobby Joe returning?" Court tried to keep his tone neutral. They already had enough battles to fight without his adding some disbelief to that.

"Not afraid," Rayna said in a whisper. "I wanted to be able to stop him if he came after me again. I learned the hard way that I can't rely on others to help me with that."

Court couldn't help himself. It was a knee-jerk reaction, but he went on the offensive, something he usually did with Rayna. "I arrested Bobby Joe after you'd had enough of him and decided to press charges," he reminded her.

"Yes, and he spent less than an hour in jail. After that, he threatened to kill me, stormed out and then faked his death to set me up."

If that had truly happened, then Court felt bad that he hadn't been able to do more. But that was a big *if*. Most folks had liked Bobby Joe and gotten along with him just fine.

Court wasn't one of those folks.

Bobby Joe and he had always seemed to be bristling at each other. Maybe because Rayna and Court had dated through most of high school. Bobby Joe could have been jealous, and Court figured his own bristling stemmed from the fact that Rayna had crushed his heart when she'd broken up with him.

But that was water under a very old bridge.

"Are you ever going to at least consider that Bobby Joe could be alive?" Rayna asked.

He didn't have to figure out what his answer would

be because Clyde Selby, the lab guy, finally came back on the line. "Sorry to keep you waiting," Clyde said. "I wanted to see what we had on the second woman before I spoke to you. Anyway, the first woman, the blonde, is Hallie Ramon. She is, *was*, a college student. She was in the system because of a drug arrest when she was eighteen. But she didn't have any gunshot residue on her hands, so I don't think she's the one who shot your dad."

Court felt the slam of disappointment. Whoever had done this was still out there.

He immediately pulled up everything he had on her. There wasn't much. No record other than the drug possession. The woman was twenty-four and didn't even have a traffic ticket. But then something caught his eye.

"She was a drama student." Court hadn't meant to say that aloud, but it certainly caught Rayna's attention.

She moved to the edge of her seat. Court hated to disappoint her, but there likely wouldn't be anything else from the lab. Any new info now would come from working the case, and that meant talking to Hallie's friends to find out how she was connected to what had happened in McCall Canyon.

"You mentioned the second woman," Court prompted Clyde.

"Yes. Janet Bolin. Egan sent me her prints, and there's no match for her. Don't know who she is because unlike the first woman, she's not in the system. No driver's license, nothing."

Court groaned. That meant she'd lied when she'd applied for the waitress job. Had probably even used a fake ID. That was going to make it a whole lot harder.

Because until they knew who she was, they wouldn't be able to figure out how she was connected to this.

"Is she here?" someone yelled. "I want to see her now!"

Court instantly recognized the voice and knew this would be trouble. It was Mitch Hawley, Bobby Joe's brother. And the *she* that he was yelling about was almost certainly Rayna.

She got right up out of the chair and whirled to face Mitch. And not just face him. She went straight out into the squad room. If she was the least bit afraid of him, she didn't show it.

But she should have.

Unlike Bobby Joe, Mitch was not well liked, and he had a nasty temper. Court had had to arrest him on several occasions for fighting. That was why Court hurried to get between them. He didn't mind arresting Mitch again, but he didn't want the man hitting Rayna. Mitch was a big guy, around six-two, and he was heavily muscled. A build that suited him because he worked with rodeo bulls, but his fists could do a lot of damage.

"Why isn't she locked up?" Mitch snarled.

"Because I haven't done anything wrong," Rayna answered.

"Right. You killed my brother, and now you shot his dad." His gaze flew to Court. "Please tell me you're not covering for her."

"No need. There's no GSR on her, and at the time of the shooting, someone was attacking her. What do you know about that?"

That put some fire in Mitch's already fiery brown eyes. "Are you accusing me of something?"

"Not at the moment. Right now, I'm asking a question. Depending on how you answer it, I'll make an accusation or not."

Rayna shook her head, maybe asking Court not to fight her battles, but he wasn't. With everything else going on, he hadn't had time to work on who'd attacked Rayna, but because of their history, Mitch was an automatic suspect.

"No. I didn't go after her. Didn't have anything to do with this hell-storm that hit town today." Mitch snapped toward Rayna as if ready to return some verbal fire, but he stopped, smiled. "Looks like somebody worked you over good."

"Was it you who did it?" Court pressed, getting Mitch's attention back on him.

The man had to get his teeth unclenched before he could speak. "No. I wouldn't waste my time on a killer. But I can't believe you'd just let her walk. She had motive to shoot your father."

"Yeah, and so do you," Court reminded him. "In fact, I seem to remember you pressing my dad and the rest of us to put Rayna behind bars. We did, and she was acquitted. End of story."

"No, hell, no. It's not the end." He flung his index finger in her direction. "If she's capable of killing my brother, she's capable of anything."

"Apparently not," Rayna spoke up. "I'm not capable of convincing anyone that *not guilty* means I didn't do it." She spared Court a glance to let him know he fell into that category, too.

"Because you bought off the jury or something. I begged Warren to try to reopen the case against you—"

"There's no case to reopen," Court interrupted. He was getting a glimpse of what Rayna had been dealing with for the past three years. "She can't be tried again because that's double jeopardy."

"Then find something else. Conspiracy or tampering with evidence." Mitch paused only long enough to curse. "Next week is the third anniversary of my brother's murder, and no one has paid for that."

And no one might pay. Court kept that to himself though. Simply put, Rayna had been their one and only suspect.

"Why'd you go to my father with all of this?" Court asked.

Mitch huffed, clearly annoyed with that question. "I went to him because I don't get anywhere with Egan and you, that's why. I figured I could get him to sway you into doing something. Warren told me to let it go. To get a life. Can you believe that?"

Yeah, he could. Warren could be steel-hard and cold. Even though his father hated that Rayna had been acquitted, he hated even more that Mitch was blaming the McCalls for that.

Mitch rubbed his head. "I can't let it go. I keep dreaming about Bobby Joe. Nightmares. It's as if he's trying to tell me from the grave to get justice for him." He looked up, blinked, the expression of a man who felt he'd maybe said too much. Or maybe Mitch just hadn't wanted them to hear the raw emotion that was still in his voice.

"There is no new evidence to charge Rayna with anything," Court said. "Not Bobby Joe's murder and not my father's shooting."

"Then you're not looking hard enough," Mitch snarled. His face hardened. "And she's responsible for that. She's got you convinced that she's the same girl you loved back in high school. Well, she's not."

Mitch moved his hand toward Rayna as if he might take hold of her, but Court snagged his wrist.

"It's time for you to go," he warned him.

Mitch threw off Court's grip with far more force than necessary. "You should have known she'd pull something like shooting your dad. The signs were there. Even Janet said so."

Court pulled back his shoulders. "Janet?"

"Yeah, the new waitress at the diner across the street. I was in there earlier this week…" Mitch stopped. He must have realized Rayna's and Court's expressions had changed.

"What did *Janet* say about me?" Rayna demanded.

Some of that fire started to cool a bit, and Mitch got quiet for several long moments. "She knew a lot about you. About what'd happened with Bobby Joe. She asked me questions about it."

Court jumped right on that. "What kind of questions?"

Mitch volleyed some glances at both of them and shook his head. "Things like how often Rayna came into town and such."

Bingo. It meant she was spying on Rayna. "Did Janet ever say anything about hurting Rayna or getting back at her for some reason?" Court asked.

Mitch's eyes widened. "No. Of course not. She wouldn't have. I mean, what with her being a private detective and all."

Now Court was certain his own eyes widened. "What made you think she was a PI?"

"She let it slip, and I saw her ID once when it fell out of her pocket. I thought you knew."

Court glanced at Rayna to see if she had any idea about this. She didn't. She shook her head.

"I thought you knew," Mitch repeated. "After all, Janet was working for your father. Warren's the one who hired her."

Chapter Four

Answers. That was what Rayna needed right now. Along with another place to stay. She only hoped she managed to get both soon.

Her place wasn't exactly safe, so that was why Court had brought her to the guesthouse on the grounds of his family's ranch. She felt as if she'd slept in the enemy's camp. With her enemy, since Court had stayed the night with her. She was betting though that there hadn't been much sleeping going on. There certainly hadn't been on her part. She hadn't been able to turn off her mind. Hadn't been able to forget that someone was trying to frame her for murder.

Again.

If Bobby Joe was truly behind this, then she prayed he'd just go ahead and show his face so she could put an end to this once and for all.

Since the cabin wasn't that large, Rayna had no trouble hearing someone moving around in the kitchen. Court, no doubt, because she also smelled coffee. While she wasn't especially anxious to face him, she did need some caffeine, and maybe he would have updates that would give her those answers. Specifically, updates on his father. She needed to know if Mitch had been right when he said that Warren had hired the now dead waitress.

If he had, then maybe this was Warren's twisted way of trying to send her to jail. This time for good.

But Rayna had to mentally shake her head at that thought. From all accounts, Warren could have been killed when he was shot. If this was a plan he'd orchestrated, he wouldn't have put his life at risk like that.

Rayna took a deep breath to steady herself and walked into the kitchen. Not a long trek at all, only a few yards. She immediately saw that she'd been right about it being Court in the kitchen. Right about the coffee, too, because he was pouring himself a cup.

"You're up and dressed," he commented, sounding relieved.

That relief was probably about the being dressed part though. It would have been too much of a trip down memory lane if she'd just been wearing her nightgown—or nothing at all—since Court had brought her here a couple of times when they'd still been dating.

"I wore my clothes to bed," she said, making a beeline for the coffee. That way, if they were attacked, she would be ready to run or fight back. "I'll need to go back to my place and check on the horses."

"I sent a couple of the ranch hands over to do that. I didn't think it was a good idea for you to be out in the open like that."

No. It wasn't a smart idea, but Rayna still wished she could at least see the horses. Just being around them usually calmed her, and she desperately needed that right now.

"Thanks," she muttered. She was surprised and glad

that Court had thought to do something like that. Of course, she'd probably been on his mind most of the morning, not in a good way, either.

"In case you're still in pain." Court slid a bottle of pain meds across the counter toward her. It was the prescription stuff the doctor had called into the pharmacy for her. Apparently, someone had picked it up and brought it to the ranch.

She thanked him again but wouldn't take any. Her head was already cloudy enough without adding those to the mix. "Please tell me you have good news."

His shrug didn't give her much hope. "My dad's still not conscious, so we haven't been able to ask him about Janet or whoever the heck she is. But we did get back your results from the blood test the doctor took, and you were drugged. It was a barbiturate, definitely meant to knock you out."

Then it was mission accomplished for her attacker, and he'd likely done that so she wouldn't show up in town at the same time as Hallie Ramon, the woman in red who had been near the sheriff's office. And either the woman had been there to shoot Warren or else Hallie had been set up, just as someone had attempted to do to her.

"What about you?" he asked. "You remember anything new about the person who drugged you?"

She had a long sip of coffee and shook her head. "But last night I called the company that installed my security system. They insist no one who works for them would have given out my code to disarm the system."

"Even if they had, there's the problem with the key," Court pointed out. "There were no signs of forced entry."

"No, but getting the key would have been easier than getting the security code. I don't take my house key off the ring when I give it to the mechanic for an oil change." Though she would do that in the future. "I also don't know if the locksmith I used made a copy of the key and gave it to someone."

She knew she was sounding a little paranoid, but Rayna needed to look at all angles here. Unfortunately, there were probably other times when maybe her purse, and therefore her keys, had been out of her sight long enough for someone to make a molding of the house key.

Yes, definitely paranoid.

He paused to have some coffee, as well. "Unless you forgot to lock the door. Maybe forgot to set the system, too."

Rayna was shaking her head before he finished talking. "I don't forget those things. Not after what happened with Bobby Joe. I know you don't believe it, but he's out there."

No, Court didn't believe it. She could see the doubt in his eyes. And maybe he was right.

Rayna huffed. "If Bobby Joe's dead, I didn't kill him, and that means if he's not out there, then his killer is. That's why I lock the doors. That's why I have a security system."

He made a sound that could have meant anything. "Why did you stay if you think Bobby Joe or his killer will come back?"

She heard more of those doubts, and while Rayna didn't think she could make him understand, she tried anyway. "I wasn't born into money. And, no, that's not a dig about you and your family. It's my clumsy way of saying that I can't just pick up and leave even if that's what I wanted to do."

Which she didn't. That house was her home where she'd been raised. Where once she'd been happy. She was hoping to reach that happy status again.

"Besides," Rayna added a moment later, "training horses is something I love doing, and I'm fortunate enough that it pays the bills." That along with the money she got from boarding horses from some folks who lived in town. The occasional riding lessons, too.

Court stared at her, and he obviously had something on his mind. "You never collected Bobby Joe's life insurance money. It was for fifty grand, and he left it all to you."

Yes, he had. Considering the big blowup Bobby Joe and she'd had just weeks before his disappearance, it surprised her that he hadn't changed his beneficiary. But then if he'd truly wanted to set her up for his murder, he would have left her name on the policy.

"I have no intentions of touching that money," she said.

Court stared at her, cursed under his breath, and he paused a long time. "I'm sorry about what happened yesterday when I tackled you like that. I was half crazy when I went out to your place."

That was true, but it was a craziness she could understand. She didn't get a chance to tell him that though because his phone rang, the sound shooting through the room. Her nerves were so frayed and raw that it caused her to gasp.

"It's Thea," he said when he glanced at the screen.

He knew the call could be important, and that was why Court answered it right away. He also put it on speaker.

"Your dad's awake," Thea stated, and with just those three words, Rayna could hear the relief in the deputy's voice. "He's still pretty groggy, but I thought you'd want to come and see him."

"I do." Court reached for his keys and his Stetson. He was already wearing his holster and weapon. But he stopped and looked at Rayna.

She could see the debate he was having. He didn't want to leave her there alone, but Court probably didn't want her near Warren, either. The debate didn't last long though.

"Rayna will be with me," he said to Thea. "What kind of security is in place at the hospital?"

"There's a guard posted outside Warren's door. Egan is there, too. And so is Griff."

Two lawmen and a security guard might not sound like a lot, but in this case, Warren was well protected.

"Good. We'll be there in fifteen minutes," Court assured Thea, and he ended the call.

Since it was normally about a twenty-minute drive from the McCall Ranch to town, Rayna guessed that they'd be hurrying. And they did. Court didn't waste any time getting her into the truck parked directly in front of the cabin, and they drove on the ranch road and then got onto the highway that led to McCall Canyon.

"It won't be a good idea for you to go into my father's room," Court said several minutes later, and he didn't give her a chance to disagree with that. "You can wait with Griff while I talk to him."

Court was right. She wanted to know if Warren had hired the dead PI, but he was far less likely to own up to anything with her in the room. Still, it wouldn't be a pleasant experiencing waiting with Griff. Yes, he would keep her safe, but he was firmly on the side of Warren when it came to anything, since Warren had practically raised Griff and his sister after their parents had been sent to jail for selling drugs.

"Keep watch," Court reminded her.

Even though she was already doing that, it caused her pulse to jump. The attack from the previous day was still way too fresh in her mind. Plus, she was having some pain, especially where the idiot had injected her with that drug. The seat belt was pulling right across the tender bruise.

"Are you okay?" Court asked.

He was frowning and glancing at her midsection. That was when Rayna realized she was holding her side. She was probably wincing, too. She nearly lied and told him everything was fine, but Rayna knew he wouldn't believe her.

"I'm hurting. I'm scared. And I'm mad. Yes, I messed up when I got involved with Bobby Joe. I should have never been with him in the first place, and I should have never stayed after the first time he hit me."

She wasn't sure how Court would react to that and expected him to dismiss it. He didn't. Even though he only glanced at her, she saw something in his eyes. Sympathy, maybe. If that was it, she didn't want it.

"I was a fool," she added. That not only applied to her relationship with Bobby Joe. She'd also been a fool to choose him over Court.

"Why exactly were you with him?" Court asked.

The burst of anger had come and gone, and now Rayna got a dose of something else that was familiar. Shame. There were plenty of emotions that came with the baggage of being in a relationship with someone like Bobby Joe.

"Because I didn't think I deserved anything better," she said. She certainly hadn't deserved Court.

He frowned. "What the heck does that mean?"

She hadn't expected him to understand. "You're a McCall from the right side of the tracks. You have a father and mother who love you." Rayna didn't have a clue who her father was, and her mother had dumped her at her grandmother's when Rayna had been in first grade.

Court's frown continued, and he added some profanity to go along with it. "You're telling you think you deserved to be with a jerk because you had some bad breaks in life?"

"I know it doesn't make sense to you." She looked at him. "It doesn't make sense to me now, either. I finally had, uh, well, an epiphany after Bobby Joe hit me the second time, and I knew if I stayed with him, the violence would only continue. Probably even get worse. That's when I ended our engagement." She paused. "And you know the rest."

Whether he believed the *rest* was anyone's guess, and there wasn't time to ask him. That was because he pulled to a stop in front of the hospital. He didn't use the parking lot. He left his truck by the curb, directly behind a cop car, and he hurried her inside.

Egan was right there to greet them.

One look at the sheriff's face, and Rayna knew something was wrong. She prayed that Warren hadn't had complications from the surgery. Or worse, that he'd died. She wasn't a fan of his, but she didn't want him dead. And that was partly because she knew how much Egan, Court and their sister, Rachel, loved him.

"What happened?" Court asked.

But Egan didn't respond. He made an uneasy glance around the waiting room, where there were several patients as well as some medical staff, and he motioned for Court and her to follow him. They did, and Egan went in the direction of the patients' ward, but he stopped in the hall. However, Rayna could see Rachel, Griff and Court's mother, Helen, just outside the door. It was no doubt Warren's room.

Egan looked at her as if trying to decide what to do with her. Clearly, he wanted to have a private conversation with his brother, but there was no way they could leave her alone.

"Dad didn't stay awake for long before he lapsed back into unconsciousness. But he did manage to say something," Egan said after he dragged in a long breath. He paused. "It's bad, Court."

And that was when Rayna heard something just up the hall. Something she didn't want to hear. Rachel and Helen were crying.

Chapter Five

Chapter Five

Court had already had a bad feeling before he saw his mother and sister crying, but that feeling went up a significant notch.

"Is Dad…" But Court couldn't even bring himself to finish the question.

"He's alive," Egan assured him.

The relief came, but the bad feeling remained. That was because of the tense look on Egan's face.

"In the few minutes that Dad was conscious," Egan went on, "he kept repeating one thing. A woman's name. *Alma.*"

Court shook his head. "You think that's maybe the real name of the dead PI he supposedly hired?"

"No." Egan took in another of those breaths. "According to Griff, it's the name of dad's longtime mistress."

That bad feeling fell like an avalanche on him. "No. Dad wouldn't cheat on Mom," he insisted.

"That's what I said, too, but Griff says it's true, that Dad's been carrying on an affair with this Alma for thirty-five years. Dad recently broke off things with her though." Egan turned back to Rayna. "And that's where you come in. It's possible this woman hired someone to kill Dad and set you up to take the fall."

"Hell," Court growled, and that was all he could manage to say.

His stomach was in knots. His heart, in his throat. And he figured Rayna wasn't feeling exactly great right now to hear confirmation that someone had set her up to take the fall for his father's attack. That part made sense—especially since they'd found Hallie dead. But none of the rest of this was sinking in.

"Alma," Court repeated. He glanced at Griff. "And he is certain it's true, that Dad cheated on Mom?"

Egan nodded, scrubbed his hand over his face. "He apparently found out a few months ago and said he told Dad to come clean. Dad obviously didn't do that, but he did break off things with this woman."

"The woman who maybe tried to set me up. I want to see her," she insisted.

Egan nodded. "You will. I'll have her brought into the sheriff's office as soon as I can arrange it." He motioned toward Rachel and their mom. "Needless to say, they're upset." He paused again. "Griff also told me that Warren had a son with Alma. I didn't say anything about that to Mom."

Court hadn't figured there'd be any other shocks, but that certainly was one. All of this was coming at him too fast. Of course, this wasn't something he could absorb with just a conversation. And he was sure there would be backlash. How the devil could his father have done this?

"The son's name is Raleigh Lawton," Egan added a moment later. "He's a year older than you."

Court belted out another "Hell." Because he knew

the man. *Sheriff* Raleigh Lawton was from a small town just one county over. Warren and he had worked on a murder case about three years ago, and Raleigh had visited McCall Canyon several times. Court thought of something else that'd happened.

"Wasn't Raleigh involved with Thea?" Rayna asked.

"Yes," Egan confirmed. "But they broke things off a while ago. I'm not sure if Thea knew he was Warren's son, but Griff says that Raleigh didn't know. He thought his father died in the military before he was born."

So, the lies had extended to not only their family but to Alma's, as well. Yeah, he definitely wanted to talk to this woman. Wanted to talk to his father, too.

"Are you okay?" Rayna asked. She touched his arm and rubbed gently.

No, he wasn't okay, not by a long shot, and Court figured things were about to get worse when he glanced at Rachel again. Griff had tried to put his arm around her, but Rachel practically pushed him away. She said something to their mom, something that Court didn't catch, and then his sister started toward Egan, Rayna and him.

"Egan told you?" she asked Court. There were fresh tears in her eyes and other tears spilling down her cheeks.

He nodded, tried to hug her, but Rachel waved him off. "I just need to get out of here. Away from Dad and away from Griff," she added. Her voice was shaking now. "He knew, and he didn't tell me."

"Maybe he didn't know how," Egan said.

"Then he should have found a way," she snapped. "He definitely should have found a way before—" She stopped, waved that off, too. "I need to go. Please. I just need to leave."

"I'll drive you," Egan volunteered. "Mom, too. Just wait here for a second until I can get her."

Egan started toward their mother, and Court went with him. Rayna stayed behind with Rachel. Which was good. As upset as the woman obviously was, she might try to leave on her own. If she did, at least Rayna could alert them. It wasn't safe for his sister to be out there alone.

Court went to his mother and pulled her into his arms. Unlike Rachel, she didn't push him away. She dropped her head on his shoulder.

"Warren loves me," Helen muttered. There was some anger in her voice now. "Why would he do this?"

Court didn't know, and he wasn't sure he'd get any answers from his father, either. "I'm sorry" was all he could think to say.

Griff was clearly sorry, too. The man was shaking his head and mumbling some profanity. Neither would help. But then, there wasn't much that could help this situation right now.

Helen pulled back and looked Court in the eyes. "You think that woman could have shot him?"

"Maybe," he admitted. "But we're looking at Mitch for this, too. He hates Dad as well as the rest of us."

Still, if his father had hired that PI, then he must have believed that Alma could be some kind of threat.

"Mom, I want to take Rachel and you home," Egan insisted.

Helen didn't argue with that. She didn't look as if she had the strength to argue with anyone. In fact, she seemed broken.

"I'll stay here and help guard Warren," Griff offered. "Just tell Rachel that I'm sorry. I'm so sorry," he repeated to Helen.

But Court wasn't sure his mother heard Griff's apology. Even if she had, it wouldn't be nearly enough to help her get through this. Still, it hadn't been Griff's place to tell them.

That blame was squarely on his father's shoulders.

Egan slipped his arm around Helen to get her moving, and Court followed them. "Why don't you take Rayna to the sheriff's office?" Egan told him. "I'll meet you there after I've driven Mom and Rachel to the ranch."

Court was still feeling stunned, but he forced himself to get moving. The sooner Rayna and he got to the sheriff's office, the sooner Egan and he could get Alma in for questioning. Not that Court was especially looking forward to meeting the woman, but this might be the start of getting those answers they desperately needed.

"Did you ever meet Raleigh or Alma?" Court asked Rayna as they walked toward the exit.

"No, but I remember the talk about Hannah Neal, the woman whose murder Warren and Raleigh were investigating. She was a surrogate who'd recently given birth, and she was killed around the same time Bobby Joe went missing."

Yeah. Hannah had been murdered in McCall Canyon, but her body had been dumped in Durango Ridge, Raleigh's jurisdiction. That was why both Raleigh and his father had been investigating it. All of that had happened just a few months before his father retired.

"You don't think Alma could have been connected to Hannah's murder, do you?" Rayna pressed.

He was about to say no, but then Court remembered that Warren had been very close to Hannah. She'd been the daughter of his best friend, a single-father cop who'd been killed in the line of duty. As Warren had done with Thea and Griff, he'd taken Hannah under his wing. So, maybe Alma had gotten jealous of that. After all, if she was the one who'd hired someone to shoot Warren, then it was possible she'd killed Hannah, too.

Yeah, he definitely needed to talk to this woman.

Egan led Rachel and their mother out the exit first, and he took them straight to his cruiser, which was parked just ahead of Court's truck.

"Will your mother be okay?" Rayna asked.

Good question. But Court wasn't sure. She'd already been teetering on shaky ground with Warren's shooting, and now this. Court made a mental note to call her doctor and have him go to the ranch to check on her.

He motioned for Rayna to follow him. However, before he could even get the doors unlocked, Court saw the blur of motion from the corner of his eye. And he immediately pulled Rayna down with him.

Just as someone fired a shot at them.

RAYNA HIT THE ground hard, much as they'd done the day before in her house, and the pain from the fall sliced through her. It robbed her of her breath.

For one heart-stopping moment, she thought she'd been shot.

But no, it wasn't that. The pain had come from the

bruise on her side. It hurt, but it was far better than the alternative of having a bullet in her. Or in Court.

She checked to make sure he hadn't been hit. He didn't seem to be, but he dragged her beneath the truck and drew his gun. Ready to return fire.

Rayna took out her gun, too, from its slide holster. Not that she was in position to shoot back. She was on her stomach, and Court had positioned his body in front of hers.

Protecting her.

Something she wished he hadn't done. Rayna didn't want him to die because of her.

She waited, listening and praying. Rayna also tried to figure out what to do. If either Court or she reached up to open the truck door so they could get inside, the gunman could shoot them.

If there actually was a gunman.

There had only been the sound of that one shot, making her wonder if what they'd heard was a vehicle misfiring. That was what she wanted it to be anyway, and she hadn't actually seen a shooter.

"Call Egan and let him know what's happening," Court shouted out to someone. "But I don't want him bringing my mother and sister back into this."

Rayna caught a glimpse of a medic in the doorway before the guy took out his phone and hurried back into the hospital.

"You're sure it's a gunman?" she asked.

But it wasn't necessary for Court to answer. She got confirmation of it when there was another shot. This one slammed into the back tire of the truck just inches from where they were. That caused her heart to skip a couple of beats because the bullet could have easily hit one of them. And now they had a flat tire, which would make it harder for them to drive out of there if they did manage to get inside the truck.

"Move," Court told her. He didn't wait for her to do that though. He pushed her farther beneath the truck. He also cursed. "I should have put you in the cruiser with Egan."

She wanted to remind him that hindsight was twenty-twenty and that he hadn't known this was going to happen. But there was no way Court would believe her. No, he would feel responsible for this.

Whatever *this* was.

Was it part of the earlier attacks against Warren and her? Or maybe it was all connected to the two dead women?

They really did need to question Alma and find out if she was the one who'd hired this gunman. If she was, then it was possible that Rayna wasn't the primary target. Court could be. Because Alma could want to hurt Court to get back at Warren. That didn't mean either of them were safe though, and Court was the one taking most of the risks. He leaned out from beneath the truck, no doubt trying to see the gunman.

"Keep watch on your side," Court instructed.

Rayna was trembling, and still in pain, but she managed to get turned around so that her back was to Court's. And she immediately saw something. There were several people cowering by the sides of their vehicles.

"Stay down," she called out to them.

Another shot slammed into the truck. But the angle was different on this one than the other two. The gunman was moving. Court obviously realized that, too, because he cursed and shifted his position so that she could have a better view of the back of the truck.

"You see the gunman?" Rayna asked.

"No." But she immediately felt Court's muscles tense. "Yes," he amended. "He's directly ahead on the other side of a white car."

Rayna could see the car but not the shooter. Not at first anyway, but then he came out from cover, fired a shot, and she got a glimpse of him then.

He was wearing a ski mask, and even though she hadn't gotten a look at her attacker, Rayna sensed this was the same person. The build and height were right, anyway. But why did he want her dead now? He couldn't set her up for Warren's attack. Maybe he just thought she was a loose end, someone who could possibly ID him.

She couldn't.

But maybe he didn't know that.

The man leaned out again and fired another shot at them. This one slammed into the pavement and then ricocheted into the truck. Court rolled out from cover, too, and he sent two rounds the gunman's way.

A sound on her right caught her attention, and Rayna pivoted in that direction. Not a gunman but a car. One that she recognized because it was Whitney's. Her friend braked to a loud stop directly behind Court's truck. That meant Whitney was now in the gunman's line of fire.

"Hell, what is she doing?" Court grumbled. "She must have heard the shots."

Yes, there was no way to miss that. But maybe Whitney thought she could save them or something. If so, it wasn't a good plan because Whitney could be killed.

Plus, it blocked their view of the gunman, making it impossible for them to return fire.

"Get in," Whitney called out to them.

Court and she couldn't do that, of course. It would be too risky for them to run to Whitney's car. If they were going to take that kind of chance, it would be better for them to just get in the truck, since it would take less time for them to be out in the open.

"Hear that?" Court asked her.

For a moment Rayna thought he was talking about Whitney. He wasn't. Because she heard another sound. It was a car engine. Since they were in a parking lot, it could just be someone leaving, but then there was the squeal of tires on the asphalt. Someone was driving out of there fast.

"He's getting away," Court said, and she could hear the frustration—and hesitation—in his voice.

Court no doubt wanted to go after the shooter, but it would be a huge risk. Because if it wasn't the gunman, then he could be shot. Still, he must have thought it was a chance worth taking because he rolled out from beneath the truck, his attention zooming to Rayna's right.

She lifted her head enough for her to see the car. It hadn't been the one the guy was using for cover though. This was a dark green sedan, and it was cutting across the parking lot only a few yards from them. Close enough for Rayna to catch just a glimpse of the ski-masked driver before he sped away.

"Stay put," Court warned her.

And with his gun aimed, he got to his feet and took off running.

Chapter Six

Court ran as fast as he could, and he kept his eyes on the green car. At best he figured he would get one shot before the shooter disappeared.

But he didn't even get that.

The car drove over the curb of the parking lot and shot out onto the road. Before Court could even stop and take aim, the gunman was already out of sight. That was not what he wanted. He needed to catch this guy so he could find out what the heck was going on.

While he ran back to Rayna, he took out his phone and texted Egan. His brother no doubt had deputies on the way, but Court wanted someone to go in pursuit of the person who'd just tried to kill them.

"Are you okay?" Rayna asked him the moment he made it back to her. She was crawling out from beneath the truck, but Court motioned for her to stay put. For a few more seconds, anyway. Just in case the shooter returned for a second round. Plus, he wanted a moment to ask Whitney one critical question.

"Why the hell did you drive into gunfire like that?" he snapped.

Whitney shook her head, her eyes widening. "I heard the gunshots and thought you needed some help."

He had. But not from a civilian. "You saw the gunman?"

Another shake of her head. "No. I only heard the shots."

Strange that most people's reaction would have been to move away from the gunshots. "You should have stayed back. Because you could have been killed." Well, she could have been if the shooter had continued to fire those shots. He hadn't. In fact, he'd stopped as soon as Whitney had driven up.

Her mouth trembled a little, and she looked as if she was about to cry. He hadn't wanted to bring her to tears—there'd already been enough of that today from his mom and sister—but he didn't want her doing anything like that again.

"You can't drive your truck on that flat tire," Whitney said. "And I don't think you want Rayna staying out here any longer than necessary. Come on, I'll give you a ride to the ranch."

Normally, Court wouldn't have given it a second thought to agree to have Whitney take them to the station, but he was having a lot of second thoughts today. Maybe because he'd nearly gotten Rayna killed along with having his world turned upside down.

Court didn't have to decline because a cruiser pulled into the parking lot and came directly toward them. Thea was behind the wheel, and she lowered the passenger-side window as she came to a stop.

"Ian and John are going after the shooter," Thea said.

Both men were deputies with plenty of years wearing a badge. Maybe their experience and some luck would help them nab the gunman.

"Is she going with us?" Thea asked, tipping her head to Whitney.

"No." Court answered so fast that it had Rayna looking at him.

He decided to soften his tone a little when he turned to Whitney and continued talking. "Go home or wherever else you're headed. You shouldn't stay around here. I'll call you about coming in to give a statement."

Whitney went stiff as if displeased with that order. Maybe because she'd already told him that she hadn't seen the gunman, but people often remembered other details when questioned.

The moment Court got Rayna into the back seat of the cruiser, Thea took off. Rayna was still trembling, of course. She probably would for a while, and he found himself slipping his arm around her before he even realized he was going to do it. Worse, Rayna moved right against him as if she belonged there.

Not good.

The last thing Court needed right now was to let down the barriers between Rayna and him. It would cause him to lose focus, and besides, he didn't have time to deal with the old baggage that existed between them.

"Griff called and told me about Warren," Thea said, pulling his attention back to her. Like Court, Thea was also keeping watch all around them as she drove to the sheriff's office.

Court figured this conversation should wait, especially since he was only minutes out of a gunfight, but it was a subject he'd planned to discuss with Thea eventually. "Did you know about my dad's affair?"

He cursed Thea's hesitation, but he had to hand it to the deputy. She didn't dodge his gaze. She made eye contact with him in the rearview mirror. "I suspected. I accidentally overheard a conversation once between Alma and Warren. It seemed—" her gaze slid between Rayna and him "—intimate or something."

Court wanted to curse twice. Once because Thea had obviously picked up on the unwanted attraction between Rayna and him. He wanted to curse a second time because Thea should have told him about that conversation she'd overheard. Of course, she would have never done that. Thea was fiercely loyal to Warren and wouldn't have ratted him out. But that did lead Court to something else.

"You used to date Alma's son, Raleigh," Court said. And he waited.

Thea nodded. Paused. "Raleigh and Warren had a, uh, falling-out. I don't know about what. Maybe it involved the case of the dead surrogate they'd investigated together. Maybe because Raleigh learned the truth. Either way, it caused things to become tense between Raleigh and me, so we stopped seeing each other."

Court glanced at Rayna, and despite the hell they'd just been through, he could tell she wanted more info from Thea.

"Is it possible Raleigh could be behind these attacks?" Rayna asked.

"No," Thea said without hesitation. "Even if he hated Warren, he's not the sort to bend the law, much less break it."

Court would have pressed for even more, but Thea pulled to a stop in front of the sheriff's office. She didn't get out though. She turned in the seat and looked at them. "As soon as I got Griff's call, I started asking around about Alma. I'd made some friends and contacts in Durango Ridge, where she lives. Anyway, last month Alma took some firearms-training classes."

That got his attention. "She has a permit for a gun?"

Thea nodded. "A permit to carry concealed." She blew out a frustrated breath. "You asked me if Raleigh could be behind this. No. But I can't say the same for his mother."

And that was why Court had to get Alma in for questioning. For now though, he didn't want to sit outside with Rayna any longer. He threw open the cruiser door and got her inside.

"I'm pretty sure Egan took your mom and Rachel straight home," Thea said when Court glanced around the nearly empty squad room. The only other person there was a reserve deputy, Dakota Tillman, and he was on the phone. "Griff's going to get someone to fill in for him guarding Warren, and then he'll come here."

Good. Griff wasn't a deputy, but it appeared they were going to be short of manpower for a while. Still, he didn't want Egan back here, not until he had Helen and Rachel safely back at the ranch. It wasn't a good idea for them to be in town with that shooter on the loose.

Since Rayna was still looking pretty shaky, Court took her to the small break room at the back of the building, and he got her a bottle of water from the fridge. While she made her way to the sofa, he called one of the deputies, Ian, for an update on the shooter.

But Ian didn't answer. Hopefully, that was because he was making an arrest.

"If you want to go out looking for the gunman," Rayna said, "I'll be fine here."

No, she wouldn't be. She was probably close to having an adrenaline crash, and what he was about to tell her wouldn't make that better. "The shooter could come to the sheriff's office."

She inhaled a quick breath, almost a gasp. Yeah, that adrenaline crash was closing in on her. Court went to her, and keeping a safe distance away, he sank onto the sofa next to her.

"He probably won't come here," he added. "But right now, we don't know which one of us is his target. Either way, he'll probably guess this is where we'd go."

Rayna groaned, pressing the back of her head against the sofa. "If he does show up, at least one of us can shoot him. But if he gets away, he'll just regroup and come after us again."

Court couldn't argue with any part of what she said. That was all the more reason to find out the person behind this. Maybe that was Alma. Or Mitch. But there was someone else on Court's radar now.

"Do you think it's odd that Whitney showed up at the hospital when she did?" he asked.

That brought her head off the sofa, and she stared at him. "You think she could have put together an attack?" Her tone made it seem as if that would be impossible, but then she huffed. "What would be her motive?"

Court had to shrug. "You tell me. Are things solid between you two?"

"Yes." But Rayna hesitated. "No. They haven't been the same since Bobby Joe disappeared."

Court had picked up on that vibe, but he'd wanted to hear Rayna confirm it. "Is that because Whitney believes you killed Bobby Joe?"

"Possibly," she admitted. "Whitney really liked Bobby Joe. She used to tell me how lucky I was to have him. Of course, that was before he hit me. After that, she didn't seem to be so much in his corner."

He gave that some thought. "Is it possible that Whitney had feelings for Bobby Joe, that maybe she could have been jealous of you?"

Rayna opened her mouth as if to deny that. She didn't. "Possibly," she repeated. "But it's a stretch to go from jealousy to attempted murder."

True, but jealousy could be a motive. "Bobby Joe's blood was in your house." Of course, she knew that, but Court wanted to look at this in a different light. "Blood that had been cleaned up."

"Yes, and the prosecution said I'd done that after I killed Bobby Joe. Since I didn't kill him, I'm guessing he put his own blood there and did the shoddy cleanup so that I would be arrested. But now you're suggesting that Whitney could have done that?"

"No. Just wondering if it's possible. Whitney would have had access to your house."

"At the time, so did Mitch." Rayna groaned softly. "Besides, what's happening now might not even be connected to Bobby Joe. It could be happening because of Warren. If so, then Whitney couldn't be a suspect."

Maybe. But Court was going to keep her on the list just in case. Whitney not only had access to Rayna's place three years ago, she had access to it now. She could have possibly even gotten the code for the security system.

"I know this isn't comfortable for you." Rayna's voice was a rough whisper now. "It's okay if you put me in someone else's protective custody."

No. It wasn't okay. He refused to let their past play into this. "I'll do my job," he said, but he hated that it came out rough and edged with too much emotion. "Or rather I'll do my job better than I have so far. I nearly let you get killed."

"You nearly got yourself killed protecting me," she corrected. "I don't want anything happening to you because of me." That certainly wasn't a whisper, and she looked him in the eyes when she said it.

That riled him. And gave him an unwanted jolt of memories. Memories of what used to be between them. Memories of Rayna. She'd always been a little fragile. Probably because of her troubled childhood. And while she was trying her hardest not to look fragile now, she still was.

She continued to look at him as if she expected him to say that he would be pawning her off on someone else. But then her expression changed, and he saw something more than the feigned strength in her eyes.

Hell.

Rayna had almost certainly gotten a jolt of those memories, too.

Court didn't move. Neither did she. That wasn't good. Because he was thinking about doing something, like kissing her. Thankfully, his phone rang, and it was the reminder he needed that kissing should be the last thing on his mind. Especially when he saw Rachel's name on the screen.

"Are Rayna and you okay?" Rachel asked the moment he answered.

"Yes." That was probably a lie, but his sister had already had too much bad news. "How about Egan, Mom and you?"

Rachel gave a heavy sigh. "We're at the ranch, and the shooter didn't come after us. But Mom is, well, hysterical. Egan is with her now, but I had to call her doctor to come out here."

Court's stomach tightened. He wanted to be there. No way though could he risk taking Rayna out into the open. "Tell Egan to stay there with her," Court instructed. "The other deputies are out looking for the shooter, and I have Rayna here at the station. Griff should be here soon."

Silence. Except it wasn't an ordinary silence. Rachel was obviously angry that Griff had known the truth about their father and hadn't told them. Court wasn't too happy about it, either, but he was going to cut the guy some slack on this. Yes, Griff should have told them, but the person who was at fault here was Warren. And now Helen might be falling apart because of what he'd done.

"I don't want to see Griff," Rachel added a moment later. "Please let him know he's not welcome at the ranch."

Court wanted to refuse to do that. After all, the McCall Ranch was Griff's second home, but he'd go with Rachel's wishes on this. Still, there seemed to be more going on that his sister wasn't saying.

"Is there something else you want to tell me?" Court came out and asked.

He got another round of silence from Rachel. "No. I just made a mistake with Griff, that's all. A big mistake."

Court definitely didn't like the sound of that. Griff and Rachel had been skirting around an attraction for years. Mainly because Warren hadn't thought they'd be a good match. But maybe something had happened. If they had indeed landed in bed without Griff telling Rachel the truth, then, yeah, it would have been a big mistake.

"Let me know if there's anything I can do," Court settled for saying. "And call me after the doctor has examined Mom. I'll be here if you need me."

He ended the call, and he glanced at Rayna. A reminder that Griff and Rachel weren't the only ones who'd been skirting attractions. Rather than sit there and continue to let the heat build, Court stood, ready to find out if there was any news on the search for the gunman. However, before he could do that, the break room door opened, and Thea stuck in her head.

"I just got off the phone with Alma Lawton," the deputy said. "She's on her way here now."

Good. That was a start. Now Court only hoped he could keep his emotions in check around the woman.

"Alma's not coming alone," Thea added a moment later. "Her son and lawyer will be with her."

Court amended his earlier thought of "good." He figured he'd have enough on his plate just dealing with his father's mistress, but apparently that dealing was also going to include his half brother.

"If she's bringing her lawyer, Alma must realize she's a suspect in the attacks," Court pointed out.

Thea nodded. "She says she's innocent."

"Of course," Court grumbled, and he didn't take out the sarcasm. "Did she say anything else?"

Thea nodded again. "Alma says she has proof of who shot your father." Then Thea hesitated. "She says it was your mother."

Chapter Seven

Rayna had no trouble hearing what Thea had just said. And she supposed it wouldn't be much of a surprise that Warren's mistress was accusing his wife of attempted murder. Helen might be making the same accusations against Alma.

But Alma had to be wrong about this.

Judging from the way Court cursed, he felt the same way. "My mother didn't know about the affair until today, a day after my father was shot."

Thea held up her hands in a "you don't have to convince me" gesture. "Alma wouldn't say what kind of proof she had, but they should be here any minute." She stared at Court a moment. "You want me to be the one to interview her?"

It was a reasonable request, since it was obvious that Court wouldn't be objective about this, but Court shook his head.

"We need to keep everything by the book," Thea reminded him. "Remember, she'll have her sheriff son and her lawyer with her."

Yes, and they might be looking for anything they could use to have any possible charges dismissed against Alma. Court cursed again and then nodded. "I'll watch from the observation room."

Thea headed back toward the squad room, no doubt so she'd be there to "greet" Alma and her entourage. Court started there, too, but then he stopped and turned to Rayna. "You can watch the interview with me."

Rayna wasn't sure why Court was including her, but then if Alma was guilty of trying to kill Warren, then that meant Alma had also been the one to try to set Rayna up. She definitely had a vested interest in hearing what the woman had to say.

She thanked him and followed Court into the squad room just as the front door opened, and someone walked in. But it wasn't Alma.

It was Mitch.

Rayna groaned. She so didn't have the energy to deal with this hothead today. She braced herself for Mitch to start throwing insults and accusations their way, but he stopped in front of them, sliding his hands into his pockets. Court noticed what Mitch had done because he stepped protectively in front of her.

"I'm not armed," Mitch grumbled, but his comment didn't have his usually venomous tone to it. "I just wanted to find out if you'd learned anything new about Janet."

"No." Court huffed. "Rayna and I have been busy dodging bullets."

"I heard. And no, I don't know who it was doing the shooting." He also didn't sound the least bit concerned, either. "Like I said, I'm here about Janet."

Court stared at him a moment. "You seem awfully interested in this woman that you hardly knew. Is there something you didn't tell us about her?"

Now Rayna saw the familiar fire in Mitch's eyes. "I'm interested because someone murdered her. Just the way someone murdered my brother." He shifted his attention to Rayna. "I just want justice."

Court drew in a long breath before he answered. "I want justice, as well. But for that to happen, I need more information. And right now, you're the only person in town who seems to have known her."

"Your father did," Mitch quickly pointed out.

Court lifted his shoulder. "I haven't been able to confirm that. Right now, I'm more concerned about what you know about her. Were Janet and you *together* or something? And I'm not talking about chatting over coffee at the diner. Oh, and before you say no, I'll remind you that you said you saw her ID when it fell out of her pocket. I doubt she had that in her waitress uniform."

Mitch's eyes were already dark, and they stayed that way. "So? We were *together*. That doesn't mean anything."

"It means plenty," Court argued. "Since Janet was possibly the one who help set Rayna up, then she could have been working for her lover. *You.* Not my father. You could have been counting on Warren never waking up so that your secret would stay safe."

"There is no secret," Mitch said through clenched teeth. "This is just another case of the McCalls putting themselves above the law."

With that, Mitch turned to leave, but he practically stopped in his tracks when he saw the three people who were approaching the building. A dark-haired woman with a slender build flanked by two men. One was in a suit, and the other was dressed like a cowboy. A cowboy with a badge pinned to his chest.

This was no doubt Alma, her son, Raleigh, and her lawyer.

The corner of Mitch's mouth lifted, and he looked back at Court. "Things are about to get fun around here. Don't guess you'd let me stay for the show?"

"How do you know those people?" Court snapped.

Mitch blinked as if he'd said too much. "I don't. They just looked like the fun-causing sort." He strolled out, heading up the street away from their visitors.

"Mitch is lying," Court muttered. "I'll get him back in here after Alma's interview."

Rayna completely agreed with the lying part, and she watched to see if Alma or the men would have a re-action to Mitch. However, if they saw him, there didn't seem to be any signs of recognition. Of course, Alma wasn't exactly looking at Mitch. She had her attention zoomed right in on Court.

Raleigh opened the door, and Alma stepped in. She never broke eye contact with Court, but she swallowed hard. "I didn't expect you to look so much like Warren," she said, her voice a delicate whisper.

Actually, the rest of her looked delicate, too, with her pixie haircut and pale skin, and she was wearing a gauzy light pink dress. Rayna's first impression was that Alma looked much too young to have a son who was in his thirties.

Court ignored her observation and instead turned to Raleigh. Neither man said anything, but they seemed to be sizing each other up. Rayna did that as well, and she could see the strong resemblance. Both of them favored Warren.

She silently cursed. For Court's sake and the sake of his mother and sister, Rayna had been hoping this affair was all some kind of misunderstanding. Judging from his scowl, Raleigh had hoped the same.

"Sheriff," Court greeted.

"Deputy," Raleigh greeted back. "Who'll be interviewing my mother?"

"It won't be you," the guy in the suit said before Court could answer. "I'm Alma's lawyer, Simon Lindley."

Thea came forward and shook her head. "I'm Deputy Thea Morris, and I'll be doing the interview."

Raleigh and she exchanged a long look. The kind of look former lovers gave each other. Rayna was certain she'd given Court that same look a time or two.

"I would have thought your brother, the sheriff, would have wanted to be here for this," Simon remarked.

"He's busy." Court's tone was as icy as his expression. "My mother isn't doing well, and my father is unconscious in the hospital. You might have heard someone murdered two women and tried to kill him." His gaze shifted to Alma when he added that last part.

Alma nodded. "Yes, I heard about Warren." She didn't offer any opinion about that and didn't ask how he was doing. The woman walked to Thea. "Perhaps we can go ahead and start?"

Simon looked as if he might stay and sling a barb or two at Court. He didn't. He hurried after Thea and Alma as they went up the hall to the interview room. Raleigh, however, stayed put.

"I'd like to listen," Raleigh said. "I suspect you'll want to do the same."

Court nodded and started for the observation room. Raleigh lagged behind and fell in step with Rayna. "You're a person of interest in Warren's shooting."

"Not anymore," Court answered before she could say anything. "Rayna was being attacked and drugged at the time of the shooting, and she was miles away at her house. No. I'm looking more at your mother for doing this." Now there was some anger lacing his words.

"And my mother is accusing yours of doing the same." No anger in Raleigh's voice, but he did take in a weary-sounding breath.

"My mom didn't do this," Court insisted. "I don't care what Alma says because my mother had no idea my dad was cheating on her."

Raleigh made a sound that could have meant anything, and the three of them went into the observation room. In the interview room, Alma and Simon were having a whispered conversation. Thea was already at the table, waiting for them.

"Did you know about the affair?" Rayna came out and asked Raleigh. She wished she hadn't said anything though because Raleigh gave her a sharp look. Maybe because he thought she had no right to be here. But Rayna stayed put.

"No," Raleigh finally answered. His jaw clenched. "We raise horses, and apparently Mom was meeting Warren on her so-called business trips."

"And you didn't suspect?" Court pressed.

"No. Did you?" Raleigh fired back.

Even though they both had practically growled those responses, it seemed to bring them to some kind of truce. No, they didn't like what had been going on, maybe didn't even like each other, but they hadn't known this train wreck was about to happen. By now though, they probably knew plenty about each other. Rayna figured they'd both used their law-enforcement channels for some background checks.

"You're not going in the interview room with your mother?" Court added to Raleigh a few seconds later.

"No." He paused, and she could have sworn his jaw got even tighter. "I'm guessing you were upset when you learned about the affair." Raleigh didn't wait for Court to answer. "Now imagine if you found out you were born on the wrong side of the sheets to a man who hasn't acknowledged you or the affair for thirty-five years."

Court didn't actually jump to offer an opinion on that, but Rayna figured he could understand that Raleigh wasn't in a good place right now. He'd been lied to his whole life about his father, and now his mother was a murder suspect.

Yes, definitely not a good place.

The three of them turned their attention back to Thea once she began the interview. The deputy started with simple questions, asking Alma to state her full name and address. Rayna had been through enough interrogations to know what Thea was doing. She was establishing baseline responses of a potential suspect. Like many people, Alma's eyes went to the right when she answered truthfully. Now Thea had created a body-cue lie detector she could use for the harder questions.

And Thea jumped right into that.

"Tell me about your relationship with Warren Mc-Call," Thea said.

"There is no relationship. Not any longer," Alma insisted. "We ended things two months ago."

"We?" Thea questioned. "Did you end it or did Warren?"

Alma glanced at Simon before she answered. "Warren. But it was time. All that sneaking around is fine when you're as young as you are, but I was tired of it. I wanted something more out of life. Something that Warren couldn't give me."

Thea jumped right on that. "So, you weren't upset when the breakup happened?"

Alma made another glance at her lawyer. "I suppose I was. At first. But then I got over it. I certainly wasn't so enraged that I would plot to kill Warren."

"And it's ridiculous that you'd bring my client in for questioning about something like that," Simon added.

Thea ignored him, and she opened a folder she'd brought into the interview room. She extracted a photo of Hallie. Obviously, the woman was dead, and it caused Alma to gasp. Raleigh didn't have a verbal reaction to that, but Rayna could feel the tension practically flying right off him.

"Do you recognize her?" Thea asked.

"No." Alma closed her eyes and shook her head. She also dropped her head on Simon's shoulder.

"Showing her that wasn't necessary," Simon growled. "You could have just asked Alma if she knew the woman."

Thea ignored that, too, and she took out a second photo. This one was of Janet. "How about her?"

Simon slipped his arm around Alma as if to turn her away from the grisly picture, but Alma not only opened her eyes, she leaned in to have a closer look.

"I know her. That's the woman who's been following me." Alma shifted her attention to Thea. "Who is she?"

"We're trying to confirm that now. When did she follow you?"

Alma huffed. "She's been doing it for the past couple of weeks. I got so worried that I took some firearms training."

Court turned to Raleigh to see if he would verify that, and Raleigh nodded. "She told me about someone following her, but I never saw the woman. You really don't know her identity?"

"Janet Bolin," Court answered after a long pause. "She was a PI."

Raleigh moved closer to the glass, staring at the picture. "Cause of death was a gunshot wound to the head." It wasn't really a question, but Court made a sound of agreement.

Even though Court didn't add anything about Warren possibly hiring the PI, it might make sense if Warren was concerned about how Alma might take the breakup.

Alma tapped Janet's picture. "She was carrying a gun the last time I saw her. I guess she thought it was concealed, but I could see the outline of it in the back waist of her jeans."

"Where and when did that happen?" Thea asked.

Alma's brow furrowed. "About a week ago, maybe less than that. She was at the coffee shop in Durango Ridge." She paused a heartbeat. "Helen McCall was with her."

Court cursed and moved as if he might charge into the room, but Rayna took hold of his arm. She didn't remind him that Thea would get the info they needed, but Court must have remembered that he wouldn't be doing his mother or him any favors if he went in there and accused his father's mistress of lying.

Alma tapped the photo again. "This woman and Helen were talking. I know it was Helen because I've seen a photo of her in Warren's wallet. That's why I got so worried. I mean, my ex-lover's wife was chatting with an armed woman who'd been following me. And when I heard Warren had been shot, I figured these two had something to do with it. Specifically, I thought Helen had hired this woman to kill Warren."

Court cursed again. Obviously, this was hard to hear, and it wasn't making sense.

"I saw Helen minutes after she'd learned of the affair," Rayna said, "and she was genuinely upset. If she'd known for a week, those emotions wouldn't have been so raw."

Thankfully, Raleigh didn't argue with that, but he probably wasn't as convinced of Helen's innocence as Rayna and Court were.

"Any idea why Helen McCall was in your hometown?" Thea asked the woman.

"I just assumed Warren had confessed all to her and that she was there to confront me or something. She didn't. And I never saw her again."

"You knew Helen was there?" Court asked Raleigh.

"No," he answered without hesitation. "But then if my mother had told me about Helen, she would have had to spill everything about Warren. It's my guess she wasn't ready to do that."

No, and Raleigh didn't seem happy about that, either. Alma's secret affair was also his secret paternity.

"Did Helen or Janet see you when you spotted them at the coffee shop?" Thea asked Alma.

Alma quickly shook her head. "But I went in through the side entrance and sat at a table on the other side of the wall from them. I couldn't hear much because it was noisy that day, but I did catch a word or two. They both mentioned Warren, of course. Oh, and a woman named Rayna."

That put a heavy feeling in her stomach, and she exchanged glances with Court. Uneasy glances. Because why would his mother and a dead PI have been talking about her?

"What did the two women say about Rayna?" Thea pressed when she continued with the questioning.

"I didn't hear that part," Alma insisted, "only the mention of her name."

Rayna wanted to believe they were talking about someone else. Or maybe that Alma had just misheard. Heck, all of this could be a lie.

But it didn't feel like a lie.

Mercy, had Court's mother been the one responsible for all this violence?

"I'll call the ranch and talk to my mom," Court insisted. He took out his phone and stepped into the hall. However, it rang before he could press the number.

Rayna was close enough to see Griff's name on the screen, and that put some fresh alarm in Court's eyes. He answered it on the first ring.

"Is something wrong?" Court immediately asked.

"Yeah," Griff answered. "Someone just tried to kill Warren."

Chapter Eight

Court's first reaction was to jump into a cruiser and head straight to the hospital. Someone was trying to kill his father—again.

His dad was in danger.

But Court forced himself to stop and think. This could be some kind of trap. Not for his father but for Rayna and him.

"Is Dad okay, and who tried to kill him?" Court asked Griff.

"Warren's fine. As for the intruder, I'm not sure who he is, yet, but we did stop him before he could actually get into the hospital room. I just cuffed him. But I can't take him anywhere because I don't want to leave Warren with only the security guard."

Neither did Court. He glanced around to see if he could come up with a solution. There were only two deputies in the sheriff's office, and Thea was still questioning Alma. The other deputies were out chasing down the shooter.

"We should go to the hospital," Rayna insisted.

Considering they'd just been attacked there, it surprised him that she would be so accommodating, but maybe Rayna didn't like the idea of staying behind with Alma. Court didn't like that, either.

"I'll be there in a few minutes," Court told Griff, and he ended the call.

Court turned to Raleigh, not sure of what he should say to the sheriff. Not sure what Raleigh would say, either. He'd likely heard what Griff had said and now knew that there'd been another attempt on Warren's life. However, if Raleigh had any reaction to that, he didn't show it.

"If you don't question your mother about what you've just heard in the interview," Raleigh said, "then I'll request the Texas Rangers do it. Helen Mc-Call needs to explain why she was talking with a now dead person of interest in this case."

It bothered Court that Raleigh was dictating to him how to do his job, but at this point anything the man said or did would probably bother him. There wasn't much about this situation that Court liked.

"I'll question my mother," Court assured him. Though it probably would be smart to have a Ranger do it. Not Griff, either. But someone who could be objective about all of this. Of course, his mother might not be in any shape to hold up to a full-blown interrogation.

Raleigh nodded, tipped his head to Alma. "I'm sure Thea will call you if there are any problems with the rest of the interview," he added.

It was pretty much a blanket invitation for Court to leave, so that was what he did. He took Rayna by the hand, hurried her to a cruiser that was just outside the door, and he prayed they wouldn't be shot at along the way.

Court's phone rang again, and this time he saw Rachel's name on the screen. He took the call on speaker, tossing his phone on the seat so his hand would be free. Court also kept watch around them, something that Rayna was doing, as well.

"Egan just told me about Dad," Rachel said the moment she was on the line.

"Yeah. I don't know anything yet, but I'll be at the hospital soon." Court debated if he should even bring this up now, but it was a conversation that needed to be started. "Once I'm sure Dad is okay, I'll need to talk to Mom. Alma Lawton said some things about her during her interview."

Rachel groaned. "I hope you don't believe anything Dad's mistress would have to say."

In this case, he did believe her. Either that or it was a stupid lie on Alma's part, since his mother's meeting with Janet was something that could be easily verified. Well, easily if his mother wasn't coming unglued.

"I just need to talk to Mom," Court settled for saying. "I'll call you when I have info on the intruder. All I know right now is that Griff was able to stop him, and he's still with Dad right now."

"Griff," Rachel repeated like profanity. "Call me the minute you know anything."

Court assured his sister that he would, ended the call and pulled to a stop in front of the hospital entrance. As close as he could, anyway. The CSIs were there, and so were several Texas Rangers. Obviously, that was Griff's doing, and Court made a mental note to thank him.

He threaded Rayna through the crime scene tape and got her into the building as fast as possible. There was another Ranger posted just inside, and the waiting room had been cleared. Good. The fewer people, the better.

"No way would your mother have done something to put you in danger," Rayna said as they walked.

Court believed that, too, but there might be another side to this. If Helen had found out about the affair sooner than she had let on, she could have wanted to harm Warren. Court hated to even consider it, but it was something he had to do. It sickened him though to think his mother might have had any part in this.

The moment they were in the patients' hall, Court spotted Griff and the security guard, David Welker, someone who Court knew and trusted. He also saw the man they had on the floor. The guy was on his stomach, his hands cuffed behind his back.

"How's Dad?" Court asked Griff first off the bat.

"Still unconscious."

That was better than the alternative or his father being bedridden and aware that someone had come back to finish him off.

Court looked down at the intruder. So did Rayna, but she shook her head, indicating that she didn't know him. Neither did Court, but he pulled the man to his feet so he could have a face-to-face talk with him. Except it wasn't really a man. The guy looked to be a teenager, but he was also dressed like an orderly.

"Did he have any ID on him?" Court asked Griff.

"No. The only thing in his pocket was this." He took out a small Smith & Wesson handgun. "He doesn't work here. The badge he's wearing is a fake."

The badge looked real enough, but something must have alerted Griff. "What made you stop him from going into Dad's room?"

"A bad gut feeling. That, and he looked too young to be an orderly."

He did, and Court thanked Griff before he turned back to the kid. "Who are you?" Court demanded.

The kid lifted his head, making eye contact with Court, and the deputy cursed. "He's high on drugs or something."

"That was my guess, too," Griff agreed.

The corner of the kid's mouth lifted. "I only had a pill or two." His words were slurred, as well.

"Who are you?" Court repeated, and this time he got right in the guy's face. His scowl must have been mean-looking enough because it caused the kid's smile to vanish.

The kid shook his head. "You don't know me. My name won't mean anything to you." He glanced over Court's shoulder at Rayna. "Might mean something to her though."

Rayna went stiff. "I have no idea who he is."

The kid shrugged. "Figured you would, since you're the one who hired me to come here and all."

"I didn't," Rayna snapped, and she repeated it, her gaze volleying between Court and Griff.

Court grabbed on to the guy's shirt, and the last scowl was a drop in the bucket compared to the one he gave him now. "I want to know your name."

"Bo Peterson," he finally answered.

That meant nothing to Court, and judging from Rayna's reaction, it meant nothing to her, either.

"When did I supposedly hire you?" Rayna demanded.

"Yesterday morning. You were wearing a red dress then."

Rayna groaned. "Hallie hired him."

"She said her name was Rayna." Bo leaned in, blinking and trying to focus on her face. "But you don't talk the way she did. And you don't look the same."

"Because she's not that woman," Court fired back. "In fact, that woman is dead. Someone murdered her and a second woman. Since you just tried to kill my father, you're my number one suspect in those killings and several attacks. That means you could get the death penalty."

Bo's eyes widened, and he suddenly looked a lot more alert than he had just a few minutes ago. "I didn't kill anyone. And I wasn't supposed to kill the person in that room. I was to put the gun behind the toilet."

Court's stomach tightened. That meant someone planned to retrieve the gun later and use it. Probably on Warren. Of course, that would have happened only if Bo was telling the truth. Court wasn't anywhere near convinced of that yet.

"I didn't kill anyone," Bo said when Court, Rayna, David and Griff just stared at him.

"Even if you didn't, you're still an accessory to murder and attempted murder. That carries the same penalties."

"No," Bo practically shouted. "I didn't know anyone was going to get killed." He snapped back toward Rayna. "That other woman is really dead?"

She nodded. "And that's why you have to tell us everything you know about her."

"I don't know anything." He shook his head and tears watered his eyes. "Several times she told me her name was Rayna."

She'd done that no doubt so Bo would remember it. "What else did she say, and how did she pay you?"

"She paid me in drugs. Oxy and Ecstasy. But I screwed up. I was supposed to put the gun in the room yesterday, but I took some of the pills and got a little messed up."

"What time yesterday?" Court pressed.

Bo's forehead bunched up, and he groaned. "Around nine or so. She didn't know what room number. She said I was to find out what room number Warren McCall was in and plant it there."

So, maybe Hallie had met with Bo shortly after the shooting. That would have meant he was perhaps the last person to see her alive. Of course, Bo could have also been the one to kill her.

"Who was going to use the gun you were supposed to hide behind the toilet?" Court continued.

"She didn't say, and I didn't ask."

That last part didn't surprise Court. Bo had likely been in a hurry to down those drugs he'd been given as payment.

"Can I go now?" Bo asked.

Court didn't even bother to laugh and he looked at Griff. "Any chance one of your Ranger friends can drive this clown to the sheriff's office so he can be locked up?"

"Locked up?" Bo howled. "But I didn't do anything. I didn't even make it into the old man's room."

Yeah, thanks to Griff and David. That was why Court had to continue to make sure whoever had hired Hallie and Bo wouldn't send someone else to try to finish off Warren.

"I'll wait in your dad's room," David said when Griff led Bo away.

Court thanked him and took out his phone to call

Rachel and Egan, but first he looked at Rayna to make sure she was okay. She wasn't. She was looking shaky again, so he had her lean against the wall.

"Who's trying to set me up?" she muttered, but it didn't seem as if she expected him to answer. Good thing, too, because Court still didn't know.

Court pulled her into his arms, intending for it to be just a quick hug, but it didn't stay that way. That was because Court realized Rayna wasn't the only one who'd just felt as if the rug had been pulled out from beneath them.

"Bobby Joe," she said. "He's the only one who hates me enough to do this."

Maybe. But this might not be about Rayna. "Or you're the perfect scapegoat because of the bad blood between you and the McCalls."

Of course, at the moment that bad blood didn't look so bad. After all, Rayna was in his arms, and when she lifted her head and looked up at him, it put their mouths much too close together. The memories came. The good ones. Of other times when he'd kissed her and she'd responded.

Much like she was responding now.

Her breath kicked up a notch, and he could see her pulse fluttering in her throat. And he caught her scent. Something warm and silky. Definitely nothing that had come from a bottle, and it stirred him in a very bad way. That was why Court stepped back before he made a mistake both Rayna and he would regret.

Well, they'd regret it afterward anyway.

He was certain there wouldn't be much of anything but pleasure during the actual kissing.

"We keep doing that," she said.

He didn't ask her to clarify. Because he knew. They kept moving much too close to giving in to this heat. That reminder caused him to take yet another step away from her, and before he could go back and play with fire, he made that call to Rachel. But it wasn't his sister who answered.

It was his mother.

"Rachel left her phone by my bed when she went to make me some tea," his mother said. "She won't be long though. Is everything okay? Egan and she are whispering."

Court wanted to assure her that everything was okay. But it wasn't. Far from it. "Dad is still asleep," he said.

"I guess that's good. He probably needs to rest and heal. If Warren really did do this to me, then I can't forgive him."

"Just give it some time," he said, because Court didn't know what else to say.

"Time won't fix this. I'm sorry," she added. "They gave me some pills, and they've made me a little woozy. Did you want me to get Rachel for you?"

"No, I need to talk to you." And because he had no choice, Court had to pause and take a deep breath. "We brought Alma Lawton into the sheriff's office for questioning."

"I see." His mother paused, too. "Did she know about me?"

Court went with the truth on this. "Yes. She also admitted to the affair."

Another sob. "Oh, God. It's true."

"According to Alma. But you still need to talk to Dad about it." In fact, Court definitely wanted to hear a confession from his father's own mouth, and part of him wouldn't fully believe it until he heard it.

"No, I can't talk to him. If Warren did have an affair with that Alma, then he had a child with her. A son."

Court was a little surprised that his mother could put all of that together—especially considering she'd been given those sedatives. It also made him wonder who'd told Helen about Raleigh. Maybe she'd overheard it in one of those whispered conversations she'd mentioned.

"Yes, they possibly had a son," Court admitted, but he didn't give her a chance to ask him any more about that. He jumped right into his question. "Alma said you had coffee with a woman named Janet in Durango Ridge. Did you?"

"No. I don't know a Janet." She didn't pause that time.

Court felt the relief. He could see that relief in Rayna's eyes, too, since she was still close enough to hear the phone conversation. But the relief didn't last because Court knew that Janet might not even be the PI's real name.

"Did you meet with a woman in Durango Ridge?" Court pressed.

"Yes."

There went the rest of his relief. At least his mother hadn't denied it, and that meant he might be able to get the truth from her. He only hoped the truth didn't lead to her arrest.

"I met with a reporter named Milly Anderson," Helen added a moment later. "She said she was working on the old Hannah Neal murder case. You know, the one that's troubled your father for the past three years."

There was no need for his mother to add that last

sentence. Because Court definitely knew about Hannah's case. Her murder was still unsolved. "Why did Milly want to talk to you about Hannah?" Court asked.

"Because she's an investigative reporter. You know, one of those journalists who digs through cold cases. She didn't really have anything new. I guess she thought maybe I would remember something that would help her."

Court doubted that. No, Janet or whatever her name was had probably had a different agenda in mind. Court just didn't know what that was.

"Did you tell Dad about this chat with Milly?" Court continued.

"I mentioned it to him. He said I shouldn't talk to any other reporters, that Hannah's murder was a police matter. He seemed really angry or something. God," she quickly added, "you don't think Milly had anything to do with Alma, do you?"

Court intended to find out. That meant digging more into Alma's background and talking to Raleigh. He might have run into Milly, as well.

"Oh, here's Egan," his mother said. "He's motioning to talk to you."

"I just got off the phone with Thea," Egan explained the moment he came on the line. "She told me what Alma said. You asked Mom if it was true?"

"Yes, she met with Janet in Durango Ridge."

Egan cursed, causing their mother to scold him, and Court heard footsteps, letting him know that Egan was taking this conversation out of Helen's earshot.

"Janet told Mom she was a reporter," Court added when he could no longer hear his brother moving around. "How is Mom, by the way?"

"Upset. Dr. Winters wants her to have a psych eval, and he's set her up an appointment."

That caused his chest to tighten. "You think she needs that?"

"Yeah."

Court wished he'd heard some doubt in Egan's voice. He didn't.

"I'll keep you posted on that," Egan went on. "In the meantime, the CSIs tested the guns at Rayna's house, and none had been fired recently. That's good news. For her, anyway."

Yes, it was, and while Court figured that pleased her, it also wasn't a surprise. Rayna had been adamant from the start that she hadn't fired a weapon. Especially one aimed at Warren.

"Thea said other than Mom's meeting with Janet, she didn't get much else from Alma," Egan continued. "Alma did agree to have her hands tested for gunshot residue. There wasn't any. And she also said the CSIs could test the weapons she owned."

Court was betting those wouldn't be a match, either. If Alma had been behind the attacks, she wouldn't have used her own gun. And she would have taken precautions to make sure there was no residue.

"What's going on between Rayna and you?" Egan came out and asked.

The question threw Court. It threw Rayna, too, because her eyes widened in surprise. "What do you mean?" Court grumbled.

"You know what I mean. Are you two involved again? And no, it's not just me being nosy. I don't care who you take to your bed. I just want to make sure you're not sleeping with a woman who's neck deep in a murder investigation."

"I'm not sleeping with her." Though Court had thought about it. Those thoughts had come shortly after their near kiss. Heck, they were still coming now.

"Good. I just wanted to make sure you hadn't lost your mind." Egan paused. "I'm guessing Rayna thinks Bobby Joe is responsible for the attacks."

"Yes," she answered.

Egan didn't seem surprised that Rayna had been close enough to Court to hear what they were saying. "I figured as much. Of course, I don't believe it, but I'll take a harder look at Mitch. Once this situation with Mom is settled." And with that, Egan ended the call.

"I'm sorry," Rayna said. "I probably shouldn't have let Egan know I was listening."

"He already knew." Court wished that weren't true, but Egan was definitely aware of the attraction between Rayna and him. Aware, too, of the problems that it could cause.

"Let me check on my dad, and we can go back to the station," Court told her. "I want to question Bo."

He opened the door to his father's room and came face-to-face with David. "I was just coming to get you." The guard stepped back. "Your father's awake."

Chapter Nine

Rayna stopped in her tracks after hearing what the guard said to Court. *Your father's awake.* That meant Court was finally going to get to question Warren about the affair and the attack, and he almost certainly wouldn't want her there to hear it.

Or so she thought.

Court motioned for her to follow him. "It'll be safer in here. Bo might not have been working alone."

That caused her throat to snap shut, and she wondered why that hadn't already occurred to her. It was because there was a tornado of emotions going on in her head right now. In her heart, too. But Rayna tried to push all of that aside for the possible firestorm they were about to face.

"I'll let the nurses know he's conscious," David said, heading out into the hall.

"Dad," Court greeted. "You know why you're here in the hospital?"

Warren nodded. "Someone shot me."

Rayna stayed back against the wall as Court walked to his father's bed. She'd hoped that Warren wouldn't even noticed her.

He did.

Warren looked past Court and directly at her. Court followed his father's gaze and shook his head. "Rayna's not the one who tried to kill you."

"No. But it looks as if someone tried to kill her." He'd no doubt seen the injury on her head before Warren's attention shifted to Court. "I know you'll ask, but I didn't see the person who shot me."

Too bad. Rayna was hoping they could have cleared all of this up right now.

"I felt the bullet go into my chest." Warren touched that part of his body. "I fell, and the only thing I remember after that is bits and pieces of conversations I've heard from the nurses and guards."

"What did you hear?" Court pressed.

Warren groaned softly and closed his eyes for a moment. "That there was another attack. Are you two okay?"

"Fine." Court sounded disappointed. And probably was. If that was all his father could recall, then there was going to be a lot more information they'd need to gather. "What about you? Are you in much pain?"

Warren shook his head, but that was probably a lie, since the head shake caused him to wince a little. That was the only reaction he managed to have, because the door flew open and one of the nurses came in. Rayna knew the woman, Ellen Carter, and she made a beeline to Warren, immediately checking one of the monitors.

"I'll let the doctor know you're awake." Ellen glanced at both Rayna and Court. "I know you'll want to question him about the shooting, but don't overdo it."

Court nodded but didn't say anything. Neither did Warren until the nurse was out of the room. "How's your mother? Is she here?"

"Not at the moment." Court didn't pause too long before he said that. "She's at the ranch with Rachel and Egan."

"Egan," Warren repeated. "Yes, he should be with her. Rachel, too." He looked up at Court again. "Do you have the person who shot me in custody?"

"No." Court took a deep breath. "But we have two dead bodies. Both women. One was an actress that we believe was posing as Rayna to set her up to take the blame for your shooting. The second one was perhaps a PI who was linked to you. She was using the name Janet Bolin."

For a man who'd just again regained consciousness after surgery, Warren suddenly seemed very alert. And frustrated. Because he groaned. "That's not her real name. It's Jennifer Reeves."

She couldn't see Court's face, but he did pull back his shoulders. If Warren knew the woman's real name, then he was indeed linked to her.

"You said she's dead?" Warren questioned.

"Murdered," Court clarified.

Warren grimaced and then cursed. "How? Did the person who shot me also kill her?"

"We're still trying to sort that out." Court dragged up a chair and sat next to his father's bed. "After surgery, you kept saying someone's name. Alma."

And the silence began. However, Warren did have a response. The shock, followed by a mumbled "Ah, hell."

That probably wasn't what Court wanted to hear. Maybe he had still held out hope that the affair was some kind of misunderstanding.

Warren looked Court straight in the eyes. "Your mother knows?"

Court nodded. "We all know. Griff filled in a few blanks for us."

Warren's mouth tightened. "He had no right. If I'd wanted all of you to know, it should have come from me."

"But it didn't," Court quickly pointed out. There was anger in his voice. Understandably so. That "if" probably didn't set well with him, and it meant that Warren hadn't planned on confessing to the affair anytime soon.

"That's why your mother's not here," Warren added. He also added some more profanity. "Call her now. Tell her I want to see her."

"That's not a good idea." Court didn't break eye contact with Warren when he said that, either. "The doctor sedated her, and she needs some rest."

Warren threw back the covers as if to get up, but Court quickly stopped him. "You need your rest, too. And I need answers. You really had an affair with Alma Lawton for thirty-five years?"

Warren stared at him almost defiantly. Obviously, he wasn't a man accustomed to being challenged, but Rayna saw the exact moment he mentally backed down. Warren stared at his hands. "What else do you know about her?"

Rayna wanted to groan. Even now after he'd been caught, Warren wasn't ready to spill everything.

"I know Alma gave birth to your son Raleigh," Court readily answered. "And that you and Alma only ended things a couple of months ago. I believe you were concerned Alma might go to Mom, and that's why you hired the PI." He paused. "How am I doing so far?"

Warren's mouth tightened even more. "Alma and I didn't end things. I did. I stopped seeing her, and she was upset about that. So, yes, I thought she might go to your mother."

"Why would Jennifer aka Janet meet with Mom in Durango Ridge?" Court pressed.

Warren lifted his head. "She wouldn't have."

"She did. Or rather according to Alma, they did. She said she saw them at a coffee shop there."

"You've already talked to Alma?" Warren snapped.

"Thea interviewed her. You have to know that she's a suspect. You really think she could have been the one to shoot you though?"

"No." But Warren immediately shook his head. "Alma's never done anything violent before."

That didn't mean she hadn't done this. It depended just how riled Alma was. Warren's scorned lover could have shot him, set up Rayna to take the fall, and when that didn't work, she could have hired someone to shoot at Court and her.

But that still didn't explain why the PI that Warren had hired would meet with Helen.

The door opened, and the doctor came into the room. He no doubt noticed the agitation on his patient's face because he huffed and turned to Court. "I need to examine Warren now. You two can wait out in the hall."

That definitely had a "get out of here" tone to it, and Rayna couldn't blame him. Yes, Warren had messed up big-time, but he was still in serious condition. Just a day earlier, he'd been at death's door, and the doctor probably wanted to give Warren some time to mend.

Court and she went out of the room, and he immediately took out his phone. He pulled up Egan's number, but he didn't press it. Court just mumbled some profanity and looked at her.

"I'll get you out of here soon," he said.

She got the feeling that he'd wanted to say something else. Maybe an apology or something. She didn't want one. Because none of this was his fault, and it was obvious that what his father had done was tearing him apart.

Court stared at her a moment longer before he finally pressed Egan's number, and this time he put the call on speaker. Court opened his mouth, probably to tell Egan that Warren was awake, but Egan spoke before he could speak.

"Mom swallowed a bunch of pills," Egan blurted out. "I've already called an ambulance, but she's unconscious."

Oh, mercy. Not this. Court and his family already had enough on their plates.

"When did this happen?" Court snapped.

"I'm not sure. Rachel's the one who found her. Are you still at the hospital?"

"Yeah. Dad is finally awake. I'll talk to you about it when you get here. You are coming in the ambulance with Mom, aren't you?"

"I am, but I'm not sure they'll keep her there. Once they've pumped her stomach or whatever the hell it is they'll do, she'll probably have to go to a place that has a psych ward."

Court groaned, scrubbed his hand over his face. "I'll meet you at the ER. How soon before you get here?"

"Soon. The ambulance is already on the way out here."

Still, that could be a good thirty minutes by the time the medics picked up Helen at the ranch and brought her in.

Court got them moving when he ended his call with Egan. Maybe because he needed to put some breathing room between his father and him. Also, he might not want to have to tell Warren about this.

He stopped just short of the ER waiting room, and they peered around the corner. The Rangers were still there, so hopefully that meant a gunman wouldn't be stupid enough to show up there.

"I'm sorry," Court said.

Since she was about to tell him the same thing, Rayna lifted her eyebrow. "For what?"

"Everything. You could be in the middle of this danger because of my father's affair." He didn't say the word *father* with too much affection. However, there was plenty of anger. "I can't believe he did something like this."

After everything Warren had put her through with the trial, Rayna wanted to say that she had indeed thought he was capable. But yes, even she was surprised. Warren could be a bulldog when it came to seeking justice, but he'd seemed to genuinely love his wife and family. And now he was tearing them apart.

"If my mom dies…" Court started.

But Rayna didn't let him finish that. She stopped him by brushing her mouth over his. In hindsight, kissing him hadn't been the right thing to do. But it certainly caused the heat to slide right through her.

She leaned back, their gazes connecting, and this time she saw more than the worry and fatigue. There was some confusion. And a little fire.

"Have only good thoughts about your mother," she warned him. "Or I'll kiss you again."

Despite everything going on, the corner of his mouth lifted. "Not much of a threat." But then he huffed, and she understood what he meant.

In some ways, kissing was the greatest threat of all.

And that was why she stepped back. Just like that, the moment was lost, taking the fire right along with it. Unfortunately, Rayna knew it would return.

His phone rang, and since he still had it in his hand, she had no trouble seeing the screen. Not Egan this time but rather Thea. He put this one on speaker, too.

"How's Warren?" Thea immediately asked.

"Awake. He confirmed the affair with Alma."

"I see." Thea sounded very disappointed about that. "Griff is here with the prisoner. I'll send the gun he had on him for testing. Anything specific you want me to look for?"

"Fingerprints or some DNA," Court answered. "It's possible this gun was going to be used to set someone up."

He looked at Rayna then, and she knew the someone might be her. She didn't remember touching a gun that wasn't hers, but it was possible someone had gotten a sample of her DNA.

"I finished the interview with Alma," Thea added a moment later.

"Yeah, Egan told me."

"Figured he had. Alma will be back tomorrow though to go over her statement. If you or Egan wanted to question her, you could do it then."

Court made a sound of agreement. "We don't have any grounds to arrest her. Not yet. But I need to look into her possible connection to the dead PI. According to my dad, her real name is Jennifer Reeves. And yes, he did hire her. Can you see what you can pull up on her?"

"Sure." And Rayna could hear the clicking of the computer keys. "Alma said Jennifer met with your mother. Do you know why?"

"No idea, and it might be a while before I can ask her." Judging from the sudden tightness in his jaw, that was all he wanted to say about that right now.

"Jennifer Reeves," Thea repeated a moment later. "Yes, she was a PI. Thirty-four. No record. She owns… *owned* an agency in San Antonio but didn't have any other employees. Let me check her social media and see if I find any connection to Helen."

"And check connections to Alma, too," Court insisted.

"You think Alma could have been lying?"

"I don't know, but if Alma is on some kind of vendetta, then she might have used Jennifer to do it. Alma could have found out my father hired Jennifer and then paid her more money to set him up."

Yes, because after all, it'd been Jennifer who'd taken the photo of the woman who resembled Rayna. But then Rayna thought of something else.

"Maybe you'll find a connection between Jennifer and Mitch," Rayna threw out there.

Thea made an immediate sound of agreement.

"There did seem to be something going on between those two, and Mitch is definitely someone who'd want to get back at Warren and you." She paused. "I'm not seeing anything on her social media, but I'll see about getting her case files. It's possible… Oh."

Rayna definitely didn't like the sound of that "oh." Thea wasn't exactly the sort to be easily surprised.

"What is it?" Court asked when Thea didn't continue.

"I think we should be looking into someone else," Thea finally said. "I'm sending you a photo that I found on Jennifer's page. You want me to bring her in for questioning?"

It took a few seconds for the photo to load on Court's phone. It was a shot of two women, and they appeared to be at some kind of party. When Rayna looked at their faces, it felt as if someone had drained all the air from the room.

The woman on the left was definitely Jennifer. But Rayna recognized the other woman, too.

Because it was Whitney.

Chapter Ten

Court definitely didn't like this latest turn of events. Why the heck had Whitney not mentioned that she knew Jennifer?

From all accounts Jennifer had been working at the diner for a couple of weeks, and Whitney lived in town. As small as McCall Canyon was, she would have likely run into her, seen her friend and then been very concerned that her *friend* had turned up dead. The very friend that from all appearances had tried to set up Rayna for a crime she didn't commit.

Court drove away from the hospital while Rayna tried to call Whitney. They were alone in the cruiser but not alone on the road. He hadn't wanted to risk that. Deputy Dakota Tillman and a Texas Ranger were in a second cruiser behind them, and Court hoped that three lawmen would be enough to deter another attack.

"Whitney's still not answering her phone," Rayna said. It was her fifth attempt to get in touch with the woman, but each of the calls had gone straight to voice mail.

Court figured that wasn't a good thing no matter which way they looked at this.

"You think it's possible Whitney got wind that you learned she was connected to the dead PI?" Rayna asked.

"Yeah," he admitted. Since Whitney was a dispatcher for the sheriff's office, she could have heard and might now be avoiding them.

Or…

There was another possibility. One that he didn't want to mention to Rayna just yet. If Whitney had gotten involved in some kind of scheme to kill Warren, a scheme that involved Jennifer and Hallie, then she could be dead, too.

"I keep going back to what Whitney did earlier in the hospital parking lot," Rayna said. "She pulled her vehicle between us and the shooter."

Whitney had indeed done that, and while that alone wasn't an indication of guilt, she was starting to look very suspicious. "I'll question Whitney as soon as she checks in with us." And the woman had better do that soon. She'd also better have the right answers.

Rayna glanced at the sheriff's office as they drove past. "You can leave me there if you want, and go back to the hospital and be with your mother."

"Rachel and Egan are there, and the doctor said he didn't want her to have visitors for a while. Even if she were allowed, I'm not sure I should be answering questions she'll have about my dad's affair. It would only upset her even more."

It had certainly upset Court. And worse, he didn't know what to do about it. Part of him hated his father for this, but hating wasn't going to fix the danger. Or his mother. No. He had to focus on getting the person responsible for the attacks and then make sure his mom had the kind of help she needed to get better.

His phone dinged with a text message, and Court handed it to Rayna so she could read it to him.

"It's from Thea," she relayed. "No signs of the shooter. Also, Bo is only seventeen, and he lawyered up."

The first wasn't a surprise, since the shooter was probably long gone by now. But seventeen! That meant Bo was a juvenile and might not be charged as an adult. That could be especially true if Bo didn't have a record. Of course, he had tried to slip a gun into a hospital room, and that was a serious enough charge that he might end up with some actual jail time.

"Text her back," Court instructed, "and ask her to question Bo as soon as his lawyer arrives. I want to find out if he knows who hired Hallie to give him the gun and the drugs."

Bo probably didn't know the answer to that, but they had to try. Right now, Bo was the only living link they had to the dead woman.

Rayna was about to hand him back his phone, but it rang before she could do that. This time it wasn't a number he recognized, and he motioned for Rayna to answer it. She did and put it on speaker. Court braced himself in case this was the shooter, but it wasn't.

It was Raleigh.

"I've got something that I'm sure you'll want to see," Raleigh immediately said. "The coffee shop here doesn't have a security camera, but there's one at the bank across the street. I'm emailing the footage to you now."

That was a pleasant surprise. "Is my mother's meeting with the PI on the footage?" Court asked.

"Yeah. It's grainy because of the glass window that's between them and the camera, but you can see their faces well enough. At first, your mother doesn't appear to be agitated, but that changes at about the five-minute mark. She appears to start crying."

Hell. That could mean that Jennifer had told Helen about the affair. But why would the PI have done that?

"I don't see any exchange of money or anything," Raleigh went on. "And your mother didn't stay long in the coffee shop after that."

So, a short meeting. One that had upset his mother. Coupled with the fact that Helen hadn't mentioned the meeting until he'd asked her about it, it wasn't looking good.

"You'll let me know what your mother has to say about this after you've viewed the footage?" Raleigh asked.

"That might be a while." Court debated how much he should say and then went with the truth. After all, Raleigh would be hearing it soon enough, anyway. "My mother tried to kill herself. Pills. I won't be able to question her until I get the all clear from her doctor."

"Sorry about that." And even though Raleigh had muttered it, he sounded genuine. "We're in a bad place right now with our mothers. Alma hasn't tried to end her life, but she's not as strong as she looks."

"Is she strong enough to have hired a killer?" Court blurted out. He wished though that he'd toned it down a little, since Raleigh actually seemed to want to get to the bottom of this.

"As her son, I'll say no. As a cop, I'll say anyone is capable of pretty much anything. But ask yourself this—if my mother was so upset at Warren, then why would she have waited two months to go after him?"

"Maybe because it took her that long to put a plan together." But Court had to shake his head. "How long ago did my mom meet with the PI?"

"Four days," Raleigh readily answered.

That meant Helen had had that meeting three days before Warren had been shot. If his mother had learned of the affair at the meeting, it was possible she'd somehow gotten Jennifer to help her with a plan. It sickened Court to think that might be true because the plan had included setting up Rayna. Plus, both Rayna and his father could have been killed along with the two women who'd been murdered.

"I'm not saying either of our mothers killed anyone," Raleigh went on, "but we have to consider they could have hired someone who went rogue. Someone they can no longer control."

Yes, and that someone had maybe fired shots at Rayna and him.

Court's phone beeped with an incoming call, and when he saw John Clary's name on the screen, he knew he'd need to talk to his fellow deputy. "I'll review the footage and get back to you," he told Raleigh and switched over the call.

"Please tell me you found the shooter," Court immediately said.

"No. But we do have a problem. Someone tripped the security alarm at Rayna's house. And since it's still taped off as a crime scene, I came here to check it out. There's someone here all right, but he or she ran into the barn when they spotted the cruiser. I just wanted to make sure it wasn't Rayna or someone she sent out here."

"It's not me," Rayna assured him. "But this morning Court had some of his hands go over and tend my horses. Maybe it was one of them."

"Seems funny though that the person would take off running like that," John commented.

It did, and it put an uneasy feeling in Court's stomach. Besides, those hands would have been long finished by now and back at the McCall Ranch.

"Every now and then some kids will come out to my place," Rayna added. "I think I'm the local bogeyman, since many people believe I killed Bobby Joe."

She glanced away from Court when she added that. It was a reminder that her life probably hadn't been so great in the past three years.

"So, you think it might be just a prank or something?" John pressed.

"I don't know," Rayna said after a long pause. "The kids don't usually go in my barn."

None of this was giving Court assurances that all was well. "Are you alone?" he asked John.

"Yeah. I was headed back to the office when I got the call. You think I should get some backup?"

It wasn't an easy question to answer. The sheriff's office was maxed out, and Rayna and he were only a couple of miles from her place. Court turned in that direction, but he definitely wasn't sure it was the right thing to do. He also motioned for the other deputy and Ranger to follow them.

"Just stay put," Court told John. "I'll be there in a few minutes." He ended the call and immediately looked at Rayna. "You won't be getting out of this cruiser. Understand?"

She didn't argue with that, but she huffed. "You really think the shooter would be stupid enough to go to my house?"

"He might if he thought he'd left something when he attacked you."

That put some new fear back in her eyes, and Court nearly turned around to get Rayna out of there. Then he saw a familiar car on the road just ahead of them.

Whitney.

Rayna immediately took out her phone and tried to call the woman again. Again, it went straight to voice mail.

Court had another decision to make. He wanted to talk to Whitney, but he wasn't sure it was worth putting Rayna at risk this way. That decision was taken out of his hands though when Whitney pulled off onto the shoulder of the road. She got out of her car, and she'd obviously seen them because she started flagging them down.

"Stay inside the cruiser," Court repeated to Rayna. He drew his gun and pulled up behind Whitney. However, he didn't get out, and he only lowered his window a couple of inches. Dakota stopped his vehicle behind them and did the same thing.

"What are you doing out here?" Court snapped when Whitney ran up to the car.

She practically stopped in her tracks, and she pulled back her shoulders. "What's wrong? What's going on?" She looked at Rayna when she asked that second question.

"You tell us. Why are you here?" he repeated.

She opened her mouth, her attention volleying between Rayna and him. "Mitch. Did he call you, too?"

Mitch? Court certainly hadn't expected her to say that.

"No," Rayna answered, "but I've been trying to call you for the past half hour."

"I know. I'm sorry, but the battery died, and—"

"You didn't tell me you knew one of the dead women," Rayna interrupted.

Whitney shook her head. "I don't."

"You do," Rayna argued. "I saw a picture of you with her. Her name was Jennifer Reeves."

It took several moments for Whitney to process that. Or maybe she was pretending to process it. "The dead woman is Jennifer? I thought her name was Janet."

"She was using an alias," Court explained. "So, you did know her?"

"Of course." Whitney's voice was barely a whisper now, and if she was faking it, she was doing a darn good job. "Jennifer's dead?"

Court verified that with a nod. "When's the last time you saw her?" And that was the first of many questions he had for her.

She shook her head again, pushed her hair from her face. "Months. Maybe longer. We met on a cruise about ten years ago and have stayed in touch." She uttered a hoarse sob. "I can't believe she's dead."

Again, her shock seemed genuine, and later he intended to question her more about her friendship with Jennifer. For now though, there was something more pressing. "What does Mitch have to do with you being out here?"

Whitney paused again as if trying to gather her

thoughts. "He called me, and he sounded frantic. Maybe scared. It was a really bad connection with a lot of static, but I thought he said there was something in Rayna's house that he had to get."

"Something?" Court questioned.

Whitney glanced away. "He didn't say exactly what, but I think he maybe meant a gun. He could be looking for the gun that he thinks killed Bobby Joe."

Both Court and Rayna groaned. "And why did Mitch think the gun would be there after all this time?"

"I don't know. That's about the time my phone battery completely died, and I started driving out here. I was afraid the Rangers would still be here, would see him and think maybe he was the person who'd shot at Rayna and you."

They might have indeed thought that, but it was still no reason for Mitch to run.

"Get in your car and go to the sheriff's office," Court told Whitney.

"But what about Mitch?"

"I'll take care of him."

Whitney didn't look at all comfortable with that. *Well, welcome to the club.* Court wasn't comfortable with it, either, but he didn't want Mitch trespassing on a crime scene, especially with another of their suspects around.

And Whitney was indeed still a suspect.

She'd had explanations as to why she hadn't told them about Jennifer or answered her phone, but Court wanted to do some more digging into her story.

"You want me to take Rayna back to the station with me?" Whitney asked.

"No." Court couldn't answer that fast enough. He

raised his window and drove off, leaving Whitney there to gape at them. Probably to curse them, too, since she didn't look very happy with Court's obvious mistrust of her.

Court considered calling John to let him know that Mitch was likely the intruder, but he decided against that, since they were nearly at Rayna's house. Plus, it might not be Mitch at all, and he didn't want John walking into the barn and finding a gunman waiting for him.

"Keep watch around us," Court reminded Rayna, though he was certain she was already doing that. They were both on edge.

When her house finally came into view, he had no trouble seeing that the front door was wide-open. He also spotted John. The deputy had taken cover behind his cruiser and had his gun drawn. And Court soon realized why.

Mitch had his hands raised in the air, and he was coming out of the barn. "Don't shoot," Mitch called out to them.

Court parked next to John so that the deputy's cruiser would also be between Rayna and Mitch, and he took aim. Behind him, Dakota and the Texas Ranger did the same thing.

"Mitch, are you armed?" Court asked.

Mitch tipped his head to the barn. "I was, but I left it in there. Didn't want either of you getting trigger-happy when you saw me trying to do your jobs."

Court didn't like the sound of that, but then he rarely liked anything Mitch said. "And doing our job includes trespassing on private property and breaking and entering?" Court fired back.

"Yes, in this case. I didn't get a chance to try the security code or the key. The door was busted open when I got here."

That didn't make sense, and Court was about to demand more, but Mitch looked past John and Court and into the cruiser where Rayna was sitting.

"You might not have actually murdered my brother, but you're not off the hook," Mitch said to her, and he smiled.

That brought Rayna out of the cruiser. "What are you talking about?" It was the exact question Court had been about to ask.

"Are you admitting Rayna didn't kill Bobby Joe?" Court demanded.

Mitch nodded.

That nod might have been a simple gesture, but Court could hear the sound it caused Rayna to make. She gasped. "He's alive," she muttered.

Mitch nodded again, and he stopped when he was about ten feet from them. "I need to get my phone from my pocket, and I don't want you to shoot me when I do that." He waited until Court nodded before Mitch took out his cell. "Bobby Joe left me a message. That's why I called Whitney and told her to come. She'll want to hear this, too."

"She can hear it later," Court snapped.

Mitch nodded, pressed the play button, and he held the cell up in the air for them to hear. It didn't take long before Court heard the voice.

"It's Bobby Joe. Meet me at Rayna's."

There was a lot of static, and the message was choppy as if he'd been thinking about each word before he said it.

"The security code is seven-six-two-one," the message continued, "and there's a spare key in the birdhouse on the end of the porch." The static got even worse. "I want to show you where she hid the gun. The gun she used to try to kill me."

Chapter Eleven

The message kept repeating through Rayna's head, and she couldn't make it stop. Bobby Joe was alive.

But now he was accusing her of attempted murder.

She'd denied it the moment she'd heard the message, and she thought Court believed her. Not Mitch though. But then, he'd always thought the worst of her. And would continue to think it, too, now that Mitch had heard the accusation from his own brother.

"There is no smoking gun," she said to Court. "So why would Bobby Joe tell Mitch to meet me at his house?"

"Maybe to plant something to incriminate you," Court said without hesitating. Which meant that message was likely replaying in his head, as well.

Not necessarily a good thing, since they were both trying to focus on the drive back to the sheriff's office. Dakota hadn't followed them for this part of the trip. That was because Court had wanted the Ranger to go ahead and take Mitch to the sheriff's office so that Dakota could stay behind and search for Bobby Joe. Rayna had wanted to do that, too, but it wouldn't have been very smart, since Bobby Joe could have just gunned her down. Of course, maybe he wanted to torment her first, to punish her for breaking off things with him.

"Everyone knows now that you didn't kill him," Court said. "I'm sorry for not believing you in the first place."

"There was a lot of circumstantial evidence," she reminded him. Evidence that Bobby Joe had planted. "He must have stockpiled some of his own blood that he put in my kitchen."

Court made a sound of agreement. "And he made sure he cleaned it up in such a way to make us believe you'd tried to cover up the crime scene." He stopped, cursed. "It could have worked, too. You could be in jail right now."

Since it was obvious he was beating himself up about that, Rayna touched his arm. "It's okay. Right now, I'm more concerned about what Bobby Joe's going to do next."

"He'll try to kill you," Court quickly answered. "That's why you'll need to stay in protective custody. That's why we have to find him. We might get lucky and be able to trace his call to Mitch."

Yes, and that brought her back to the message Bobby Joe had left on Mitch's phone. Why risk bringing in anyone else, even his brother? Why not just plant the gun and then arrange for someone to find it? And why do the whole gun-planting thing if Bobby Joe was the one behind the attacks? Why not just continue the attacks until he was successful?

A thought that twisted her stomach into a knot.

But there was something else about this that didn't fit.

"The security code," Rayna said. "The one Bobby

Joe gave Mitch. It was the old code. That's why he tripped the security alarm when he tried to get in."

"Did you know about the key in the birdhouse?" Court asked.

"No, but if he was telling the truth about that, it would have been the old one, too. I changed the locks after the trial."

And Court obviously picked up on where she was leading with this because he cursed. "It means Bobby Joe wasn't the person who broke into your house and drugged you."

No, because whoever had done that had the correct key and code. With everything else going on, she hadn't followed up on finding who could have gotten those things, but she had to move that to the front burner.

Well, as soon as she dealt with the news of Bobby Joe's return.

Even though she'd known he was alive, it was another thing to deal with the proof of it. Plus, he was out there, probably trying to figure out his next move. He probably hadn't counted on that move including Mitch ratting him out.

They pulled to a stop in front of the sheriff's office, and Rayna immediately saw the cruiser the Ranger had used to bring back Mitch. What was missing was Whitney's car, but Rayna held out hope that her friend had parked elsewhere and walked to the station. She didn't want to accept just yet that Whitney could be avoiding her because she'd had something to do with those attacks.

"The Ranger had to leave and go back to the hospital to guard your dad, but Ian just went in the interview room with Mitch to take his statement," Thea said the moment Court and Rayna walked in. "Is it true? Is Bobby Joe really alive?"

"It's true," Court verified.

But he didn't stop to add more. With his arm hooked around Rayna's waist, he kept her moving to Egan's office, where he had her sit in a chair next to the desk. He also shut the door.

He stared at her as if waiting for something, and that was when Rayna realized he was looking at her hands. They were shaking. Heck, she was shaking. And before she even knew it was going to happen, the tears came.

The emotions hit her all at once. For three years she'd been battling the stigma of being branded a killer, and that wasn't just going away despite the fact of Bobby Joe's return. She'd hated him for a long time now but never so much as in this moment. Bobby Joe had taken her life and torn it into little pieces, and he was still tearing it, still trying to break her.

"I don't want to cry," she insisted. But that didn't stop the tears.

Court grabbed her some tissues, but instead of just handing them to her, he wiped her face. Their eyes met. And she saw more of that frustration and guilt in his expression. Yes, she could see that even through the tears.

He muttered some profanity, pulled her to her feet and eased her into his arms. "You can yell at me if it'll make you feel better."

She didn't want to yell at anyone. Especially Court. Right now, he was the only sane thing in her life.

That stopped her.

And Rayna felt herself go stiff. Court obviously

felt it, too, because he looked down at her. Again, he seemed to be waiting for something, but she didn't know what exactly.

Not until he kissed her, that was.

Even though she figured he was doing this to comfort her, Rayna instantly got a jolt of other emotions. Familiar ones. Because the kiss spurred the old fires between them. And it kept on stirring it because he continued to kiss her. This went well past the comforting stage, especially when he pulled her against him.

Court made a sound, a grumble from deep within his chest. It seemed like some kind of protest, maybe a plea for him to stop. But he didn't. He continued the kiss until the taste of him was sliding right through her.

Yes, this was a cure for tears, but it soon gave her a new problem. The touch of his chest against her breasts, the way he took her mouth…that only made her want him even more.

Rayna found herself slipping her arms around his neck to bring him even closer. Not that she could actually do that. Not while they were clothed anyway, and there was little chance of them stripping down in Egan's office. However, there was still a chance of things escalating.

Court backed her against the door, and the kiss raged on. Until they were out of breath. Until Rayna was certain she could take no more. Only then did he pull back from her, and she braced herself. Court would almost certainly curse and remind her that kissing her had been a huge mistake.

He didn't.

But she saw something else in his eyes that she hadn't wanted to see. Sympathy. He was feeling sorry for her, maybe because he and his father hadn't believed her about Bobby Joe. Maybe because he knew she was probably very close to losing it. Either way, she didn't want that from him, and that was why she moved to the side.

"We should review the security footage Raleigh emailed to you," she managed to say. Not easily. It was hard to talk with her breath thin and her head light. "And talk to Mitch. Plus, Whitney will be here soon."

She would have gone back into the squad room to his desk if Court hadn't caught her hand. He looked at her as if trying to figure out what was going on in her head. Then he cursed.

"That wasn't a pity kiss," he snarled. "Trust me, when I kiss, it's for just one reason, and it doesn't have anything to do with pity."

That pretty much took care of what little breath she had, but he didn't give her a chance to respond. He threw open the door and went to his desk.

Thea glanced up from her computer screen but then quickly looked away. She could no doubt see what was going on between them and had wisely decided to stay out of it.

"Any updates on my father?" Court asked Thea. He sat at his desk and started downloading the email from Raleigh.

"Nothing, but I'm hoping in this case that no news is good news."

Rayna agreed. "What about Whitney? Have you seen her? She was supposed to come in."

That was definitely a surprise to Thea. "No sign of her. Should I call her?"

"No," Court answered. "I'll deal with Whitney, but

I am going to need you to run that trace on the phone call he got from his brother. Did Mitch ask for a lawyer before Ian went in to take his statement?"

"No. I suspect he will though if he really did break into Rayna's house."

"He claims someone else did the actual breaking in," Court said. "What about Bo's lawyer?"

"Not here yet, either. He called and said he was stuck in San Antonio, so it might be a couple more hours."

Rayna wished they could get the answers from the teenager now, but it was possible that Bo was going to be a dead end when it came to helping them with this investigation.

While Thea got to work on the phone trace, Court loaded the security footage. "Raleigh said my mom's demeanor changed at the five-minute mark, but I want to watch it from the start."

He pulled up a chair for her, their gazes connecting again when she sat. "For the record, I didn't let you kiss me out of pity," she whispered.

The corner of his mouth lifted for just a second, but that seemed to indicate they'd declared some kind of truce. Rayna was okay with that, especially since the images loaded on the screen, and she knew that had to push kissing, and thoughts of kissing, to the side. That didn't mean this heat was going away though.

Rayna leaned in closer to the monitor when she spotted Helen making her way to the coffee shop. She certainly didn't look upset.

As Raleigh had warned them, the images weren't so clear when Helen went inside, but they could still see when she greeted Jennifer with a handshake. After that, the women sat at a table so that only the sides of their bodies were facing the camera.

"Too bad this doesn't have sound," Court mumbled as they reached the five-minute mark.

Rayna agreed because there was definitely a difference in Helen's body language. "Maybe your mom was just upset about reliving the details of Hannah's murder."

"Maybe." But he didn't sound especially hopeful about that.

They watched as Alma came in through the other entrance, and as the woman had said, she stayed back behind a half wall that would have hidden her from view of Helen and Jennifer. Alma hadn't been in the shop very long when Helen stood. She took something that Jennifer handed her, perhaps a business card, and slipped it into her purse before she hurried out.

Once Helen was outside, it was easier to see her face. She wiped at her eyes as if wiping away tears and then disappeared out of camera range. Court reached to turn off the footage but then stopped.

They both zoomed in on the man who was outside of the coffee shop. He was in position to have watched the meeting between Helen and Jennifer, and now he was watching Helen as she left. And the man was someone they both recognized.

Mitch.

"Mitch sure as hell didn't mention any of this," Court grumbled, and he got to his feet. "I think it's time to question him."

"So do I, but why would he have been spying on them? You think Jennifer told him about the meeting?"

"That's my guess. I'm betting Mitch knows a lot

more about Jennifer than he's letting on." He started for the door but then stopped when Rayna's phone rang. "If that's Whitney, tell her to get her butt in here right now."

But it wasn't Whitney's name on the screen.

It was Unknown Caller.

She hadn't thought her stomach could tighten even more, but it did. Rayna showed the screen to Court and waited until he got out his own phone to record the conversation before she answered the call and put it on speaker.

Nothing. Not for several long moments.

"Hey, Rayna. It's me," the caller said.

Bobby Joe.

Like the message he'd left for Mitch, this one was filled with static, too.

"Can't wait to see you," Bobby Joe added.

Rayna could have sworn her heart went to her knees, and she fired glances outside the window. There was a trickle of people on the sidewalks, but there was no sign of Bobby Joe.

"Where are you?" Court snapped.

There was a long pause. "Rayna's gonna pay for what she did."

Rayna hated that he could still get to her like this, and she mustered up as much steel as she could manage. "Is that a threat?"

Bobby Joe didn't confirm that, but after another hesitation, he just laughed.

It did indeed feel like a threat. And there was nothing she could do about it. Not unless they caught Bobby

Joe, that was. Then he could be charged with fraud for trying to frame her for his murder.

"Bye, Rayna," Bobby Joe added. "See you soon." And the call ended.

Chapter Twelve

Court could feel the dangerous energy bubbling up inside him, and he hated what this was doing to Rayna. All those feelings and energy were so strong that they almost overshadowed his lawman's instincts.

"Something's not right," he said.

That caused Rayna to fire glances all around them again.

"No, I don't think Bobby Joe is nearby," Court added. "In fact, I'm not sure that call was actually from him. I think it was a recording of old conversations that have been spliced together."

She opened her mouth as if she might dispute that, but then Rayna frowned. She was obviously going back through what she'd heard. "Maybe."

"That would account for the static and the long pauses in between some of the words."

Rayna shook her head. "But who would do that? Why would someone want to make us believe it was Bobby Joe?"

"Maybe to rattle us." And if so, that had worked. But Court got the feeling there was much more to it than that.

He handed his phone to Thea. "I recorded a call

that Bobby Joe supposedly just made. I need the voice analyzed on it. Also the voice on the message left for Mitch."

Thea nodded. "I've already started working on tracing that call to Mitch. It came from a burner, so no luck."

That was too bad. A burner was a prepaid cell phone that couldn't be traced.

"But I did find something strange," Thea added a moment later. "Using that same burner, someone called Mitch three times before leaving that message. It appears Mitch answered the other three calls, but Bobby Joe or whoever it was didn't talk to him. Or if he did, they were very short conversations. It appears the only time the caller actually communicated was through the message he left on the fourth call that Mitch didn't answer."

Yeah, that was strange, and it was right in line with Court's theory about Bobby Joe's conversation being spliced together. Maybe someone had taken old recordings and used them.

But again. Court didn't know why.

"I'm done with his phone," Thea added. "I've gotten everything I can from it—including copying the message from Bobby Joe. Now I'm just waiting on the phone company to email a complete record of all the calls and texts he's made in the past couple of months."

It might take a while to get that, especially since Mitch wasn't being charged with a serious crime.

"I can give Mitch back his phone when I talk to him," Court said, taking it from her.

Thea nodded again. "It can't wait until Ian is done taking his statement?" she asked. Her concern wasn't because she had doubts about his interrogation skills. It was because Mitch was a hothead who could set off Court's own temper.

"No. I'm not going to interview him right now. I just want to ask him about that message."

Thea still looked a little skeptical. So did Rayna, and she followed him to the interview room. Ian was typing something on a laptop. It was no doubt Mitch's statement.

Mitch immediately got to his feet when Court opened the door. "Did they find Bobby Joe?"

Court shook his head and quietly apologized to Ian for interrupting the interview.

"You're sure your brother is actually alive?" Court asked Mitch. He put the man's phone on the table next to him.

The surprise went through Mitch's eyes. "Of course he is. You heard the message."

"I heard what could have been something recorded years ago. Something that was put together to make you believe it was actually from Bobby Joe."

"It was from him," Mitch practically shouted. But then he stopped and slid glances at both of them. "Is this some kind of trick?"

"You tell me," Court argued.

"If you're accusing me of…whatever the hell this is, then I want a lawyer." Mitch's voice got even louder, and his hands went to his hips. "And I want bail. You can't lock me up for trespassing."

Well, he could put him in jail, but Court couldn't hold him for long, since right now the only charge he could make against Mitch was a misdemeanor. But maybe there was another way of going about this.

"Can you think of a reason why someone would want you to fake that message?" Court asked.

"No! My brother wanted to meet me. He wanted to show me the gun that Rayna has hidden somewhere."

Not likely. There'd been plenty of searches of Rayna's place that should have already revealed a gun if there was one. Of course, Bobby Joe could have hidden it as he'd maybe done when he'd put the key in the birdhouse.

And that led Court to an idea.

Bobby Joe might not try to see Mitch as long as he was here, but if he was indeed alive, he might contact Mitch as soon as no cops were around.

"You'll be able to leave as soon as you're done with the interview," Court told Mitch.

Ian made eye contact with Court and seemed to know what Court was thinking. "We're done. Well, unless you're going to press charges against him for trespassing," Ian said to Rayna.

She glanced at all of them. Paused. Then shook her head. "No charges unless we prove Mitch actually broke down the door."

"I didn't," Mitch insisted.

Maybe he was telling the truth, but it didn't matter. "Just stop by Thea's desk," Court told Mitch. "She'll print out a copy of what Ian just typed up so you can read through it and sign it. Will you need a ride?"

"Thanks, but no, thanks. I left my truck on a trail near Rayna's, but I'll find a way to get home." Mitch grabbed his phone and hurried out of the room.

"I know it's a risk, letting him walk," Court said to Rayna.

"But it might help us catch Bobby Joe," she finished for him. "If he's really alive, that is."

Yes, that was the million-dollar question, but Mitch might be able to give them the answer to that.

"You want me to follow him?" Ian asked the moment that Mitch was out of earshot.

Court nodded. "But I don't want you to go alone. And we don't have another available deputy." He didn't like this much, but it was a temporary solution until he could get some Rangers in place to pick up the tail on Mitch. "Rayna and I will go with you."

Ian didn't look so certain about that. Neither was Court, but he had no intentions of leaving her at the sheriff's office, where Thea already had her hands full.

"It'll be okay," he told Rayna. Without thinking, he brushed a kiss on her cheek.

He immediately cursed himself for doing that. Yeah, that other kiss had definitely broken down some barriers that should have stayed in place. At least until this investigation was over.

Court texted Thea to let her know what was going on, and Ian, Rayna and he went out the back to one of the two unmarked cars they kept there. It was reinforced just like a cruiser, but maybe Mitch wouldn't recognize it was a cop car. Ian got behind the wheel, and after Court got in the back seat with Rayna, Ian pulled to the side of the building so they'd be able to see when Mitch left.

Court was so caught up in keeping watch that it gave him a jolt when the sound of his phone ringing shot through the car. Not Unknown Caller this time. It was Rachel.

"How's Mom?" he asked the moment he answered.

"Not great. They're transferring her to the hospital in San Antonio." Rachel was crying. No doubt about that. Court could hear her sobs. "They'll commit her there until she can have some evals done."

"You need me there?" Though he wasn't sure how he would manage it. Still, he would if necessary.

"No need. We won't be here much longer, and Mom won't be allowed visitors for a while at the other hospital."

That meant Court wouldn't be able to question his mother anytime soon about what he'd seen on the surveillance footage. However, there might be a way around that. "By any chance did Mom bring her purse to the hospital?"

He could tell from Rachel's slight huff that the question had surprised her. "No. It's at the house. Why?"

Court hoped he didn't alarm Rachel unnecessarily with this, but it was something they had to know. "I believe she might have gotten a business card or something from the murdered PI, Jennifer Reeves. That was a couple of days ago. I know it's a long shot, but I need to see if she still has it."

Rachel's slight gasp let him know that he'd alarmed her after all. "I'll be going back to the ranch when Mom is transferred. I want to get some things and go to the hospital in San Antonio. I can check her purse as soon as I'm back at the house."

"Thanks. But I don't want you driving alone."

"Egan's already told me that. He'll take me back, and then we'll drive to San Antonio together. He's arranging to have some local cops guard me."

Good. He thanked her again and ended the call when he saw Mitch finally come out of the building. The man didn't even look their way. He immediately took out his phone, made a call and started walking on the sidewalk away from them. Ian eased out of the parking lot so they could follow him.

Mitch had made it only about a block when Court's phone rang again. For a moment he thought it was Mitch calling him, but it was Whitney's name on the screen. Court pressed the answer button, ready to blast her for not coming directly to the sheriff's office as he'd ordered her to do. However, Whitney spoke before Court could say anything.

"Oh, God. You've got to help me!" Whitney blurted out. "Oh, God. There's a fire."

And then Court heard something on the other end of the line that he definitely didn't want to hear.

The sound of a gunshot.

RAYNA HAD NO trouble hearing the sound. Or Whitney's bone-chilling scream that quickly followed the blast from what had to be a gunshot.

"Whitney?" Court yelled into the phone. "Where are you? What's going on?"

"You have to help me," Whitney begged. "I'm just up the street by the hardware store."

That was the direction Mitch was walking. The direction that Ian went as well, and both Court and he drew their guns.

The hardware store was about two blocks away, but the moment Ian pulled out of the parking lot, Rayna saw the smoke. It was thick and black, billowing in the air, and the wind was blowing it right toward them.

Mitch obviously noticed it, too, because he turned and started running back to the sheriff's office. Maybe he would stay there instead of trying to get to Bobby Joe. That way, someone could still follow him after they took care of this situation.

"I'm calling the fire department," Ian said, and he did that while he continued to drive closer to the smoke. It wouldn't take the fire department long to get there at all. Well, it wouldn't take long if there wasn't any other gunfire.

"Get down on the seat," Court told her, and he handed her his phone. "Try to find out exactly where Whitney is and who fired that shot."

Rayna did get down, and she tried to level her voice. Whitney had sounded terrified, and it wouldn't do the woman any good if she heard the panic in Rayna's tone, too.

"Where are you?" Rayna asked.

Whitney started coughing, which meant she was probably very close to the smoke. Maybe in the middle of it. "I think I saw Bobby Joe."

So, not just a message or phone call this time but a possible sighting. Of course, Hallie had posed as Rayna, so someone could be doing the same when it came to Bobby Joe. "Where did you see him?"

"In the alley by the hardware store." Whitney coughed some more. "I'm not sure he saw me, so I went running after him. I saw a car parked back there, but that's when the fire started. The flames just popped up right in front of me, and I couldn't get to him."

Which meant someone had almost certainly set it. Before Rayna could ask her who'd fired the shot, there was another one. Then another. They sounded much too close, which was probably why Ian pulled off the street and into a parking place outside the bookstore.

"Everyone, take cover now!" Court shouted when he lowered his window.

Rayna could hear people running and shouting. She prayed that none of them would be hurt.

"Where are you?" Whitney said on another of those sobs. "I need to find you. And we need to find Bobby Joe so he can clear your name once and for all."

"No. You need to go inside the nearest building and stay put," Rayna assured her. "You could be shot."

Whitney said something that she didn't catch, and the line went dead. Rayna didn't try to call her back because she didn't want the sound of a ringing phone to cause a gunman to home in on Whitney. Maybe she had done as Rayna told her and had taken cover.

Behind them, she heard the wail of the sirens from the fire engine. But she also heard a fourth shot. It was even closer than the others had been.

The fifth one slammed into the front windshield.

Both deputies cursed, and Court pushed her even farther down on the seat. "You see the shooter?" Ian asked.

"No." But Court was glancing all around them. "Tell the fire department not to approach. It's too dangerous."

Another shot cracked through the air, and this one hit just a few inches from the previous one. The glass held, but it was cracked enough that other bullets might be able to get through.

"Get us out of here," Court told Ian.

The deputy did. The moment he finished with radioing the fire department, Ian threw the car into Reverse and hit the gas. He didn't get far though, probably because of other vehicles.

"Hold on," Ian told them.

His warning came only a few seconds before he made a sharp turn, causing Court and Rayna to slam against each other. She lifted her head enough to see that Ian had turned around in the middle of the street and was now heading back in the direction of the sheriff's office.

The shooter fired a flurry of shots at the car, all slamming into the back windshield.

"I see the guy," Court said.

She followed his gaze to the left side of the street. The same side as the fire. But she was too far down on the seat to see what had captured his attention.

"It's a man wearing a mask," Court added.

It was probably the same person who'd shot at them at the hospital. But had he also been the one to set the fire? And if so, why? Maybe he thought it would conceal him, and if so, it'd worked. The guy had managed to get off at least ten shots before Court had spotted him.

"You want me to go back?" Ian asked.

She saw the quick debate in Court's eyes. He wanted to catch this guy and would have almost certainly gone after him if she hadn't been in the car. "No. Let's take Rayna to the sheriff's office. We'll regroup and go after him."

Which meant Court was going to put himself in the line of fire. Of course, that was his job, but it sickened her to think that he could be hurt or worse because some goon was after her.

Ian screeched to a stop in front of the sheriff's office, but none of them got out. They sat there, no doubt waiting to see if the shooter would continue. If he did, it wasn't safe for them to run inside. Even though they would be out in the open only a couple of seconds, that would be enough time for them to be gunned down.

Rayna lifted her head again. Thea was in the doorway of the sheriff's office, and she had her gun drawn. There was no sign of Mitch, but Court's phone rang again, and she saw Whitney's name on the screen. Rayna answered it as fast as she could.

"Please tell me you took cover," Rayna told her.

"I couldn't. For your sake, I had to find Bobby Joe."

Rayna groaned. "No, you don't. There's a gunman out there."

"Yes. I saw him. Are you sure it was a man? I thought maybe it was a woman wearing a ski mask."

That gave Rayna a jolt of adrenaline. It wouldn't be Court's mom, since she was on her way to a hospital in San Antonio, but it could be Alma. Still, that seemed like a stretch. If Alma wanted them dead, she could have just hired someone. That included a female assassin.

Whitney gasped, the sound coming through loud and clear. "Rayna, tell Court he needs to get here. He needs to see this."

That didn't help with the adrenaline, either. "See what?" Rayna pressed.

"Oh, God. There's a body in that fire."

Chapter Thirteen

Court didn't like anything about this, but there wasn't much else he could do but stand and watch as the fire department finished up with what was now a crime scene.

One with a body.

Once they were done, the medical examiner and CSIs could get in the alley and maybe figure out what had gone on here. He could question not only the fire chief, Delbert Monroe, but also help track down possible witnesses. Until that happened, Court could only speculate. And worry about Rayna.

He'd left her at the sheriff's office with Thea and Ian, and Egan was on the way now that he'd put the ranch on lockdown. Three lawmen would hopefully be enough to keep her safe, but she was in the building with not only Bo but Whitney, as well. At least Bo was still locked up, but he couldn't do the same to Whitney because there were no charges against her. Still, that didn't mean Court trusted her.

Ditto for Mitch.

But Court hadn't heard a peep from the man since he'd left shortly before the fire. He wasn't answering his phone, and no one had seen him. That meant Mitch could have been the person who'd worn a ski mask and shot at them. He would have had time to duck into the alley and do that.

Whitney had said though that she thought the shooter was a woman. So far, no other witness had managed to corroborate that, but it didn't mean she was mistaken or lying. That was because their other suspect—Alma—wasn't answering her phone, either.

No, there wasn't any part of this he liked.

Plus, there was the whole problem of an unidentified shooter. There hadn't been any shots fired in over an hour, so that probably meant the gunman was long gone. That didn't mean he wouldn't be back though.

Court took out his phone to call and check on Rayna, but he finally saw Delbert making his way toward him. He was sporting a weary expression, along with soot and ashes on his clothes.

"Our DB is male," Delbert said right off the bat. "We didn't touch the body, of course, but it's badly burned. Too burned to make a visual ID."

That didn't surprise Court because the vehicle that had contained the body was a charred mess. "I smell gasoline," Court pointed out.

Delbert nodded. "An accelerant was used. I suspect it was poured over the car and then lit. Most of his clothes burned off, but there's some tissue remaining. Plus, his teeth are in good shape. We can compare them to dental records."

Good. Because the person's identity might lead Court to finding out why he was dead. "Any signs that the guy struggled to get out of the burning car?"

"No. He was lying on the back seat."

That possibly meant he was unconscious or even

already dead before the fire. Often criminals tried to use fire to cover up any DNA or trace evidence they might have left behind. Of course, it would be bold for a criminal to do that in broad daylight.

Or maybe not bold after all.

Court motioned to the blackened strip on the concrete between the dead guy's car and them. It was where a second fire had been set, and it was a good fifteen feet from the other deadly one. "Can you think of any good reason why someone would do that?"

Delbert immediately shook his head. "No, but I can think of a bad one. A strip fire like that would conceal whatever was going on in the car."

Yeah, that'd been Court's theory, too. If the person who'd set it had been behind the first set of flames, it would have made it very hard for someone on the street to see him or her. Then the person could have escaped through the back alley.

There were no cameras back there, either.

"I went ahead and called in the CSIs," Delbert went on. "They'll be here soon." He hitched his thumb back to the alley. "Just thought you should know there's a cell phone on the ground. It's not a fancy smart one. Just one of the cheap ones you can buy just about anywhere. Again, we didn't touch it, and it might not even belong to the vic."

Court would definitely have it collected and tested. If it was the vic's though, he wasn't sure why it was out of the car when the body was inside.

Delbert glanced around the street, which was empty now. But Delbert wasn't looking at the sidewalks. He was studying the buildings and the streetlight that was to their right.

"There aren't any cameras," Court told him.

Of course, Court would check to see if anyone had recently added one, but this area of Main Street was essentially a dead zone when it came to surveillance. Alma might not have known that, but Whitney and Mitch likely would have.

Ditto for his mother.

That was because it'd come up in a discussion when there'd been a robbery at the hardware store a couple of years ago. Many people then had lobbied to get security cameras for all of Main Street, but it hadn't been in the budget.

Court wanted to exclude his mother as a suspect, but he kept going back to the point that Raleigh had made. Whoever had hired the shooter might no longer have a leash on him or her. If that proved to be true, then his mom was still a possible person of interest.

When Court saw the CSI van pull up, he figured it was time for him to go back to the station. He could do a lot more good there—including keep watch on Rayna—while the CSIs processed the crime scene. However, he did remind both the CSIs and Delbert to call him the moment they had anything on the body or the phone. Too bad Court couldn't just take it now, but he couldn't touch it until the CSIs had gotten pictures.

Court drove his cruiser back to the sheriff's office, parking behind the shot-up unmarked car. Just seeing it made him feel sick and riled him to the core. Once again, Rayna had come close to being killed, and they still didn't know why.

"Anything?" Rayna asked the moment he stepped inside. She was in the doorway of Egan's office, her hands bracketed on the jamb. Her knuckles were white.

"We'll know something soon," he assured her and hoped that wasn't a lie.

Rayna wasn't alone. Both Thea and Ian were in the squad room, but there was no sign of Whitney.

"Egan got here about fifteen minutes ago, and Whitney's in the interview room with him," Rayna said. "She seemed really upset." Court didn't miss the *seemed*, and he wondered if that meant Rayna was having doubts about her friend.

Because he thought they could both use it, he went to Rayna and pulled her into his arms for a hug. Yeah, he needed it all right, and that was why Court lingered a moment before he eased back from her—along with easing her deeper into Egan's office. Not so he could kiss her, though that was something he suddenly wanted to do. No, it was because the shooter was still at large and could try to fire through the windows of the sheriff's office.

"Did Whitney say anything to you before Egan got here?" Court asked her.

"Not really. She was crying a lot. I asked her why she didn't come straight to the sheriff's office after you told her to, and she said she had to pick up some meds first. She'd felt a migraine coming on."

Since Whitney did indeed suffer from migraines, it wasn't much of a stretch that she'd need meds for the headaches. Still, the timing was suspicious.

"Come on." Court took Rayna by the hand. "We'll go to the observation room and listen to what she's saying to Egan." That was better than standing there with all this energy still zinging between them. "I'll also try again to track down Mitch."

He took out his phone, but it rang before he could

make the call. However, this one could be important, since it was from one of the CSIs, Larry Hanson. Court put the call on speaker and hoped it wasn't bad news. They'd already had enough of that for the day.

"I went ahead and photographed the phone," Larry said right off. "I was about to bag it when I saw there was a missed call on the screen. I don't have the password to see if there's a voice mail, but I got the name of the caller."

"Who?" Court immediately asked.

"Alma Lawton. You know her?"

Hell. "Yeah. I know her." And he was going to get her right back in here for questioning. "I don't suppose you can tell whose phone that is?"

"Nope. Not without the password. I'll get it to the lab though to see if they can come up with something. We might have something on the body soon, too."

That got Court's attention. "Dental records?"

"We'll try those, sure, but it seems as if the back of the body might still be intact. The ME thinks he can see a wallet in the back of the guy's jeans. We won't know though until we can lift it, but that shouldn't be much longer."

If there was a wallet, there might be an ID. Of course, it didn't mean the ID or, for that matter, the wallet belonged to the dead guy. However, it could be a good break if it did.

Court thanked Larry and went back into the squad room so he could get Alma's number from the computer.

"It must not be Alma's phone they found, since she was the caller," Rayna said. "But I don't think she knows any of our other suspects. Not personally, anyway," she added.

Rayna was no doubt referring to his mother. Alma had definitely heard of her, but neither Alma nor Helen had mentioned being in contact with each other.

The moment he had Alma's number, he tried to call her. It went straight to voice mail, so Court left a message for her to get to the sheriff's office ASAP for questioning. He tried Raleigh next, but the deputy who answered said the sheriff was in the process of arresting a burglary suspect. Since Court had struck out with both Alma and Raleigh, he made another call to his sister. Unlike the other two, Rachel answered on the first ring.

"Are you okay?" Rachel asked before he could even say anything.

"We're fine. You?"

"I'm as well as can be expected. Egan said there was a body, that that's why he had to go in."

"There is. The CSIs are working on the ID right now." He gathered his breath for the next question. "By any chance, did Mom have a new phone? Not the one we got her for Christmas but a cheaper one?"

"I don't think so. But I can look in her purse. I was going to do that anyway because you said you wanted me to check for a business card."

"Yes. Could you do that now?"

Since Rachel was the daughter and sister of lawmen, she knew that wasn't a casual question and that it likely had something to do with the investigation. "What's this all about?"

"Just checking to see if she called anyone."

It was a pretty sorry explanation, and Rachel made

a sound to indicate she wasn't buying it. Still, she was obviously looking because several moments later she added, "Her phone's not on her nightstand." Court could hear her moving around. "I'm looking through her purse now. No phone. You think she lost it?"

He hoped not, and he hoped even more that she hadn't bought another phone and used it to call Alma. Of course, even if she had, that wouldn't have explained why it would be in that alley.

"There's a card," Rachel added. "Yes, it's for Stigler Investigations. You think Jennifer Reeves works for this PI agency?"

No, that hadn't come up at any point, so he sandwiched his phone between his shoulder and ear, went to his desk and typed in the name on his computer. It was another agency all right.

One that specialized in getting proof of cheating spouses.

That felt like a punch to the gut. Because it meant that his mother had likely known about Warren's affair days ago. That would have been plenty enough time to hire someone to fire that shot that'd gone into his father's chest.

"Do you have access to Mom and Dad's bank account?" Court asked.

"No," Rachel answered, hesitation in her voice. "But I'm sure I can get it. Why?"

Court didn't go with the full truth on this. "I just want to see if maybe Mom hired a PI, too. It might have gone on her credit card if she hired someone over the phone. Also, look for a check."

"Now, are you going to tell me what this is all about?" Rachel demanded.

"Just making sure there's not another PI out there to interfere with this investigation." But what he really wanted to know was if there was enough money missing for his mother to have hired a gunman. "Call me if you find anything." With more of that skepticism in her tone, Rachel assured him that she would.

Since it might take a while for Rachel to do that, Court led Rayna to the observation room. Egan and Whitney were there, and Whitney was still crying. He wanted to give her the benefit of the doubt, not only because she was Rayna's friend but also because she worked at the sheriff's office. He hated the possibility that he'd been working with a would-be killer after all these years.

Rayna stared at her friend through the glass. "Whitney hasn't been the same person since my trial. She's been, well, distant."

Maybe because Whitney had thought Rayna was really a killer. But there was another angle on this. "You think Whitney could have had feelings for Bobby Joe?"

"It's possible." Since Rayna hadn't hesitated, it meant she'd given that some thought. Then she shrugged. "But there were times when I felt as if Whitney wanted me to ditch him. Whenever we'd have a girls' night out, she was always trying to fix me up with other guys."

Again, that was maybe because Whitney wanted Bobby Joe for herself. She did seem to be genuinely upset, and maybe that was because of the possible Bobby Joe sighting.

"Who do you think set the fire?" Egan asked her.

Whitney's head whipped up. "You're not accusing

me of doing that, are you?" There was some bitterness in her voice.

"Just asking," Egan calmly clarified.

"Well, I don't know. I told you the flames just shot up right in front of me. I would have caught up with Bobby Joe if it hadn't been for that."

If she was telling the truth, it meant someone had put that line of gasoline there before Whitney had even gone into the alley, and it was possible someone had triggered it with a remote device.

But why?

That was the question Court was asking himself when his phone rang, and he saw Larry's name on the screen.

"We got the wallet from our dead guy," Larry immediately said. "And there was a driver's license. The name on it is Dustin Clark, but the photo is one I'm sure you'll recognize. I'm texting it to you now."

Court knew Larry was right the moment he loaded the photo and saw the man's face.

Bobby Joe.

HE WAS FINALLY DEAD.

For the first time in three years, Rayna actually believed that was true—that Bobby Joe was no longer a threat to her. Of course, they'd have to wait for more proof of the dental records, but she didn't need anything else.

"You should sit down," she heard Court say.

He didn't wait for her to do that though. He practically put her in the chair in the observation room. That was when Rayna realized she was wobbling some and wasn't feeling very steady. Court probably thought she was about to collapse. She was, but it was from relief.

That relief didn't last long though.

"Will people once again think I killed Bobby Joe?" she asked.

Court shook his head, sighed and brushed a kiss on the top of her head. All of those gestures eased some of the gut-wrenching tension inside her. "You were with Ian and me when that fire started."

True, but since many people in McCall Canyon thought she was a killer, they might think she'd set this up in some way.

"Who would have killed him?" Rayna pressed.

Court shrugged. "For us to know that, we'll have to figure out what he's been doing all this time. I doubt this was suicide, so that means either someone killed him in the car and set fire to it or they put him in the vehicle after he was already dead. Either way, it's murder."

Yes, and she couldn't rule out the rogue gunman who was running around shooting at them. The person wearing that ski mask would have had time to set the fire before launching this latest attack against them. For that matter though, so would Mitch, Whitney and maybe even Alma.

"Wait here," Court instructed.

Since she didn't trust her legs, Rayna didn't have a choice about that. She watched as Court went into the interview room to whisper something to Egan. He was no doubt telling his brother about Bobby Joe, but Court didn't wait around for Egan's or Whitney's response. He left and went back to the squad room. A few seconds later, he returned with a bottle of water and a laptop.

In the interview room, Egan was breaking the news to Whitney, and Rayna watched the shock wash over the woman's face. More tears followed, but Rayna didn't focus on that. She turned her attention to Court, who was running a computer check on Bobby Joe's alias, Dustin Clark.

"That's all there is on him," Court said, pulling up the driver's license. "No record. Not even a parking ticket."

Probably because Bobby Joe had been living under the radar, waiting for his chance to come after her again. Of course, she still didn't know why he'd waited all this time.

"I'll check the address he gave the DMV," Court added, but he stopped when they heard the sound of voices in the squad room.

Alma.

"Why would Deputy McCall leave a message like that for me?" Alma snapped. She sounded angry. Looked it, too, when Rayna saw the woman after Court and she stepped out into the hall.

"Because I need to talk to you about a possible murder," Court answered. He sounded angry as well, but Rayna knew there was also plenty of frustration. Each thing they found only seemed to lead them to more questions.

Alma gave him a flat look. "Murder? Really? Did Warren die?"

Court matched her look with a scowl. "Not Warren, but a man you called shortly before he was murdered."

Alma started shaking her head before he'd even finished. "The only person I've called today was one of my former hands, Dustin Clark."

Bingo. Well, at least she hadn't claimed it was a setup.

Court motioned for Alma to follow him to Egan's office, and once the three of them were inside, he shut the door. Bobby Joe's picture was still on the laptop, so Court turned it in Alma's direction.

"Is that the Dustin Clark you called?" he pressed.

Alma had a closer look at the screen. "Yes. Did something happen to him?" If she was concerned about that, she didn't show it. She could have been discussing the weather.

"He's dead. Now, tell me how you know him and why you called him. Then you can explain how you got here so fast. You didn't have enough time to drive from Durango Ridge."

"I was already here in McCall Canyon," Alma admitted. "I was coming to pay Dustin what I owed him. He's been working for me out at my ranch."

It didn't sound like a coincidence that Bobby Joe would be working for someone with ties to the McCalls.

"There's no record of his employment with you," Court pointed out.

"Because I paid him in cash. That's the way he wanted it, and I was happy to oblige. He was good with the horses." She glanced at the screen again. "You're sure he's dead?"

"We have a body that we believe is his. When's the last time you saw him?" Court continued without even pausing.

Alma huffed, and she frowned. "Maybe about a

week ago. He was at my ranch and told one of the other hands that he had to leave to take care of some personal things. He didn't come back. That's why I called him to make arrangements to meet him so I could pay him."

"And he answered that call?" Rayna wanted to know.

"Yes. Like I said, that's why I'm here in town." Alma's attention shifted back to Court. "Is this about your father?"

Court pulled back his shoulders. "Why do you ask that?"

"Because Dustin hated Warren, that's why. He never did tell me why, but a few months ago Dustin saw Warren picking me up at the ranch, and he pulled me aside later and said Warren couldn't be trusted, that he'd been a dirty cop when he was still sheriff here. I got the feeling there was some bad blood between them, but when I mentioned it to Warren, he said he didn't know anyone by that name."

And he wouldn't have, since Bobby Joe was using an alias. Still, it made Rayna wonder why Warren hadn't followed up on that. Or maybe he had so many people who disliked him that it wasn't anything that concerned him.

"Dustin's real name was Bobby Joe Hawley," Court provided. "Ever hear him mention that?"

She quickly shook her head. "I only knew him as Dustin." She stopped, looked at Rayna. "That's the man you were accused of murdering. The one that Warren was certain you'd killed," she added. "Since you were acquitted, that means you couldn't be tried for his death now."

"I didn't kill him," Rayna insisted. She kept her stare on Alma.

"Well, neither did I." Alma huffed again. "What possible motive could I have for wanting him dead?"

"Maybe you hired him to shoot my father," Court answered. "Or maybe Bobby Joe found out you'd hired someone to do that and he was trying to extort money from you. This is a long way to come to pay a ranch hand some wages. You could have just mailed him the money."

Alma's mouth tightened. "I always pay my debts." And since she'd said it through clenched teeth, it sounded like some kind of threat. But she glanced away, her expression softening a little. "Dustin... Bobby Joe or whatever his name is...said he didn't have an address here. Nor a car. He asked me to meet him."

Court and Rayna exchanged another glance, and Rayna could almost see the thought going through his head. He was wondering if Bobby Joe had been planning to set up Alma in some way. Though that still didn't explain who'd killed him.

"Bobby Joe hated my father and Rayna," Court said to Alma. "It's possible he hated them even more because she wasn't convicted of his murder. Now, think back to your dealings with Bobby Joe. Did he ever ask you any questions about Warren or Rayna?"

"Not Rayna," she answered right off. "But like I said, we did discuss Warren after he'd come to the ranch. Bobby Joe was upset, but after what I've just learned about him, maybe he was just trying to make sure Warren didn't come back. If he was supposed to be dead, he wouldn't have wanted Warren to recognize him."

True. In fact, it'd probably given Bobby Joe a jolt, or maybe a secret thrill, when he'd seen Warren.

"But Bobby Joe did mention Helen," Alma added a moment later.

Rayna saw Court's muscles go stiff, and he motioned for Alma to continue.

She did not until she'd taken a deep breath first. "It was after Warren's visit. Bobby Joe told me that Warren was married, and that his wife, Helen, was the darling of McCall Canyon. *Darling*, that's the word he used. Bobby Joe didn't come out and say it, but I could tell he suspected an affair between Warren and me." She paused. "I lied and said Warren was there on ranching business and that there was absolutely nothing going on between us."

If Bobby Joe had truly been suspicious of the affair, Rayna wondered why he hadn't exposed it. He couldn't have personally done that, but he could have sent Helen or someone else an anonymous note or maybe even pictures of Warren's visit to the Lawton ranch.

"Anyway, I told Warren it wasn't a good idea for him to visit me at my house again," Alma continued. "Warren and I ended things shortly after that."

Court stayed quiet a moment, obviously processing that. "And you didn't mention *Dustin* or what he'd said to you about my dad?"

"No." She paused again. "I didn't want to know anyone was suspicious. I mean, I could feel Warren already pulling away from me, and I didn't want to give him a reason to break things off."

That was the first time Alma had admitted that she'd wanted to stay in the relationship.

And, of course, it was also her motive for Warren's attempted murder.

It was hard for Rayna to stand there so close to the woman who might have tried to kill Court and her, but if Alma had indeed done that, then things hadn't gone according to plan. After all, Court, Warren and she were all still alive.

"Am I free to go now?" Alma asked. "Or should I call my lawyer?"

Court gave that some thought. "I don't have a reason to hold you, yet. But I'll be checking your phone records. Now would be a good time to tell me if there's something else you want to add about Bobby Joe, or anything else for that matter."

Alma's mouth tightened again. "I haven't done anything wrong, and the next time you want to speak to me, call Simon." With that, she walked out.

"You believe her?" Rayna said the moment the woman was out of the sheriff's office.

Court shrugged. "I'd love to pin this on her, but I don't think I'm objective when it comes to Alma."

No, neither was she. The woman had basically been living a lie for over thirty years, and she could be lying now.

"I meant it when I said I'll be checking out her story," Court said, "but I can do that at the ranch. I doubt you want to stay around here much longer."

She didn't. Rayna was exhausted and was now dealing with the aftereffects of the spent adrenaline. "But what about the gunman? And what with the fire and attack, I doubt Egan can spare a deputy to go with us."

"I can have a couple of the hands come here and then drive back with us. The ranch is already being guarded."

Yes, but that didn't mean it was safe. Of course, the sheriff's office wasn't exactly safe, either. Someone could easily fire shots into the building.

"Let me talk to Egan before I call the hands," Court added. But his phone rang before he could do that. "It's Larry."

Since this was the CSI, Rayna definitely wanted to hear what he had to say, and thankfully Court put the call on speaker.

"We found something," Larry said as soon as he was on the line. "Court, it's another dead body."

Chapter Fourteen

Court stared out the window of his house. It was something he did often as the sun was setting, something that usually relaxed him. But it was going to take more than familiar scenery to take this raw edge off him.

Four murders. Probably all connected, and yet they still didn't make sense. Now he could add the latest body to the "not making sense" category.

Mitch.

One of their top suspects was dead, shot at point-blank range, two bullets to the head. Since the PI and Hallie had been killed in a similar way, it was possible it'd been the same shooter. But if it was, Court didn't have any proof. All he had were those damn questions that just wouldn't stop going through his mind.

Who'd killed those people? And why? Of course, one of the biggest questions of all—was his mother involved?

So far, Rachel hadn't found any unaccounted-for funds in Helen's checking account. No missing cash, either, from the safe at the family home. But there were other ways people could get cash. His mom could have sold some jewelry or had money stashed away that no one else had known about. The fact she'd known about the affair and had even gotten that business card from Jennifer were red flags that he couldn't ignore. The problem was it was going to be days, maybe even weeks, before he could question his mother.

"You're going to drive yourself crazy, you know that?" Rayna asked.

Her voice cut through some of his mind-clutter. So did the sound of her footsteps as she walked toward him. She'd showered and looked less tense than she had when they'd arrived back at his place. But then, if she'd looked more tense, he would have had to call the doctor because she'd been right on that edge. With reason.

She was probably the killer's next target.

Judging from the other attacks, so was he.

She came closer, and he caught the scent of the soap and shampoo she'd used. *His* soap and shampoo, but it smelled better on her than it ever had on him. She'd dressed in the jeans and blue top they'd gotten from her house. And she was holding the gun he'd given her.

The gun had been a compromise. Court hadn't wanted to give her one because he hadn't wanted her to do anything to put herself in even more danger. If there was another attack, he wanted her to get out of harm's way rather than returning fire.

But that wasn't practical.

The truth was someone could get on the ranch. Yes, the hands were watching the road, but someone could get to his house using the back trails. Heck, a gunman could climb over the fence. Rayna knew that. And that was why she now had the gun.

"Any updates?" she asked. She tucked the gun in the waistband of her jeans at the small of her back, poured herself a cup of coffee and joined him at the window.

This wasn't exactly a topic to keep her nerves steady, but Rayna needed to know. "We don't have a dental match ID on the dead guy in the car, but the other body they found is definitely Mitch. No one heard gunshots, but there was a lot of commotion what with the fire."

"Yes," she said as if giving that some thought. "The unidentified gunman could have killed him. He could have set the fire, too."

"Or Alma or Whitney could have done it," Court quickly pointed out.

Rayna flinched, probably because it was hard for her to hear that her former friend could be a cold-blooded killer. It was especially hard since they weren't sure what Whitney's motive would have been for that.

Alma was a different story though.

"I've gone through Alma's phone records," he explained, "and she did call Bobby Joe aka Dustin three times." That wasn't a large number, and the calls could have been legit if Bobby Joe had actually been working for her.

"What about her financial records?"

He shook his head. "I haven't gotten those yet, but even when I do, I'm not expecting much. If Alma has been putting this plan together for months, then she probably would have been smart enough not to use funds that would create a money trail leading right back to her."

"True."

Court didn't think it was his imagination that she was waiting for more. "Nothing on my mother, either," he added. "Warren also hasn't been much help. He says he didn't know about Mom meeting with the PI."

"You think he could be covering for your mom? He

might feel so bad about the affair that he doesn't want her punished."

That was possible, of course, but Court just couldn't buy it. "If the attacks had only been limited to Dad, he might have covered for her. *Might.* But no way would he sit back and not spill something that involved four murders. Plus, there were the attacks on us. My dad might not have valued his marriage vows, but he'd do anything to protect his kids."

She had a sip of her coffee. "You're right."

That caused him to breathe a little easier. It was already hard enough to accept his mother might have had a part in this without believing the same of his father.

"What about Bo and Whitney?" she asked. "Did Egan get anything from them when he questioned them?"

"No. Whitney stuck to her story about not having a clue what was going on. And Bo didn't say anything that he hadn't already told us. The DA plans to charge him as an adult. That might spur him to spill something new." If there was anything new to spill, that was. Bo did seem like a pawn in all of this.

Like Hallie. Maybe Jennifer, too. And since they were both dead, it meant Bo needed to be in protective custody.

The sun finally dipped below the horizon, so Court went to the foyer, turned off the interior light and turned on the ones outside. There were about a dozen of them, and they went all around the house and grounds. When he'd had them installed though, it hadn't been with the idea of seeing an intruder. It had been to try to keep the coyotes and other wildlife away. Now it might keep that gunman from trying to sneak up on them. Just in case he did, Court made sure the security system was armed and ready. It was.

"Rachel is at the hospital with my mom," Court continued. "Egan's at the main house. Or at least he will be when he finishes up at the office."

Whenever that would be. Court figured it'd be a late night for his brother, and he was feeling guilty about that. Still, someone needed to stay with Rayna at his house, and it might as well be him.

That thought stopped him for a moment.

He *wanted* to be the one to stay with her.

Hell, that wasn't a good sign. Coupled with those kisses he'd been doling out to her, it meant he'd had a big-time loss of focus. He looked at her, to warn her about that, but one look in her eyes, and he realized no warning was necessary. Rayna knew exactly what was going on.

"Sometimes, it feels like we're back in high school," she murmured. Rayna set her coffee cup back on the counter. "Well, with the exception of someone trying to kill us, that is."

She managed to make that sound, well, light, and it caused Court to smile. She smiled, too, but then she quickly looked away as if trying to remind herself neither smiling nor looking at him that way was a good idea.

It wasn't.

Court stayed in the foyer on purpose. Best to keep some distance between them. But Rayna didn't go along with that. She went to him, her steps and body language hesitant. There was nothing hesitant about the feelings going on inside him.

He wanted her.

And no distance between them was going to remedy that. Silently cursing himself and cursing Rayna, Court strode forward to meet her and pulled her into his arms.

RAYNA HAD KNOWN the kiss was coming even before Court's mouth landed on hers. Still, she hadn't been prepared for the shock of the sensations that went through her. Yes, in some ways it did feel as if they were back in high school, but she also hadn't remembered anything this intense when they'd been teenagers.

"You know this is a big mistake, right?" Court asked when he broke away from her for air.

She did know that. So did he.

But apparently knowing wasn't going to make a difference here because he went right back for a second kiss. Rayna had been hesitant about that first one, since it'd thrown her off guard a little, but with this one, she just gave in to the moment and kissed him right back.

Rayna slid her hands around the back of his neck, pulling him closer until they were body to body. Along with the new slam of heat that gave her, it also tapped into some old memories. Of other times when Court had kissed her.

And made love to her.

He'd been her first, something she wouldn't have been able to forget even if he hadn't been doling out some mind-blowing kisses.

Court stopped again, easing back so they could make eye contact. It seemed to be his way of giving her an out. He was giving her time to put a stop to this. But Rayna had no intentions of stopping it. That was why she pulled him right back to her.

He deepened the kiss, stoking the fire between them. And he stoked it even more when he took those kisses to her neck. It didn't take her body long to realize it wanted a lot more of what Court was giving her.

Years ago, Court and she had kissed like this for hours, driving each other crazy, until they'd finally become lovers. All of that came back now and upped the urgency even more.

She reached for the buttons on his shirt, but his hands got in the way. That was because he pulled off her top, tossing it onto the floor. In the same motion, he kissed her breasts. First, the tops, and then he shoved down her bra to kiss her the way Rayna wanted. He'd remembered those were sensitive spots for her, and he made sure he gave her as much pleasure as possible.

But soon, it wasn't enough.

Rayna went after his shirt again and managed to get enough buttons undone so she could kiss his chest. Apparently, that upped the urgency for him, too, because Court pulled her to the floor.

There were no lights on inside, but the exterior lights were enough for Rayna to see his face. Mercy, he was hot. Always had been, and that hadn't changed. If anything, the years had made him even better, and she regretted the time she'd lost with him.

Regretted, too, that she might never have him again like that.

That tugged at her heart, but Rayna didn't have time to dwell on it. That was because the kisses continued. The touches, too, but it was obvious that foreplay wasn't going to last much longer. That was okay with Rayna. For now, she just needed Court to soothe the fierce ache inside her. She needed him to make her forget all the bad things that had been happening.

Of course, she wouldn't forget for long, but that didn't matter.

All that mattered right now was having him.

Court did his part to speed things along. He took out her gun, placing it on the floor next to them, and he shimmied her out of her jeans. Since he'd already taken off her bra and top, it made her aware of just how naked she was. He wasn't. So, she rid him of his shirt and tackled ridding him of the rest of his clothes.

It wasn't pretty, but she was about to get him unzipped and shove off his jeans when he stopped her by sliding his hand over hers.

"Condom," he managed to say. He rummaged through his back pocket to get his wallet and took out a condom from it.

She groaned because she hadn't even remembered safe sex. Then she groaned again, this time in pleasure, when Court started kissing her again.

Those wildfire kisses didn't make it easier for her to move around, but Rayna managed to get him unzipped, and Court broke the kiss long enough to put on the condom.

He looked at her again, and Rayna thought maybe she saw some hesitation in his eyes. But no. There was no hesitation whatsoever when he pushed into her.

She got another huge jolt of pleasure, and it just kept coming when Court started to move inside her. This was familiar but also new. He'd obviously learned more about how to please a woman since their make-out sessions in high school. He seemed to know just how to touch her. Just how to move. Just how to make her crazy with need.

The need couldn't last, of course. That meant the pleasure couldn't, either.

When the pace became harder and faster, it pushed Rayna right over the edge. There was nothing she could do but hold on to Court and make sure he went over the edge with her.

Chapter Fifteen

"I'm getting too old for floor sex," Court grumbled.

Though it really wasn't much of a complaint. His body was slack and practically humming, but if Rayna and he stayed on the hardwood floor much longer, that slackness was going to be replaced with some back aches. That was why he got up, scooped her up in his arms and carried her to the bedroom.

Rayna made a sleepy moan of pleasure and kissed him before he headed to the bathroom. Once he was done, he fully intended to slide right into bed with Rayna and maybe make another mistake tonight.

And it had been a mistake.

Still, he wasn't seeing how he was going to stop himself from making another one. He wanted her, and Court doubted anyone would be able to talk him out of that. Maybe Rayna would get a sudden dose of common sense and tell him to go back to keeping watch.

Or not.

When he went into the bedroom, she patted the spot next to her, motioning for him to join her. She also had a sly smile on her face. Couple with the fact that she was naked, and it erased any chance of him putting a stop to this.

He got on the bed, automatically pulling her into his arms and kissing her. The kiss would have gone on a lot longer if he hadn't heard the ringing sound. It wasn't in his head, either. It was coming from his phone, which he'd left in the foyer. Since it could be a critical call, he bolted from the bed and ran to get it.

Rachel's name was on the screen.

"Is everything okay?" Court immediately asked.

"Fine. Well, you know that's a lie. What I should say is that Mom and I are safe. What about Rayna and you?"

"We're safe, too," he settled for saying.

He really wanted to enjoy seeing Rayna naked a while longer, but when she came into the foyer to gather up her clothes and start dressing, Court did the same. He also put the call on speaker for her.

"Good." Rachel hesitated, and Court wondered if his sister had sensed what'd just gone on. If she did though, she didn't mention it. "Mom is all settled in her room here. It looks like a regular hospital room, but it's, well, noisy. Lots of people coming and going, and every now and then I can hear someone shout. Apparently, they have patients in here who get agitated easily."

His sister wasn't painting a good picture of the place, but maybe his mom wouldn't have to be there for long. "What about security?"

"There's a Texas Ranger in the hall and another out front. I've come to the cafeteria for a while so we can talk about that business card she had. Mom's been sedated since we got here, but I asked her if she hired someone." Rachel paused. "She did. His name is Abraham Stigler. But she insists he didn't really do much for her."

Court replayed that last bit word for word. "But he did do something?"

He could hear more chatter along with Rachel's frustrated breath. "Stigler apparently wanted to try to lure Dad into a compromising position with Alma so he could get photographs. Of course, Stigler wanted her to use those pictures to launch into a divorce where Mom could get a better settlement than she otherwise would have gotten. Mom refused. Stigler got mad and stormed off."

He definitely didn't like the sound of that. "Is it possible this Stigler is unhinged? Because that doesn't sound like the behavior of a professional PI. If so, he could be the triggerman in these attacks."

"I asked Mom about that in a roundabout way, but she didn't think he would do anything violent. She said he was just frustrated that she was going to let herself be treated like that. Apparently, his dad cheated on his mom, so it's a sore spot for him. Anyway, I've got my laptop here, so I did some checking and didn't find anything on him, either."

That didn't mean there wasn't something to find. "Thanks, sis. I'll let you know if I come up with anything. Try to get some rest," he added.

Since checking on the PI could take a while, Court gave Rayna another kiss. One that he hoped would let her know that…except he didn't know what he wanted her to know. That was because he didn't have a clue where this was going. Worse, he really didn't have time to figure it out.

"Work on the PI," Rayna prompted. "I'll make a fresh pot of coffee."

Coffee wasn't much of a substitute for kissing, sex

or even a "where is this going?" discussion, but she was right. It could wait.

Court called the sheriff's office to get someone to access the computer, and Ian answered. However, Ian spoke before Court could say anything.

"I was about to call you. The dead guy in the car had a receipt in his wallet. One for the Lone Star Inn here in town. The CSIs found out that a person matching Bobby Joe's description had a room there, and they're going through it now. Court, they found something."

Judging from Ian's tone, that *something* wasn't good. He tried to steel himself, and he waited for Ian to continue. He didn't have to wait long.

"The dead guy has to be Bobby Joe because he has some recordings saved on a laptop, and I'm emailing them to you now so you can see for yourself," Ian explained. "Uh, is Rayna with you?"

"Yes."

"Okay. Well, the recordings will probably upset her. Just thought you should know that up front."

Hell. Court wished there was a way to keep this from her, but he couldn't. After everything Bobby Joe had put her through, she deserved to know the truth.

Since it sounded as if Ian had his hands full, Court decided to wait on having the deputy check on the PI. Instead, he ended the call, and with Rayna right there next to him, he went to his laptop and accessed the file. It didn't take long for the images to appear on the screen.

Bobby Joe.

Yeah, it was him all right. Court could tell that even though Bobby Joe wasn't looking directly into the camera. He had also grown a beard. Court checked the date on the recording, and it'd been made just three days ago. Or rather that was when it'd been uploaded.

"It's time to make Rayna pay," Bobby Joe said. He was resting against the headboard of a bed and drinking a beer. "Revenge is best served up cold, you know."

Someone else in the room said something that Court couldn't hear. It was a mumble, and whoever had said it wasn't on the screen.

"Because she made a promise to love me forever, that's why," Bobby Joe snapped in response to whatever the other person had said. There was pure venom in his tone. "That's what you promise when you accept a marriage proposal. It's like a lie when you break a promise, and no one's gonna get away with lying to me."

Rayna's breathing became faster, and she inched closer to the screen. "I'm not sure he knows he's being recorded."

Neither was Court, but he was surprised that Rayna could pick up on that, considering the hatred in Bobby Joe's voice.

The other person mumbled something else, something that caused Bobby Joe to bolt up from the headboard. "It matters," he snarled. "It was fun, watching her always looking over her shoulder. Living like a monk because she was too scared I'd come jumping out at her."

Rayna shuddered, and Court knew why. This meant Bobby Joe had indeed been watching her all this time.

"Rayna's gonna have to pay," Bobby Joe grumbled after downing some more beer. "I'm gonna burn that bitch alive."

That was obviously a little more than Rayna could take because she dropped back a step. Court slipped his arm around her. It wasn't much, but then there wasn't much they could do except finish listening to what this snake had to say.

"That'll teach her to file charges against me," Bobby Joe went on with his rant. "That'll teach her what happens when she breaks a promise."

The recording ended, but it was more than enough to let Court know that Bobby Joe had indeed been out to kill Rayna.

"Someone intentionally left this recording for us to find," Court said.

"Yes." She agreed so quickly that it meant she'd come to the same conclusion. "Is there any chance there can be a voice analysis done on the other person in the room with him?"

"Maybe." And considering this had been recorded three days ago, it could have been any of their suspects. "Ian's probably already sent it to the Ranger Crime Lab, but I'll make sure." He paused. "Whoever was in that room, Bobby Joe felt comfortable enough with him or her to admit to conspiracy to commit murder."

She nodded. "Plus, the recording might not even be recent." Rayna motioned toward the background of the shot Court had frozen on the screen. "I've never been to the inn, but I'm not even sure that's where this was recorded."

No, and if it hadn't been, maybe someone had planted the laptop with the recording in the room. For that matter, the person could have planted the receipt, as well.

Court's phone rang, and with all the things that'd been going on, he expected it to be Ian calling with more bad news of something they'd found at the inn. But it wasn't. It was Rachel.

Since his sister could have her own version of bad news, something else she'd perhaps learned from their mother, Court took a deep breath before he answered.

"You have to come right away," Rachel said, her voice filled with panic. "Mom's missing. I just got back to her room, and she's not here. God, Court, I think someone kidnapped her."

RAYNA KNEW THIS could be some kind of setup. A ruse to get Court and her out of his house. But the problem was, it was going to work.

Because there was no chance Court was going to stay put if his mother was in some kind of danger. That was why they'd practically run to his cruiser when they'd heard what Rachel said, and Court had started driving the moment they were inside. He'd also had Rayna use her phone to call Ian and tell the deputy to meet them on the road that led from the ranch to San Antonio. That way, they would at least have some backup.

"Rachel, tell me exactly what happened," Court insisted. He still had her on the line, and he'd put the call on speaker.

His sister didn't answer right away though, something she'd been doing since her bombshell of Helen being gone. That was because Rachel was also answering frantic questions from people who most likely were the staff and the Texas Ranger.

"Rachel?" Court said in a much louder voice.

He wasn't panicking like his sister, but he wasn't exactly cool and calm, either. That lack of calmness wasn't just limited to his mom though. His gaze fired all around them, keeping watch, and he motioned for Rayna to do the same. She did, and she also kept a firm grip on the gun he'd given her.

She prayed she didn't have to use it, but it was nearly an hour's drive to San Antonio, and plenty could go wrong between here and there. Maybe it wouldn't take Ian long to join them. Of course, someone could attack them while Ian was with them, but at least they'd have an extra gun if things went wrong.

"No, I don't know where she went," she heard Rachel say. "I've already told you that a dozen times. Now find her." Rachel made a hoarse sound before she came back on the phone. "Court, I don't know where she is. They think I helped her escape, but I wouldn't do that."

"I believe you. Now, tell me what happened."

"I'm not sure." Rachel made another of those sobbing sounds. "I was in the cafeteria making some other calls, and when I came back to her room, Mom wasn't there."

"But you said you thought someone kidnapped her," Court pointed out.

"Someone did. I should have never left her alone."

"You thought she was safe. You didn't do anything wrong," Court said, and he somehow managed to speak calmly. "What about the Ranger? Who is he and how did someone get past him?" His voice got a little harder on those two questions.

It took Rachel a moment to answer. "The Ranger's name is Marcus Owen, and he said someone dressed like a janitor walked past him and hit him with a stun gun. After he was down, the guy used pepper spray on him."

That tightened Rayna's chest. The memories of her own attack came flooding back, and the man who'd gone after her had used a stun gun, too. No pepper spray, but Helen McCall hadn't gotten a syringe of drugs pumped into her. "Mom's room is a mess, like there was some kind of a struggle," Rachel said. "Items had been knocked off the stand next to her bed. Her things are still here, so I don't think robbery was the motive."

Neither did Rayna. "What about the Ranger? Did he see the face of the man who used the stun gun on him?"

"I don't think so. Ranger Owen's still coughing from the pepper spray, so he might remember more once his head is clearer."

Court cursed. "What about security cameras? They should be all over that place."

"They are, and someone's trying to get the surveillance footage from them now. The ones in the parking lot, too."

That was a start, but even if they could identify the guy, it didn't mean they could stop him. By now, he could have already taken Helen out of the hospital. Plus, since the woman had been sedated, it was possible she wouldn't be able to figure out a way to escape. Even if she did fight off the sedation, her attacker could obviously use the stun gun or pepper spray on her.

"Mom must have screamed or something," Court added. "No way would she just let a stranger take her."

"She wouldn't have. I think that's why the room looks as if it's been trashed. Oh, God. Court, you don't think he would hurt her, do you?"

"No, I don't," Court quickly answered, but judging from his suddenly tight jaw muscles and the death grip that he had on the steering wheel, he was considering the same thing.

"Whoever took her probably wants to use her for leverage," Rayna suggested. "That means he won't hurt her."

"Leverage for what?" Rachel asked.

"I'm not sure," Rayna lied. But she had a strong inkling this was either tied to Warren or Court and her. "Did you let your dad know what's going on?"

"I called his guard," Rachel said. "I wanted to make sure he hadn't been taken, too, but he's okay. I told the guards to make sure it stayed that way."

"Thanks for doing that," Court told her. "Are the local cops out looking for this guy who took Mom?"

"I think so. If not, Egan will make sure they are when he gets here. How long before you can come?"

"I'm on the way now. Whatever you do, don't leave the hospital, and don't go looking for Mom. Just stay put until Egan and I get there, and we can figure out what to do. Don't worry, we'll get Mom back."

Rayna knew that Court would do anything in his power to make that happen, but this might be beyond what he could do. She hadn't wanted to mention it with Rachel on the phone, but the moment Court ended the call, she knew she had to say something.

"This could turn into some kind of ransom demand," Rayna told him.

Court nodded. "For either us or Dad." He cursed again and continued to keep watch. "There's another thing to consider. We're not sure that burned body is actually Bobby Joe. He could be the one behind this."

"Yes," she admitted, "but that doesn't explain the recording on the laptop." Rayna hated to even consider that Bobby Joe might be innocent in this, but she had to force herself to at least consider it. "The recording on the laptop could have been made years ago, and now someone could be using it to set up Bobby Joe."

"I agree," Court answered several moments later. "Since someone used Hallie to try to set you up and then murdered her, the person could have done the same to Bobby Joe."

She hated Bobby Joe for what he'd done to her, but he didn't deserve to be murdered. If that was what had happened. It was entirely possible that the body in the car wasn't his. Maybe it belonged to someone else that this unidentified killer had eliminated to tie up some loose ends.

"Call Ian so we can find out his location," Court instructed.

Rayna did, putting the call on speaker and holding the phone so that Court would be able to speak to his fellow deputy. Ian answered on the first ring.

"We're about five miles from the exit to the highway," Court said abruptly.

"I'm on my way there now, too. I should arrive in just a couple of minutes. If I make it ahead of you, I'll wait."

"Good." Court opened his mouth to say more, but he stopped. "What the hell?" he grumbled, and he hit his brakes.

It took Rayna a moment to realize why he'd done that. It was because someone had stretched a spike strip across the road. It was the kind of thing that cops used to stop bad guys from getting away. They ran right over it, the spikes tearing through the tires.

The cruiser jolted from the impact, and Rayna immediately felt something she didn't want to feel.

The tires were quickly going flat.

And that made Court and her sitting ducks.

COURT DIDN'T TAKE the time to curse, but that was what he'd do later. For now though, he got the cruiser to the side of the road so he could stop and draw his gun. Rayna had hers ready, and like him, she was looking all around, trying to find out who'd just set this trap for them.

"What happened?" Ian said from the other end of the line.

"Spike strip. Head this way, but approach with caution. I'm betting the person who put it there is still around."

Rayna pulled in a hard breath. Of course, she'd already known that, but it was probably unsettling to hear it said aloud.

"I'll get there as fast as I can," Ian assured him.

Court ended the call and put his phone back in his pocket. That way, he'd be ready when Ian arrived. He didn't want anything slowing him down when he moved Rayna from his cruiser to Ian's.

"Do you see anything?" she asked. Her voice was shaky, but he had to hand it to her, she was looking and sounding stronger than he'd expected. He hoped that she wasn't actually getting used to being put in danger like this.

"No," Court answered.

But it was hard to see much of anything. There was only a sliver of a moon, and even though the headlights were cutting through the darkness, that allowed them to see only directly ahead. It was pitch-dark behind them. It also didn't help that there were ditches and plenty of trees in the pastures on both sides of them. It'd be easy for someone to hide out there and wait to attack.

"No way could the person who took Mom have made it out here already," Court said.

He was talking more to himself than Rayna. But it could mean that the man who'd previously attacked them wasn't behind this. Well, he wasn't if he'd been the one to take Helen.

"It could be another hired gun," Rayna muttered.

Yeah. A hired gun who was enjoying watching them squirm. Now that their car was disabled, why hadn't the person come after them? Why wait when he or she would know that backup had to be on the way?

His phone rang again, and Court glanced at the screen to see Rachel's name there. He was debating whether or not he should answer when he saw something. A blur of motion to their right, on the passenger's side of the cruiser.

Someone was in the pasture.

"Get down on the seat," he told Rayna.

"You need me to keep watch," she argued.

He hated that she was right. Hated even more that he might need her help to get out of this.

Rayna already followed his gaze to the pasture, but Court could no longer see anyone moving out there. He kept watch. Not just there, but he looked around them, too, in case there was more than one person involved in this.

"There," Rayna said. She motioned toward the road just ahead. "I think someone just got in that ditch."

Court hadn't seen it, but it was possible, especially

since the headlights weren't focused on the ditch. He put the cruiser into Drive, knowing he wouldn't get far, but he wanted to move the vehicle only enough to shine some light in that specific area.

And it worked.

He saw the person then. Whoever it was, he or she was definitely in the ditch.

"I could lower my window enough to try to get off a shot," Rayna suggested.

But he was already shaking his head before she even finished speaking. "Not a chance. Just keep watch to the side and behind us." That way, he could deal with this snake.

The windows were bullet resistant. That was both the good and the bad news. It meant the guy in the ditch wouldn't be able to execute an immediate kill shot. He'd have to fire enough to tear through the glass. But it also meant Court wouldn't have an easy shot, either.

Even though it was a risk, he lowered his window a couple of inches and aimed his gun out the narrow space. He put his finger on the trigger.

And he waited, his attention nailed to the spot where he'd last seen the person. He doubted this was some hunter or innocent bystander out for an evening stroll. No, this was the person who'd put out the spike strip. The person who probably wanted them dead.

The seconds crawled by, but it didn't take him long to get a whiff of something in the air.

Gasoline.

Rayna obviously smelled it, too, because she practically snapped her head in his direction.

"It could be coming from the cruiser," he told her. Though there was a slim to none chance of that being the case. Still, Court held out hope that maybe the spike strip had somehow flipped up when he'd driven over it and punctured the gas line.

His phone rang, and again it was Rachel. It was a bad time to be talking on the phone, but Court hit the speaker button anyway.

"We got a call," Rachel blurted out the moment he answered. "God, Court. It's really bad."

His chest went so tight that it was hard for him to breathe. "Is Mom okay?"

"I don't know. The caller said he'll exchange her for Rayna."

That definitely didn't help with the tightness. "I want that call traced."

"Ranger Owen's trying to do that now." His sister sounded even more desperate now than she had earlier. "The kidnapper said he'd kill Mom if we didn't hand over Rayna in thirty minutes."

"I can't get there that soon," Rayna said, and Court knew then that she was indeed planning on surrendering to the kidnapper to save his mother.

"There's no guarantee the kidnapper will let either you or my mother live," Court pointed out.

"We have to try. Someone disabled Court's cruiser," Rayna said in a louder voice to Rachel. "But as soon as Ian is here, I can get to San Antonio. Tell the kidnapper when he calls back."

Rayna looked at Court. "We have to try to save your mother."

Court was certain he would have come up with an argument for that, but he saw the headlights ahead. Then his phone dinged with a message from Ian.

"Rachel, I have to call you back," Court insisted, and he switched his screen to the text.

Is it safe to approach? Ian texted.

No, it wasn't. Someone's in the ditch to your left, Court answered back.

He waited for Ian's response, and since Ian was a lot closer to that particular section of the ditch, he might be able to see the person. The moment that thought crossed his mind, there was another blur of motion.

Then Court heard the swooshing sound.

As a wall of fire shot up right in front of them.

Chapter Sixteen

From the moment the cruiser had hit the spike strip, Rayna had known they were in trouble. Now that trouble had just escalated.

"I can't drive off because of the flat tires," Court grumbled under his breath, and he cursed.

No, and that meant if the fire started to come toward them, they would have no choice but to get out of the cruiser and run. That would no doubt make it much easier for them to be gunned down.

If the smoke and fire didn't get to them first, that was.

Because of the direction of the wind, the smoke started to come right at them. Using the cruiser's AC would help, but not for long. Worse, the smoke was making it very hard to see anything.

Court's phone rang. It was Ian, and he answered it without taking his eyes off their surroundings.

"I'm going to try to drive through the fire to get to you," Ian said. "Maybe the flames will conceal you enough so you can jump in."

He didn't sound very hopeful about that, and neither was Rayna. Any hope whatsoever vanished when there was a gunshot. It was a loud blast, and judging from the sound, it went in the direction of Ian's cruiser. A few seconds later, another sound followed the gunfire.

The hiss from the new flames that flared up between Ian and them.

Also on the side of them, too.

The ditch across from the driver's side of the cruiser burst on fire, too.

Now there were two new walls of flames and smoke, these latest ones even higher than the first. That would make it too dangerous for Ian to drive through it because if he got stuck, it could cause his gas tank to explode.

Court cursed again, and he started coughing. "Whoever's behind this had to have put more than just accelerant on the road. There has to be incendiary devices."

Yes, ones that were probably operated by remote control, since Rayna didn't see anyone close enough to set the fire by hand. However, the person had to be nearby, waiting for them.

And Rayna didn't have to guess the location.

There was only one path—to her right—that wasn't on fire, and that was almost certainly where their attacker wanted them to go. It meant that was where an ambush had to be waiting for them.

The smoke started to smother her and burn her eyes. Again, it was exactly what their attacker wanted. They couldn't sit there much longer.

"I called the fire department," Ian said. His voice was laced with frustration and fear, and he was also coughing from the smoke. "When they get here, they might be able to get close enough to put out the flames."

Not likely, since they wouldn't be able to approach if there was gunfire.

And that meant Court, Ian and she had to figure out a way to find the fire starter and take him or her out of commission. If the fire jumped the road and ditch, it could start burning the pastures and the nearby ranches. Of course, that didn't seem so urgent as the danger that was right on top of them.

"Can you go in reverse?" Court asked Ian.

"I can, but I'd rather get closer to Rayna and you. I can maybe help you."

"That's too risky," Court warned him. "Put some distance between the fire and you."

"I'll try… Wait, I've got another call coming in," Ian said.

So did Court. It was Rachel again, and Rayna could see that he was hesitant about answering it. She knew why, too. He probably didn't want to tell his sister about their situation. Rachel was already frantic enough about their mother, and hearing this wasn't going to help. Still. Court hit the answer button, and as he'd done with Ian, he put it on speaker and continued to keep watch.

"Where are you?" Rachel blurted out.

Court hesitated, obviously trying to figure out how to say this. "Rayna, Ian and I are trapped on the road. Someone set fires, and that means I'm not going to be able to get to you right away."

A sob caught in Rachel's throat. "Are you okay?"

He didn't even attempt a lie. "No. If the kidnapper calls back, negotiate for more time for Mom. I'll call you when I can."

Court ended the call just as another wave of smoke came at them. Now it was impossible to see anything, and even though the flames weren't advancing on them, the cruiser was getting hotter with each pass-ing second.

"We can't stay here." Court looked Rayna straight in the eyes when he said that, and she saw the apology that she hoped he wouldn't say.

Because this wasn't his fault.

It was the fault of that snake out there who'd put all of this together. Rayna only hoped she learned the reason for all of this. While she was hoping, she also wanted to catch the person and put an end to this dan-ger once and for all.

"What do you need me to do?" Rayna asked before Court could add that *I'm sorry.*

"Put your phone in your pocket so you don't lose it and then switch places with me," he said through the coughs. He tipped his head to the ditch on the pas-senger's side of the cruiser. "I'll go out first. You'll be right behind me. We'll take cover and try to shoot this guy before he shoots us."

It was a simple enough plan, and they might get lucky. *Might.* But there were plenty of things that could go wrong. As thick as the smoke was, their attacker could be already waiting right outside the door, and Court and she wouldn't know it until it was too late.

Court sent a text to Ian, no doubt to tell him what they were about to do. Maybe Ian would be able to help in some way, but at this point, the deputy just needed to figure out a way to get out of that fire and be safe.

Rayna pushed back the seat as far as it would go to give Court space to maneuver. It wasn't easy now that they were coughing nonstop. Plus, Rayna felt on the verge of panicking. It was hard to breathe with the rising heat and the adrenaline. Even harder to catch her breath when Court brushed a quick kiss on her mouth.

"Stay safe," he said.

She repeated that to him and prayed that both of them and Ian could manage to do just that.

Court threw open the cruiser door, and they immediately caught another wave of the smoke. No bullets though, so maybe the visibility wasn't so good for the shooter, either.

Using the door for cover, Court got out, and while staying in a crouched position, he inched closer to the ditch. He glanced around, but she could tell from the way he was blinking that the smoke was doing a number on his eyes.

"Let's move now," he whispered.

He took hold of her wrist, pulled Rayna out of the cruiser. In the same motion, he hurried toward the ditch. They didn't make it far.

Before the shot came right at them.

Court shoved Rayna into the ditch as fast as he could, but it hadn't been quite fast enough.

The shot slammed into the ground, kicking up the dirt and sending some of it into his eyes. Not good. He was already having a hard enough time seeing as it was. And now his heart was beating so fast that it felt as if his ribs might crack. That was because he wasn't sure if the bullet had ricocheted and hit Rayna.

She could be hurt.

Rayna made a sharp sound of pain, and Court caught her in his arms, dropping down as far as they could go. The ditch was soft from the recent rain, and it helped break their fall a little. Still, it was a hard landing.

"I'm okay," Rayna said. Though she certainly didn't sound okay. "I just hit my head."

That wasn't good, since she already had an injury there, but it was better than the alternative. They could have been shot. Hell. How had he allowed it to come to this?

Because he was stupid, that was why.

He'd let the news of his mother's disappearance cloud his mind, and now Rayna might pay for that mistake.

Since he didn't know where the shooter was, Court adjusted his position so that Rayna's back was against the side of the ditch and he was in front of her and facing the pasture. The lower ground helped with the smoke, too, and thankfully the wind seemed to be blowing some of it away. That was a good thing because he needed to be able to catch his breath in case they had to run.

Court tried to pick through the smoke and darkness to spot their attacker. Nothing. Nor did the person fire any other shots. Normally, that would have been a good thing, but it could mean the person was moving closer—maybe trying to get in place for a kill shot.

His phone buzzed with a text message. It was Ian, again. But Court didn't answer it. He didn't want to be distracted even for a second, so he passed it to Rayna so she could read it to him.

"Ian says he's going to try to go back up the road and find a way to get into the pasture where we are," she whispered.

That was beyond risky, but at this point, everything they did fell into that category. If Court had been alone, he would have told Ian to get to safety, but since Rayna was involved, Court was willing to take all the help he could get.

Behind them, the fire snapped and hissed, but it didn't seem to be burning itself out. Not good. Because the flames could still reach the gas tank on the cruiser. If it exploded, Rayna and he were plenty close enough to be hurt or killed.

"We have to move," he said, keeping his voice as soft as he could manage. And there was only one direction in which to do that. Too bad it would mean moving away from Ian, but he had to get Rayna away from the fire. "Stay behind me and try to keep watch," he added.

She nodded, and he could feel the tightness in her body. Her too-fast breath on his neck. As a lawman, he'd faced danger, but Rayna shouldn't have to be going through this. Unfortunately, they didn't have a choice about that right now.

With him still in front of her, they started moving to their right. Inch by inch. It was very slow going because they had to stay crouched down. They made it about two feet before Court saw something.

A person darted behind a tree directly in front of them.

Because of the smoke, he couldn't tell if the person was a man or a woman, but he definitely saw the gun. A rifle. If it had a scope, which it probably did, it was going to make it much easier to target Rayna and him. Court instantly got proof that he'd been right.

The next bullet tore into the ditch, and if Rayna and he hadn't ducked down, it would have hit them. That was way too close for comfort.

It didn't stay just one shot, either. A second one came. Then a third. All of them were ripping into the dirt just above them. Court had no choice but to pull Rayna back down to the ground. That meant he no longer had a visual on the shooter.

Behind them, he heard another hissing sound, and almost immediately new flames shot into the air. This fire was even bigger than the others and jumped up right next to the ditch. If the ground caved in any more from the shots, it would send that fire spilling down on them.

"How much ammo do you have?" Rayna asked.

That wasn't a question he especially wanted to hear. Because it sounded as if she was thinking about doing something he wouldn't like.

"I have two extra magazines plus what's in my gun," Court answered. "Why?"

"Because we can't stay here. If we can pin down this guy, then we can get farther down the ditch and away from the smoke and heat."

She was right about the "staying here" part, but there was no way he wanted her high enough out of the ditch to return fire. But he did have an idea.

A risky one.

It might work though if there was only one shooter. If there were more than that, well, things were going to go from bad to worse.

Still, it wasn't as if they had many options here, and those options decreased when their attacker started sending more shots their way. Each bullet was slamming into the very dirt that could bury them in that fire.

Court tipped his head to their right. "Stay low but move as fast as you can," he told Rayna.

He couldn't see her expression, but he felt her tense even more—something that he hadn't thought was possible. "What about you?" Her voice was shaking now, too.

"I'll be right behind you."

Or at least he would be once he was certain he'd pinned down the shooter enough for him to do that. For now, his goal was just to get Rayna as far away from that fire as he could manage.

He doubted she believed that "right behind you" part, but she moved out from behind him. "Just be careful," she whispered.

Court nodded, told her to do the same. "Go now," he instructed.

He came out from cover, lifting his head and gun high enough so he could send a shot in the general direction where he'd pinpointed the shooter.

The gunman fired back.

Court dropped down, and from the corner of his eye he saw Rayna doing exactly what he wanted her to do. She was practically on all fours and was scrambling down the ditch away from him. She wasn't nearly far enough though, so he came out from cover and fired another shot.

That was when Court finally got a glimpse of the shooter. The person immediately darted behind a tree that was about twenty yards from them. Unfortunately, there were plenty of trees and underbrush on each side of their attacker, so Court had no way of knowing which way he would go.

There was a slash of bright lights to his left, and Court whipped his gun in that direction. But he didn't think it was a gunman. It was hard to tell with the smoke, but he thought it might be Ian, and that he might be seeing the headlights from the cruiser.

Court glanced at Rayna again. She was still moving. Still staying down. And so the shooter would stay pinned down, too, Court fired another shot where he'd last spotted him.

Nothing.

He doubted that meant the guy had just left, though it was possible the headlights had given him second thoughts about leaning out to shoot.

The lights came closer. Yeah, it was Ian all right. Maybe the deputy would get in position to help them. But that hope barely had time to register in Court's mind when there was another hissing sound.

Much, much louder than the others. The flames came. Not just on the road this time, either.

But into the ditch.

The line of fire flared between Rayna and him. And the flames came right at Court.

Chapter Seventeen

"Watch out!" Rayna called out to Court.

But it was too late.

She'd seen the new flash of fire, but she hadn't been able to warn Court in time for him to get out of the way. Rayna turned to hurry back to him, and that was when she realized she couldn't.

Because the line of fire was coming in her direction, too.

Whoever had set this latest fire had obviously meant to burn Court and her alive in the ditch. Well, Rayna had no plans to die, and she wanted to make sure Court didn't, either.

Since she couldn't move very fast on all fours, she got to her feet and started running. She hated putting more distance between Court and her, but maybe she'd be able to get into the pasture and then double back for him. Something that he was hopefully doing as well, since Rayna didn't want him staying near that fire. Of course, being in the pasture wouldn't exactly be safe, either.

The line of fire finally stopped moving behind her. Probably because there was no more accelerant to fuel the flames. She stopped and ducked back down in the ditch. Low enough for cover but high enough so she could try to spot the shooter.

Nothing.

The smoke and darkness were acting like a thick, smothering curtain all around her. Worse, the sound of fire might be able to mask the footsteps of anyone trying to sneak up on her. That was why she stayed facing the pasture. If the attacker came at her, that was the direction he'd likely come from.

Rayna could see the headlights from Ian's cruiser to her left, but she had no idea where the deputy was. Maybe Court would be able to get to him, and they could use the cruiser to come after her. At least then they'd be protected from gunfire.

Her phone buzzed with a text, and even though it meant taking her eyes off the pasture, she glanced down at the screen, since it could be important.

It was.

Get as far away from the fire as you can, Court texted her. I'll come for you soon.

Despite their god-awful situation, relief flooded through her. Court was okay. For now, anyway. Rayna prayed that it stayed that way. But it didn't last.

A shot blasted through the air.

The bullet wasn't fired in her direction though but rather had gone near Court. She doubted either Court or Ian had fired it, since it'd seemed to come from the area by the trees.

There was another shot.

Then another.

Rayna ducked down even farther into the ditch, but with the fourth shot, she was better able to pinpoint the location of the shooter. The person was moving away from Court and in her direction. Since the line of trees continued almost to the ditch, she had to keep watch not just in front of her but also to the side.

In the distance she heard sirens. Probably from the fire department. They wouldn't be able to help, but at least they'd be close enough to put out the fires once the shooter was no longer a threat. Whenever that would be.

Her phone dinged again. It wasn't from Court this time but rather from Ian. And the message he sent her had her stomach going straight to her knees.

Court was hit, Ian texted.

Rayna forced herself not to scream and bolt from the ditch to hurry to him. That was exactly what the shooter wanted her to do, and he would almost certainly gun her down. But while she could make herself stay put, she couldn't stop the strangled groan that made its way through her throat.

No. This couldn't be happening.

Somehow, she had to get to him, had to help him, but she couldn't just go running into the pasture. Rayna forced herself to stop, and breathe, so she could try to think this through. It was hard to think though with the worst-case scenarios going through her head. And that was when she realized something.

She was in love with Court.

That was why she was reacting this way. That was why losing him suddenly seemed unbearable.

Maybe part of her always had been in love with him, but it had taken something like this to make her see it. Now she might not even get the chance to tell him how she felt.

How bad is he hurt? Rayna texted back. No way

could she ask if Court was dead. She refused to believe that could happen.

The seconds crawled by, turning into what felt an eternity. Because her legs suddenly felt as if they couldn't support her weight, Rayna leaned her back against the wall of the ditch. And waited. Even though she was expecting it, the jolt of surprise still went through her when her phone dinged.

Court says it's not bad, that it's just a flesh wound, Ian finally answered. He'll be okay.

Rayna had no idea if that was true or if Court was merely trying to prevent her from panicking. If so, it wasn't working.

Can you get Court into the cruiser? she texted Ian.

She didn't have to wait nearly as long for a response. No. We tried to get to it, and that's how he got shot. But Court wants me to try to get to you.

Of course he did. But Rayna had to nix that with a semi-lie of her own. I'm safe where I am, she answered.

She definitely didn't want Ian leaving Court alone, especially since Court might not be able to defend himself.

Thea and John will be here soon, Ian added a moment later.

Good. Two more deputies might help them put an end to this. Again though, they might not be able to get close because of the fire.

Rayna slipped her phone back in her pocket so she could free up her hands, and she looked around the pasture again. There was no more gunfire, no glimpse of anyone in the trees. That didn't mean someone wasn't out there, but for now they were staying hidden.

That surprised her.

She would have thought the shooter would have wanted to go ahead and put an end to this, since he had to know that backup was on the way. Maybe it meant the guy had pulled the plug on this attack and had fled. Even though she wanted to catch this snake, right now her priority was helping Court.

When the next minute crawled by without any other gunfire, Rayna figured it was now or never for her to get to Court. Since she couldn't risk the pasture in front of her, that meant taking an alternate route. She could hurry into the pasture on the other side of the road, skirting along the edges of the fire until she could get to a clearing to cross back over.

She got her gun ready and looked over her shoulder at the road behind her. The only thing she could see was thick smoke, and Rayna knew the moment she stepped into it, she'd start coughing, something that would slow her down. That was why she took a deep breath and turned to scramble out of the ditch.

But turning was as far as she got.

Someone wearing a gas mask reached out from that smoke, and that someone had a stun gun. Before Rayna could move or make a sound, the person rammed the gun against her neck.

The jolt went through her. So did the pain, and even though she heard her phone buzzing with a text, there was nothing she could do about that, either.

Rayna had no choice but to fall back into the ditch.

"RAYNA DIDN'T ANSWER," Ian relayed to Court.

Court knew that wasn't good. Especially since Rayna had answered the other texts from Ian. And this one had been important because it had been an order for her to stay put.

Where the heck was she? And why hadn't she answered?

Court grimaced and bit back some profanity. He could feel the blood on his arm. Could feel the pain, too, where the bullet had sliced across it. It wasn't a deep cut, but he would need stitches. Eventually. But for now, he just needed to get to Rayna.

Everything inside Court was yelling for him to get to her. Because he knew something was wrong.

Ian had sent that first text before Court could stop him, and Rayna now knew that he'd been shot. Despite Ian's assurance that it wasn't serious, she probably thought he was dying and would try to help him. That would almost certainly put her in danger, and unlike him, she didn't even have any backup. Heck, he wasn't even sure she knew how to defend herself if it came down to it.

"You know you shouldn't be doing this," Ian warned him when Court climbed out of the ditch.

Yeah, he did, but that wasn't stopping him. Nothing would.

"You should wait here," Court told Ian, but he knew that wasn't going to fly. This was a stupid idea, but Ian wasn't going to let him go out there alone.

Something that Court had allowed to happen to Rayna.

He cursed the fire that had shot up between them. He cursed their attacker, too, for putting them in this situation. Now he only prayed he could get to her in time to stop whatever was happening.

Somehow, Court made it out of the deep ditch onto

the pasture grass. And he immediately got slammed with a wave of smoke. He had no choice but to cough, which only made his arm hurt even more. He ignored both the pain and the coughing and started moving. He also kept as low as he could while keeping watch of that treed area where he'd spotted the shooter.

No sign of the person now.

That didn't make Court feel better. Because it could mean their attacker had gotten to Rayna.

That caused him to hurry. Well, hurry as much as he could, anyway. Everything seemed to be working against him, and it didn't help that he didn't know how far she'd managed to go. Hopefully, though, she had stayed in the ditch where he could find her. But even if she was close by, it wouldn't be easy to spot her with the smoke and darkness.

The fire was dying some, but there were still some flames in spots being fanned by the wind. There was still enough of a threat from the shooter, too, that he couldn't give the fire department the green light to enter the area. But when Thea and John arrived, they would almost certainly get as close as they could. In some ways that would make this situation even more dangerous.

Because Court didn't want the deputies hit with friendly fire. Ditto for the deputies shooting toward Ian and him.

Court and Ian were both on edge and braced for a fight. Not the best conditions for having other lawmen arrive on the scene. Especially since Ian and he were having to keep watch all around them.

Court stopped when he heard a sound. It was like a gasp, and it had come from just ahead of them. He stopped for a second to see if he could pinpoint it. And he did hear something else. A thud. As if someone had fallen.

That got him moving even faster, but Court was well aware he could be walking into an ambush. At least there were some trees to his left that he could maybe dive behind if the shooter was lying in wait for them.

He got a break from a gust of wind that cleared a section of the smoke, and he saw some movement in the ditch. He heard another moan, too.

Hell, it sounded as if Rayna had been hurt.

Nothing could have stopped him at that point. He readied his gun and ran toward that sound. The wind stopped cooperating though, and the smoke slid right back in front of him, stinging his eyes and blocking his view.

The moment he made it past the fire, Court climbed back down into the ditch. It was clearer there, and he finally saw more than just movement.

He saw Rayna.

She was on her feet, and at first he thought she was okay. Then Court saw someone standing behind her. And that someone had a gun pointed at her head.

Before Court could even react, that someone pulled the trigger.

He watched in horror as Rayna fell, and for several heart-stopping moments he thought she'd been shot.

But she hadn't.

She had dropped down just as the shot had been fired. She was moving, trying to get away, but it was as if she was dazed or something. Her attacker had no trouble latching on to Rayna and dragging her in front of him.

Except it wasn't a *him*.

With the gun back at Rayna's head, the shooter yanked off the gas mask she was wearing, and Court got a good look at her face.

Whitney.

Rayna glanced back at her, too, shock and then anger going through her. But Court got only a split-second glance of both Whitney and Rayna before Whitney turned the gun on him.

And she fired.

RAYNA TRIED TO shout a warning to Court, but her mouth still wasn't working well just yet. That stun gun hit had caused her muscles to spasm, and if Whitney hadn't dragged her to her feet, she'd probably still be on the ground.

On the ground and fighting to save Court.

Thankfully, Court and Ian climbed out of the ditch and scrambled behind some nearby trees, but before they could make it to cover, Whitney shot at them again. Since the gun was right against Rayna's ear, the sound was deafening, and she groaned in pain. She prayed that groan didn't send Court racing toward her though. Because Whitney would almost certainly shoot him.

But why?

Rayna didn't know why a woman she'd once considered her friend would now want Court and her dead. One thing she did know was that Whitney was trapped—something she probably hadn't planned on happening. No. By now, she'd likely thought she would have been able to kill Court and her and then escape.

"Backup's on the way," Court shouted out. "Let Rayna go, and we can talk."

"Talk," Whitney repeated like profanity. "It's a little late for that. Rayna should already be dead, but if I shoot her now, then you'll shoot me."

Rayna hadn't thought for a second that the shot Whitney had aimed at her had been some kind of bluff. No. It was meant to kill her. Except Rayna had managed to fall just in time. She might not get that lucky again.

She wiggled her fingers and toes, trying to get back the feeling in her body so she could fight off Whitney if she tried to pull the trigger again.

"Why are you doing this?" Rayna had to ask. But as soon as the question left her mouth, she thought she had the answer. "Bobby Joe. You're the one who helped him hide all this time."

Whitney didn't jump to deny that. "I was in love with him," she told her "And he threw it all back in my face. He was coming back to town to confess everything."

That didn't make sense. "You mean confess that he'd tried to frame me for his murder?"

"No. To confess that *I* had tried to frame you for his murder."

Oh, mercy.

She couldn't imagine that being true. Until she remembered how Whitney had changed after Bobby Joe's disappearance. And that'd happened because Whitney had fallen in love with him.

"Bobby Joe helped with the framing, at first," Whitney added a moment later, "because he had to collect some of his own blood. But then he had *a change of heart.* That's what the SOB called it. A change of heart, and he was coming here to try to win you back."

Rayna felt the sickening feeling wash over her. "It wouldn't have worked. I would have never gotten back together with Bobby Joe because I've always been in love with Court."

A burst of air left Whitney's mouth. A laugh, but definitely not from humor. "Too bad Bobby Joe didn't know that before he died."

"You mean before you killed him," Rayna snapped.

Whitney didn't deny that, either.

All the missing pieces suddenly fell into place. Well, many of them, anyway. Whitney would have had the chance to get both a spare key to Rayna's house along with the code for her security system. That would have made it easy for Whitney to send a hired thug to break in, drug her and then set her up for Warren's shooting. That same hired thug had probably been the one who'd fired shots at them at the hospital.

The same one maybe who'd taken Court's mother.

Unless the guy was out here somewhere. But Whitney didn't seem to be waiting for her own version of backup. No. Her jerking motions and gusting breath told Rayna that Whitney had been backed into a corner and was now looking for a way out.

"You thought if I was in jail for Warren's murder that Bobby Joe wouldn't try to get back together with me," Rayna concluded.

Still, no denial, and every bit of that silence cut Rayna to the core. She'd been a fool to trust this woman.

"Whitney?" Court called out again. "This is the last warning you'll get. Put down that gun."

Rayna couldn't be sure because she was still light-headed, but she thought maybe Court had moved farther to the right. Whitney must have thought so, too, because the woman shifted their positions, putting her back to the ditch while keeping Rayna in front of her.

"If you try anything, Rayna dies," Whitney shouted back. "Since she just confessed to me that she's in love with you, I doubt you want her dead."

That caused Rayna's chest to tighten even more than it already was. Whitney's outburst wasn't something she wanted Court to hear. Not like that. And not now. He didn't need any more distractions.

"I didn't want my father shot. Or Jennifer and Hallie dead, either," Court responded. "But you killed them. Killed Mitch and Bobby Joe, too. You know what that makes you, Whitney? A serial killer. And people aren't going to go easy on you just because you work for the sheriff's office."

Whitney made a loud sob, and Rayna didn't think it was fake. No, that was real emotion, and Whitney was probably just now realizing the horrible things she'd done. A string of murders that had all started because she wanted to keep Bobby Joe away from Rayna.

There was some more movement, and even though Whitney was crying now, she still pointed the gun in those trees. Which meant she was probably pointing it at Court or Ian. No way was Rayna going to let her claim another life.

Rayna knew she still wasn't steady, but that didn't stop her. She could tell from the way that Whitney tensed her arm that she was about to pull the trigger. That was why Rayna gathered all the strength she could and rammed her elbow into Whitney's stomach.

Whitney howled in pain, cursed.

And she turned the gun on Rayna.

Even in the darkness Rayna could see the hatred in the woman's eyes. Could see that Whitney was going to kill her.

The shot came. Blasting through the air. And Rayna braced herself for the pain. It didn't come though. But there was pain on Whitney's face. Along with some shock. That was when Rayna saw the blood spreading across the front of Whitney's top.

Court stepped out from the trees. He had his gun in his hand, and it was aimed at Whitney.

The woman looked down at the blood, then at Court before she laughed again. Like the other one, there was no humor in it.

But there was *something*. Something evil.

"You might have put a bullet in me," Whitney said, "but you'll never see your mother again. By the time you get to her, she'll be dead."

Whitney dropped to the ground, gasping on the last breath she would ever take.

Chapter Eighteen

Court's mind was shouting for him to do a dozen things at once. He needed to get to his mother, to save her, but he had to make sure Rayna was safe, too. Whitney appeared to be dead.

Appeared.

But since the woman had already murdered at least four people, Court didn't want to take any chances. He scrambled into the ditch so he could get Rayna out of there.

"Your mom," Rayna said. "We have to find her."

Yes, they did, but first they had to confirm that Whitney was indeed dead. Court kicked the woman's gun away from her hand and touched his fingers to her neck to see if he could feel a pulse.

Yes, she was dead all right.

"She hit me with a stun gun," Rayna muttered.

So, that was why she was so wobbly, but it could have been worse. Whitney could have used a real gun, and the only reason she hadn't was because she'd intended to use Rayna as a human shield to try to make an escape. And now even though Whitney was no longer a threat, she still could claim another victim.

His mother.

Ian hurried out from the trees, his gun pointed at Whitney. He didn't get in the ditch with them. He stayed in the pasture keeping watch. He also gave the all clear for backup and the fire department to come closer.

Because they could possibly use it to track the person who'd kidnapped Helen, Court went through Whitney's jeans pockets and located her phone. Actually, there were two of them. One was probably the one she regularly used, and the other was likely a burner cell that couldn't be traced. He put them both in his pockets.

"You're bleeding," Rayna added when he scooped her up and lifted her out of the ditch. Not easily. His arm was still throbbing, but he had to take her to the cruiser so that she wouldn't be out in the open.

The night was suddenly filled with flashing lights from the approaching deputies and the fire engine. With Rayna still in his arms, Court started moving with Ian right behind them.

"You shouldn't be carrying me," Rayna protested. "You've been shot."

That was true, but Rayna wasn't in any shape to run and probably wouldn't be for at least another couple of minutes. Those were minutes he didn't want to risk her being in the pasture.

The moment Court reached Ian's cruiser, he got her in the back seat, and Ian took the wheel. The deputy radioed backup to let them know they were about to drive out of there. Good move, since Court didn't want the other deputies thinking they were perps trying to make an escape.

Despite Rayna still being shaky, that didn't stop her

from checking his arm. It was still bleeding, which was probably why she made a slight gasping sound.

"Here's a first-aid kit," Ian said, passing it to her when he took it from the glove compartment. Rayna immediately got to work applying a bandage to Court's arm to slow the bleeding. "Should I take you directly to the hospital—"

"No. To San Antonio. I need to help Egan look for our mother."

Neither Rayna nor Ian argued with him about that. Probably because they figured it wouldn't do any good.

Because he needed it, Court brushed a quick kiss on Rayna's mouth. She looked up at him, their gazes connecting for just a second before he took out his phone and the two he'd taken from Whitney.

"Glance through those and see who Whitney called," Court told Rayna.

He'd put his own phone on vibrate when he'd gone into cover by the trees and had three missed calls. Two from Rachel and another from Egan. He pressed in Egan's number. And his heart sank when his brother didn't answer. He tried his sister next, and unlike Egan, she answered on the first ring.

"Court," Rachel said on a rise of breath. "Are Rayna and you okay?"

He'd expected her to blurt out some bad news about their mother, so the question was somewhat of a relief. "We're fine. Ian, too." He paused a heartbeat. "Whitney's the one who had Mom kidnapped."

"Whitney?" Rachel repeated, and her tone said it all. She was as shocked as Court and Rayna had been. "Why would she do that, and where does she have her?"

He didn't want to get into the "why," but he had also been hoping that Rachel would know the "where."

Hell.

"God, Court. Why did Whitney do this?" she repeated.

"To get back at Rayna. Maybe to get back at me, too, for helping Rayna." Or Whitney could have been hoping to set up Helen some way and pin the murders on her. "When's the last time you heard from Egan, because he's not answering his phone?"

"About fifteen minutes ago. He said he was getting ready to meet with the kidnapper."

Now it was Court's turn to be shocked. "Meeting with him? How'd Egan find out where he was?"

"The guy made a ransom call to Egan. It was a man, and he sounded frantic, like maybe things weren't going as planned."

Maybe because he'd realized that the woman who'd hired him was dead or about to be dead.

Rayna held out Whitney's phone for Court to see. "Is that the kidnapper's number?" she asked.

Court read off the number to Rachel. "Yes, that's it," Rachel verified.

Whitney had called the man multiple times in the past two hours. And not just during that time frame, either. When Court scrolled through the history, he saw that Whitney had been calling the man often for the past two days. That was the link they needed to prove that Whitney had hired him. And it was the reason the woman had no doubt used the second phone. It almost certainly wasn't a number assigned to her actual name.

"The kidnapper's using a burner cell so Egan

couldn't trace it," Rachel went on, "but the guy wants Egan to meet him and give him some money."

That was good news and bad. Good because the kidnapper would almost certainly keep his mother alive if he wanted to ransom her. But it was bad, too, because it meant Egan could be hurt or killed in an exchange like that.

Court debated if he should call the kidnapper's number, but he decided to wait a few more minutes. Until he'd heard from Egan. If he called now, he might distract his brother at a critical time. It could make things even more dangerous than it already was.

"Please tell me Egan didn't go alone," Court said.

"No. Griff and another Texas Ranger are with him. Egan said I was to wait here, but I'm going crazy. I have to do something to help Mom. I have to do something to stop this."

"You can help her by staying put." Court made sure he sounded like a lawman giving an order and not just like a big brother. "Rayna and I are on the way there to the hospital. I'll drop Rayna off with you and go out and help Egan. Do you know his location?"

"No. He wouldn't tell me."

Probably because Egan hadn't wanted Rachel to try to follow him. But Court could track Egan through his cell phone, since it wasn't a burner.

"Court was shot," Rayna blurted out. "He should see a doctor."

"It can wait," Court said at the same moment Rachel said, "Shot? You said you were fine."

"I will be," Court assured his sister. "Or at least I will be once Mom and Egan are safe." And after he'd made sure that Rayna was okay. Then there'd be time for stitches. "We're about thirty minutes out."

"Forty," Ian corrected.

"Light up the sirens and get us there in thirty," Court told him.

"Stay put," he repeated to Rachel, and he ended the call so he could try Egan again.

Still no answer.

Rayna gave his bandage another adjustment, and when he looked at her, Court saw the tears in her eyes.

"I'm okay, really," he assured her.

She shook her head and blinked back more of those tears. "This is all my fault."

Court had known she was going to say that before the words had even come out of her mouth. Since it wasn't her fault, and he didn't want to hear her continue with an apology, he kissed her.

All in all, it was an effective way to put an end to it. An effective way to make him feel instantly better, too. He was still in pain, but he no longer cared. After several moments, he didn't think Rayna cared, either, because she moved right into the kiss, and she only broke it when she took in a huge gulp of breath.

"You're trying to distract me," she said with her mouth still very close to his. Close enough for him to kiss her again, so that was what he did.

"Yeah," he admitted. "But I need distracting, too." After all, his mother was a hostage, and his brother was out there trying to rescue her. Something that Court wanted to be doing.

Rayna nodded, eased back even more, and he saw the look in her eyes. She was about to apologize again. This time it would no doubt be for his mother.

"None of this was your fault," he said. "Put the blame right on Whitney where it belongs."

She nodded again, but the agreement didn't seem very believable. "I shouldn't have trusted her. I mean, I always knew she had feelings for Bobby Joe, but I thought it was just a crush. I had no idea she was in love with him."

"That seems to be going around," Court muttered.

Her eyes widened. Because she knew they weren't talking about Whitney now. They were talking about her.

"You told Whitney you were in love with me," Court reminded her, though he was certain it wasn't a reminder she needed.

Those words were no doubt as fresh in her mind as they were in his. But it might not be true. The fear and the adrenaline might have caused her to blurt that out.

"Yes," Rayna answered.

She glanced in the front at Ian, but the deputy was on the phone with Thea. Besides, Ian had almost certainly heard what Rayna had said to Whitney.

"It's true. I am in love with you." Rayna's voice was barely a whisper, but Court still heard it loud and clear.

"You're in love with me?" he said just to make sure. Though he didn't want her to take it back.

She nodded but didn't add more because a ringing sound cut through the silence. It wasn't his phone though but rather one of Whitney's. And it was the kidnapper's number that appeared on the screen.

Court steeled himself as much as he could. Even though he wanted to rip this guy limb from limb, he reined in his temper and hit the answer button.

"Whitney?" someone said. But it wasn't the kidnapper. It was a voice Court recognized.

"It's Court," Court answered. "I have Whitney's phone. She's dead."

"Good. Because I just found out from this piece of slime that Whitney's the one who hired him."

Court hoped that meant Egan had not only the kidnapper but their mother, too. "Is Mom okay?"

"She's shaken up but fine. Not a scratch on her even though she did try to fight off the kidnapper. Griff is taking her back to the hospital right now."

"She's alive," Rayna said, her breath rushing out.

"Yeah," Egan verified. "And it's good to hear that Court and you are, too. What happened?"

Rayna shook her head, obviously not trusting her voice and motioned for Court to give the explanation. He would, but since he didn't want to repeat a lot of the details in front of Rayna, he just kept it simple.

"Whitney killed Jennifer, Hallie, Bobby Joe and Mitch. Then she tried to kill Rayna and me." The woman had almost succeeded, too.

"That's what I got from her hired thug. By the way, his name is Burris Hargrove, and he's talking even after I read him his rights."

"Good." Because Court was sure they would need some details filled in, and Hargrove was the only one who might be able to do that. "How'd you catch him?"

Egan took a deep breath first. "I met Hargrove at the drop site he arranged. It was a gas station about two miles from the hospital. We'd agreed that I would bring thirty grand in cash."

Not much, considering the McCalls were worth millions, but then maybe Hargrove had asked for such a small amount because he'd figured Egan would be able to get it together quickly. Then he could have used it for a fast getaway.

"When I got to the gas station," Egan went on, "I had Griff and Ranger Jameson Beckett come up behind Hargrove. He had Mom gagged and tied up in his car, so Griff got her out of there before Hargrove even knew what was happening. Jameson moved in behind Hargrove so we could trap him. I offered him a choice. He could put down his gun or I'd kill him." There was plenty of anger in Egan's voice. "He put down his gun."

So, Egan had managed to rescue Helen without any shots being taken around her. That was something at least. But he was certain these nightmarish memories would stay with his mother for a long time. They'd certainly stay with him, and he could add nearly losing Rayna to those memories.

"Did Mom say anything?" Court asked.

"Plenty. She was mad Hargrove took her, and she tried to punch him. I let her get off a swing before I pulled her back."

Even though he hated that his mother had been through that ordeal, this was a normal reaction, and he much preferred it to her breaking down again. Maybe that meant this situation wouldn't interfere with her treatments and healing while she was trying to get her mind back in a good place.

"What about Dad?" Court pressed. "Was it Hargrove who shot him?"

"He says no. He claims the only thing he did was fire shots at Rayna and you, but that he didn't intend to kill you. Yeah," Egan snarled when Court huffed, "I'm not buying that, either. I think Whitney got riled because her plan to set Rayna up wasn't working, and she gave Hargrove the order to kill her. That order probably included you if you got in the way. Which you would have done."

Definitely. No way would Court have just stood by while some snake attacked Rayna.

Rayna's forehead bunched up. "But why did Whitney stop the attack at the hospital?" she asked. "Hargrove had us pinned down. He could have carried through on her orders to kill us."

Court figured he knew the answer to this. "We had backup moving in fast. It wouldn't have been but another few minutes before the deputies would have gotten to him. Whitney wouldn't have wanted us to catch—and interrogate—her hired thug because he might have implicated her."

Rayna made a sound of agreement. "That way Hargrove could regroup and come after us again. Which he did."

Yes, he had. Well, maybe the man had done that. They might never know if it was Whitney or Hargrove who'd fired at them near the sheriff's office. Or set that fire in the alley. And it really didn't matter. Whitney was dead, and whether Hargrove realized it or not, he'd be charged with accessory to murder, which would carry the same penalties as murder itself. The man would probably get the death penalty.

Court was going to make sure that happened.

"The CSIs are still going through Bobby Joe's room at the inn," Egan explained. "But I'll get a team out to Whitney's place, too. I'm betting we'll find some other pieces to this puzzle there."

Probably. And one of those pieces might explain the

recording they'd found on Bobby Joe's laptop. Court was betting that Whitney made the recording so that it would look as if Bobby Joe still wanted to go after Rayna.

He hadn't.

Though it did sicken him to think that Bobby Joe had come to town in an attempt to win Rayna back. There'd been no chance of that happening, but Bobby Joe might have turned violent again when Rayna turned him down. No way would Court have allowed the man to get away with something like that.

"I need to get Hargrove to jail," Egan went on a moment later. "Ranger Beckett will help me with that. You're on your way to the hospital now, right, so you can check on Mom?"

"We are. We'll be there in about twenty minutes, maybe less. And before Rayna says anything, I probably need a stitch or two. I got grazed by one of the bullets Whitney shot at us."

"The cut is deep, and he's bleeding," Rayna corrected.

Egan cursed. "Make sure my knot-headed brother sees a doctor as soon as he gets to the hospital."

"Don't worry, I will," she answered right before Egan ended the call.

Since she sounded adamant about doing that, Court figured he wouldn't be able to delay getting those stitches. That meant he needed to finish up whatever he was going to say to Rayna now, because once they arrived at the hospital, things could get hectic fast.

"I'm glad you told Whitney you were in love with me," he said. "And I'm especially glad you meant it. It saved me from asking you how you felt about me."

She stared at him, obviously waiting for something, and he was pretty sure what that *something* was.

"I've cared about you for a long time," he added and would have said more if she hadn't interrupted him.

"Yes, but that stopped when you thought I got away with murder."

"No, it never stopped." He was certain of that. "So, this isn't exactly love at first sight. It's me finally coming to my senses and admitting something I should have admitted to you ages ago—that I'm in love with you, too."

He'd been so sure she had expected him to say that. Judging from her shocked expression, she hadn't.

"Uh, should I pretend I'm not hearing this?" Ian asked.

"Yes," Rayna and Court answered in unison.

Rayna continued to stare at him, and despite everything they'd just been through, she smiled. Then she kissed him. The kiss was a lot hotter and went on a lot longer than it should have, considering that Ian was only a few feet away from them.

When she pulled back from the kiss, the smile was still on her mouth. "You're in love with me," she said as if that were some kind of miracle.

"Oh, yeah," he assured her.

It wasn't a miracle, either. She was a very easy person to love. Not just for this moment. But forever.

And that was why Court pulled her right back to him for another kiss.

* * * * *

THREE
COURAGEOUS WORDS

ELLE JAMES

To my husband, who swears he doesn't have a creative bone in his body, for giving me the idea to have a villain warlord who conscripts young boys into his terrorist army. When I ask my husband for help brainstorming, I see the fear in his eyes.
This time, he came through!

Chapter One

"R&R is over, team." Navy SEAL Corpsman Graham "Buck" Buckner clapped his hands together as he walked across the fourth floor of the bombed-out apartment building in Bentiu, South Sudan. "It's time to do what we do best."

"Yeah, Buck." Diesel lay prone, staring through the sight of his M4A1 rifle with the SOPMOD upgrade. "And what's that? Lying around in the heat, waiting for something to happen?"

"Men, we're here on an important mission." Buck grinned. "So what if it's hotter than Hades outside and we haven't had a breeze in over a week? We're here to get our man. Let's do this."

"Shut up, Buck," T-Mac said. "Nothing's stirred in this godforsaken town since we got here."

"That doesn't mean it won't. The intel guys said we'd find Koku here. My gut tells me it won't be long before something happens."

"Your gut is telling you that you're hungry." Pitbull tossed a packet of meals ready to eat at Buck. "Feed your gut."

Buck ducked, letting the MRE packet fall to the floor, unheeded. "Seriously, we've been in worse situations where we all almost died. This isn't that bad."

"At least our enemies weren't boring us to death," Pitbull said. He pulled a photograph from his pocket and stared down at it. "We could have spent two more days at the All Things Wild Resort, enjoying our last little bit of rest and relaxation." He sighed. "I wonder if Marly's packing her apartment in Nairobi right now. I'd like to have been there to help her."

Harm snorted. "You're just afraid she'll say, *What the hell was I thinking, falling for a navy SEAL?* She might change her mind and stay in Africa."

Pitbull's lips twisted. "Yeah. I guess I am afraid of that. Why would she give up her life here in Africa to be with me?"

"Yeah, who'd want to give up a life in Africa?" T-Mac quipped. "It's such a bowl of cherries, what with pirates, warlords and tribal wars everywhere you turn. Think of the excitement she'll be missing."

"And why wouldn't she want to be with you?" Diesel asked. "Some women like ugly mugs like yours."

"Hey, you found a woman here," Pitbull reminded him. "And you're no Mr. *GQ* yourself."

"Ha! Wait until she realizes he snores like a freight train," Big Jake murmured from his position on the other side of the room, holding a pair of binoculars to his eyes. "You and Diesel are just mad you didn't get to spend more time with your women—now that you *have* women." He glanced back at them. "Get over it. Like Buck said, we have a job to do. Let's do it."

Buck crossed to where Big Jake leaned his elbows on the rubble that had once been a wall. "Anything?" he asked, staring out at the buildings they'd been surveilling since they'd arrived.

"Not much," Big Jake said. "Our old man with the mule cart is passing in front of the compound now. You could set the clock by that man. Same time every day."

"I'll take watch for now," Buck offered.

"Good. My eyes are crossing." Big Jake handed the binoculars to Buck. "If you're not going to eat those MREs, I will."

"Knock yourself out." Buck rubbed a hand over his flat abs. "My belly isn't over the brisket with au gratin potatoes I had for breakfast."

"We tried to warn you about them," Harm said.

Buck couldn't deny it. Harm had told him it would mess him up. His stomach was still burbling four hours later. "Yeah, well, I'll listen next time." He lifted the binoculars to his eyes and focused on the structure on the other side of the bombed-out marketplace.

The intel guys had identified the compound as one that General Ibrahim Koku frequented—a local government facility where he had friends conspiring with him to make life hell for the people of Sudan and South Sudan.

The general was a defector from the South Sudan Army and the self-appointed leader of the Sudanese People's Resistance Army, which had been terrorizing South Sudan for the past fourteen months, killing entire populations of villages and conscripting children to be part of his army. As if that wasn't bad enough, he was also the primary reason US aid wasn't getting to the starving people in refugee camps in Sudan's Darfur region, or anywhere else, for that matter. He'd stolen food, medical supplies and even the vehicles transporting them.

And when US money was being thrown away on aid, the American government sent in their boys to fix it. So, instead of enjoying a full week off for much-needed rest and relaxation, the SEAL team had been called back to duty from their Kenyan safari vacation two days early. And for what? To sit in the heat of the sub-Saharan desert and roast like pigs on a spit.

They didn't know when the general would show up, just that their mission was to take him out when he did.

Buck expanded his view to take in more of the surrounding area. A couple blocks to the south, a crowd of women gathered, growing in number as the woman in the center raised her fist to the sky, probably shouting something. From the distance, Buck couldn't hear what was being said, but the crowd responded, chanting something he couldn't understand. As one, the crowd turned and marched down the middle of the street, headed north on the same boulevard where the general's compound stood.

In the opposite direction, a number of blocks away, a motorcade of black SUVs sped south, on a collision course with the women staging a protest.

"Heads up," Buck said to his teammates. "Things are about to get interesting. Motorcade coming from the north."

Diesel shifted his body and weapon. "Got the vehicles in my sights."

"And what looks like a riot coming from the south," Buck added.

"A riot?" Harm asked and hurried to where Buck stood to see for himself.

Big Jake, T-Mac and Pitbull took up positions against the crumbling walls.

"Holy crap, if those women are on a mission to protest our favorite general, they're going to be slaughtered."

"What can we do?" Buck asked.

"Nothing," Big Jake said. "We're not here to stop them from protesting. We're here to take out Koku."

Buck glanced toward the oncoming motorcade. "Yeah, but—"

"No buts," Big Jake said. "We're here to stop Koku's reign of terror. The end. No side trips to the mall, no flirting with the local girls."

Buck lifted the binoculars again and focused on the woman leading the march. Unlike the others, who were dressed in brightly colored head scarves and dresses, the woman's head was bare. She had dark hair, dark eyes and much lighter skin than the other women marching. And she wore faded blue jeans and a white T-shirt with a red design and black lettering. "Guys, is that woman wearing a Doctors Without Borders T-shirt?" He handed the binoculars to Harm.

"Damn. She is," Harm said. "And she's not Sudanese."

"What the hell is she doing?" T-Mac asked.

"I don't know, but I'm going to get closer before all hell breaks loose," Buck said.

"Stand down, Buck," Big Jake said.

"If that woman is American, she'll be worse than killed," Buck said. "Let me get close enough to find out. If she's American, I'll—"

"You'll what?" Big Jake shook his head. "You can't jeopardize this mission because some do-gooder has decided to march against a murdering terrorist."

"I can't do nothing." Buck lifted the binoculars again. Something about the woman seemed familiar. Maybe it was the way she walked or flipped her hair back over her shoulder, but whatever it was brought back memories he'd thought long forgotten. "I'll get her out of the way before the motorcade gets there."

Big Jake's eyes narrowed. "You can't do anything to make us miss this opportunity to take down Koku."

Buck stood and held up his hand as if swearing in court. "I promise."

Big Jake jerked his head to the side. "Go. But don't do anything stupid, and don't give yourself away. We've got your back, but don't force us to expose our position. There's too much riding on this mission's success."

Buck pulled on one of the long white robes called a dishdasha, worn by Sudanese men, and settled a white turban on his head as he ran for the stairs leading to the ground. He only had a couple minutes to get to the marching women and decide what to do before the motorcade arrived.

Keeping to the shadows, he ran along the walls

of the bombed-out building between their hideout and the compound. If he were spotted, his white skin would stand out, even though most of it was covered. His tanned face and hands were not nearly dark enough to match the skin of the Sudanese men.

As he arrived near the street where the women were marching, the motorcade of black vehicles rolled into sight.

Buck cursed. If he made any kind of move to get out in front of the mob of women, he'd be picked off immediately.

Instead, he waited in the shadows for the leader of the march to pass. As she neared, a knot formed in his gut next to the one created by the MREs.

He knew her. Buck knew the woman leading the march. At least, he'd known her back in Chicago, what seemed like a million years ago.

How in the hell did she get here, half a world away from where he'd first met her?

Now more than ever, he had to get to her, to pull her out of harm's way before the motorcade reached them.

Women in brightly colored clothing passed him, filling the streets, all chanting. Some were carrying signs Buck couldn't read.

Ducking low, Buck melted into the crowd, working his way to the front where the woman led the march, yelling loud and clear in that voice he'd recognize anywhere.

When there were only two people between them, he made his move. He dashed up behind her, spun her around and threw her over his shoulder, then ran back through the women in the crowd. He did it so quickly, the women didn't realize what was going on until he had her back by the building, in the shadows, yelling at him.

He shot a glance over his shoulder at the women who'd been marching. They'd stopped shouting and were scattering in all directions as the black vehicles rolled up to the compound.

"Put me down!" Buck's captive said. She pounded his back and kicked her legs, squirming so wildly he all but dropped her on her feet.

As soon as she had her legs under her, she cocked her arm and smacked him upside the head.

She hit him hard enough to make his ears ring.

With the motorcade so close to where they stood, Buck didn't have time to explain. He spun her around, her back to his front, clamped a hand over her mouth and dragged her deeper in the shadows.

She fought, kicking, scratching and finally biting his hand so hard she almost drew blood.

"Damn it, Angela! It's me," he whispered. "Graham."

DR. ANGELA VEGA STILLED. Her pounding heart stopped for a fraction of a second before racing ahead, for an entirely different reason than fear. "Let go of me," she demanded.

"Only if you promise not to run," he said in that deep voice she remembered all too well.

She hesitated a moment, her pulse pounding, and then said, "I promise."

Her captor released her.

Angela spun to face the man who'd turned her world upside down years ago, while she'd been in medical school. So many questions ran through her head, like what was he doing here? And why was he dressed like a Sudanese man? But she had more immediate issues. "Why did you stop me?" She spun toward the road he'd yanked her off. "I was leading those women in protest. I need to be out there."

His lips thinned. "They scattered. You won't get them back together any time soon."

"Damn it, Graham. They need food and medicine. We needed our voices to be heard by the local government officials."

"Not there, you don't." He gripped her hand in his. "Come on, we have to get out of here, ASAP."

"I'm not going anywhere with you. I work with those women. They need our assistance. Their entire families need help. And the local government is working with Koku, a bastard of a warlord, stealing the aid packages that are supposed to be going to the refugee camps."

"And you think a protest is going to make a difference?" Buck shook his head.

"We had to do something," Angela said. "The local government wasn't helping."

"I'm not here to argue with you. I'm just telling you that you're in danger."

She jerked her hand free of his and squared off

with him, her shoulders back, her chin held high. "We knew that when we started. It was a risk we were all willing to take."

"Yeah, well, the only way to reason with a man like Koku is with force."

"We were protesting the local government, not Koku," Angela insisted.

"Since they're in cahoots with him, it's the same thing." He narrowed his eyes and took a threatening step toward her. "Now, are you coming with me peacefully, or am I going to have to carry you out of here?"

Angela backed up a step, then another. "I don't have to go with you. I have to get back to my practice."

"You're not going anywhere without me until we know what's happening. And the longer we stand here arguing, the greater chance there is of one of Koku's men finding us and settling our argument with bullets." He lunged toward her, bending as if to scoop her up.

"Hold it right there, buddy," she said. "You don't have to carry me like a Neanderthal."

Sounds of gunfire erupted.

Angela ducked, her heart pounding. Maybe he was right. Now wasn't the time to argue. "Fine. I'll go with you. For the time being…"

Graham grabbed her hand and ran, leading her away from the street and into the shadows of a crumbling wall. They followed the wall until they came to the back of the building, which was no more than a pile of rubble.

"Where are we going?" she asked. "And what the hell is happening back there?"

He nodded toward the damaged apartment building. "We're going there. And I don't know what's happening. Hopefully, we'll find out when we meet up with the rest of the team."

"Team?" she asked but was cut off when he practically yanked her arm out of its socket, dragging her toward the damaged apartment building.

Just as he started to climb a set of stairs leading up, five men came running down.

"Abandon ship," one of them said and raced past them.

"What's going on?" Graham asked.

"If the motorcade belongs to Koku, he's not here to schmooze with the locals," the second man down the stairs said. "He's here to destroy it and the people inside."

The man behind him continued speaking. "We think the trailer that just pulled up in front of the compound is full of explosives." He kept running.

A big blond guy with massive shoulders was the last one out. "Run!"

Graham and Angela raced after the departing men. As they neared the structure on the back side of the abandoned apartment building, an explosion rocked the ground, spewing chunks of concrete, rock and splinters of wood into the air.

Angela fell to the ground and covered the back of her neck.

Graham fell on top of her, using his body as a shield to protect her. When the debris stopped falling, he was back up, dragging her to her feet.

The rapid report of gunfire sounded behind them.

The men didn't stop until they reached a beat-up old van a couple blocks away.

The first guy there threw open the side door, leaped inside and crawled into the driver's seat. The others piled in after him.

When Angela reached the van, Graham lifted her and tossed her in like a load of laundry. He dived in behind her, landing on top of her, and someone slammed the door shut.

Angela could barely breathe with Graham's weight pressing her into the metal floor.

The popping noise of automatic weapons sounded close by.

"Go! Go! Go!" someone shouted.

The man behind the steering wheel shifted into Drive and spun out, leaving a layer of rubber on the street. Something hit the side of the vehicle.

Graham grunted and stiffened, letting out a string of curses.

Finally, he rolled off her and sat up.

Angela dragged in a deep breath, filling her lungs, and then pushed to a sitting position.

Two men sat in the seats up front. The bigger guy had sandy-blond hair. The driver had black hair. Three other men besides Graham crowded into the back, sitting or squatting with their backs to the walls of the van.

When her gaze came back around to Graham, he held his hand over his arm, his lips pressed tightly together.

"Damn, Buck, you're bleeding," one of the men said.

Angela looked again at the hand holding his arm. Blood leaked through his fingers and dripped onto the floor.

Her pulse leaped. "Why didn't you say something?"

"I was too busy getting off you so you could breathe," he said. "Besides, it's just a flesh wound."

Angela moved closer. "Let me see."

He removed his hand from the wound. Blood oozed from the injury, but not at an alarming rate. Still, she needed to stop the bleeding.

"Anyone have a knife?" she asked.

Four wicked-looking knives appeared in front of her.

She selected one, ripped the hem of the robe Buck wore and tore a length along the bottom all the way around. She folded it into a tight pad and applied it to the wound. "Use that to apply pressure."

Buck forced a smile. "Yes, ma'am."

She tore another length off the robe and used it to tie around his arm, knotting it over the wound to maintain the pressure. Some blood soaked through, but not enough for her to be worried about it.

"When we get back to the refugee camp, I'll sew you up."

"Let's get this straight," Graham said. "We're not going back to the refugee camp."

Angela stared around at the others. "But we have to. All of my equipment and supplies are there."

"We're not even supposed to be in South Sudan," said the big blond guy in the front seat. "We can't go to the refugee camp. We'd be too exposed and our mission would be jeopardized, if it hasn't already been." He glared at Graham.

Angela sensed he wasn't happy with her former boyfriend. But she couldn't be worried about that. She had a job to do. "Then let me out at the next corner," Angela said. "I'll get to the camp by myself."

Graham shook his head. "Not happening."

"What were you doing leading a protest against Koku?" the big guy in the front said. "Oh, and by the way, I'm Big Jake. Diesel's the one driving." He then pointed to a man with close-cropped brown hair leaning against the wall of the van. "That's Pitbull, and the one beside him is Harm." Harm had black hair and dark eyes. Big Jake nodded to the man in the very back with auburn hair and green eyes. "That's T-Mac. And I guess you met Buck."

"Buck?" She frowned at Graham.

Graham shrugged. "Short for Buckner."

"Do any of you have real names?" she asked.

"When we need them," Pitbull said.

T-Mac grinned. "On our paychecks."

"Well, Big Mac," Angela said. "I need to get back to the camp outside town, as soon as possible."

The men laughed.

"No can do," the man in the passenger seat said. "And it's Big Jake."

"Seriously, I have to go back. My nurse is there. If the raiders who attacked the government office make it out to the refugee camp, they might take her. So, if you're not taking me there, at least let me out and I'll walk." She moved toward the door and placed her fingers on the handle.

"Hey." Graham reached out with his injured arm and winced but grabbed her wrist anyway. "You can't jump out of a moving vehicle."

"If that's the only way to get back to the refugee camp, I'll do it. I won't leave my nurse to be terrorized, killed or sold into slavery." She spoke louder. "So if you don't stop this vehicle now, I'm going to jump."

Chapter Two

"Hold your horses. We'll take you to the camp," Diesel said. "Just let me get us far enough away from what's going on downtown."

"Jump from a moving vehicle?" Buck chuckled, then stopped when he realized Angela hadn't been kidding. He shook his head. "You're as stubborn as you always were."

Angela lifted her chin. "It's what keeps me going here. My stubbornness got me through medical school and my internship."

She didn't say it, but Buck could hear the comment she didn't make: *Unlike you.*

Buck felt the cut like a knife to his gut. "I had my reasons for leaving," he said and ended it there.

"Where's the refugee camp?" Diesel asked.

Angela turned away from Buck and focused her attention on Diesel. "Southwest of town."

Using less-traveled streets, Diesel drove the van to the edge of town. Before they left the cover of the buildings for the open landscape, Big Jake glanced back.

"No one behind us for now," T-Mac confirmed.

Diesel shot out of Bentiu and into the open.

Not far from the town was the beginning of a city of tents and poorly erected shelters made of scrap plywood and tin.

"We can't drive right into camp," Big Jake said. "Remember, we're not supposed to be in this country."

Angela nodded. "Our tent is on the back side of the camp. There are some buildings past that where you can hide the van and let me off." She directed Diesel past the camp and a little farther, to where a stand of shanties stood.

Diesel parked behind one that appeared abandoned.

When Angela reached for the door, Buck gripped her wrist. "I'm going with you."

"There's no need," Angela said with her fingers curling around the handle. "I'm not coming back."

"The hell you aren't," Buck said.

"I'm not here to argue. I have to check on my nurse." She shoved the sliding door open and dropped to the ground. Without waiting, she took off toward the camp at a slow jog.

Buck shot a glance at Big Jake. "I can't let her go it alone."

Big Jake jerked his head toward Angela's departing figure. "Then go. We'll wait here as long as we're not discovered." He tapped the earbud headset. "Stay in touch. I'll send a couple men out to keep watch for bad guys."

"I'll keep you informed." Buck jumped out of the van and ran to catch up with Angela.

She didn't slow for him but kept jogging toward her destination. "You didn't have to follow me," she said. "I know what I'm doing."

"Humor me." He raised a hand to the makeshift bandage on his arm. "Besides, I need you to patch me up better."

"How do you know I didn't do a good job?"

"I'm the corpsman, the medic for the team. It's my professional opinion that you need to clean the wound and apply a fresh bandage to keep it from becoming infected."

Her eyes narrowed. "Right. You're a medic. Do it yourself."

"I can't perform surgery on myself, now can I?"

She sighed and kept moving. "Fine. It wouldn't hurt to clean the wound and apply sterile bandages."

Buck suppressed the smile threatening to spread across his face. He'd scored a very minor victory, but one that would give him a little more time to convince her to leave an extremely volatile area.

As they approached the sprawling camp, they circled around a large white tent to the entry at the front where a canvas sign was tied over the door. The red, white and black lettering stated Médecins Sans Frontières, which translated to Doctors Without Borders.

Buck knew all about this international nongovernmental organization known for humanitarian relief in war-torn or developing countries with little or no medical services available to the general population. He'd hoped one day to be one of the doctors to volunteer his time to help others less fortunate. He'd had lots of dreams when he'd started medical school.

A woman with graying blond hair stepped out of the tent and frowned when she saw Angela and Buck. "I heard an explosion in town. That wasn't anywhere close to your demonstration, was it?"

Angela's lips pressed together. "Brenda, we need to prep for stitches. I'll fill you in on what happened while we're sewing up this man."

Brenda smiled at Buck. "Hi, I'm Brenda Sites. And you are?"

"Graham Buckner, but you can call me Buck." He nodded toward the tent. "We don't have time for stitches," Buck said. "A clean pressure bandage will do for now."

Angela shook her head. "No, we need to close the wound to keep it from getting infected. I can do it in less than five minutes, if you'll shut up and let me get busy."

"All right, sweetheart. You don't have to be so bossy." Buck's lips twitched as he followed Angela into the tent, his gaze taking in the neat little hospital complete with a few beds and a separate room for more advanced procedures.

His curiosity always piqued when he was around medical equipment and medicine. More than anything, he wished he'd been able to finish his degree and residency. Alas, his past had caught up with him, and he'd had to leave school or risk exposing the people he cared most about to the murdering, scum-of-the-earth gang members he'd grown up with in Chicago.

He'd left school, Angela and his dreams behind to get away from his past and to get his past away from Angela. He couldn't regret that. She'd deserved to finish her schooling without being stalked, harassed and potentially harmed by Buck's old gang members.

The only way Buck had gotten the gang to leave him and Angela alone was to give up his dreams and leave Chicago all together.

"Have a seat." Angela indicated a folding chair in front of a small field desk.

"Really, we could just clean the wound, bandage it and be done in a lot less time," Buck said. "If you'll give me whatever you use to clean with, I can try to do it myself."

"Didn't you say you couldn't perform surgery on yourself?" Angela washed her hands, dried them and pulled on a pair of latex gloves, while her nurse spread out sterile drop cloths across the table, then laid out scissors, gauze, Betadine and tweezers. She used the scissors to remove the makeshift bandage from his arm. Blood oozed from the wound.

Angela inspected it. "See? You need stitches." She took over after the nurse completed removing the bandage and irrigated the wound with a syringe.

The nurse patted it dry with gauze and applied Betadine to the skin around the wound.

Angela threaded the needle with suture line, her movements quick and efficient. "We're short on local anesthetics. Hell, we're out of most medications."

Angela met his gaze with a steady one of her own. "You'll have to hold very still and grin and bear it."

If he wasn't mistaken, she almost looked like she was enjoying taunting him with the threat of pain. He nodded. "Just do it quickly. We don't know when or if Koku's men will show up and cause more trouble."

Before the last word left his mouth, she stuck the needle into the edge of one side of the wound and looped it through the other. She talked softly as she worked, informing her nurse of what had occurred in Bentiu.

Buck stared at the top of Angela's head while bracing his jaw to keep from cursing. It hurt like hell, but he wouldn't jerk his hand away or let loose any of the choice words he wanted to say at that moment. Instead, he focused on Angela, taking advantage of her concentration on his arm to study her.

She hadn't changed much in their years apart. If anything, she'd become even more beautiful. Her dark hair framed her face, her olive-toned skin was a little darker and the confidence she exuded was palpable. The woman had matured into a self-assured, capable doctor with a steady hand.

Buck's heart swelled with pride for her. "I always knew you'd make it," he said softly.

Her hand stilled for a fraction of a second before she tied off the first stitch. "That's what happens when you stay focused."

Her comment hurt. He shouldn't have let it, but it did. Angela hadn't known how much he wanted to stay at school and be with her. He hadn't told her, figuring a clean break would be better than leaving her holding out hope for his return. "I had my reasons for leaving."

"Yeah. And it doesn't matter, does it? You left. I stayed. We lived our own lives." She slipped the needle into another section of the wound. "Separately."

Buck winced and bit down on his tongue. He figured Angela was right. Why bother rehashing the past? It was over. What he needed to do was concentrate on getting her out of the camp before Koku's men came looking for another place to shake up.

Angela and Brenda worked on his arm with quiet efficiency.

By the time Angela tied off the last stitch, Buck could swear he'd ground at least a quarter of an inch off his back teeth. He released the breath he'd held and stood.

"Now, let's get you out of here." Buck reached for her wrist.

Angela stepped backward, avoiding his hand. "I told you, I'm not going. I can't leave these people."

"You saw what happened in Bentiu. Those guys could come here next."

"These people need us. We can't abandon them." Angela peeled the gloves from her hands.

Buck's jaw tightened. He couldn't walk away and leave her here, in danger. "You're not safe."

"*They're* not safe." She laid the gloves on the table and captured his gaze in an unflinching one of her own. "I'm not going."

Big Jake's voice came over Buck's headset. "We've got company."

"You may not have a choice," Buck said. "My guys say Koku's men are coming into camp as we speak."

No sooner had he made the announcement than a burst of gunfire could be heard outside, followed by women screaming.

"If you don't leave for *me*—" Buck nodded toward her nurse "—leave for Brenda. We need to get both of you out of here. Now." He took Angela's hand and dragged her toward the door.

More gunfire erupted.

Angela dug in her heels and pulled her hand free. "You're a SEAL. You can stop them."

"Not if we're outnumbered. And sometimes that only causes more casualties when so many civilians are involved."

"Seriously, guys," Big Jake said into Buck's ear. "They're headed straight for your tent."

"My men say Koku's men are headed directly for this tent. Are you coming with me or staying to argue with a killer?"

ANGELA HAD SPENT so much of her time working with and healing the people in the refugee camp. To leave them would be like abandoning her own children.

"Dr. Vega." Brenda touched her arm, her eyes rounded, her hand shaking. "We can't help anyone if we're dead."

Her nurse's words hit hard. If Brenda was scared,

Angela owed it to her to get her out. She turned to Buck. "Take my nurse and get her to safety."

He shook his head. "I'm not leaving without you."

One of the women Angela had been training to assist with medical treatments ran into the tent. "Dr. Angela! Dr. Angela! The men. They're coming for you. They're coming for the doctor." She took Angela's arm and hauled her toward the door. "You have to go. You go. Now."

Angela's gaze met Buck's over the woman's head. "Okay. We'll go."

Buck touched his headset. "We're on our way." He stepped in front of Angela before she could leave the tent. "But not that way." He pulled his Ka-Bar knife from the sheath on his belt and strode through the tent to the back, where he jabbed the knife into the fabric and slit an opening large enough for a person to get through.

Then he stepped out and held the fabric wide. "Now you," he said, waving for Brenda to come next.

The nurse ducked through and moved out of the way.

While Buck and Brenda were making their way out of the tent, Angela got busy throwing equipment, supplies and medication into her backpack.

Buck stuck his head back into the tent. "Angela, we have to go now. They're almost on us."

Angela shot one final glance around the tent she'd called home for the past six months, tossed in a couple bottles of water and dived out of the tent.

Loud voices could be heard from the men storming through the refugee camp toward the hospital tent.

Her heart thundering against her ribs, Angela ran.

Buck grabbed the backpack from her arm and slung it over his shoulder. Then he took her hand and urged her to go faster.

By the time they reached the deserted shack, Angela could barely breathe. T-Mac and Harm were waiting at the sliding door, where they lifted Brenda off her feet and into the van. They did the same for Angela and then clambered in after them. Buck was last inside, slamming the door as the vehicle took off.

Angela stared through the back window of the van at the camp she was leaving behind. Smoke rose from the tent they'd just vacated, the fabric succumbing to the flames shooting into the sky.

Men in black clothing ran toward them, firing their rifles.

But by then, the van was far enough away, and the bullets fell short.

"We don't have much of a lead on them," Buck said. "Once they get their trucks rolling, they'll be after us."

"Then we need to keep rolling," Big Jake said. "The faster, the better."

Diesel pressed his foot to the accelerator, taking the van as fast as it would go, fully loaded with SEALs and the women.

"If we're lucky, the sun will set before they catch up to us," Big Jake said. "The 160th is on standby for extraction as soon as we give them the coordinates."

"In the meantime," Diesel tossed over his shoulder, "any suggestions on a place around here to hide a van and eight people?"

Angela thought hard. For the most part, she'd been confined to the hospital tent, working nonstop with masses of people living in the terrible conditions of the refugee camp. But there was one time she and Brenda had been asked to help a village elder in another small town nearby. She glanced out the window. They were headed that direction. "I know of a place."

Leaning through the gap between the two front seats, she watched the road ahead, trying to remember where they'd turned to get to the village.

Brenda squeezed in next to her. "Are you taking them to Abu Hanafi's village?"

She nodded. "The turnoff to the village should be coming up soon."

"Remember, it was where the abandoned tank tracks were," Brenda said.

"Right." Angela turned to Diesel. "There should be some buildings coming up soon and a field beside the road with what looks like a pile of junk metal. It's actually the tracks from an army tank."

Diesel nodded. "I'll be on the lookout."

Angela glanced back through the van's rear window, her pulse pounding. As she turned back to the front, her gaze skimmed across Buck. Her heart did a backflip. When she'd first realized who'd plucked her out of the middle of the protest, she'd been too angry to fully appreciate what had happened.

In this totally different part of the world, why had fate brought Graham back to her? At that very moment?

He was the same Graham she'd known and loved in medical school, yet different.

His body was honed, his muscles tight and strong, and his eyes...those gorgeous blue eyes she'd fallen into on their first group project were somehow different. Although still the same blue, they appeared to see more and have more depth than before. The lines around the corners of his eyes added character, and the scar on his chin made her want to reach out and touch it.

As quickly as the thought sprang into her mind, she pushed it away and returned her attention to the road in front of the van.

Ahead, on the left, was a field of long grass with a patch of dirt next to the road. Rusted metal lay in a heap in the middle of the dirt.

"There!" Angela pointed to the dirt road past the tank track. "Turn there."

Diesel only slowed enough to negotiate the turn and then sped along the bumpy road, barely more than a rutted track.

Big Jake's brow crinkled as he glanced her way. "Are you sure this is the way?"

"Positive." She nodded toward a blue tin shack. "I remember that blue building."

"And the one with the orange roof," Brenda added, pointing to the structure.

"The village is another mile or more along this road, and it's tucked into the side of a hill."

"As long as the dust settles before the rebel attackers get to where we turned off, they won't have a clue we came this way."

"*If* the dust settles," T-Mac said.

Angela glanced back at the cloud of dust rising up behind them.

Buck touched her arm. "It'll settle."

She gave him a hint of a smile and turned away. So many forgotten emotions welled up inside her. Why did he have to come back into her life? Why now? But if he hadn't, she might be dead. The protest she'd staged against the local government could have ended a lot worse. She prayed the women who'd gone along with her had made it back to safety.

Leaving behind the refugees she'd grown to care for was killing her. But like Brenda had said, she couldn't help people if she was dead.

Soon, they came to the little village tucked into the side of a hill. Shacks and huts lined the road, with barely clothed children playing outside.

"Let me out," Angela said. "I'll speak to Abu Hanafi. He might not want us in his village if we bring trouble with us."

"Tell him we won't stay any longer than it takes to get airlifted out," Big Jake said. "And we'll arrange pickup away from his village so as not to draw too much attention to it."

Angela nodded and hopped out of the van. Buck followed.

"It might be better if I go alone," Angela said.

"Not happening." He gripped her elbow and marched forward.

Angela shrugged free of his hand. Every time he touched her, that same jolt, like an electrical current, ran through her, reminding her of the connection they'd had when they were much younger.

She tightened her jaw. That was the past. "I got along fine without you for six months in this country. I can do this on my own."

"Then do it on your own, just with me. I won't say a word. You'll barely know I'm there."

She snorted. "You're over six feet tall. Much taller than many of the people in this village. I think I'll notice you. And I won't be the only one." As much as she protested, she did feel protected when he was around.

Angela led the way to the mud-and-stick building at the center of the little village. A woman wearing a faded red-and-gold dress with a red scarf draped over her head and shoulders stood in the doorway with a toddler on her hip.

With a smile, Angela addressed the daughter of the village elder. "Uluru, how are you and your children?"

She knew from the last time she'd been here that Uluru spoke perfect English she'd learned at a missionary school when she was much younger. At twenty-one years old, she had three children, the youngest of which she was holding.

"They are well. I am teaching Kamal his letters. He will go to school one day."

Angela nodded. "Your children will be smart as well as beautiful, like their mother."

She snorted softly. "If they live that long and are not stolen away by Koku's army." Uluru moved out of the doorway. "You are here to see my father?"

"Yes," Angela said.

"And this man with you, who dresses like one of our men?"

"He is my…" Angela almost said *boyfriend*, but that was so many years ago.

"I'm her fiancé," Buck said and cupped Angela's elbow. "We are to be married soon."

Angela swallowed hard to keep from disagreeing out loud. Now that he'd said it, she couldn't deny it without appearing wishy-washy in front of Uluru and her father.

Uluru's gaze swept over Buck from head to toe before she nodded. "As the doctor's betrothed, you are welcome in our home."

Inside, the structure was cast in shadow, with no electrical lighting in use.

Uluru passed through the house and out into a small courtyard where an old man, dressed all in white much like Buck, sat cross-legged on the ground in the shade of a tree.

Angela waited for the man to invite her forward.

When he did, she sat cross-legged across from him, and Buck sat beside her.

Uluru joined them, setting the toddler on his feet. The child wandered off to play with a stick.

Angela studied the man, searching his face for any signs of illness. "You are well?" she asked.

Abu Hanafi nodded, his gaze going to Buck and back to Angela. "Who is this white man who dresses like one of our people?"

Buck sat up straight, meeting the man's gaze with a strength and confidence Angela had to admire. "I am Dr. Vega's fiancé."

The elder continued to stare at Buck for a long moment, as if sizing him up. Finally, he gave a single nod. "Why are you here?"

Angela realized the elder wasn't speaking to her, but to Buck. In deference, she let Buck respond.

"There was an attack on the government building in Bentiu. We believe it was Koku. Then his men attacked the refugee camp," Buck said. "My men and I got Dr. Vega and her nurse out before they could be harmed. We all need a place to hide until after the sun sets, at which time we will leave."

Abu Hanafi's brow furrowed. "You have brought danger to my village?"

"We hope not," Buck said. "But we will leave as soon as we can."

"Or we could leave now, if you think we have endangered your people," Angela said softly.

A long silence stretched between the elder, Angela and Buck. Finally, Abu Hanafi nodded. "You will stay until dark. However, if trouble follows you, you will leave sooner. Too many of our children have been stolen by Koku and his men."

"Koku has taken children from your village?" Buck questioned.

"He takes our young boys to fill his army," the elder said. "We are forced to hide them in the bushes when Koku is in the area."

"I'm sorry to hear that," Angela said. "I wish we could do something to stop him."

"You have to know where to find him," Buck said, "in order to do anything to stop him."

Once again, Abu Hanafi studied Buck. "You are not a doctor."

Buck shook his head. "No, sir."

"You are an American soldier?"

Buck tensed beside Angela. "No, sir."

That penetrating gaze pinned Buck to his spot. But Buck wasn't giving the man any more than he already had. "Sir, we should move our vehicle before Koku's people see it and report back to him."

Abu Hanafi waved his hand. "Go."

When Angela rose to her feet, he touched her arm. "My people owe you a debt we cannot repay."

"You owe me nothing," Angela assured him.

The elder dipped his head. "I can only repay you in friendship."

"Which is the most important payment of all." She held out her hand to the man. He took it in both of his. "Thank you for saving my life."

"You're welcome."

Uluru led them through the house and back to the van. "You can park in the trees at the base of the bluff," she said.

"Thank you." Angela strode back to the van, anxious to get away from Buck and the chemistry he seemed to be stirring up inside her. The faster they resolved the issue with Koku, the quicker she could get back to helping others.

She hoped it happened sooner rather than later, because all those old feelings she'd had back in medical school seemed to be bubbling up inside. Losing him the first time had been bad enough. She feared the more time she spent with Buck, the more dangerous he became.

To her heart.

Chapter Three

Buck and Angela returned to the van, where several of the SEALs stood outside the vehicle.

Having taken over the conversation with Abu Hanafi, Buck allowed Angela to take the lead this time.

"We can stay only until after dark," Angela jumped in without preamble. After informing them of where Uluru had indicated they could park the van out of sight of the road, Angela announced, "I'll walk."

"I'll walk with you," Buck said.

The only hint she wasn't happy with his announcement was the tightening of her lips. "Suit yourself." And she started toward the hillside.

Diesel cranked the van's engine, the SEALs piled in and the van passed Angela and Buck on the way to the hiding place.

Angela waited until the people in the van were well out of hearing distance before she said, "Did you ever consider I might not want you to walk with me?"

"Yes." He lifted a shoulder. "And I ignored it. I don't feel comfortable leaving you anywhere alone."

"You left me in Chicago," she shot back.

The anger and hurt in Angela's voice twisted a knife in Buck's gut. "We're in South Sudan, a volatile nation filled with murderous people" was all he could push past the tightness in his throat.

"Like Chicago?" Again, she was quick with her comebacks. Sadly, she was right.

"I had reasons for leaving when I did," he said.

Angela spun around in front of him, stopping him in his tracks. "I wouldn't know, now would I?" She poked a finger at his chest. "Because you didn't bother to tell me what they were, or even that you were leaving. I had to find out from your roommate, *after* you were long gone." She smacked her palm flat against his chest. "You'd think any kind of man would have the decency to tell his girlfriend he was skipping town, quitting college and joining the navy. But then, you weren't even decent—"

Buck grabbed the woman's arms and yanked her against him, crushing her lips with a bruising kiss. He'd never wanted to leave her, would rather have slit his own throat than hurt her. And now, seeing her in front of him, her eyes alight with fury, her cheeks blooming with righteous indignation, he couldn't resist.

This was the woman he'd never been able to forget. The kiss started out raw and angry but quickly turned hungry and desperate. He remembered her lips, the way they felt beneath his mouth, the curve of her body against his and the way she leaned into him when she gave her whole self to the kiss.

At first she was stiff in his arms, her palms on his chest. But she didn't push him away. Slowly, almost imperceptibly, she loosened up until she was leaning into him, giving back every bit as much as he gave.

When at last he was forced to surface for air, he drew in a deep breath and rested his forehead against hers.

"Don't think this changes anything," she said, her fingers curling into his shirt. "I'm still angry with you. And I'm still staying in Sudan." Then she did push out of his arms, turned and ran after the van.

Buck followed at a slower pace, wondering what the hell had just happened. He'd never intended to pick up where they'd left off all those years ago. Angela had her life, and he had his. Nothing between them would ever work.

Granted, Chicago was not an issue anymore. From what he understood, his old gang had been disbanded with the arrest and incarceration of their leader. The man had finally been caught and convicted of murder.

Once the team had the van hidden behind old buildings and trees near the base of the hillside, they climbed out and prepared to lie low until after sunset.

Harm and Diesel went south, and Pitbull hiked to the north, each going around the hill. Big Jake and T-Mac climbed to the top, all of them searching for potential threats and the coordinates to give the helicopter crew for their extraction.

They left Buck to guard the two women.

"Tough job, but someone has to do it," Diesel said as he left with Harm.

Word must have gotten out that the doctor was in the village. Before long, women brought children to the base of the hillside, seeking assistance for minor injuries, skin infections, lacerations and more.

Working out of the side door of the van, Angela, Brenda and Buck treated the patients.

All the while, Buck kept a close watch on the surrounding area and scrutinized every patient, searching for hidden weapons. But they were all what they appeared to be…people sincerely in need of help.

As the sun dropped to the horizon, the line of people dwindled to two, then one.

The last one, a bone-thin woman dressed in a faded gold dress and scarf, waited to speak until the others had all gone. "Dr. Angela, you must come with me." She took Angela's hand and tried to drag her away.

Buck stepped between them and loosened the woman's grip on Angela's hand. "The doctor isn't going anywhere. What do you want?"

"She must come," the woman insisted.

Angela placed a hand on Buck's arm and stepped around him. "What's your name?"

"I am Fatima." She turned, waving her hand to the side. "Please, you must come."

"Can't we talk about your problem here?" Angela asked.

"Not me," Fatima said. "My son needs you."

Angela frowned. "What's wrong with your son?"

Fatima glanced around furtively. "He is injured."

"How was he injured?" Angela asked.

The woman looked from Angela to Buck and over

her shoulder, as if afraid of something or someone. "Please, my son needs your help."

The sun had set, and the grayness of dusk enveloped them.

Big Jake, T-Mac, Harm, Diesel and Pitbull all appeared out of the shadows.

"What's going on?" Diesel asked.

Buck tilted his head toward Fatima. "This woman wants the doctor to go to her son."

"I don't recommend it." Big Jake glanced down at his watch. "Our extraction is scheduled for T-minus five minutes. We'd better move to the other side of the hill. And make it fast."

The men headed in that direction. Buck started to follow, but Angela wasn't at his side.

She stood with her feet planted firmly on the ground. "I can't leave this woman without help."

"You can't stay," Buck said. "Koku could be back at any moment."

"Please…" The woman took Angela's hand again, her eyes pleading. "My son is injured. He needs your help. He has been beaten by Koku's men."

Even Buck, a hardened SEAL, couldn't ignore the woman's desperation. "How far is it to your son?"

"On the other side of the village. It will not take long. He has suffered so much. Please help him."

The thumping sound of rotors beating the air made Buck's heart leap. Their transport neared. "We can't do this," he said to Angela.

She stared up into his eyes. "I can't *not* do this."

Buck turned to the woman. "Can you bring your son here?"

"No. My son traveled a long way. He escaped from Koku's camp. His action is punishable by death. He cannot risk being seen and recaptured."

"Wait." Buck's heart rate ratcheted up. "Your son escaped from Koku's camp?"

She nodded. "It is very bad there. He does not wish to return."

Excitement rose like a tidal wave in Buck. "But he knows where Koku lives?"

The woman frowned. "Yes, but he does not wish to return," she repeated. "He was one of many young boys taken to fill Koku's army."

Angela squeezed the woman's hand. "I will help."

Big Jake trotted back to where Buck and Angela stood. "Hey, are you two coming? We have to get around this hill to our extraction point. It's time to move out."

Buck turned to Big Jake. "This woman's son escaped Koku's camp. He knows where we can find Koku."

Big Jake frowned, and he stared at the woman in the deepening dusk. "Your son knows where Koku lives?"

The woman nodded.

Big Jake glanced at his watch. "We'll have to come back to follow up. Right now, we're scheduled for extraction."

"And you need to go and take my nurse back to

safety," Angela said. "But I'm staying to help this woman's son."

Big Jake's frown deepened. "I can't force you to come with us. But you realize the risk you're taking?"

She nodded. "I do."

"And I'm staying with her," Buck said.

"You can't," Big Jake said. "You're part of the team. We leave no man behind."

"Give me the radio. I'll be a one-man recon element scouting out Koku's location." Buck talked fast, the idea coming to him as he spoke. "When you get the nurse to a safe location, you can come back. Hopefully by then, I'll have Koku's exact coordinates. We can complete our mission."

For a long moment, Big Jake stared at Buck. Finally, he said, "I don't like it."

"You don't have to like it, but it makes sense for me to go with this woman and check out her son's story. If it pans out, we'll get a lot farther a lot faster than we have in the past week." Buck nodded toward the sound of the approaching helicopter. "You need to hurry. They won't wait long."

Big Jake nodded to T-Mac. "Give him your ground-to-air radio and go."

T-Mac unclipped the radio from his belt and handed it over to Buck. "Don't do anything to get yourself killed." T-Mac spun and ran toward the sound of the helicopter.

Big Jake stuck out his hand. "What T-Mac said."

Buck clasped the man's hand and was pulled into a bear hug.

Then Big Jake was gone, running after T-Mac.

Buck watched as the last two men of his team disappeared around the side of the hill. Moments later, the thumping sound of the rotor blades intensified and then faded into the distance.

For all intents and purposes, Buck was stranded in South Sudan, without his team to provide backup. Whatever happened from here on, he'd be on his own until he called for extraction. His lifeline was the radio in his hand.

"Please," the woman said. "My son needs you."

Angela slipped her backpack of supplies over one shoulder and said in a calm, quiet voice, "Show me the way."

Buck grabbed his gear bag from the back of the van. Keeping a close watch on his surroundings, he followed.

ANGELA COULDN'T BELIEVE Buck had actually remained behind with her. She hadn't expected him to. Hell, she hadn't really thought through her *own* plan. All she knew was that she couldn't let some poor injured boy lie in pain because she was in a hurry to get out of the country.

Fatima skirted the village, keeping to the deepest shadows that a night sky full of stars couldn't penetrate. Once they were past the jumble of huts and tin shacks, she led them another half mile to what appeared to be a huge junk pile of tin and scraps of worm-eaten lumber.

When she pushed aside a sheet of corrugated roofing metal, she waved for Angela to enter.

The small cave-like structure's interior was pitch-black. Angela hesitated at the entrance, trying to remember whether or not she'd brought a flashlight in the backpack she'd hastily loaded.

A soft click sounded and a beam of light cut through the darkness.

She smiled. Trust Buck to have a flashlight handy. He'd always been good about being prepared. He must have been a Boy Scout in a past life.

He stepped around her and shined the light into the structure.

A young boy, around ten years old, lay on a pile of rags, his face caked with dried blood, one of his arms bent at an odd angle.

The shack was small and rickety. Angela didn't know how she'd manage to work on the boy in the cramped space. When she bent to enter, a hand shot out to stop her.

"We'll have to move him out into the open," Buck said. "This hut doesn't look like it'll stand up to a strong wind."

"I'm smaller. Let me move him," Angela said.

"No way." Buck handed her the flashlight. "Just give me some light to work in."

Angela held the beam steady as Buck hunched over and ducked into the shack.

The boy moaned but didn't fight when Buck gently laid his injured arm over his chest. Then he lifted him into his arms and maneuvered the child and his own big body through the narrow entrance and out into the balmy night air.

Fatima spread her scarf on the ground. "Place him here."

Buck eased the boy to the ground, careful not to jolt his arm or cause him more pain.

His mother hovered close by, looking over her shoulder, fear evident in the whites of her eyes. "You will fix this?" She pointed to the boy's bent arm.

"I'll have to reset the bone. It's going to hurt. What is your name?" Angela asked the boy.

When the boy didn't answer right away, Fatima twisted her hands together. "He is Mustafa."

Using the flashlight, Angela shined the beam into the boy's eyes, testing his pupils' response. No indications of concussion, despite the blood on his head and face. She checked his vital signs. His pulse was strong, his blood pressure right for his size and age. "Mustafa," she said, her tone low, calm and gentle. "What I'm about to do will hurt, but then your arm will feel better. Do you understand?"

The boy nodded, probably in too much pain to do more.

Over the light's beam, Angela caught Buck's attention. "You'll have to hold his upper arm while I apply traction."

He nodded, sat behind the boy and leaned over to grip the child's skinny arm. "Ready."

Angela slowly straightened the arm.

The boy bared his teeth in silence, his body tensing.

Once she had it straight, Angela pulled gently but

firmly until the bone jutting at an odd angle beneath the skin moved back in line with the other end.

Mustafa's back arched and his jaw clenched to keep him from crying out.

Angela hated to cause another human so much pain, but she knew it was necessary and that he'd feel better once they were done.

The boy squirmed and squeezed his eyes closed, perspiration shining on his forehead. Then he went limp.

"I believe he passed out," Buck whispered.

"Good, then maybe he won't be in as much pain." She continued to apply strong downward pressure, easing the bone back into place. Once she had the bone where she wanted it, she held the arm steady. "I need something for a splint."

"Do you have him?" Buck asked.

"Yes," she said. "Go."

Buck released the boy's shoulder and took the flashlight. A few moments later, he came back with two flat, straight sticks about the length of the boy's forearm. He laid them on the ground beside Angela and dug in her backpack for roller gauze and scissors.

While Angela held the arm and spoke to the boy in a soft monotone voice, Buck placed the two flat sticks on either side of the boy's arm and wrapped the roller gauze around and around until he was certain it would be sufficient to keep the arm immobile. When he finished, he cut the gauze and secured the end.

"Well done," Angela said. "You look like you've done this before."

He shrugged. "Like I said, I'm the team medic. We've had a few bumps, bruises and broken bones."

Angela nodded. She would bet he'd seen a lot more than that, including gunshot and shrapnel wounds.

The boy woke before they finished and watched the proceedings with interest, no longer tense with pain.

Angela gave him a mild painkiller and one of the bottles of water she'd stashed in her bag. "He should sleep now."

Buck touched her arm and motioned for her to move away from the boy and his mother. "We need to question him about Koku's location before he goes to sleep."

He leaned so close to her, she could feel the warmth of his body. A shiver of awareness slipped across her skin. She almost didn't register what he said. "He's been through a lot."

"We can't wait. We don't know if Koku will come back through tonight or tomorrow looking for the van and the people who were in it."

Still, Angela hated to disturb the boy. He'd been in so much pain.

"I know you want your patient to recover, but we also put the people of this village at risk just by being here," Buck reasoned. "We need to leave as soon as possible. Preferably at night, to avoid being seen in that van."

Angela knew he was right. The longer she held off questioning the child, the more likely he'd fall asleep before they could. "Fine. Question him. But how is a child going to be able to give you directions?"

"I don't know, but I have to try." He returned to the boy and squatted on the ground beside him. "Are you thirsty?"

Mustafa nodded.

In the glow of the flashlight, Buck held the bottle of water to the boy's mouth. When he'd had enough, Buck capped it and set it beside the child. "Mustafa, your mother says you were in Koku's camp?"

The boy's eyes widened and his gaze darted around.

"It's okay." Buck rested a hand on the boy's arm. "We won't take you back there. But we want to know where to find Koku. Can you tell us how to get there?"

The boy's eyes closed for a moment.

Angela thought he'd gone to sleep. Then he opened them and nodded. "I will show you." He sat up with help from Buck, leaned over the side of the scarf he lay on and drew his finger in the dirt.

"It is a long way. Ten days' walking." He dragged his finger in a fairly straight line for a while, then he poked a dot next to the line. "There are one…two—" he poked another dot, then another "—three…four… five villages along the way. The first one is very small, even smaller than my village. The second one is small, too. The third is a town with a church at the center. The missionaries have gone, and the building has been damaged, but it still stands, and it gave me shelter for one night."

Again, the boy's eyes closed and he grew silent.

Then he opened his eyes as if doing so took great effort. "The next two villages are very much the same as the first—small. The fourth one has an old abandoned truck beside the road—black, like fire burned it. I slept beneath it one day to hide from sight of Koku's soldiers."

Angela's heart squeezed in her chest at the thought of the little boy hiding beneath the burned-out hull of a truck, fearing for his life. He shouldn't have to be afraid. He should be in school learning to read and write. He should be playing with his friends, able to be a kid for a while longer. Her eyes burned with the hint of tears.

"The fifth town is much larger, like Bentiu, with buildings, houses, stores. There are many of Koku's men in those streets. It was not safe. I did not enter. I hid in the bushes outside the town. When the sky became dark, I circled the town and continued to follow the road all the way back to my home."

"After the big town, is that where we will find Koku's camp?"

The boy shook his head. "There is a place where the one road becomes two." Mustafa drew a fork in the road that formed a Y. "To get to Koku's camp, you must take this road." He pointed at the fork to the left. "I watched when we were taken. I knew that if I escaped, I would have to know the way to return to my home." The boy lifted his chin. "Koku's camp is another day's walking from the fork in the road. Half of a day on the road, another half heading west into the setting sun on a smaller, rougher road, leading into the hills."

His mother laid a hand on his shoulder. "My son is all I have. If we have to, we will leave our home and find another place to live."

"You might need to," Buck advised. "If Koku learns we were here, he might search the entire village and surrounding area."

After treating so many patients and then having a helicopter land on the back side of the hill where the village was situated, it would be hard to keep the secret that an American doctor and six military men had been there.

For the villagers' sake, Angela hoped Koku didn't find out. But she wasn't banking on it. Now that she had Mustafa on the road to recovery, she realized it was time to move on. And like Buck had said, moving at night made the most sense.

Buck. Calling him Buck made it seem like he was a different person from the one she'd known back in medical school. Perhaps it would help to keep her from falling for him all over again.

Angela gave Mustafa and his mother instructions on how to take care of the broken arm until it was fully healed in six to eight weeks.

Then Buck helped Mustafa into the ramshackle hut, tried to shore up the posts holding the roof up and stepped out.

Angela turned to the boy's mother. "Fatima, will you be all right taking care of Mustafa?"

The woman nodded. "Now that Mustafa is home, we will make sure we he is not captured again."

Angela glanced at the hut where the boy lay nestled in the darkness. She understood what would happen to the boy should he be recaptured. Most likely, he'd be shot or tortured to death as a message to others who might attempt escape.

Buck cupped her elbow, his touch sending a spark through her system. "We need to go before the light of dawn," he said.

Having done all she could for the child, Angela nodded and followed Buck back toward the village.

When they reached the van, a ghostly figure in white robes hovered by the driver's side. As they neared, the starlight revealed their visitor as Abu Hanafi.

His face was grave. "You said you would be gone by now."

Angela stepped forward. "We are the last two to leave. We will be gone soon."

When Buck tried to get around the elder to the driver's door, the man stood in his way. "This van will be recognized if you try to take it now," Abu Hanafi said.

"It's the only transportation we have," Buck said.

"You have helped my people. I would help you with an alternative to the van."

Angela shot a glance toward Buck. "What alternative?"

"Follow me." Abu Hanafi led the way to a mud-and-stick hut on the edge of the village. Unlike most huts, this one had a sturdy door with a lock hanging from a hasp. The elder used a key to unlock the mechanism.

Buck switched on his flashlight.

The hut contained a variety of items, including sacks of grain, seed and farm implements. In the far corner of the hut stood a relatively large item covered in old cloth.

The village elder grabbed the end of the cloth and yanked it to the side, revealing a shiny red racing motorcycle beneath.

"Uh…this?" Angela shook her head. "I don't think so."

"The van belongs to you?" Abu Hanafi asked Buck.

Buck nodded. "We paid cash for it."

"The motorcycle was a gift from a man we helped hide over a year ago. We haven't used it. I cannot drive it. What we need more is a van for the people of this village. I would trade the motorcycle for the van." The elder's eyes narrowed as he stared across at Buck. "You know how to ride a motorcycle?"

"Yes, sir." Buck grinned. "Although it wasn't as nice as this one, I had one when I was in college."

A smile tugged at Angela's lips at the memory. "I know. You took me on several dates on the back of that bike." Angela crossed her arms over her chest. "But we're talking South Sudan, not Chicago." She waved toward the bike. "There's no protection against bullets."

"Bullets can go through the metal of the van,"

Buck countered. "Besides, this will be faster. And if we're being chased by men in trucks, we could go off-road and get away much more easily than in the van."

Everything he said was correct. The motorcycle would make it easier and faster to get around. A big van would be far too noticeable and hard to hide. As much as she hated the thought of traveling in this fashion, she could see its merit.

"What do you say?" Buck asked.

She drew in a deep breath and let it out slowly. "Thank you, Abu Hanafi. We accept your offer."

Chapter Four

Buck walked the bike out into the open and then checked out the motor, the wires and the brakes. He filled the tank from the fuel jugs the elder had on hand and cranked the engine. It started on the second try and roared to life.

He breathed a sigh of relief. If a motorcycle sat unused for too long, the carburetor often gummed up. But the engine ran smoothly. It would use less fuel and get them around in places a van might not be able to go.

All that was left to do was strap his gear bag and Angela's backpack to the back of the bike and climb on.

After securing their bags, Buck got on first, straddling the seat with both feet on the ground to balance. The engine was powerful enough to handle two riders and not lose speed or degrade the bike's ability to make turns.

Angela's gaze went from the bike to the man and the gear. "Are you sure there's room for me?"

Buck scooted forward. "It'll be tight, but doable." He tipped his head to the side. "Hop on."

With a deep breath, she slid her leg over the seat and placed her feet on the footrests. She couldn't get any closer to Buck unless they were both naked. His pulse sped and his body heated everywhere it touched hers. Which was just about everywhere from his thighs to his back.

"This isn't going to work." Angela started to get off.

He put out his hand, stopping her. "It'll work. I promise."

She sat down hard, but at least she didn't get off. "You could just leave me here and come back for me when you're done scouting," she suggested.

"I don't dare leave you. After they torched your tent at the refugee camp, I don't trust what Koku would do to you if he found you here, unprotected."

Angela shivered. "You have a point. I don't have to like it, but it makes sense."

Buck handed over the keys to the van to Abu Hanafi. "I don't suppose you have helmets?" he asked the elder.

Angela latched on to the only excuse that seemed within her reach. "Ah, see? We shouldn't take the bike. It's too dangerous to ride without a helmet."

Abu Hanafi darted to the corner and unearthed one red helmet that matched the bike. "I have only one."

"Hopefully, it'll fit Dr. Vega." Buck twisted around to help the elder fit the helmet over Angela's head and buckle the strap beneath her chin.

It fit perfectly, and she was so darned cute with the frown on her face framed by the helmet. Before he could resist, he bent forward and kissed the tip of her nose. "You'll be all right." Then he pulled the face shield down over the front and straightened to address the elder. "Thank you for your assistance. We hope we don't cause your people trouble by having been here." He reached out a hand.

Abu Hanafi shook it and let go. "You need to go before the sun rises."

Buck checked his watch. They had a couple hours before dawn, but they needed to get as far down the road as possible before stopping for the day. They'd have to do all of their movement at night to stay under Koku's radar.

"Ready?" he said.

"No." Angela sighed. "Yes."

Although Buck eased the throttle on the handle, the powerful motorcycle still leaped forward. Angela squealed and flung her arms around his waist to hold on.

Buck chuckled as he pulled away from the village and onto the road leading south, the direction from which Mustafa had said he'd come.

Angela might be better off hiding in the village, but Buck couldn't leave her. Though Abu Hanafi had offered them shelter and a place to hide, he could do nothing against Koku's armed men. And Buck didn't want to imagine what would happen to Angela should Koku find her in the village. Would they respect the fact that she was a doctor? Or just look at her as a woman to be handled any way they wanted?

Buck wasn't willing to test any theory involving Koku, his men and Angela. He'd take care of Angela and do his best to keep her safe.

He drove the motorcycle along the main road without using the headlights. The stars shining down from the heavens provided sufficient illumination to see the road and any obstacles in the way. No one stirred in the huts they passed on their way out of the village, and soon, they left the village behind.

The nights were cooler than the heat of the day. Buck preferred to travel through the countryside at night when most people slept. However, he had to be wary of animals wandering across the road. No sooner had he picked up a decent amount of speed than he had to slam on the brakes to avoid plowing into one of the long-horned cows the Dinka people raised. It lay in the middle of the dusty road along with twenty more.

Buck wove through the herd, careful not to get too close to the horns or to run over or disturb them enough to start a stampede.

Angela clung to him, her hands locked around his waist as he leaned left, then right, then left again. She was getting better at going with the motion of his body and maintaining the correct balance to keep the bike from falling over.

Once past the herd, Buck picked up speed. Already the sky was lightening in the east, the gray glow of predawn creeping over the horizon. They would have to stop soon or risk being seen.

Buck slowed, taking time to scout out a good rest stop. On the outskirts of the second small town Mustafa had described, Buck found a small knoll several yards off the main road. It was surrounded by bushes, leafy trees and nothing else that he could see in the early-morning light.

He drove off the road and across a grassy field to reach the knoll.

Angela must have fallen asleep, because she jerked upright and said, "What? What's happening?"

He briefly covered her hand with his. "We're stopping before sunrise."

"Can't we keep going?"

"Not if we want to remain undetected. Besides, we both need some sleep."

She yawned and nodded, her helmet bumping against his back. "I suppose so. You must be exhausted."

As they reached the knoll, Buck brought the motorcycle to a stop. "Think you can stand while I stash the bike in the bushes?"

"Of course I can stand," she said confidently.

"Go easy. You're not used to riding for a long time. It can be hard on a body."

She slipped to the side and planted her foot on the ground, then brought the other leg over the top. Immediately her knees buckled.

Buck reached out to catch her before she fell and pulled her against him with one arm, while the other balanced the motorcycle. He chuckled softly. He couldn't get over how good she felt pressed against his chest.

He loosened the strap beneath her chin and slid the helmet off her head. "A little wobbly?"

She laughed. "A little. Ouch. I didn't realize how sore I'd gotten until I moved."

"I'll be the same. Maybe we should have kept the van."

Angela shook her head and straightened away from him. "You wouldn't have been able to drive it through the cattle or off the road like you've driven the bike. You made the right call."

Buck dismounted. His legs were a little shaky, but they held up while he worked the kinks out of them and his backside. He figured it was like riding a horse—you built up calluses the more you rode.

Once he was steady on his feet, he pushed the bike behind thick bushes and unstrapped his gear bag and her backpack and carried them to the top of the rise. There, they could see the low structures of the small village. At the moment, they were nothing more than dark shadows on the horizon. At least they could watch from where they were without disturbing the inhabitants or alerting them to their presence.

Buck couldn't be certain the villagers would be quiet about them being there. If Koku's men had threatened them, they might expose any outsiders to prove their loyalty to the local warlord, rather than be cut down for hiding a potential enemy.

Angela followed Buck up the rise and dropped to

the ground, wrapping her arms around her knees. "We didn't get very far, did we?"

"Far enough away from Abu Hanafi's village that hopefully he won't catch any flak."

"Do you think the people we treated will tell Koku's men we were there?" she asked.

"I doubt it." Buck dug in his gear bag, drew out a pocket-size package and unfolded the contents.

Angela lifted her head. "What's that?"

He shook out what appeared to be an aluminum sheet. "It's a Mylar thermal blanket. It's not cold enough to worry about heat loss, but it'll be nice to lie on something other than the dirt while we sleep."

He spread it on the ground, sat on one side and patted the space beside him. "We'll have to take shifts sleeping. I don't want some goat herder to wander by and report our location to Koku."

"Since I fell asleep on the back of the motorcycle— and how I did that, I'll never understand—I can take the first shift." Angela dropped down beside him.

"Deal. But first, we should eat something to keep up our strength. I have four packages of MREs. If we're smart about it, we can make them last for two to three meals each, between us."

"I have a couple of bottles of water and a twelve- pack of protein bars," Angela offered. "I wish I'd thought to bring more."

"We were in a little bit of a hurry getting out of the refugee camp. I was surprised you got out with any of your medical gear." Buck pulled out an MRE package and tore it open, spilling the contents onto the blanket.

He opened the largest pouch and sniffed. "It's Italian food. I love the spaghetti and meatballs almost as much as the shredded barbecue." He glanced across to Angela. "We'd have to use precious water to heat the meal, or we can suffer and eat it cold. It's up to you. If we use the water, we can save it for the next meal in a marked bottle."

She shook her head. "I've eaten MREs. I can take them cold, when necessary. The point is to keep our bodies fueled." She took the plastic fork and the packet of food from him, stabbed a meatball and shoved it into her mouth. After chewing for a few moments, she gave him a weak smile. "See? Not bad."

He took the packet and ate the next one. He, too, was used to eating whatever he could, whenever he could, knowing it might be a long time before his next meal. The flavor of the marinara sauce was much more palatable when warm, but he couldn't feel bad about eating cold food. Plenty of people in the refugee camps went hungry for days before the aid trucks arrived. *If* they arrived, and weren't waylaid by ruthless thieves and warlords like Koku.

They finished the spaghetti and meatballs and saved the crackers and peanut butter for a snack later.

Angela dug in her backpack. "I have two bottles of water left."

"I have—" he glanced in his gear bag "—three, and my CamelBak is full."

"CamelBak?" she questioned.

"It's like a backpack you can fill with water. There's a straw you can use rather than pulling out a bottle or canteen. So you can drink on a march or run." He pulled a small pair of binoculars from the bag and handed them to Angela. "You might want to keep an eye on what's going on in the village. If anyone starts this way, wake me. We might have to make a run for it."

She took the binoculars and raised them to her eyes, staring out over the field to the village. "No one is awake yet," she said.

"Good." Buck stared at Angela in the starlight. "Are you sure you're up to standing watch on only a few minutes of sleep?"

"I'm awake. I might as well be useful." She continued to look through the binoculars. "Sleep. I'll wake you if I need you."

He lay back on the Mylar blanket and laced his hands behind his head. A long silence stretched between them.

Buck was good at taking whatever catnaps he could snag, whenever he could. Sleep was yet another way to fuel your body for the task ahead.

But Angela was sitting next to him, and her mere presence was keeping him awake. He wanted to reach out and touch her, as if to make sure she was real and not something made of his dreams.

This woman had haunted him from the moment he left Chicago to the moment he found her protesting in the streets of Bentiu.

He'd fallen in love with her when he witnessed her

compassion toward other students, patients and anyone she came into contact with. She was everything the life he'd led in the gang was not. Angela was good and pure and out to help the world, not tear it apart.

Buck's chest tightened. He'd never stopped loving her, even when he was half a world away. But she'd been better off without him weighing her down. He'd had to believe that in order to leave the way he had. And seeing her again, the proof of her success and continued compassion only made him love her more.

ANGELA HAD BEEN sitting in silence, staring through the binoculars at the tiny village but not seeing a single hut through the lens. Her memories overlaid her vision with images of medical school, studying long hours with Buck and falling asleep in his arms on the couch in her apartment.

She'd given her heart to this man without holding anything back. And he'd left. No note. No explanation. Just left. How her heart had broken. She'd feared he'd been kidnapped or murdered when he hadn't shown up for class. Her calls went unanswered and his phone was finally disconnected. If she hadn't cornered his roommate and demanded to know what had happened to him, she wouldn't have known he'd dropped out of school and joined the navy.

Angela never understood. Why had he left her without a word? Why had he joined the navy? And he hadn't been around to give her any answers. Her eyes stung with a hint of the tears she'd shed for days back then. She'd had a hard time concentrating on her studies. The medical licensing exam had passed in a blur. How she'd passed, she hadn't a clue.

"I always knew you'd be a great doctor." Buck's whispered words jolted her back to the present.

"Quitting wasn't an option," she shot back automatically. After the pall of sadness lifted, she'd gone through an angry stage, much like the stages of grief. She'd wrapped herself in her anger, using it to push through her internship. No, she didn't take her anger out on her patients. She also didn't date, preferring to remain focused on her goal—to become a licensed physician and get the hell away from the place that reminded her of her first love.

"One question," she said. "Then you can sleep."

"Shoot."

"What happened with that gang…was that what made you leave?" She lowered the binoculars and turned toward him.

Buck lay with his eyes closed without responding.

At first Angela thought he might have fallen asleep.

But he finally opened his eyes and met her gaze. "I didn't tell you at the time, but I used to belong to that gang."

She frowned. "Those horrible people who nearly killed our classmate?"

He jackknifed to a sitting position and shoved a hand through his hair. "Those bastards who nearly killed you. Yes. I was a member of that gang when I was in high school and the summer after I graduated."

She shook her head. "I thought you knew them,

but I didn't realize you were a member of their gang. I can't see you being that cruel."

He lay back down and stared up at the sky. "Yeah, I was a hoodlum. I never told you that part of my life. I didn't want you to think any less of me. The dirt on me is that my parents divorced when I was five. My mother worked two jobs to keep a roof over our heads and put food on the table. My father disappeared. He never paid child support, so it was up to my mother to handle everything." Buck glanced down at his hands. "She wasn't around much."

Angela reached out to touch his hand. "You never talked about her."

"She was so proud of me, going to college when she hadn't even finished high school." His jaw tightened. "She died of cancer the year I graduated with my bachelor's degree. She didn't even get to see her only son walk for his diploma."

"I'm sorry," Angela said.

"For what? You didn't give her the cancer."

"I'm sorry she didn't get to see you earn your degree and get accepted into medical school."

"Anyway, when I was in high school, I didn't have brothers and sisters to keep me company while my mother worked her two jobs, so I went out and found friends." He laughed, though there wasn't any humor in the sound.

"The gang?" Angela asked softly.

He nodded. "They accepted me for who I was. Or at least I thought they did. They really accepted me to become what they were—thieves, thugs and miscreants."

"Why didn't you tell me this when we first met?"

"I didn't tell you everything about my life before college. I didn't think it was relevant to who I was when I met you. I'd left that life behind when I went to college. I wasn't that person anymore."

"It was most certainly relevant. You are shaped by the events of your past and the people around you." She turned to fully face him. "You made a conscious decision to leave that way of life, and you were a better man for it."

He snorted. "It didn't keep the past from catching up to me."

"What do you mean? I thought they arrested the gang members."

"Some of them. But it didn't stick long enough. Their leader had a rule—once a member, always a member, until death."

Angela shivered in the warm morning air. "Is that why they came after us?"

Buck nodded. "I went to college in a small town, far enough away from Chicago that the gang didn't bother to come looking for me. But when I came back to Chicago for medical school, I knew I risked running into them. Even then, I'd been in medical school for a couple years without confrontation. So I got sloppy. I wasn't as vigilant. And then the chance encounter that night told them I was still around. Their leader decided he needed to enforce his rules and make an example out of me."

"Couldn't you go to the police?" she asked.

"And tell them what? Until they actually hurt someone, I could do nothing."

"And then they did hurt our friend." Angela remembered arriving at their friend Brandon's apartment and finding him hurt and bleeding. And the gang being there, having set a trap to lure Buck to them.

Buck had fought hard. He'd wanted her to run, but the leader of the gang hit her, knocking her to the ground. That's when Buck had turned into a raving maniac and nearly killed every one of the gang members in Brandon's apartment.

Even the leader had suffered a broken nose and broken ribs from Buck's defense.

Angela had never seen Buck that crazed. But she'd thought it had all ended up well in the long run.

"I remember," Angela said. "The police hauled off the members of the gang, including their leader. They went to jail. We were so happy we didn't have to worry anymore. I thought it was all over." They'd celebrated in her bed, making love through the night.

"Our relief was short-lived. Their leader was out within a week," Buck said, his tone flat.

"So? Not all of them were out, were they? He was just one man."

"No, not all of them were released. But he wasn't going to forget that we caught him, and that he had to spend a week in jail. He was out for blood." Buck's jaw tightened. "Mine. And anyone who meant anything to me."

Angela's pulse leaped. "So you left?"

"I left to take away any reason they might have to hurt me. And I severed all ties so they wouldn't come after you or anyone else at the school."

Her throat tightened, and she had to swallow hard to force words past her vocal cords. "You could have told me."

"I couldn't. I turned off my phone and cut all ties to Chicago. If they wanted to hurt me, they'd have had to come to the naval training base to do it." Buck lay with his eyes closed, his face turned to the sky. "I did the only thing I knew would keep you safe—I got the hell out of your life."

Angela stared at his taut face. "You left to save me." She remembered how hurt she'd been, and she never wanted to feel that sad again. She'd turned her hurt into anger and worn it like a shield to guard her heart from ever being broken again.

How could she forget that lesson so quickly? He'd stormed back into her life, but he couldn't storm back into her heart. No. Just no. Her chest was tight at the memory. She couldn't go through that again.

Angela snorted, rebuilding the barriers that had helped her make it through those dark days after he'd left. "I don't buy it. You didn't even ask me if I wanted to go with you. That, to me, says you ran away from commitment. We were getting too close. You couldn't stand the heat, so you got out of the fire." She lifted the binoculars to her eyes. "I didn't ask you to save me, so don't give me that bullshit. Just go to sleep. We need to be rested for when we get back on the road tonight."

Angela resisted turning to study Buck's face for a reaction to her comments. The anger that had seen her through her residency was back and in fine form. She sure as hell had better hold onto it and keep it close like a shield, or she might fall into that pathetic habit of believing him again.

After all the years apart, after she'd congratulated herself on getting over this man, why did he have to come back into her life when she was doing just fine without him?

Chapter Five

"Buck." A voice called to him as if from a long distance away.

Buck had struggled to get to sleep after Angela had told him how she felt about him leaving her.

She had a right to be angry and to feel like he'd skipped out on commitment. He'd gone over and over his decision, wondering if she'd been right and he'd run from responsibility and from giving his heart to someone. His parents hadn't set the best example for handling relationships. What made him think he could make one last?

All those thoughts roiled through his mind as he lay with the sun in his eyes, trying to fall asleep. Eventually, he must have nodded off, though he felt as if he'd only slept for a few minutes when he was awakened by her soft voice.

A warm hand shook his shoulder. "Buck, wake up. We might have trouble."

In a fraction of a second, he went from completely out to on his feet, in a crouched fighting stance. "What's going on?"

Angela handed over the binoculars. "A truck full of what might be Koku's men just pulled into the village. They're rounding up all the people."

He stared through the lenses, adjusted to clarify and saw what Angela was talking about.

A group of about a dozen men wearing military-style black clothing and wielding rifles herded men, women and children into the center of the village.

One of the gunmen was shouting at the villagers. Even from the distance, Buck could hear the echo of his raised voice, though he couldn't understand what he was saying.

He was yelling at a man dressed in the white robes of a village elder. When he didn't get the response he evidently wanted, he hit the elder with the butt of his rifle.

The man fell to the ground and lay motionless.

Angela gasped. "Did he just kill that man?"

"I don't know." Buck counted all of the men and made a mental note as to their positions.

"We have to do something," Angela said. "We can't let them kill all those people."

"There are only two of us and a dozen of them."

"You have a rifle, don't you? Can't you shoot them?"

He frowned at her. "You're a doctor. What about the Hippocratic oath?"

"I didn't say *I'd* kill them, but you could." She pointed to the village. "They're taking the children."

Buck raised the binoculars to his eyes again. Just

as Angela said, they were rounding up the young boys and loading them into the back of the truck.

"We have to stop them." Angela started down the knoll, her mouth set in a grim line. "If you aren't going to do something, then I am."

Buck hurried after her and grabbed her arm. "If you go down there and confront them, they'll shoot you."

"Better me than those little boys," she said, her voice choking on a sob. She tugged at her arm, trying to break free of his grip. "You saw what they did to Mustafa. How many of those kids won't make it back to their families?"

"I want to stop what Koku is doing as badly as you do, Angela. But charging into a situation where we're outnumbered will solve nothing. We'd be killed and my team will still not know where to find Koku."

Angela stopped struggling and looked up into his eyes, her own glassy with unshed tears. "How can people be so cruel?" she asked. "To children, for heaven's sake."

Buck pulled her back into the shadows of the trees and bushes and enveloped her in his arms. "Those men don't think the same way you do. To them, people are like cattle. Slaughtering them doesn't faze them in the least. Not everyone is as compassionate as you are." He held her close, stroking her hair, reveling in how good it felt to have her so near. All the while, he kept his gaze on what was going on in the village.

The good news was that no shots were fired. The elder was still lying on the ground when the truckload of soldiers and little boys pulled onto the road and headed south.

"The village elder got up," Buck said. "I think he's going to be okay."

"Thank goodness," Angela whispered against his chest. "That was going to be my next suggestion, to go to him and see if there was anything we could do to help."

"That would have exposed us. You know we can't let Koku know we're heading his way."

"I understand. But you know me. I couldn't stand by and do nothing."

Buck hugged her tighter. "At the very least, we know we're heading the right direction. Mustafa was pretty clear about his directions so far." He pulled away from Angela slightly, holding her at arm's length. "We'll free those boys. But we have to get Koku out of the picture, or he'll continue to terrorize villagers and steal children to man his army."

Angela nodded. "They were so young," she whispered. "I feel like I should have done something to stop them."

"You can't. Those men were Koku's men. Koku is giving the orders. We have to take him out to stop this insanity."

Her lips tightened. "Then let's find that bastard and put an end to his reign."

Buck chuckled. "That's my girl." Before he could think about what he was doing, he bent to sweep a gentle kiss across her lips.

Her eyes widened, but she didn't resist.

That little bit of a lip buss wasn't nearly enough, so he did it again. This time, he gathered her closer in his arms and cupped the back of her head. His mouth crushed hers in a kiss that he'd waited for since he left Chicago. Like someone who'd been stranded in the desert, he drank his fill of Angela.

She moved her hands from his chest to lace at the back of his neck, and then she rose up on her toes to get even closer.

Buck traced the seam of her lips. When she opened to him, he swept in and claimed her tongue in a long, sensuous caress.

He'd missed her. Even before he'd made his decision to leave Chicago, he knew he would. All the years between, he'd never found another woman who'd made his heart pound so hard in his chest, or one who left him wishing for more.

When he finally raised his head for air, he stared down at her, his pulse still racing, his heart swelling against his ribs. "I missed you."

She looked up into his eyes, her dark eyes even darker with desire. Then her face changed, her lips thinned and she backed away. "You knew where to find me."

"I didn't think you'd ever want to see me again, especially after I'd left without a word of explanation."

She shrugged and turned away. "It doesn't matter. What we had is in the past. What we have now is a partnership that will last only as long as it takes to find Koku. After that, you can go back to your job in the navy, and I'll go back to…" She raised a hand. "Well, whatever I can do to help people."

Buck reached out to take her hand.

Angela stepped even farther away, shaking her head. "We shouldn't have kissed. Nothing will come of anything between you and me. We weren't meant to be together."

But he wanted something to come of them. Now that he'd found her again, he realized what had been missing in his life.

Her.

And he wanted her back. "Angela—"

"Please, Buck, let's just focus on the task. And unless we're leaving now to follow that truck, I want to get some sleep. I think we'll have a long night ahead of us."

Buck didn't push. He suspected the night ahead would be even longer than either of them could imagine. Being so close to Angela and unable to hold her would be the most difficult challenge he had to face.

On a brighter note, based on the way she'd responded to his kiss, she wasn't immune. Definitely scared to get involved, especially after the way he'd treated her…but not immune.

ANGELA COULD HAVE kicked herself. What had she been thinking to return Buck's kiss? When he'd left Chicago without a word, he'd proven he didn't trust her to understand the situation. He didn't care enough about her feelings to give her an explanation. The man had disappeared out of her life, only to show up again years later in South Sudan, of all places.

And just because he was back in her life now didn't mean he'd stay. He'd joined the navy to get away from his old life. Well, his old life had included her. He'd gotten away from his gang affiliation, and he'd gotten away from a relationship with her. Since he hadn't returned, she had to assume that all he'd felt for her was lust. She'd been the one who'd fallen hopelessly in love with her fellow classmate. In medical school, that was never good. The training was intense. Love had nearly derailed her studies.

She'd counted it off as young love and fought her depression to get on with her life, telling herself he hadn't been worth the tears she'd cried. In the back of her mind, and deep in her heart, she'd still mourned her loss. She'd read first love was always the hardest to get over.

Angela thought she'd done a pretty good job moving on and living without him. Throwing herself into completing her studies and internship had helped. She'd volunteered for additional shifts at the hospital and worked with clinics on the side to fill her time. Anything to keep from going back to an empty apartment, where she'd stare at the walls for hours and wish she wasn't so darned lonely.

She'd missed him terribly.

She stretched out on the Mylar blanket and turned her back to Buck. It helped a little. But she knew he was there, and she couldn't deny the desire she'd felt in that kiss.

Holy hell, she could easily slide right back into that trap again. Falling in love with a man who didn't return the same level of feelings was a no-win situation. She'd be better off focusing on the task ahead. Save the boys and get back to her work with Doctors Without Borders.

SHE MUST HAVE fallen asleep, because when she woke, the sun was on its way toward the horizon. The day had passed and night was approaching.

Angela sat up and looked around. Her gaze sought Buck. When she didn't find him, her pulse quickened and she pushed to her feet. Where could he have gone? Surely, he hadn't left her to head out on his own. He wouldn't do that, would he?

Angela descended the little hill to where they'd stashed the motorcycle and breathed a sigh. The bike was still wedged into the bushes. Buck couldn't be too far. She raised her head and peered over the bushes toward the village. A slight movement caught her attention. There. In the tall grass. A dark head popped up, barely above the seeded fronds waving in the wind.

She'd recognize the dark hair and the stealthy way he moved anywhere. The man was like a cat, all sinew and grace. He was working his way back toward her.

Her pulse slowed and her breathing returned to normal. In the back of her mind, she'd thought, *he left me once—he could do it again.* But like he'd said, he'd left her to save her from being targeted by his old gang. She believed him, but she couldn't let that soften her heart. Soft hearts were easily broken.

For now, she needed him to help stop Koku from hurting the people she'd come to help, and to keep her safe in the process. Yes, he'd left her in Chicago all those years ago, and in the back of her mind, she wasn't sure she trusted that he wouldn't do it again. She didn't think he would, but still, she prayed he wouldn't leave her alone in a foreign country. Even Buck couldn't be that cruel.

Her stomach rumbling, Angela hiked to the top of the knoll and dug out the crackers and peanut butter and a bottle of water. They'd have to be careful and ration their food to make it last. She had no idea how long it would take to get to Koku's camp. Mustafa had walked for ten days to make it home. On a motorcycle, traveling at night, they should be there in a lot less time. Maybe even as soon as early morning. They'd only driven for two hours the previous night, due to everything that had happened in Abu Hanafi's village.

Buck pushed his way through the bushes and emerged on the grassy knoll. "Ah, good, you're awake, and I see you cooked dinner." He winked. "What are we having, steak and baked potatoes?"

"Crackers à la peanut butter." Angela slathered peanut butter on one of the big crackers and handed it to Buck. "What were you doing?"

"I wanted to make sure none of Koku's men stayed behind in the village."

"And?"

"I'm happy to report only villagers remain."

Angela could imagine the mental state of the families. The women would be heartbroken about losing their sons. "Did you see the village elder?"

"He was sitting outside one of the huts. He seemed all right. But what concerned me was that someone came to visit while I was watching."

Angela's gaze met his. "A visitor?"

"From what I could tell by all the hand gesturing, he was from another village." Buck's jaw tightened. "I think Koku's men came through their village as well, and Koku's thugs weren't nearly as nice in the other village as they were here."

"What do you mean?"

"The man had been beaten and his clothes were bloody."

Angela's heart sank. "Should we go now and see if we can help?"

Buck shook his head. "Not until dark. Our mere presence in a village could be dangerous to the villagers."

"Sounds like even when we aren't there, the villagers are in danger." Her instinct was to immediately go to where her medical skills were needed. Waiting was killing her. But for Buck to get the coordinates he needed, they had to keep their current location as secret as possible. Koku couldn't know they were headed his direction. If he learned they were coming, he might end their journey before they could pass on the information the SEALs needed to eliminate one of the most ruthless warlords in South Sudan.

Resigning herself to waiting until dark, she spread

the rest of the peanut butter over the second cracker. "Are we leaving as soon as it's dark?"

"As soon as the sun sets, we'll push the motorcycle past the village before we start the engine."

Angela bit into the cracker and peanut butter, surprised at how good it tasted. She was glad Buck was sitting beside her. He made her feel safer just by being there. His skills as a SEAL would prove useful in the night to come. She glanced at him from beneath her lashes.

Buck's gaze zeroed in on Angela's mouth as she chewed her cracker.

Heat rose up her throat and into her cheeks. Was he going to kiss her again? Even though she'd rebuffed him the last time, her heart still raced in anticipation of his lips meeting hers. Why was it so hard to resist this man?

Buck leaned forward. "Angela," he said softly and reached out his hand.

She blinked, her breath catching in her throat. She swayed toward him, her lips puckering.

He cupped her cheek in his palm and swept his thumb across her bottom lip. "You had peanut butter on your lip." He brought his thumb to his mouth and sucked the peanut butter off. Then he popped the last bite of his cracker into his mouth and chewed, a smile tugging at the corners of his mouth.

Angela sat back, her cheeks burning, her mouth dry. How could he be that close and not kiss her? She'd been halfway to him, caught in his trance.

What a fraud she was. She'd been the one to shut

him down the last time they kissed. And here she was, practically salivating for another.

She jammed the last of the cracker and peanut butter into her mouth and nearly choked, trying to chew it. Somewhere between staring at Buck's lips and falling into his dreamy gaze, she'd lost her appetite. But she had to eat and conserve her strength. The next leg of their journey would be grueling and long. She needed energy and her wits about her. If not to fight off Koku's men, then to fight her own attraction to this man who'd stolen her heart once before.

After dusting the crumbs from her fingers and swiping her hand over her mouth to remove any debris there, she pushed to her feet. "The sun just set. We need to gather our belongings and be ready to go as soon as the residual light wanes."

Buck nodded, drank from one of the water bottles and handed it to her. "It's dry in this part of South Sudan. You need to keep hydrated."

She drank from the bottle, recapped it and stored it in her backpack. "I'm ready when you are."

He stood, folded the Mylar blanket to a small rectangle no bigger than a man's wallet and slid it into a pocket in his gear bag. "Ready."

They walked in silence down the little knoll to where Buck had stashed the motorcycle in the bushes. He pulled it out into the open and secured the bags to the back seat. "We'll have to swing wide of the village to avoid detection. Not all the villagers have gone to bed yet."

"Should we wait until they do?" she asked.

"I think we can get around them without being spotted. Are you game?"

She nodded, ready to see this mission through. "Let's do this."

Chapter Six

Buck pushed the motorcycle in a large circle around the tiny village, taking twice as long than if they'd gone down the road. They had to dodge bushes and trees, push through tall grass, and circumnavigate the outlying huts.

By the time they reached the road on the other side, Buck was ready to blow the dust off their clothes. He climbed aboard the motorcycle and waited while Angela slid on behind him.

Her thighs wrapped around his and she fit snugly against him.

His body heated immediately. The woman set his world on fire. Their kiss had resurrected all the old feelings he'd harbored since he'd met her in medical school. After all those years, he'd thought he'd be over his crush. What it proved to him was that Angela had been anything but a crush. He'd loved her deeply, to the very core of his being. And he still did.

Not a day went by, nor a night, that he didn't think of her and second-guess his decision to leave.

Could he have confronted the gang and told them to leave her alone?

No.

That would only have made them more determined to torment her, and in the process, torture him. No one left the gang on his own two feet. Until Buck. Thankfully, that world was well and truly behind him. The gang leader had gone to jail for murder. He wouldn't be getting out any time soon. In spite of that knowledge, Buck had no desire to return to Chicago. He'd thought he would eventually end up somewhere out west—Colorado, Wyoming or Montana. Someplace far enough away from Chicago where his past wouldn't come close to following him.

And maybe, just maybe, he'd apply to medical school again. He'd finish the course and become the doctor he'd always dreamed of being.

Assuming he made it back to the States. In the wilds of Africa, with a warlord to locate, he had a lot to do between now and retirement to start thinking along those lines.

"Are you going to start the engine?" Angela asked.

Pulling his head out of his thoughts, he started the motorcycle. The engine roared to life, the noise a sharp contrast to the peace and quiet of dusk.

"Hold on," he called out and twisted the throttle, shooting the motorcycle forward along the road toward Koku's camp. He had to keep his focus on the mission in order to protect Angela and see that she made it out of South Sudan alive.

Not long after they got underway, they came across

another of the small villages Mustafa had told them about. They smelled it before they reached the outer edges. Smoke lingered in the air from the wreckage of several huts that had been burned to the ground.

Buck pulled off the road and into tall grass before he shut off the engine and listened.

Behind him, Angela removed her helmet.

The sound of a woman wailing carried all the way out of the village to their location.

"We have to help," Angela said.

A fire still burned in the center of the village. The people he could see silhouetted against the flames were moving bodies and laying them out in the firelight. There appeared to be a number of injured, and possibly even more dead. His fists clenched. Koku's work. The warlord had to be stopped.

"I have to help." Angela untied her backpack from the motorcycle seat and started toward the village.

Buck grabbed her arm. "What's to keep them from telling Koku we were there?"

"The same thing as with Abu Hanafi's village. If we help them, they will help us." She shook off his arm. "You don't have to come. But I can't stand by and do nothing."

Buck sighed. She wasn't going alone. "Give me a second to mark the spot in this grass, or we'll never find the motorcycle when we need to."

He moved the bike closer to a lone tree in the middle of the field and laid it on its side. Find the tree, and he'd find the motorcycle. He jogged back to where Angela stood, staring toward the fire. Taking her hand in his, he hurried with her into the village, wondering if he was making a terrible mistake and putting Angela into a lot more danger than he should.

Once they entered the village, Angela took charge and went to work doing what she did best—helping people.

At first the villagers were afraid of the strangers, but they soon realized she was a doctor, there to help.

She quickly triaged the injured and determined who needed the most immediate attention and who could wait. With Buck's help, she stitched wounds, treated burns and set bones. What Koku had done to these people was horrible.

From what Buck could gather, the villagers had refused to let him take their children. They'd fought to keep their sons. All that had bought them was torched buildings and six dead adults. One of the dead had been the village elder, and they had many more injuries than they could afford to deal with and still work to keep food on their tables.

Angela and Buck worked through the night, stitching cuts, bandaging wounds and setting broken bones. By the time morning light edged up the horizon, they had seen and treated all who needed help.

Buck was exhausted, but he could keep going. His BUD/S training had prepared him for long nights of grueling work and little sleep.

Angela was a different story. Dark circles shadowed her eyes. She packed what little was left of the medical supplies she'd grabbed on her way out of the refugee camp and her medical equipment into her backpack and met his gaze. "Are we leaving now?"

He nodded. "We need to. If Koku's people come back, we can't be here."

She sighed and lifted her backpack.

Buck took the bag from her and slung it over his shoulder.

The villagers gathered around them. Small children tugged at their clothes. An elderly man with stooped shoulders and weathered skin stepped forward and held out his hand to Angela. "Thank you for helping us."

"You saved us," said a woman with a sling fashioned out of a scrap of fabric. She reached out to touch Angela's arm with her good hand.

A little girl with a big lump on her forehead tugged at Angela's trousers. "Please, stay," she said, staring up at Buck and Angela with big brown-black eyes. She appeared to have been viciously hit or kicked in the head by one of Koku's thugs.

Buck's heart melted. He never understood how anyone could be cruel to children. He bent to get eye level with the girl. "Sorry, sweetheart, we can't."

Angela stared into the eyes of the elderly man. "You can't let Koku's men know we were here. It could be bad for us, but I'm more concerned about you and your people. If Koku finds out we were here and you didn't tell him, he could kill all of you."

He nodded, along with all the other adults. "We will keep your secret safe."

A shout rose up from somewhere behind Buck.

Everyone, from the young to the old, ducked low as if expecting bullets to fly toward them.

Buck spun to face a young man limping toward them, leaning heavily on a long stick. Dressed in the black outfit Koku's men wore, he had a rifle slung over his shoulder and a rag tied around his leg, blood oozing through the fabric.

Men, women and children gasped and cried out in fear, backing away from the man.

Buck pulled his handgun from beneath his jacket, ready to shoot the man if he made a move to fire on them.

Angela touched Buck's hand. "He's not here to shoot us."

"How do you know?" Buck asked, his hand steady, his gun aimed at the man's chest.

"He's injured." Angela started toward the man.

Buck reached out to snag her arm. "What if he's faking it?"

"Why would he?" Angela shook free of Buck's grip and hurried toward Koku's man.

Before she reached him, he stumbled and fell, landing in a heap in the dirt.

Buck ran forward, reaching him before Angela. He checked the man for other weapons and took his rifle, sliding it well out of reach. Finally, he checked for a pulse.

The man was alive, but weak.

"Help me roll him over," Angela said.

Together, they gently rolled the man onto his back. Immediately, Buck could see the problem. The man had a wound on his leg and it was still bleeding. He'd probably lost a lot of blood.

"Good Lord, he can't be more than seventeen." Angela held out her hand. "I need scissors."

Buck slid her backpack from his shoulder and dug inside for her kit of surgical equipment, found the scissors, and handed them over.

She quickly cut the trousers away from the guy's leg and spread the fabric wide.

He had a four-inch gash, all the way through the skin to the bone.

"Give me the bottle of water."

"It's the last one," Buck warned.

She held out her hand. She'd give her last scrap of food to someone in need. It was who she was.

He handed over the bottle. She filled a large syringe with the water and flushed the debris out of the wound.

Meanwhile, Buck dug out the suture line and a needle. Using an alcohol pad to sterilize the needle, he then threaded it and handed it to her.

As she stitched, he dabbed at the blood with a gauze pad, keeping the edges of the skin visible. Within a few minutes, Angela had the man's leg sewn together and the bleeding stopped. She applied a gauze pad to cover the wound and wrapped it tight enough to hold the pad in place.

Koku's thug groaned and blinked his eyes open.

"What's your name?" Angela asked.

"Kaleel," he muttered. He stared up at her and then

around at the faces of the villagers. His eyes rounded and he tried to sit up.

Angela pressed a hand to his shoulder. "You need to lie still and let your body heal. You lost a lot of blood."

His gaze shot to his rifle, being held by one of the older men. "That is my gun."

The old man shook his head. "Not anymore."

Kaleel looked around at the angry villagers and lay back. "Why did you let me live?"

The old man's mouth pressed into a thin line. "You are lucky the good doctor reached you first, or you would not be alive now."

The teen stared up at Angela. "You should have killed me."

She smiled. "I'm a doctor. That's not what I do."

He rested his arm over his eyes, blocking out the glare from the rising sun. "If I do not return soon to Koku, I will be dead anyway."

"You need to let your leg rest," Angela said. "And your body needs to recover and regenerate the blood you lost."

The young man peeked from beneath his elbow at the villagers standing around.

"They won't hurt you," Angela said. She glanced around at the people and gave them a stern look. "This man is injured. You will leave him alone."

The women and older men glared at Kaleel.

Angela held gazes with the old man who seemed to have assumed the role of village elder.

Buck nearly laughed. Angela had the heart of an

angel, but when she gave that look, she had people agreeing to anything she wanted.

Finally, the old man nodded. "Because of all you did for us, we will leave him alone. But if he tries to hurt anyone…"

Angela nodded. "Fair enough."

The elder glanced at the sun rising in the sky. "You need rest. You can stay in my home," he offered. "Until dark."

Angela frowned and glanced around at the village and its people. "We need to be moving on."

"Koku's men patrol the road passing through our village. You will be seen if you leave now."

Angela met Buck's gaze.

He made the decision. "We'll stay until dark. But we need someone to be on the lookout for Koku's men."

The new village elder nodded toward two women. "Samya and Nahla will be in charge. But we will keep watch while you sleep."

Buck dipped his head. "Thank you."

"I don't like that our being here puts these people in danger," Angela said.

"There's too much of a chance of running into Koku's men in broad daylight," Buck said. "Besides, you need rest."

"I don't need rest," she said and then yawned.

Buck chuckled. "Right." He glanced toward the old man. "We would like to rest in your home. Thank you."

The old man dipped his head. "You are welcome."

"We need to move Kaleel out of the open," Angela said. "If Koku's men drive by and see him lying here, they might come and ask too many questions."

Buck bent and looped the younger man's arm over his shoulder. Then he scooped him up and carried him deeper into the village.

A woman stood in front of a hut, waving him toward the entrance. "In here."

Buck carried Kaleel into the hut and laid him on a mat on the floor. "You give this woman any trouble, and you'll have to answer to me," he warned the young man.

Kaleel shook his head. "I won't cause trouble," he promised.

Satisfied with the young man's answer, Buck straightened and left the hut. He didn't like being away from Angela for long.

Back out in the open, he found Angela standing with the new village elder outside a mud-and-stick building. She waved for him to join her.

When he did, she motioned toward the door of the hut. "Munawwar says we can sleep here. He says not to worry—he will have the entire village watching for Koku's men."

"I'll stay awake while you sleep," Buck said. "Go on. You need rest."

"Yes, I do need rest," Angela agreed. "And so do you."

Buck shook his head. "I can go days without sleep."

"Maybe so, but you aren't as effective and alert."

She had a point. And he was tired. But leaving their safety in the hands of the villagers…

"They'll watch." Angela grabbed his hand and led him through the door. "You need your sleep, too."

Munawwar's woman had arranged a neat pallet of straw covered with woven blankets on the floor of the hut.

Buck let Angela lead him to the pallet. He dropped her backpack to the ground and shed his jacket and the holster beneath.

Angela knelt on the blanket and then stretched out to lie on her side. "Pardon me while I go right to sleep," she said with a yawn. She laid her head in the crook of her arm and closed her eyes.

Buck smiled down at her. He drank in the sight of Angela curled up on the pallet. He wanted to lie down with her, but he was afraid to let his guard down and trust others to keep watch for them.

But he couldn't resist. He lay down behind her, curled his body against hers and pulled her back to his front, resting his hand on her hip.

She scooted back, pressing herself even closer. "Thank you for helping."

"You're an amazing doctor," he said. "I'm happy for you." And he was proud of all she'd accomplished.

"You're every bit as good. I'm just sad you didn't finish," Angela whispered and yawned again.

Buck felt that pang of regret he always felt when he thought about all he'd given up. But holding Angela in his arms now was worth all of his sacrifices. Had he stayed in Chicago, his old gang might have killed her to prove a point to him. He couldn't regret that they hadn't had that chance.

"Buck?" Her voice was as soft as the warm air in the hut.

"Yes, Angela?"

She yawned before continuing. "Will we see each other again after all this?"

He wanted to say yes, but he hesitated. He was a navy SEAL, and she was a doctor with the Doctors Without Borders organization. How often would they be on the same continent?

"We'll see," he finally said. "Sleep, sweetheart. We have a long way to go."

"Mmm," she murmured. "Buck?"

He chuckled softly. "Yes?"

"I love you." The words came out so quietly, he thought maybe he'd imagined them.

"What did you say?" He tipped his ear toward her, hoping that when she repeated herself, he'd catch the words this time.

Her breathing grew deeper and her body was limp against his. Angela had fallen asleep.

Buck's heart squeezed tightly in his chest. Surely he'd heard her wrong. How could she love him after all these years? Hell, he'd left her without a word. Seriously, he must be half-asleep himself. He laid his head down, fully intending to get up after a few minutes and go back outside to stand guard over her.

Before he could do that, he drifted into a deep sleep, dreaming about white picket fences and half a dozen children with dark hair and blue eyes, running around a yard with deep green grass and a sky so blue it almost hurt his eyes.

His heart was so full, he could hardly breathe. He knew it was only a dream, but he couldn't help wishing it was real.

"MISTER! DOCTOR!" a voice cried.

A movement beside Angela made her jerk awake.

Buck was on his feet, gun in hand, heading for the door as it was flung open.

A young girl, around ten or eleven years old, stood there, her eyes wide, her breathing ragged.

"What's wrong?" Buck asked.

"Kaleel…" She drew in a breath and rushed on. "Kaleel left."

Angela pushed to her feet, blinking the sleep out of her eyes. "He shouldn't be moving about. How long ago?"

"I don't know. He was there, and then he wasn't," the girl admitted. "I was supposed to watch him." Her eyes filled with tears. "I was playing with my doll. I didn't know he left until he was already gone." She reached for Angela's hand. "I'm so sorry."

Angela shook her head. "It's okay." But she knew it wasn't. If Kaleel headed back to Koku's camp, he could tell Koku where they were. She looked to Buck.

He nodded. "We need to leave." He glanced at the watch on his wrist, his lips pressing into a thin line. "I can't believe we've been sleeping all day. It'll be dark soon."

"Then we should be ready to roll as soon as dusk

settles." Angela reached for her backpack, but Buck grabbed it first and looped it over his shoulder.

"You aren't leaving us, are you?" the girl asked, tears rolling down her dark cheeks. "This is all my fault. You would not be going if Kaleel had stayed."

"No, we should have left hours ago," Angela said. "Your people aren't safe as long as we are here."

"But you helped my family," she said. "You are good and kind. Not like Koku. He is evil. He took my brother Jamal. I miss my brother."

The old man whose house they'd slept in appeared behind the girl and laid a hand on her shoulder. "You cannot keep the doctor here. It is too dangerous."

The girl straightened her shoulders and wiped away the tears. "Yes. You must go. We would not want Koku to find you."

Angela didn't tell the old man and the girl they were searching for Koku's camp. To them, heading into Koku's camp would sound crazy. Why would anyone go near Koku if they had a choice?

As Angela and Buck left the hut and walked through the village, the sun sank below the horizon, casting the huts in deep shadows.

Children ran around their legs and the adults reached out to touch them as they passed, thanking them for all they had done to help their injured.

Angela smiled and squeezed several hands as she worked her way through the throng of villagers to the edge of the town.

Dusk quickly turned into dark, and stars slowly began twinkling in the night sky.

Buck took her hand and guided her through the tall grass to the tree where he'd left the motorcycle. He strapped her backpack on top of his gear bag and pushed the bike toward the road.

She followed close behind. The stars had not quite lit the sky sufficiently for her to see where she was going. She tripped once but caught herself before she fell to the ground.

Buck paused and turned back. "You all right back there?"

"I am." She hurried to come up alongside him.

"Did you get enough sleep?" he asked.

"Yes, I did," she lied. She could have slept for an entire day and night; she'd been that exhausted.

"You needed it."

"And so did you," she said. "I'm glad you got some sleep as well."

"I should have stayed awake." Buck's voice was tight. Almost curt. "Kaleel could have snuck in and murdered us both in our sleep."

"But he didn't," she reminded him. "We helped him. He returned the favor."

"By not killing us?" Buck snorted. "He might well be on his way to Koku to report our whereabouts."

"Do you think he will?" Angela asked.

"If he's loyal to Koku, he will."

"I hope he doesn't. Not for our sakes, but for the sake of the villagers." Her chest tightened. "His people did enough damage without our visit being a factor. I can't imagine what they'll do if they know we've been there."

"Hopefully, they won't come back." He paused near the road and shook the motorcycle. "Sounds like we're getting low on fuel. We'll need to purchase gas soon. I doubt the villagers have gasoline."

"No. But Mustafa said there was a larger town after the two small villages. We should be able to find a gas station there."

"If we make it there," Buck said.

"Are we that low?"

Buck pulled out his small flashlight, twisted off the gas cap and shined the light down into the tank. "It's pretty low. We probably have enough to get us to the next town, but we'll have to fill up once we get there."

"How will we do that and not alert Koku?"

"If the town is big enough, we should be able to fly under his radar. At the very least, we should be able to get in and out before his people are notified."

Angela hoped so. She wasn't sure how much longer she could continue on. Riding a motorcycle impacted a different set of muscles than sitting in a car or standing as she examined patients. Her thighs ached from clamping around the seat and Buck's backside.

Buck started the engine and scooted forward so that Angela could slide her leg over and settle in behind him.

He twisted the throttle and sent the bike speeding toward Koku and the stolen boys.

Angela held on tight, wondering what the night held in store for them. No matter what, she had her arms around Buck, and that had to be enough for the moment.

THEY TRAVELED THROUGH the middle of the night, only slowing when they had to swing around a squatters' camp or a herd of cattle. Just when Angela thought her bottom couldn't get any sorer, they spied in the distance lights of what seemed like a newer town. As Mustafa had indicated, this was a larger settlement. It had more modern buildings made of brick and mortar, and it had electricity.

Buck pulled to the side of the road before they got too close to homes and buildings. "The gas stations likely won't open until daytime. We might as well find a place to park and catch some shut-eye."

Angela had been sitting so long, her legs had gotten stiff and her thighs were sore and achy. When she swung her leg off the seat, she nearly fell over.

Buck reached out and snagged her arm, yanking her up against him. He held her for a long moment, still sitting on the bike. "Are you okay?"

She nodded, her face pressed against his shirt, her fingers digging into him. He smelled of the wind and dust, but on him, it smelled earthy and good. Angela inhaled deeply, memorizing his scent, wishing she could be with him and smell him always.

As her legs acclimated to the standing position, she had no excuse to lean into the man, and he needed to get off the motorcycle and move his legs as well.

With a sigh, Angela straightened. "Thanks."

Buck swung his leg over the seat and stood beside her. "I should take you back to where it's safe. The closer we get to Koku, the more dangerous it will become."

"I want to find his camp as much as you. Those bastards are stealing children and killing villagers. They have to be stopped." She lifted her head to stare up into his eyes that were so dark, and yet, they shined in the starlight. "We have to find them. Then we can get your team in to take out Koku."

Buck cupped her cheek in his palm and brushed his thumb across her lips. "You're a brave woman."

She laughed. "Or just too stupid to know better."

"Never. You're also one of the smartest women I've ever known. And you always put others ahead of your own needs and safety."

She shook her head. "Which leads us back to *too dumb to know better*. And I get scared. How brave is that? Not very."

"No." He closed the distance between them and cupped her cheeks in both of his hands. "Courage is being scared but doing whatever needs to be done anyway." He bent, his lips hovering so close to hers she could practically taste them. "You're amazing."

Angela wanted that kiss so badly, she lifted up on her toes. When her lips touched his, every other thought left her head. She was where she wanted to be. In this man's arms, kissing him. Loving him like she always had.

His tongue traced the seam of her mouth.

She opened for him, meeting him with her own tongue, thrusting against his. Her hands circled the back of his neck, pulling him closer, her breasts rubbing against his chest, her hips pressing to his. The hard ridge of his desire nudged her belly, making her want so much more.

Lights blinked in the darkness, bringing her up out of the lust-filled coma she'd fallen into.

Buck's head shot up. His hands gripped her arms and he set her aside.

A vehicle rumbled toward them along the road, heading into the town. If they didn't want to be noticed, they had to get off the side of the road quickly and ditch the motorcycle.

"That's our cue." Buck grabbed the bike and started pushing it toward a stand of trees and bushes.

Angela followed.

Time to hide.

Chapter Seven

Buck found a little copse hidden in a stand of trees, surrounded by thick bushes and underbrush. He pushed the bike into the bushes and covered it with branches to keep anyone from seeing it from the road. They'd have to hunker down and wait until daylight, and maybe a little longer, before they could ride into town and put gas in the fuel tank.

The town appeared to be large enough that they might get away with acting like they were just another couple of crazy tourists riding a motorcycle on their way to South Africa.

If Angela left her helmet on, no one might even realize she was a woman until after they got their gas and got the heck out of town.

If he could get the pumps to work at night, he'd be willing to sneak in and steal the gas rather than put Angela at risk. But he wouldn't leave her alone. Not for a moment. Too much could happen in the short amount of time he'd be gone. She could be eaten by a lion, or nabbed by human traffickers. Or she could be captured by Koku himself. The man was ruthless.

Buck didn't want to think of the horrible things he could do to Angela if he caught her.

Once they were tucked into the little copse, he spread the Mylar thermal blanket on the ground and laid his bag and her backpack down for her to use as a pillow. He pulled out a packet of MREs from his gear bag and handed it to Angela. Then he fished around in his bag some more and brought out his CamelBak and shook it. "I think we're still okay on water. But we'll need to find Koku soon, or we're going to be thirsty." He handed her the CamelBak and adjusted the straw. "Go ahead and drink. Maybe we can pick up some bottled water when we get fuel."

While Angela drank, Buck pulled out the satellite phone. "I need to check in with my team. They'll be worried." He hit the numbers and waited for Big Jake to answer.

"Damn it, Buck! Where have you been for the past couple days?" Big Jake didn't waste time getting to the point.

Buck chuckled. "Sorry, dude. We've been on the road, moving at night as much as we can." He told Big Jake about Mustafa, trading the van for the motorbike and the village Koku's men had ransacked, how they'd helped the villagers and then were confronted by Koku's wounded man, Kaleel.

"He probably ran back to Koku to tell them all about you two. Tell us where to land and we'll pick you up. It'll take us a couple hours to get to you from Djibouti. You'd have to lie low until we arrive."

Buck stared across at Angela where she sat in the

little bit of light that made it through the trees. "Want to get out of here?" he asked her.

She glanced up, the whites of her eyes glowing in the darkness. "What do you mean?"

"I can have our guys pick us up now and forget finding Koku."

She shook her head. "No way."

"What did the doc say?" Big Jake wanted to know.

Angela reached up and grabbed the phone from Buck. "No. I'm not bugging out until we find Koku and stop him from hurting these people." She paused.

Buck could hear Big Jake talking but couldn't make out what he was saying.

"I'm okay," Angela said. "Yes, we have food and water. Yes, Buck's taking good care of me. I will. Thanks for asking." She handed the phone back to him. "He wants to talk to you."

Buck's heart swelled. The woman was tough and she would do the right thing, no matter how hard it was.

"Buck here."

"We think you need to get back here," Big Jake said.

"Yeah, but we haven't nailed the coordinates for Koku. As soon as we do, we'll be on the phone with you."

"Don't go all John Wayne on us and go in on your own."

"Not happening," Buck assured him. "The man has a small army working with him. I'm not that crazy."

"And don't go so long between calls," Big Jake said. "We were worried."

"I'll do a better job of communicating," Buck promised. "But for now, out here."

"Out here," Big Jake echoed.

Buck ended the call and stashed the phone in his gear bag. Then he settled on the blanket beside Angela, turned on his small flashlight and opened the bag with the MREs.

"What do we have tonight?"

"I don't know, but I could eat shoe leather at this point," Angela said. "Do you realize we haven't eaten in over twenty-four hours?"

His stomach rumbled to emphasize her words, and they both laughed.

"I promise you a steak dinner when we get to Djibouti," he said. "Well, maybe not steak, but definitely something other than MREs."

"It's a date."

A date. He hadn't had a date with her in years. What would it be like to take her to dinner and a movie? "I'd like to take you out on a real date when we get back to the States."

She paused in the process of tearing open a package of crackers. "How would that be possible? You work all over the world. I work in Africa."

"How long are you committed to Doctors Without Borders?"

"My commitment is up. I just stayed on. I can leave any time I want after giving them notice."

"What about your folks? Don't they miss you?" he asked.

She smiled. "They've been out here to visit me on a couple of occasions, and I've been back once since I've been here. They're happily retired and traveling the States in their motor home."

Buck could picture them. He'd met her parents when they'd come to visit her in Chicago. "Do they still have a place in Wisconsin?"

Angela shook her head. "They sold their house when they bought the motor home."

Buck's pulse beat faster. "I'm stationed out of Little Creek, Virginia, when I'm not deployed. What about you? Where are you when you're not in Africa?"

She sighed. "I'm headed back to Denver when I'm done here. That's half a continent away from Virginia."

Sweet heaven. She'd ended up in Colorado, where he'd dreamed of living when he retired or got out of the navy. "I could fly out to see you."

She pulled the crackers out of their airtight foil package and sat staring at them. "Who are we kidding? You have your life and I have mine. We're not even the same people we were when we were in med school. What good would it do to try to see each other?"

Pain stabbed Buck in the heart. As much as he didn't want to hear the words, he knew she was right. They were two different people. He had his job as a navy SEAL and she was a doctor. He tore open a package of Mexican-style chicken stew, not at all interested in eating. "You're right. Once we're out of here, we have no reason to see each other. But I would like to treat you to a better meal back in Djibouti before you ship out to wherever you're going next."

Angela didn't say anything for a while, taking the time to spread peanut butter onto the crackers. "I just don't want to start something neither one of us is able to finish. It hurts too much, and…well… I can't go through that again. For now, can we just be friends?"

His chest tightened so much, Buck felt as if he was having a heart attack.

She just wanted to be friends. How could he be a friend when he wanted to hold her, kiss her and make love to her? "You got it," he said, trying to sound natural when his jaw was tight and he wanted to yell out how he really felt.

They ate in silence.

Buck didn't taste anything. Or rather, it all tasted like cardboard. But he shoved it down his throat. He had to keep up his strength to see this mission through. Then he'd be on to his next assignment, and she'd be on to hers.

When they were done, he packed away the trash in his bag and drank from the CamelBak. Then he sat like a lump beside her, wishing he could take her into his arms.

She had yet to lie down and go to sleep. Instead, she sat beside him, her arms wrapped around her knees, staring into the darkness. "It's the right thing to do, isn't it?" Angela whispered.

"If you say so," he answered, a little more harshly than he'd intended.

"We'd never see each other."

"Yeah," he agreed. "My work as a SEAL makes relationships difficult."

"But some people make them work?" she asked.

"Some of my buddies are in relationships. Some are married and have kids. Though I don't know how they do it."

Angela sat awhile longer in the darkness without saying anything.

Buck couldn't think of anything to say, either, when all he wanted was to do was beg her to give him another chance.

"You should sleep" was all he could push past his vocal cords.

"Yeah," she said, but she didn't move immediately. Finally, she lay down on her side, turning away from him.

Buck sat next to her. Close enough to touch her, but feeling as far away as if she were back in Chicago. He hurt so badly, he could barely breathe. Why did she have to show up during his mission? He'd resigned himself to life without her, imagining she'd married and had a couple of kids by now. But there she was, lying next to him, single, beautiful and everything he'd ever wanted in a woman.

And she wants to be friends.

ANGELA LAY AWAKE, trying to breathe softly, listening to Buck's every movement.

Be friends? What the hell had she been thinking when that had come out of her mouth? The last thing she wanted was to be just friends with Buck. Back in med school, he'd been the love of her life. Since seeing him again, she'd realized how much she still loved him. Hell, she'd never stopped loving him. How could she ask him to be just friends?

Because she never wanted to feel the way she'd felt when she discovered he'd left without telling her he was going. Without an explanation. Without saying goodbye. Even lying beside him, remembering the pain of those days, made her heart squeeze in her chest, and her breathing became more difficult. He'd broken her heart. Shattered it into tiny pieces she'd found difficult to reassemble.

He could do it again. And she didn't want that kind of pain again. But being just friends was really not an option. When he left Africa, that would be the end of their time together. She wouldn't see Buck again. She'd have to give notice to the Doctors Without Borders organization and maybe stay on for another two weeks or a month. But then what? She'd said she was heading back to Denver, where she'd worked before coming to Africa. But she didn't really have a job or an apartment waiting for her. She'd put all of her worldly goods into a storage unit when she'd left.

She'd always known Buck had loved Colorado and wanted to live there one day. Though she'd tried to tell herself she'd only gone to Denver because she'd been offered a job there, she'd really gone there because of Buck. Somewhere in the back of her mind, she'd hoped she would run into him.

Ha! Like that had happened in any of the years she'd worked there. So she'd given up and left to work in Africa. And of all places, she had to run into him here.

Fate played cruel tricks on her heart. But she couldn't give it away to him. No. She just couldn't.

Tears slipped from the corners of her eyes, and before she knew it, she was crying. She tried not to make a sound, but she must have sobbed loud enough to get Buck's attention.

"Hey." Buck rested a hand on her shoulder. "What's wrong?"

"Nothing," she said, her voice choked. Then she sniffed loudly and could have died of embarrassment.

"You're crying." He tugged, rolling her over onto her back. "Why?"

She couldn't tell him she was crying because of him. He couldn't know how much it had hurt to ask if they could be friends. She refused to open her heart to more hurt, even though it pained her to put up barriers between them. So she told him the only thing she could think of. "Because I'm hormonal."

"Is it that time of the month?" he asked.

"No."

"Then why are you hormonal?"

"I don't know. I'm just sad." She scrambled for a reason. "I guess talking about my folks, our old house and Wisconsin made me a little homesick."

"Oh, baby." He pulled her into his arms and held

her close. "Don't cry. I can't stand it when you cry. It breaks my heart."

"I can't help it," she said and buried her face in his shirt. "I can't stop."

He brushed the hair off her forehead and pressed his lips there. "Please, don't cry."

She hiccuped and more tears slipped from the corners of her eyes. "Why do you have to be nice? I'm trying hard to hate you."

"Hate me?" He leaned back and stared down into her face.

She tried to read the expression in his eyes, but what little light made it through the leaves only shadowed his face and eyes.

"Why would you hate me?" he asked.

"Because it's the only way I can keep from falling in love with you all over again."

"And you don't want to do that, do you?" He brushed his thumb along her cheek and bent to kiss her forehead again, and then pressed his lips to her eyes, one at a time. "I told you I'd be your friend. Friends aren't supposed to hate each other. And friends aren't supposed to fall in love with each other." He traced a line from her cheek to her mouth, his thumb brushing her lips ever so lightly.

"I know." Angela's tears slowly dried, but her pulse sped. She kissed the pad of his thumb and pressed her body closer to his as he held her close.

"But friends can comfort each other and hold each other when we're down," he said, kissing the tip of her nose and finally brushing his lips across hers. "As a friend, I could kiss away your tears."

"Yes, you could," she whispered, her hands sliding up his chest as if they had minds of their own. She locked her fingers behind his neck and pulled him down to her.

"As a friend, I would be remiss if I didn't keep you in my arms through the night. It's scary where we are."

"Very scary," Angela said and she raised her face, capturing his lips with her own. "As a friend, will you keep me close?"

"I will."

"As a friend, will you comfort me when I'm sad?" She kissed him again.

"You bet," he whispered against her lips.

"As a friend, will you make love to me?" she asked, her voice fading to almost nothing.

"No."

Her heart stopped and her breath caught in her throat. She held it, waiting for his next words.

"I can't make love to you as a friend," he said. "But I can as a lover."

She let go of the breath on a sigh. "Then don't be my friend. Just for tonight."

"What if I don't want to be your friend for longer than that?"

"I can't make any promises," she said. "You hurt me once. I thought I hated you. The anger got me through medical school and my internship, but I realize it was more than hate. It was self-preservation. Tonight is all I can promise."

He hesitated a moment, his hand still on her cheek. Then he pressed his lips to hers. "Then tonight it is." He rolled her onto her back and kissed her like there would be no tomorrow.

And Angela gave back, desperate for one more night together. It had to be the last. She couldn't let him back into her heart.

But she was afraid she already had.

Chapter Eight

When Angela had asked him to just be friends, Buck's life seemed to crash in around him. Yeah, he deserved it. He'd hurt her all those years ago by leaving without explanation.

But now that he'd found her again, he hadn't wanted to repeat his disappearing act. This was the woman he'd fallen in love with and never stopped loving. She deserved better.

Her tears had torn a hole in his heart, and he couldn't keep himself from touching and holding her until she stopped crying. But embracing her had been his undoing.

If she'd told him to leave her alone, he would have found the strength to let go, but she hadn't. She'd curled into his side, wrapped her arms around his neck and pressed her lips to his in a kiss that shook his world.

She couldn't kiss him like that and not have feelings for him. It hurt his heart that she'd been crying. And the fact that she'd been crying because of him made it even worse.

He'd really thought she'd be better off without him. That's why he'd stayed away from her. She'd gone on with her life, become a doctor and was now saving lives with her skills.

And here she was, wanting him to make love to her for only a night? Holy hell, how could he do that and walk away? He wanted her for more than the night. He wanted her for the white picket fence, half a dozen kids and forever.

This was the woman he'd dreamed of since he'd met her. And he was going to make love to her under the stars of an African night.

Hell, what if she got pregnant?

That thought brought him to a screeching halt. He leaned up on his arms. "We can't do this."

"What?" She blinked up at him, her body going stiff beneath his. "Why?"

"No protection."

She laughed, the sound breathy. "In my backpack. Side pocket. I have at least a dozen."

"You packed medical supplies and condoms?"

She smiled and cupped his cheek in her hand. "I hand out condoms to the women who don't want more children to feed. They work with their husbands to get them to wear them."

He dug in the pocket she indicated and found a condom, just as she'd said. Placing it to the side, he settled in to show her how good it could be between them again. Perhaps if he rocked her world, he'd convince her to give them a second chance. The logistics of the relationship could work themselves out in the long run. He'd make it work, somehow.

Leaning over her, he stared down into her face. The light of the stars and the shadows of the leaves on the trees made her skin a dappled silvery blue. "You're even more beautiful than you were in medical school. And I thought you were pretty stunning then," he said and kissed one of her eyelids, still salty from her tears.

"We've been on the run for a few days. I have to be a mess."

"A beautiful mess," he said and kissed her other eyelid.

Angela ran her fingers through his short hair and tugged on his ears. "Shut up and kiss me."

"I like telling you—"

She leaned up and pressed her lips over his, thrusting her tongue past his teeth to caress his.

He shut up and did as he was told, laying her back against the blanket. He kissed her slowly, thoroughly, and would have gone on forever, but they had to breathe at some point. When he was forced to come up for air, he trailed a line of kisses along her cheek, across the line of her chin and down the length of her neck to the base, where her pulse beat fast and strong.

She ran her hands over his shoulders and down his back to tug the T-shirt from the waistband of his jeans. Her hands were warm against his skin and sent fire burning along his nerve endings and blood rushing to his groin.

He pushed her shirt up her torso and pulled it

over her head. Then he grabbed the back of his shirt, yanked it over his head and tossed it to the side.

She laughed, the sound light and happy in the stillness of the night. Angela sat up and reached behind her back to unhook her bra.

Buck placed his hand over hers. "Let me."

She shifted her hands to his chest and ran her fingers over the muscles there while he unfastened her bra and slid the straps down her arms.

Her breasts spilled out into his palms and he held them, their warmth seeping into his fingers.

Buck breathed in deeply, trying to pace himself. If he wasn't careful, he'd climax before he got started. He was that excited by her and her body. Slowly, he circled her nipples with his thumbs, then he laid her back on the blanket and took one of her breasts in his mouth and pulled gently.

She arched her back, urging him to take more.

He did, sucking as much of the firm orb into his mouth as he could, tweaking the tip with his tongue.

Angela clasped the back of his head in her hand and pressed him closer.

He rolled the nipple between his teeth several times and then let go to move to the other breast. There he teased and tasted, flicked and nibbled until she was writhing beneath him.

A sense of urgency made him move downward, flicking and tonguing each of her ribs, darting into her belly button and lower to the waistband of her trousers.

She reached for the button, but he brushed her hand away and pushed the button loose himself.

With excruciating slowness, he eased the zipper down, parting the fabric as he went. He peeled the jeans and her panties over her hips and down her thighs, and finally past her ankles and feet.

She lay naked in the starlight, her body covered in the softly waving shadows of the leaves.

"Beautiful."

"As are you, but you aren't nearly as naked." She tugged at the button on his jeans.

He took charge and shed his clothing and boots then lay down beside her on the Mylar blanket, the cool fabric doing nothing to chill his desire.

He traced a finger from her breast down her torso to the mound of fluff at the apex of her thighs.

Angela lifted her knees and let them fall to the sides, opening herself to him.

Buck slid between her legs and pushed her knees higher before he leaned over and pressed a kiss to her soft curls. Then he parted her folds with his thumbs and touched his tongue to the nubbin of flesh between.

Angela moaned and lifted her hips.

He took more, sucking her between his teeth, tonguing the bundle of nerves until she cried out and clutched the back of his head, her fingers digging into his scalp. Her body stiffened and then pulsed, her hips rocking again and again as she rode the wave of her release.

Several minutes later, she lowered her hips and tugged on his arms. "Please. Come inside me, now," she begged.

He crawled up her body, found the condom and tore open the packet.

Angela took it from him and sheathed him in seconds.

Then he lay down between her legs and pressed against her entrance. This was where he'd longed to be from the moment he'd found her in Bentiu. In her arms. In her life, and inside her body.

"Now," she urged. She grabbed his backside, her fingers digging into his buttocks, and guided him into her.

He thrust, long and deep, driving all the way into her, his shaft stretching her channel slickened with her juices.

Once he was all the way inside, he held steady, letting her adjust to his girth before he slid back out. He started slow, increasing his speed with each thrust, until he was powering in and out of her.

She dug her heels into the ground and raised her hips to meet each thrust with one of her own.

The heat of his release rushed through him, igniting his blood and nerve endings until he shot over the edge. He thrust one last time, burying himself deep inside Angela, dropping down on top of her, lying skin to skin until the last wave rippled through him. Then he rolled to his side, taking her with him. He wrapped his arms around her and held her close, smoothing his hand through her hair. "You are amazing."

"You're not so bad yourself," she said, her voice a soft murmur. She yawned into his chest and kissed his nipple. "Thank you."

He chuckled. "For what?"

"Thank you for being my friend," she said and fell asleep with her mouth against his skin.

Sleep was the last thing on Buck's mind. He'd just made love with the only woman he'd ever given a damn about, and she'd called him her friend.

Holy hell. He wanted to be her friend and so much more.

He had his work cut out for him if he wanted to bring her around to his way of thinking. But she was worth the effort...and then some.

Chapter Nine

Angela woke a few hours later, wrapped in nothing but strong arms and the cool of the morning air. She blinked her eyes open and looked up into Buck's wide-awake gaze.

"Did I fall asleep?" she asked.

He smiled down at her. "You did."

"And you didn't wake me to get dressed?" She snuggled closer and slipped her leg over his.

"I hated to disturb you. You seemed to need the sleep. Besides, I like you naked."

Angel's cheeks burned. "Did you sleep?"

He shook his head. "I kept watch."

"Thank you." She trailed her hand over his chest, loving the feel of his skin beneath her fingertips. "But you should have woken me sooner. I could have done guard duty while you got an hour or two of sleep."

"I'm used to little sleep." He smiled at her in the gray light of morning. "Besides, I got to watch you snore."

"I don't snore," she said and pinched the tip of his little brown nipple.

"You do. But it was cute." He pressed a kiss to her forehead and another to the tip of her nose.

Her body came alive the more she rubbed it against his. She pushed him onto his back and climbed up on top of him, straddling his hips, happy to see and feel he was as excited as she was. "Where's that side pocket?" She leaned over and dug one of the condoms out of the backpack and tore open the packet.

"I thought we were only making love for one night?" he said.

She nodded toward the gray sky, the sun still well below the horizon. "The night is not over yet."

He chuckled and sucked in a breath as she rolled the protection over his hard shaft. Then he lifted her up and positioned her over him.

Angela sank down, taking him into her, loving the feel of him filling her to the limit. She closed her eyes and drew in a deep breath, letting it out slowly. Then she rose up on her knees and came back down, and did it again.

Buck gripped her buttocks and guided her up and down, settling into a tantalizing rhythm that set her core on fire and made her nipples pucker.

Before long, she was rising and falling faster and faster.

Then Buck lifted her off him and laid her down beside him. He came down over her, parted her legs and drove deep inside her, thrusting again and again until his body stiffened and he buried himself deep inside her.

Angela wrapped her legs around his waist and dug

her heels into his buttocks, holding him as close as he could get until his shaft stopped pulsing and he collapsed against her.

Although breathing was difficult with all of his weight on top of her, Angela didn't mind. She could die like this, knowing she'd never been happier. But the sun rose above the horizon. Another day had begun, and they had to get back on the road.

Buck rose up on his hands and slipped free of her. He pressed a quick kiss to her lips and then got up. Standing in the early-morning light, his body bathed in golden hues, he could have been a Greek god.

He extended a hand to her.

Suddenly shy of her nakedness, she allowed him to pull her to her feet. When she started to reach for her clothes, he stopped her with a hand circling her waist. "Just so you know... I don't give a damn that the night has ended. I'm not ready for this to be over. I'm not ready to let you go."

Her cheeks heated and she opened her mouth to say—what? She didn't know, nor did she get a chance to speak.

Buck's mouth descended on hers, crushing her lips with the force of his kiss. His tongue slipped through her teeth and slid along hers in a long, sensuous caress that left her knees weak.

Angela clung to his shoulders long after he lifted his head, her gaze on his lips, wondering how he made her forget everything, including her words of the night before.

Just friends.

Ha! They could never be *just friends*. The passion between them was much too combustible, as evidenced by the night before.

But Angela couldn't bring herself to commit to him. He'd broken her heart once, and so completely that she wasn't sure she could live through it again.

When common sense finally returned and she opened her mouth to tell him they wouldn't be able to see each other again once they left Africa, she felt like it was too late. The timing wasn't right.

He bent to retrieve her clothing. He held her bra straps as she slid her arms through, then he turned her and fastened the back.

The more he helped her, the longer he stood before her completely naked, his shaft jutting out in front of him, still hard and thick from making love to her.

"You know I can do this by myself," she said.

"I know, but this is more fun." He held her shirt over her head until she slipped her arms into the sleeves. Then he dragged it over her breasts and down her torso, his knuckles brushing her skin as he did.

A shiver of awareness rippled across her body, making her want to remove the shirt and bra and go for another round of lovemaking in the morning sunshine.

Instead, she took the jeans from his hands. "I'll do the rest." And she stepped out of his reach.

Buck shrugged and dressed himself quickly in his jeans and T-shirt. Before long, he was wearing his boots and his light jacket. He tossed her backpack onto the back of the bike and strapped it down.

Angela lifted his gear bag and his shoulder holster with the handgun tucked inside. "Aren't you going to tie down your bag and wear your pistol?"

Buck shook his head. "I have a bad feeling about going into town. If anything happens and we're jumped, I don't want them to find my weapons or the satellite phone. As far as anyone knows, we're just a couple of tourists stopping in to get fuel before we get back on the road."

"But that means we'll have to backtrack to retrieve your bag."

"True. We'll have to come back this way before circling back to head out of town the opposite direction. We don't want Koku to know we're moving south toward his camp."

Angela nodded. "I get it."

He handed her the helmet. "You'll need to tuck all of your hair up in the helmet and wear your T-shirt untucked and baggy. It's hard to hide the fact that you're a woman, but the longer they have to guess, the better our chances of getting gas and getting out of town before they become clued in."

She nodded and carried the helmet as they pushed through the bushes to exit the little copse.

Buck led the way. He pushed a branch to the side and paused before completely emerging from the underbrush.

Angela couldn't see anything past his big body. But when he stiffened, she touched his back. "What's wrong?"

"Shh," he whispered.

Angela's pulse kicked up a notch.

"We have company." Slowly, he backed into the brush and let the branch swing in front of him.

Angela glanced through the limbs and leaves and gasped.

Beneath a nearby tree lay a pride of lions, basking in the shade and cleaning themselves.

"Holy hell," she exclaimed quietly. "How do we get past them?"

"I suggest we wait until they move," Buck whispered. "I'd rather not antagonize them."

Out of morbid curiosity, she watched the lions stretched out in the sun, their tawny hair golden and shiny. She leaned through the branches, fascinated by the beauty of the animals.

Buck snagged her arm, holding her back from pushing through the brush and out into the open. "You can't go out there," he said, keeping his voice low.

"How long do you think they'll remain unaware of us?" Angela asked.

"I don't know. It could take them all day before they decide to move out. We could be here awhile."

Angela bit down hard on her bottom lip. She wanted to get this show on the road again. To do that, they'd have to get past the lions, with the motorcycle.

"We can wait a few minutes, but we really need to evaluate our alternatives and come up with a way to get past them. In a hurry."

"How are you at driving a motorcycle?" Buck asked.

"Never have." Angela narrowed her eyes. "Why?"

"I'd let you drive and risk me being mauled, but no way am I turning you loose on the bike when you've never operated one."

She smiled. "Probably not a good idea. With my luck, I'd fall over and be eaten."

"Most likely, they'll leave when the engine starts up, but we can't be certain. They could be conditioned to hearing vehicle engines, considering how close they are to the road and town."

"True." Angela shivered. "I've heard some lions have been known to steal children from their beds at night."

Buck circled her waist with his arm. "We're armed and ready if they decide we look like lunch." He glanced around. "I just wish we could get to the bike without drawing their attention."

They'd parked the motorcycle in the bushes outside the little copse of trees before entering their own little grotto the previous night.

"Can we get to it from this side?" Angela whispered.

"We can try, but there are quite a few bushes in the way."

They moved slowly away from the lions and back into the tiny grove.

Buck carefully moved aside branches and leaves in an attempt to get to the motorcycle.

Angela held back limbs and helped where she could, but the brush was thick. Getting a man through was one thing. Getting a man and a motorcycle through…well, it didn't look promising. She tried to keep an eye on the pride, but she couldn't see through the branches to know what was going on with them. They seemed so big and lazy. Surely they wouldn't see her and Buck as a threat.

Between Angela and Buck, they eased the motorcycle through the thick brush into the tiny clearing. Buck quickly strapped Angela's backpack to the seat and hung his gear bag up on a branch, hopefully out of reach of the lions.

"Why aren't we taking yours?"

"I hate leaving it, but if we're caught in town with a bag containing a military-grade weapon, we might not make it back out."

"What about the satellite phone?" Angela asked.

"Another item I don't want someone finding on us. I think we could explain it, but if we're robbed, I'd rather not have it taken." Buck adjusted the bag so that the tree branch it rested on hid it from sight. "We'll come back here as soon as we can."

"You mean, as soon as the lions leave," Angela said.

"Yes, and as soon as we fill the gas tank and ditch anyone following us. I'd rather they thought we were heading back north, anyway."

Angela stared at the bag. "I don't like leaving the satellite phone."

"Me either, but I don't want anyone taking it from us. Plus, I don't think anyone will find it. Especially if the lions stay here much longer." He glanced around the small clearing. "I'd almost rather leave you here while I go into town for the fuel."

She shook her head before he finished speaking. "You're not leaving me anywhere."

He kissed her forehead. "You're right. I don't trust the animals around here. Two or four legged." He handed her the helmet. "Put this on and tuck your hair up inside. The less obvious it is that you're female, the better."

"I'll just be a boy on the back of your bike." She untucked her shirt and stretched it enough that it would hide her curves.

"Sweetheart, even making your shirt baggy can't hide that you're a woman." He pulled her close and hugged her to him. "Just stay with me. I don't want anything to happen to you."

"I'll be like a fly on flypaper," she said with a grin. "Like white on rice. Like stripes on a zebra, like—"

Buck chuckled softly and pulled Angela into his arms. "You're an amazing woman. I repeat, I'm not giving up on you, so expect a fight." He crushed her lips with his.

Buck kissed Angela until her toes curled and she forgot all about the lions lurking on the other side of the bushes. When he raised his head, he chucked her beneath the chin and winked. "Now, let's run the gauntlet of lions. We'll be going fast, so you'd better hold on tight."

Angela had barely caught her breath from the kiss when she slid onto the back of the motorcycle. "How are we getting out of here?"

He nodded toward a break in the bushes on the opposite side from the lions' lounging location. "We're going through there at top speed. Keep your head down, your helmet buckled and your arms around me. It's going to be a bumpy ride."

After a quick glance at the lion pride, she nodded. "They're still pretty calm."

"Let's hope they stay that way." Buck swung his leg over the seat and moved forward.

Angela slid on behind him.

"I don't like you riding on the back. If the lions come after us, they'll get you first."

"Then we'll just have to ride like the wind." Angela wrapped her arms around his waist, sucked in a deep breath and held it while Buck turned the key.

The engine rumbled to life. "Ready?" he shouted.

"Go!" Angela yelled.

Buck twisted the throttle, launching the motorcycle forward and through the branches.

Angela ducked her head and pressed it, helmet and all, into Buck's back. Branches and thin tree limbs whipped at their heads, necks, arms and legs as they blew through the barrier and out into the open.

Buck swung wide of the lion pride, circling back to the road heading into the town.

Daring to turn back, Angela spotted three lionesses running toward them. "Go! Go! Go!" she yelled.

Buck gave the engine more gas and sped toward the town.

The lionesses raced after them, gaining ground.

Buck shot forward at full throttle, building up speed and flying over the uneven ground.

Angela held on until her arms ached. The bumps

were so bad, they nearly threw her from her seat. She clamped her legs around Buck and locked her hands and wrists around his belly. If she came off the bike, she'd take him with her.

Soon, they were going so fast even the lionesses couldn't keep up. They slowed to a walk and turned back toward the pride.

Buck slowed their mad pace as they connected with the dirt road and headed into the town.

Angela couldn't help but think they were going from one lion's den into another. She prayed they didn't run into danger. This man she was holding onto for dear life meant more to her than he could possibly know. She didn't want him to die protecting her. And she was seriously considering retracting her "just friends" requirement for their relationship. She wanted the chance to tell him that when this was all said and done.

BUCK COULDN'T HAVE left Angela in the stand of trees, or he would have. Surrounded by lions, she wouldn't have been any safer than riding with him into a town that could well be occupied by Koku's men. His gut was telling him this was a bad idea, but the gas tank was telling him he was out of choices.

They had to have fuel, and this was the closest town with the potential to have a gas station.

He drew in a deep breath and drove into the outskirts of shacks and huts that gradually transformed into concrete block buildings. Before they'd gone more than a tenth of a mile into the town, a man in a long white robe stepped into the street and waved them down.

Buck's first inclination was to race past him, but then he noticed the gentleman wasn't dark-skinned like most of the people of the Sudan. He was white and he had a gray beard. And he appeared to be frantic.

"Slow down. I think he needs help," Angela said.

More interested in getting fuel, Buck slowed to a stop next to the man, his hand going to the pistol beneath his jacket, only it wasn't there. He'd left it in the gear bag back in the copse of trees outside of town.

"Do you speak English?" the man asked.

"We do," Angela responded. "Are you in trouble?"

The man gave a hint of a smile and shook his head. "No, but you two are. You need to get inside quickly."

Buck stared around at the suspiciously empty streets. "Why?"

"They're on the other side of town, heading this way." The man stepped back. "Hurry!" He waved toward a whitewashed stucco building. "Get inside and bring the motorcycle, too."

A white woman in a blue dress similar to what the locals wore opened the door and waved them forward. "Hurry!" she said.

"I don't understand," Buck said.

The man gripped the handle on one side of the motorcycle. "I'm a Christian minister. My wife and I are missionaries. Our parishioners warn us when the local warlord's men are on their way through. We hide until they're gone."

"We should go with them." Angela climbed off the back of the bike. "Even if we were willing to risk it, we might put these good people at risk."

Buck nodded and pushed the motorcycle toward the building.

"Take the bike around the back. I have a place in the shed where we can hide it," the preacher said.

His wife came out, hooked Angela's arm and led her toward the house.

Buck didn't like that they were being separated. "She stays with me."

The minister grabbed the handle of the motorcycle and urged Buck to roll it forward. "You'll only be apart long enough to stow the motorcycle. Longer if we stand around arguing."

Buck hurriedly followed the man to the shed behind the building. Calling the structure a shed was being generous. It looked more like a shack constructed of bits and pieces of lumber, plywood and tin. But there was a place to push the bike into the back behind what was left of an old truck that had been cannibalized for parts. Buck parked it beside the truck body, pulled a sheet of old tin next to it and leaned it toward the truck. If someone casually peered into the shed, he wouldn't see the bike, just the body of a rusted truck and a sheet of tin.

Once he had the bike in place, he grabbed Angela's backpack and carried it to the back door of the house.

The minister opened the door for him and closed it once he was inside, sliding a wooden bar in place to lock people out.

Buck walked through to the front room, where he found Angela and the older woman.

The minister held out his hand. "Let me introduce myself. I'm Hiram Woodby, and this is my wife, Gladys."

Buck shook the man's hand and nodded toward his wife. "I'm Buck and this is Angela—"

"His fiancée." Angela stuck out her hand. "I was just telling Mrs. Woodby about our exciting trip through the Sudan on motorcycle. We never expected to run into trouble along the way." Angela met his gaze and held it.

Fiancée, huh? Why would she want to keep secrets from the minister and his wife? But then, the less they knew, the less someone could torture out of them.

"Right, we were on a self-guided tour of Africa, hoping to drive all the way to South Africa."

The minister shook his head. "You don't realize how very dangerous it is to travel the length of Africa. There are too many warlords, rebels and pirates around to make it through safely."

Mrs. Woodby wrung her hands. "You two really need to head back north. This area is not stable. Not at all."

Her husband waved toward several cushions on the floor. "Please, have a seat. We will wait until it is safe to go outdoors again."

"How long will that be?" Buck asked.

"Sometimes thirty minutes, sometimes longer," Woodby said.

"We'd like to head back north, but we can't until

we get fuel for the bike," Angela said. "We were hoping to find some in this town. There are gas stations, aren't there?"

Mrs. Woodby shot a glance at her husband.

He reached for her hand. "There is one. But it's not safe to go there until the men have passed through."

"What men are you talking about?" Buck asked, hoping the minister could shed more light on the whereabouts of Koku's camp.

Angela sat on one of the cushions and patted the one beside her. "Sit."

Buck's lips quirked at the command, but he complied.

The Woodbys sat as well.

"As you might know, we're in predominantly Muslim territory," Mr. Woodby said. "The local warlord, Koku, doesn't appreciate our culture and would rather we depart the area. But we can't leave the people who've come to rely on us. So, they help hide us and we lie low to keep them from being punished." The minister squeezed his wife's hand and let go. "We should leave, but we don't have family waiting for us back in the States, or anyone who truly needs us more than the people here."

"Yes, the people here need us much more," his wife added. "So we chose to stay, even though we are in grave danger."

"This Koku…is he nearby?"

"He can't be too far, because his men come through often and rough up the locals, stealing food and fuel." Woodby's lips thinned.

Mrs. Woodby leaned closer and lowered her voice. "They've even stolen boys. We think they are training them to be in their evil army." She looked down at her hands. "We prayed they wouldn't, but they did. The mothers were beside themselves. Those poor children must be terrified. They were so young."

Angela reached out and patted the woman's wrinkled hands. "That's terrible. This Koku must be a monster."

"Yes, he is," Mrs. Woodby said. "So, you see, you can't stay long. If Koku's men know you're here, they'll come after you."

"How do you know?" Buck asked.

The minister took his wife's hand again. "There was a Baptist preacher who came to town a couple of weeks ago. Koku's men came through and we haven't seen him since."

"We think they might have killed him." Mrs. Woodby's voice trailed off. "He was such a nice young man. So full of hope and good intentions."

"He didn't understand how dangerous it was here. He thought he could change how things are." The minister straightened his shoulders. "I would offer you the fuel you need, but we don't have any to spare. I could ask one of our people to get it for you."

Buck shook his head. "I don't want to put anyone in danger. If all we need to do is wait for Koku's men to leave town, we can wait."

Mrs. Woodby released a long breath. "Good. No use going out into the streets now." She rose from her cushion. "Could I get you some tea? We boil the water to purify it."

"Yes, please," Angela said.

Buck stood when Mrs. Woodby did. He waited until she'd left the room and then crossed to a window that had been boarded up from the inside and peered through the slats.

At first, he saw no movement. The streets appeared to be completely empty.

But as he continued to study the road, a truck rumbled past. In the front were two black-garbed men carrying Russian-made AK-47 rifles. When the truck passed, Buck counted half a dozen similarly garbed and equipped men in the back.

Buck's pulse sped. He fought the urge to back away from the window. The men in the truck couldn't possibly see into the home with the boarded windows. But they were close. Too close for Buck to feel comfortable.

The vehicle stopped in the middle of the road, and the men jumped to the ground. Moments later, they pounded on the door of the building across the street from the Woodbys' house.

When no one answered, the men kicked the door in and rushed inside.

"How often are they breaking down doors and entering homes?" Buck asked.

"Every day." Mr. Woodby came to stand beside Buck. "At first, they just harassed the townspeople. When they grew bored of that, they would drag people out into the street, beat them and then shoot them."

"For no reason at all," Mrs. Woodby added, reentering the room with a tray filled with cups, saucers and a teapot.

The men emerged from the home across the street, empty-handed. The one who seemed to be in charge pointed to the house across from where he stood. The house was the missionaries'.

Buck's pulse leaped. "We have trouble."

The minister moved faster than Buck would have thought possible. "Gladys, take our guests into the secret room. And hurry."

"Yes, dear." Gladys set the tea tray she'd been carrying on the coffee table and turned away from the living area. "Follow me, please," she said.

"Yes, ma'am," Buck said.

She walked to a wall and touched the center and the wall slid open, revealing a staircase going down into the ground below.

"Come with me," Mrs. Woodby said, her tone short, clipped. The older woman went first, followed by Angela and then Buck. He didn't like leaving Mr. Woodby alone. If Koku's men kicked in the door, the man had no protection.

Halfway down the stairs, Buck stopped. "You two go on without me. I'm going to stay with Mr. Woodby."

"He knows what to do and say," Mrs. Woodby said. "If you're there, he'll be in more danger. Koku's men know he's here. For the most part, they leave us alone."

"I'll stay out of sight. But I don't like that he's alone and defenseless."

"He'll be in the Lord's hands," Mrs. Woodby said.

And if he were killed, Mrs. Woodby would be alone in a hostile town. She'd have a hell of a time getting out of South Sudan on her own.

"Don't worry," Buck said. "I'll be as quiet as a church mouse."

Mrs. Woodby stared at him for a moment and then nodded. "Okay. But do be careful."

Loud banging sounded on the door.

Buck ran up the stairs and closed the hidden door, hiding the women below. He hurried toward the front room and slid into the pantry cabinet with barely enough room for him to close the door.

And he waited.

Chapter Ten

Buck could see through the gap into the living room where the minister was opening the door for Koku's men.

No sooner had he removed the bar covering the door than the men burst into the room, nearly knocking down the old man.

Buck clenched his fists, his first instinct to go to the man's aid, but his wife's words echoed in his head. Just his being there would be more dangerous for the minister.

Hopefully, the thugs wouldn't rough up Woodby any more than they already had.

"Why are you still here, old man?" the leader demanded.

In a calm, even tone, Woodby replied, "This is my home."

"You are not welcome in my country. Take your beliefs and your white man's ways back to where you came from."

Woodby dipped his head without replying.

Koku's man narrowed his eyes and glanced past

Woodby's shoulder. "Are you hiding anyone?" He waved his weapon in the man's face. "If you are, we will kill them and you."

Woodby waved a hand toward the interior of the house. "You are welcome to search."

Buck cursed silently. Woodby didn't know he'd chosen to come back out of the basement hiding place. If the men found him in the pantry, they would attempt to kill him and the minister.

He braced himself for a fight.

The leader had stepped past Woodby and started toward the kitchen when a shout sounded from the street outside.

Buck held his breath, ready to spring if he needed to. The element of surprise was on his side, but he'd still be outnumbered and put Woodby in danger.

He held his course and waited to see what Koku's men would do.

Another shout sounded in the street. The man who'd confronted the minister spun and ran to the door. He yelled at the man in the street. "What?"

The man outside yelled back, his voice muffled by the walls of the building and the cabinet door.

Suddenly all of Koku's men departed the small home.

Woodby closed the door softly and slid the bar in place. He turned, leaned against the door and pressed a hand to his chest. Then he walked to the window and watched through the slats.

Buck left the cabinet and joined the minister. "Are you all right?"

The man nodded. "Shaken, but not hurt." He continued to watch the man outside. "You risked a lot by coming back upstairs."

"I know. But I couldn't leave you to handle those men. They might have gotten more violent."

Woodby shrugged. "It's part of my life. I trust the Lord to take care of me."

Buck hoped the Lord did take care of the man. He also believed the Lord helped those who helped themselves.

"They're moving on," the minister said.

"How often do they come in and do shakedowns?" Buck asked.

"More than we care for." The old man glanced out the window again. "Sometimes they just rough people up. At other times, they have been trigger-happy and shot residents." His lips thinned. "They're ruthless and godless."

Buck shook his head. "That doesn't bode well for you and your wife."

"No. But it also doesn't bode well for our parishioners."

"You have the choice to leave," Buck reminded him.

"And our people do not have that choice." The minister faced Buck. "My wife and I agreed to stay. We couldn't abandon them in their time of need." He crossed the living around and pushed on the wall, exposing the hidden doorway and the staircase leading down into the basement. "You can come up now."

Buck peered down the darkened stairway.

Angela was the first to appear. "Are they gone?"

Mrs. Woodby stepped up behind her.

"They're gone," Buck replied.

Angela stepped aside and allowed Mrs. Woodby to go up first.

When the older woman arrived at the top, she hugged her husband. "Why do they have to be so hateful?" she whispered and pressed her face into his chest. "I worry about you."

The minister stroked his wife's gray hair. "It's God's will."

"I wish God's will was to stop their reign of terror," Mrs. Woodby said.

"He will. He will," her husband assured her.

Angela stepped around the older couple and into Buck's arms. "I didn't like having you out of my sight." She held him tight. "I have to admit, I like having you around. I feel safer."

He smoothed the hair out of her face and pressed a kiss to her forehead. "I like knowing you're safe."

"You're welcome to stay as long as you like," Mrs. Woodby offered. "We can lay out a pallet on the floor in here for you two to sleep on. There's enough food in the pantry to feed us all for several days."

Buck stared down at Angela. "We can't."

She nodded. "We have to get moving."

They had to find Koku and get the coordinates to his team. The sooner they did, the better off everyone in the region would be.

Buck kissed Angela hard on the lips and stepped away. "I'm going out to get the fuel we need."

"I'm going with you," Angela said.

Buck hardened his jaw and his heart. "No. I need to know you're safe. I want you to stay here. You have a place to hide if Koku's men return."

"You said yourself you didn't like me out of your sight."

"I did. But if you're with me, I might lose focus and get us both hurt." He lifted her hand, pressed a kiss into her palm and curled her fingers around it. "Please, promise me you'll stay."

Angela stared into his eyes, her own suspiciously bright. "I'll stay, but don't be too long."

He gave her a tight smile. "I'll be back as soon as possible."

"I'm coming with you," Mr. Woodby said. "I have a gas can in the shed. We can take it instead of taking the motorcycle."

"I'd rather take the motorcycle. I need to fill it to full, if possible."

The minister shrugged. "Either way, I can show you the way to the station by taking the back streets."

The man had a point. "The station should be on a main road, right?"

"Yes, but not all of the secondary streets run straight through. You could run into a dead end getting there and back."

"Let my husband help," Mrs. Woodby implored. "If nothing else, the people of the town know him and will help you sooner than they'd help a stranger."

"Any sign of trouble—" Angela started.

Buck nodded. "Any sign of trouble and we'll find

a place to hide until it blows over." He grabbed Angela's helmet and handed it to the minister. "You'll have to use this."

Mr. Woodby grinned. "I always wanted to ride a motorcycle. The closest I've come is riding on a scooter. This will be a treat." He kissed his wife and led the way through the back of the house to the shed.

Buck followed, keeping a close watch on the corners of the building, listening for sounds indicating a return of Koku's men.

Once they had the motorcycle out of the shed, Buck mounted and waited for the minister to climb onto the back.

He started the engine and revved the throttle before easing out onto the main street running through town.

The roads were still fairly empty, with only a few men daring to get out after Koku's troops had come through.

Buck drove the motorcycle through town, coming to a halt at a building the minister assured him was the gas station. It had one old-fashioned pump Buck had only seen the likes of in photographs. He stopped the motorcycle at the pump. "It might be best if you keep your helmet on. I don't want people to know who is with me."

The minister agreed and kept the helmet buckled. He went into the building and addressed the man who owned the station. When he returned, he nodded toward the pump handle. "It's all taken care of. Fill your tank, but make it as quick as possible. Fahd is afraid Koku's men will be back through soon."

Buck plugged the nozzle into the tank and pressed the lever. The gas poured into the tank so slowly, he gritted his teeth and prayed he could get what he needed in this century.

He didn't like being away from Angela so long. Anything could happen. Koku could return to the house and kick the door in. The women would be defenseless.

The more he thought about it, the more frustrated he became at how slowly the pump was filling his tank. When it was only half-full, he gave up, stopped the pump and hung up the nozzle.

"Hey!" someone shouted behind him.

He turned to see the leader of the thugs who'd burst into the Woodbys' home earlier, surrounded by six of his buddies, all carrying AK-47 assault rifles and wearing the black outfits of Koku's shoddy army. They were young men looking for trouble.

Buck didn't have time to put up with them. He wanted to get back to Angela and get the hell out of town. But if trouble was what they were looking for... well, they'd found it.

"Mr. Woodby, go inside the building."

"I'm not leaving you to these men."

Buck purposely replaced the cap on the gas tank, ignoring the men heading his way, while keeping an eye on them in his peripheral vision. "Mr. Woodby, I need you to go inside the building and lock the door."

"But—"

"Now," he said, his tone low, brooking no further argument.

The minister hurried into the building and closed the door just as the thugs reached Buck and the motorcycle.

He glanced up and smiled. "Can I help you?"

"Yes, you can. You can give us your motorcycle."

Buck shook his head, the smile still in place, though forced.

"You want my bike? Come and get it."

ANGELA PACED THE FLOOR, wishing she'd gone with Buck instead of staying at the house, wondering what was happening on the streets of the town.

All sorts of scenarios rolled through her mind, none of them good. Had Buck and the minister run into Koku's men? Had the people of the town turned on them? Had they been shot by a sniper perched on a rooftop? The more she thought of all that could have happened, the faster she paced.

"Come. Sit. You're wearing a hole in the floor," Mrs. Woodby said. "I can warm up the tea I made earlier, and we can have some cookies I made out of the last of my flour and sugar."

"Thank you, Mrs. Woodby, but I'm not thirsty or hungry." She just wanted Buck to get back and show her he was fine.

The older woman stepped in front of her and touched her arm. "They'll be okay. You'll see."

The woman's soft smile and words of reassurance were just enough to send Angela over the edge. Tears pooled in her eyes and her lip trembled. "I'm worried about them. About him."

Mrs. Woodby opened her arms. "Come here."

Angela stepped into the older woman's embrace and laid her head on her shoulder, tears trickling from the corners of her eyes. "I know Buck can handle anything that comes his way, but I still can't stop worrying."

"I know how you feel. Every time Mr. Woodby steps outside, I worry until he's back in the house. He can be cantankerous and stubborn, but I love that man." She smoothed a hand over Angela's hair. "You love Buck, don't you?"

Angela sniffed, her heart squeezing hard in her chest. She'd always loved Buck. From the day she'd met him in medical school, she'd known he was the man for her. Even when he'd broken her heart, she'd never stopped loving him. Why, oh, why had she told him she only wanted to be friends? She loved the man with all of her heart and didn't want to live another day without him in her life.

She prayed she'd have the opportunity to tell him. In the meantime, she needed to be strong and ready to go whenever he returned.

Angela straightened and rubbed her hand over her face, drying her tears. "Thank you for letting me blubber like a baby."

"Angela, we're human. We're allowed to cry on occasion. There's no shame in emotion. Especially when we're stressed about the ones we love." She patted Angela's hand. "Now, come. Let's have that tea. It always calms me to fix a cup and sip while I'm waiting."

Angela let Mrs. Woodby lead her into the kitchen when she'd rather have stood by the window and counted the minutes Buck was away.

"How long have you and Mr. Woodby been together?"

The older woman set the teakettle on a camp stove and lit the burner. "We've been together since we were in grade school. Oh, there was a time we weren't dating, just after we graduated high school. Mr. Woodby didn't want me to wait for him while he went away to seminary. He wanted me to date other men to know for certain what I wanted in a husband." Her smile softened and her eyes grew cloudy with memories as she stared at the heating kettle.

"And did you?" Angela asked. "Did you date other men?"

Mrs. Woodby grinned. "I did. And you know what I learned?"

"What?" Angela leaned toward the woman, eager to hear more.

"That Mr. Woodby was the only man for me. He was like the other half that made me whole. Without him, my life wasn't full." The kettle heated until the steam made a whistling sound. The minister's wife filled a cup with hot water from the kettle and dropped a tea bag into it. She handed the cup to Angela and motioned for her to take a chair at a small table. She filled another cup and sat across from Angela, dipping her tea bag in the hot water. "You know what I mean, don't you? You and Buck are so in love, you must feel the same way. I see it in your eyes."

Angela's chest filled with all the love she felt for Buck, and her cheeks heated. She pressed her palms to her face. Did it show that much? Could Buck see through her when she'd said she wanted to be "just friends"? Did he know she'd been lying?

Hell, she wanted all those things she'd wanted back in medical school and more. She wanted the happily-ever-after life with the man she loved. If it meant risking her heart again for a chance to be with him, so be it. If he left her again, well, she'd already proven to herself she could survive. It would be hard, but any time with Buck was better than never seeing him again. Why hold back when she could have him now?

She lifted the cup of tea to her lips and sipped. Despite Mrs. Woodby's promise that drinking a cup of tea would calm her, she found herself wanting to leap to her feet and rush to the window. Sitting still was killing her.

Finally, she set her cup on the table and stood. "I don't know how you remain so calm. I'm not nearly as patient. I have to move."

"By all means. Each person handles stress in his or her own way." Mrs. Woodby remained at the table sipping her tea.

Angela strode to the window, anxious to catch sight of Buck and Mr. Woodby returning on the motorcycle. As she leaned toward the gap between the boards over the window, she was shocked to see more of Koku's men in front of the house, at the door. They were different men than those who'd come earlier, but dressed the same and brandishing rifles.

"We have trouble," Angela said softly enough not to be heard through the door. She turned to Mrs. Woodby, the blood rushing from her face. "Get to the basement."

Someone banged on the door and shouted for them to open the door. Mrs. Woodby set down her cup and stood, her eyes rounded. She rose from her seat at the table and went to the hidden doorway. She raised her hand but didn't get the chance to press it to the wall before the door slammed inward, the brace board over it splitting into two pieces.

Angela squealed and backed away from the men storming through the entrance.

She hadn't gotten far when one of them grabbed her arm and dragged her across the floor.

Mrs. Woodby yelled, "Leave her alone!" She grabbed a pillow from the floor and went after the man dragging Angela toward the door. She hit the man with the pillow, but its softness did little to deter the man from taking Angela.

Angela fought hard, but the man who'd grabbed her was much bigger and stronger than she was.

Mrs. Woodby hit the man again with the pillow, reminding Angela of a teenage pillow fight party. The attack with the pillow would do little to save her from being taken. But she had to give the old woman credit for having the gumption to help her.

Another man grabbed the minister's wife around the middle, lifted her off the ground and set her away from the man dragging Angela toward the exit.

The older woman made one last effort to get the man to let go of Angela, but he wasn't taking suggestions from anyone, much less an old woman with a soft, cushy pillow.

Mrs. Woodby kept swinging, but nothing was stopping the men from taking whatever they wanted. And apparently, they wanted Angela.

She kicked, bit, scratched and fought her hardest, but the men were stronger and there were more of them than she could fight off.

The minister's wife fought valiantly for her, but she and her pillow were no match for the men.

One man grew tired of her assaults and back-handed her, sending her flying across the room.

She slammed against a wall and slid to the floor, unconscious.

"Leave her alone!" Angela cried and struggled even harder to free herself to go to the old woman. She could be dead or dying for all she knew. As a doctor, she might be able to help. But only if the men holding her would let her go long enough to render aid.

They didn't relinquish their holds on her arms.

The largest man bent low, grabbed her legs and flung her over his shoulder.

With her legs trapped under his arm, all she could do was beat against the man's back with her fists. It was as if she were tickling him. He laughed and

strode through the door and out into the late afternoon sunshine.

Sweet heaven, where was Buck?

All she could think as they dragged her away was
Please, Buck, help me!

Chapter Eleven

Buck didn't have time to reach for the gun beneath his jacket. Instead, he hid his hip and hand behind the motorcycle and reached for the Ka-Bar knife strapped to his side in time to jerk it from its scabbard and jab the wickedly sharp blade into the gut of the first man to reach him.

His attacker screamed and fell to the ground, clutching at his abdomen.

When the others saw what had happened to their compadre, they launched themselves at Buck.

He dived over the top of the motorcycle, hit the ground and rolled to his feet. If he didn't strike fast, the attackers would pull their weapons and start shooting. Seven against one wouldn't last long. He'd be bullet-ridden and useless.

His only hope was to go on the offensive. Strike first and fast. Holding the knife in front of him, Buck leaped at the first man, sliced him across his throat, spun him around to catch the blade of another man and shoved him away. Moving fast, he vaulted back over the bike and planted both feet into another man's chest as that guy raised his rifle. He knocked him into the man behind him.

Both men went down, their rifles flying from their hands.

Buck snatched one of the weapons, fired and killed the two men on the ground. He dropped behind the bike and came up swinging the butt of the weapon at the head of one of the other men.

Shots rang out, one of the bullets hitting Buck. The projectile sliced through the edge of his arm, leaving a shallow, bloody trail.

Buck barely felt the pain, adrenaline pumping through his veins, making his heart pound and his pulse race. He turned the rifle on the other two men fumbling to aim their weapons and pulled the trigger, hitting them with several rounds each in the chest. Then he dived for the side of a building, out of range of other would-be assassins. From his position, he took down the rest, easy targets for a seasoned navy SEAL.

When the gunpowder smoke cleared, Buck tallied his results. Seven of Koku's men lay on the ground. But there had been more than these men in the trucks that had passed through town earlier. Had they made it back to the Woodbys' house?

Buck checked in all directions before running to the motorcycle. The first thing he noticed was the acrid scent of gasoline. The bright stain in the dirt made his gut clench. One of the stray bullets had pierced the tank. He didn't have time to waste if he planned to get back to the Woodby house on what was left of the gas in the tank.

Mr. Woodby eased out of the building, his eyes wide, his hand pressed to his chest. "I consider myself a forgiving man, but these men had long ago gone past forgiveness."

Buck didn't have time to philosophize over the dead. He had to get back to Angela, ASAP. Instinct told him something wasn't right. He felt it deep down, and the distance between him and the woman he loved was far too great.

"Going back to the house?" Mr. Woodby asked.

"I am." He slung his leg over the seat. He only had moments to get to the house before all of the gasoline leaked out of the tank. "If you're coming, get on."

The minister swung his leg over the seat and held on around Buck's belly.

Praying he didn't start a fire with the leaking gas, Buck cranked the engine and twisted the throttle, taking his chances, hoping against hope he didn't set them both aflame. He was willing to take any risk to get to Angela as quickly as possible.

He spun the bike around and headed down the back streets they'd come in on. Through the lanes and alleyways, Buck kept watch for other vehicles running the parallel main road a couple blocks away. At one point, a truck lumbered by with a contingent of Koku's men wielding rifles and shouting.

Buck was happy to avoid that bunch of thieves, thugs and terrorists. He'd had enough struggles for the day, and his body still hurt from fighting Koku's men.

When he reached the white stucco building that was the Woodbys' home, he could feel the silence stretch before him like a cloak of sadness.

He waited impatiently while Woodby slipped off the back, and then he jumped up and ran for the front door. "Angela!"

She didn't respond.

The branches on the tree beside the house waved gently in the breeze, unconcerned with the plights of men.

Even before he reached the door, he could see it stood slightly open. The doorjamb was splintered and the bar that should have been securely wedged over the door had been snapped into two pieces.

Buck ran into the building, searching for the love of his life. "Angela!"

A moan sounded from the corner of the small living space.

Mrs. Woodby lay on her side against the wall, her eyes blinking open. She touched a hand to the back of her head and winced. "W-what happened?"

"Gladys?" The minister rushed in after Buck and ran to his wife. He dropped to his knees beside her and gathered her gingerly into his arms. "Oh, my love. What have they done to you?"

Mrs. Woodby moaned. "Oh my God. I remember. Koku's men came back." She leaned into her husband, tears slipping from her eyes. "They took Angela. Oh dear Lord, they took Angela."

Buck's heart lodged firmly in his throat, choking off his air. He ran through the small house, looking for her, knowing what Mrs. Woodby said was the truth. Angela was gone. Captured by the group of terrorists he'd come to destroy.

He no longer had the time or the means to find the coordinates for Koku's camp. The warlord had to be close, though, if they were terrifying this town on a regular basis.

Buck headed for the door, his mind made up, the only course of action clear.

"Where are you going?" Mr. Woodby called out after him.

"To get help," Buck responded.

He climbed onto the motorcycle and sent a silent prayer to the heavens that the bike would make it back to where he'd stashed his gear bag and the satellite phone. He was glad he'd left it outside of town. If he'd had it on the bike, the bullets that had pierced the gas tank might also have taken out his only means of communicating with his team.

The smell of gasoline was strong, but he couldn't let that worry him. The motorcycle had to get him back to his bag. Buck held his breath and started the engine. It puttered and then engaged. Without waiting to see if it would remain running, he shifted into gear and twisted the throttle.

The bike leaped onto the road headed north out of town. He didn't care if someone followed him. If anyone got in the way of him calling for help, he'd shoot first and ask questions later. Angela had been captured by a ruthless murderer. His only focus was getting to her before the warlord hurt her.

No one tried to stop him. No one stepped into his path, and the road was clear of all traffic. A mile from town, the bike sputtered, coughed and died. All the gas he'd put into the tank had leaked out, leaving the motorcycle to function as one large paperweight.

Buck left the bike and took off on foot, running as fast as his legs would take him to the last place he and Angela had made love.

By the time he returned to the copse of trees, he was ready to run the gauntlet of the lion pride. Thankfully, the field in front of the stand of brush and trees was empty.

Buck didn't take it for granted. The pride could very easily have taken up residence in the clearing beyond the line of brush. He slowed and eased his way through the thick branches, his gun in hand, his senses heightened, his guard up in case he came face-to-face with one of the savannah's most deadly predators.

For once, fate played into his hands. The tiny clearing was empty and the gear bag was where he'd left it in the branches. He pulled out the phone, hit the buttons that would connect him with his team and waited for them to answer.

"Buck, where the hell have you been?"

The relief he felt at the sound of Big Jake's voice sent Buck to his knees. "They have her. Koku's men captured Angela."

"Damn," Big Jake said. "I hate to hear that. She's a good woman with a big heart. But…the good news is that we're on our way from Djibouti. The commander got tired of waiting for you and sent us out to bring you in."

"I'm not going back until we get Angela out of Koku's clutches."

"Understood. And you're in luck. We're fully loaded for bear and ready for a fight."

Buck let go of the breath he felt like he'd been holding since he'd left the Woodbys' house. "ETA?"

"Within the hour," Big Jake responded. "Stay where you are. We have the satellite phone on our GPS tracking device. We'll find you, and the team will take it from there."

Buck had never been more appreciative of the brotherhood that was the navy SEALs than he was at that moment. They had his back and they wouldn't let him down.

He prayed he wasn't too late to save Angela.

THE MEN WHO'D taken Angela had tied her wrists and ankles, dragged a burlap sack over her head, and thrown her into the back of a truck. They'd bumped along a rough road for what felt like a very long time but was probably less than an hour.

Every inch of her body felt bruised by the rough ride, but Angela couldn't worry about the aches and pains. She had to worry instead about being killed. Throughout the ride, she'd worked at the bindings, trying to get her hands free, but the ropes were too tight. All she managed to accomplish was to rub her wrists raw in the process.

Her ankles were a different story. She wiggled

and twisted until she was able to work the rope free. Whoever had tied them hadn't secured the binding tight enough, which worked to her advantage. She had her feet free, even if she couldn't move her hands from behind her back. All of her wiggling and twisting had the added benefit of shifting the burlap over her head. She could see light if she moved just right.

When the truck stopped bumping and the engine shut off, Angela knew she had to make a break for it, or suffer at the hands of Koku. He'd been known to rape and kill women without showing a shred of compassion.

If she could get to the edge of the camp, she might have a chance of escaping. Then she could think about how to evade the wild animals who preyed on defenseless creatures. She'd much rather face a pride of lions than Koku and his men.

Though she was scared and worried about her fate, Angela wasn't ready to give up. She would get free and go back to Buck, or die trying. Hopefully, the dying part wouldn't be the endgame. She had things she wanted to tell Buck, and she refused to die until she had the chance to let him know just how much she loved him and always had.

Men moved around her, jumping out of the truck and onto the ground.

Someone grabbed her ankles and yanked her toward the edge of the truck bed. The burlap bag caught on something and was dragged off her head, allowing her to see without obstruction and to study her surroundings before she was unceremoniously flung over a man's shoulder and carried toward a building.

She couldn't use her hands to steady the bouncing and she flopped like a rag doll, a bony shoulder jabbing into her gut. Her head smacked into the man's back as they crossed the rough ground.

They came to a building at the center of the camp, the only one with four sturdy walls and a roof. It had likely been a farmer's home until Koku had commandeered it for his operations center. All around her were pens that might once have held goats and cattle, but were now topped with concertina wire. Inside were the young men and boys who'd been taken from their families and forced into service for Koku's army.

In one area, young teenage boys were being drilled in how to march and display the proper respect for their superiors. They weren't caged like animals, having already been indoctrinated and brainwashed into loyalty toward Koku and his cause.

The man carrying her stopped in front of the building and knocked on the wooden door.

Angela couldn't see what was going on from her position staring at the man's backside.

He exchanged words with the man who opened the door. Moments later, he entered the building and walked down a shadowy hall to a room with more light.

Once inside the room, he dumped her on the floor and backed through the doorway, leaving Angela to figure out how to sit up when her arms were secured behind her back. She drew her knees beneath her and pushed to a kneeling position to face the man behind a metal desk. Two massive men stood on either side of him, each holding a rifle, their faces masks of determination.

"You are Angela Vega, the doctor who left the refugee camp in Bentiu a couple days ago." The man behind the desk didn't ask. His words were a statement, a fact.

She stiffened. How did he know who she was?

He smiled, his teeth the whitest part of his dark and dangerous face. "I sent my men to get a doctor, and they came back without one." He drummed his long fingers on the desk. "You have been a difficult person to track down."

She managed to stand, lifting her chin high. "Maybe I don't want to be tracked."

He waved his hand to the side, dismissing her words. "You have no choice. We need a doctor. You will be our doctor."

"You can't hold me forever," she said.

"And who will stop Koku?" He pounded a fist to his chest and sneered. "No one dares to stop the great Koku. They fear him."

"Do you always refer to yourself in third person?" Angela asked, though she was careful to remove all sarcasm from her tone. The man didn't appear to have a sense of humor. Angela didn't relish the idea of him being angered at her lack of respect for his inflated ego.

Koku's eyes narrowed. "What is this third person you speak of?"

"Nothing." Angela glanced around the room. "Why do you need a doctor?"

"We have sick children and injured soldiers," he said.

"Are you referring to the children you stole from their homes?"

A frown drew his eyebrows together at the center of his forehead. "I bring children here to give them a better life than if they stayed with their poor families. Here they will be fed, have purpose, learn self-discipline and become soldiers."

"Soldiers you will use to terrorize farmers, women and more children." Angela glared at the man who'd killed so many and was maniacally proud of the fact.

He studied Angela. "I see that you do not approve of my methods to bring order and calm to the chaos of this region."

"From what I've seen, you are part of the reason there is chaos."

"You know nothing of the struggles that are here in South Sudan."

"I know you steal the food destined for the refugee camps, and you take children from their parents to train for your army."

"You are from the West, where everyone is governed by one set of rules. In the Sudan, whoever is strongest makes the rules." He pounded his chest again. "I am the strongest. I make the rules."

She wasn't going to convince the man otherwise. He'd built himself up in his mind to larger than life and better than anyone else. Who was she, a female from a foreign land, to tell him he was wrong?

All she could hope for was to survive long enough for Buck and his team to find her and rescue her, along with all of the children being held hostage.

She sighed and played along with what Koku wanted. "Why do you need a doctor?"

He stood, holding a hand to his abdomen. "I have need of you to determine what it is causing me great pain in my side. And when you're done with that, we have at least a dozen men and boys who are dying, and we have been unsuccessful in determining the cause."

"I'll need my backpack with my medical equipment and supplies."

"I have everything you will need. We took things from the hospital tent at the refugee camp. I had my men construct a hospital tent specifically for administering to the people of this camp." He rounded the desk, still holding his side. His lips pressed tightly together and his back hunched with every step. The man was in a great amount of pain and was trying to hide it. "You will come with me."

She refused to move. "I will be unable to help anyone with my hands tied behind my back."

Koku barked an order to one of the men standing by his desk.

The man pulled a knife out of a scabbard on his belt and advanced on Angela.

She backed away, fearing he would jam the blade into her ribs.

Koku gave a short laugh. "He will not hurt you, as long as you do not hurt me. Be certain you do not harm me in any way. My men have orders to kill you if you do. Do you understand?"

Angela nodded. "I'm a doctor. I took an oath to help people, not hurt them."

"Oaths are mere words. I've known many people who do not live by their words."

"I'm not one of them."

The man with the knife circled her, grabbed her wrists and hacked through the ropes.

When her hands were free, she rubbed at the raw wounds where the ropes had ravaged her skin.

Koku stepped past her, walking slowly out of the building.

His two guards closed in around Angela. When one reached out to grab one of her arms, she glared at him. "You don't have to drag me. I'll go on my own two feet."

The two narrowed their eyes and blocked her from going any other direction than the way their boss was headed.

Angela followed Koku out of the building and toward a crisp white tent perched on flat ground on the other side of one of the pens.

A man met them at the door of the tent and flung open the flap, holding it to the side as Koku and Angela entered.

She thought for a moment she recognized him.

Her gaze dropped to where his pant leg was torn and stained with dried blood.

Kaleel.

He didn't meet her gaze; instead he pretended he didn't see her at all.

Of course, he wouldn't want Koku to know she had been the one to stitch his leg. If Koku knew, he'd ask him why he hadn't told him sooner where to find the doctor he'd been searching for.

Angela realized she had information she could hold over Kaleel if he decided to make her life miserable. She tucked that little bit of knowledge away and studied the hospital tent.

It appeared to be like the one the Doctors Without Borders had provided for her to use. Most likely, it had been on one of the shipments destined for another refugee camp.

Angela bit down on her lip to keep from saying something about the theft. Stealing from others didn't seem to concern Koku. He appeared to think it was his right and part of his role as reigning warlord of the region.

Not only had they stolen the tent, they'd stolen the cots and adjustable examination table. All they needed now was the generator, lights and medical equipment and they'd have a fully equipped hospital.

Koku said something to one of the men standing nearby. The man flipped a switch, and the roar of a generator filled the silence. Lights blinked on overhead, chasing out the shadows of the afternoon sunshine that couldn't quite make it through the fabric of the tent.

Angela's eyebrows rose in challenge. "Medical equipment?"

Koku waved toward a shiny white cabinet. "You will find a large collection in there."

She opened the cabinet and found enough tools and supplies to operate a field hospital for several days in a mass casualty event.

Koku hopped onto the examination table. "Now, make this quit hurting."

Angela lifted her chin, disliking the way he demanded instead of asking. "And if I don't?"

"You die." He lay back on the table, wincing as he did. "And if I die...you die."

"Sounds like I don't have much choice in the matter."

"You have a choice. You can fix what is hurting me, or I can turn you over to my men for their pleasure before they kill you." He closed his eyes, his lips pressing together into a tight, thin line.

The doctor in Angela couldn't let the man continue to suffer. She lifted his shirt and pressed her fingers on his belly.

He flinched.

After a thorough examination, measuring his vital signs and talking through his symptoms, she knew what was wrong but wasn't happy with her alternatives. "Your appendix is inflamed. You need to have it taken out before it ruptures."

"Then do it," Koku said through gritted teeth.

"I'm not a surgeon. What you need is a real hospital with a surgeon to operate."

He leaned up on his elbow and glared at her. "You will perform the surgery and you will take this appendix out."

"I told you, I'm not a surgeon. I've never performed this surgery on my own."

"But you've done the procedure with another doctor?"

"During my surgical internship. But I'm not a surgeon."

"Is the necessary medical equipment available here?"

She'd gone through the cabinet. It had what a surgeon would need to perform the procedure. "I think so."

Koku lay back on the table. "Then get started."

"You don't understand."

He waved one of his guards over to him, jerked a pistol out of a holster on the man's belt and pointed it at Angela. "What more do I need to say?"

Angela stared down the barrel of the gun. "I'll get started."

Chapter Twelve

Buck paced in the copse of trees for the next hour, counting every second of every minute until he heard the thumping sound of rotor blades whipping the air. He shoved through the branches and brush to emerge into the open. He barely remembered to look for the pride of lions. At that point, he didn't care. *Koku has Angela* played through his brain like a broken record, and the longer he had her, the worse it could be for her.

Three helicopters flew in from the north. One dropped to the ground long enough for Buck to climb on board. As soon as he was strapped in, the chopper rose into the air and headed south along the road through the town where the Woodbys lived and where Angela had been taken.

Buck filled Big Jake in on what had occurred and his suspicion that Koku couldn't be too far from where they were.

Mustafa had said five towns. They'd gone through three. Only two more remained, and then they would find Koku and hopefully recover Angela before the warlord had a chance to harm her.

Mustafa's journey on foot had taken days. On a motorcycle, keeping out of sight and moving by night had taken far longer than Buck had liked. But in a helicopter, it should be only a matter of minutes before they found Koku's camp. If the sun would stay up long enough. Unfortunately, day was quickly turning into night. Shadows lengthened and blended into the murky gray of dusk.

Before the light was completely snuffed out, Buck counted two more small villages, just like Mustafa had mentioned. Which meant they were getting close to Koku's camp.

Buck leaned over the backs of the pilot and copilot's seats to stare out at the landscape ahead. A light blinked and flickered on the ground. He didn't expect Koku's camp to have electricity. Any light would most likely come from a vehicle's headlights, a campfire or battery-operated lanterns. Unless the man commandeered generators to run electricity.

Again, he saw the flicker of lights.

"Did you see that?" He pointed toward the light.

The pilot nodded.

"Don't get any closer," Big Jake said. "If that's the camp, we need the element of surprise in order to take on a much larger force."

Adrenaline flowed through Buck's system, firing his blood and making him anxious to hit the ground and get to the business of rescuing Angela. But he knew Koku had a lot of dangerous men working for him. They needed to recon the area, find out what they were up against before they could plan the mission.

All of which took time. And time might not be in Angela's favor.

Two helicopters landed an estimated two miles from what they guessed was the target. The third chopper, containing Buck, Big Jake, Pitbull, Harm, T-Mac and Diesel, continued in a wide circle, far enough out not to alert the occupants of the camp with their engine and rotor noise. They flew close to the earth, to keep from being spotted, with exterior lights off.

Several times they saw lights blink on then off. By this time, they'd determined the lights were headlights from the trucks Koku used to transport his men.

"That has to be it," Buck said. "Angela is down there."

"We'll get her out," Big Jake assured him. "But we can't go in there like John Wayne, guns a-blazin'. We need a plan, and we need to know how many of Koku's men we'll be up against."

Buck understood what Big Jake was saying, but his heart was telling him to *go, go, go!*

He'd left Angela once and it had nearly killed him. Leaving her this time had left her exposed to Koku's men. Buck had let her down. By trying to keep her out of the line of fire, he'd left her in a vulnerable situation she had no way of escaping.

Their pilot flew back to the location where the other two helicopters had landed. The men disembarked and checked their weapons and communications. In all, there were eighteen SEALs ready to do whatever it took to take out Koku and rescue the American doctor. The helicopters would be on standby to extract them when they needed them to come. Until then, they would stay back, out of range of rocket-propelled grenades and gunfire.

The two miles into the camp wouldn't take the SEALs long to cover. They were all in top physical condition and knew the stakes. What would take time was easing up to the camp, locating any guards on the perimeter and neutralizing the chance of them alerting the rest of the camp to the infiltration.

The team had been on enough missions together to know what it took.

Buck took point, leading the team into Koku's territory. As soon as they got close, they split off, establishing their own circle to identify guard posts.

"Got one Tango on the northeast boundary," Pitbull reported. "He appears to be asleep."

"Tango on eastern edge," Harm whispered.

Buck spotted movement in the shadow of a tree. He lowered his night-vision goggles over his eyes and picked up the green heat signature of a warm body. "I've got one on the north."

"You know what to do," Big Jake said.

"Affirmative," Buck, Pitbull and Harm responded.

They would move in, quietly dispatch the guards and cover while the other bounded forward.

Buck sneaked up on his guard. The man was equipped with an AK-47 rifle, an old one probably supplied by the Russians. He didn't even have time to shout or react, and Buck was on him. Seconds later, the threat was eliminated.

"North Tango down," Buck said into his radio.

"East Tango down," Harm's voice said into his ear.

Moments later, Pitbull came over the radio. "Northeast Tango down."

"Let's do this," Big Jake said. "Cover."

"Got your six," Buck replied.

While the six of them moved forward, the others circled the camp and eliminated guard positions one by one, reporting in as they accomplished the tasks.

Buck's team moved forward, edging closer to the camp where they could get an accurate count of what they were up against.

Men moved around a fire pit, where a large spit had been erected and the carcass of some kind of deer was slowly being roasted. The smell of succulent flesh met Buck's nostrils, reminding him that he hadn't eaten a decent meal in days. His stomach growled, but he ignored it, knowing Angela was somewhere in that camp, possibly in pain, maybe tortured or raped.

His gut clenched at the thought, and it was all he could do to keep from rushing in to find her.

"I count fifty-four," Diesel said.

"I got fifty-five," Big Jake said. "There might be some lying on the ground in the shadow of that building."

"There's an entire corral full of children close to where I am," Harm reported.

"Any sign of Angela?"

"No. But there's a large tent in the center of the camp. She could be in there or in the building."

"I'll take the tent," Buck said.

"Harm, you're with Buck," Big Jake said. "Pitbull, you're with me. Diesel and T-Mac will provide cover. Give us ten minutes to locate the doctor. If we're not back by then, make some noise."

"Give me a minute to set up the noise factor diversion," T-Mac said.

"Do it," Big Jake said. "And report back."

A few moments later, T-Mac came across the radio. "Diversion fireworks are in place."

Buck touched the grenades he had strapped to his protective vest, gripped his rifle, settled his night-vision goggles in place and prepared to enter Koku's camp.

ANGELA HAD SWEAT her way through an operation she'd only assisted with on five occasions during her internship that seemed like a million years ago.

Koku insisted on being awake throughout the procedure. She could only give him local anesthesia to deaden the area where she'd be cutting through his skin. Thankfully, the medical kit that had come with the tent and equipment had an instruction book detailing some of the more common operations that could be performed in a field environment. The short review she conducted prior to setting the scalpel to Koku's belly was enough to help her remember what it all looked like, and what things to look for once she got inside.

Kaleel served as her nurse, helping to dab at the blood and hold things when she needed help. He was useless at handing her the different instruments because he didn't know their names.

Angela made it through the operation, removed the diseased appendix and sewed Koku up. When she was done, she washed her hands with alcohol, cleaned the instruments and put them back in the cabinet.

Koku lay on the table, awake, but not as forceful as he'd been before they'd started. He lifted his head just enough to look her way in the overhead light. "You'll take care of the others in the morning," he said and gave a sharp command to his guards, who'd stood back from the operating table the entire time she'd worked on their boss.

The men grabbed her arms and led her from the tent to another, smaller hut with a real door and a lock hasp on the outside.

This was where he'd keep her locked up. If she didn't make her break for it now, she'd never get away. But they had a firm grip on her arms.

Angela pretended to faint, going limp and slipping toward the ground, hoping they'd be surprised and lose their grips on her.

When they did, she rolled sideways, dived between them and made a run for it.

She hadn't gone three steps before they caught her. One snagged her hair and yanked her backward so hard it brought tears to her eyes.

The other tossed her over his shoulder, flung open the hut's door and dumped her on the dirt floor.

She scrambled toward the door, hoping to duck out before they could slam it shut, but she was too late.

The door almost caught her in the face. She fell backward to avoid being hit and landed on her butt.

She could hear the sound of someone slipping a lock through the hasp and clicking it closed.

Not a single glimmer of light made its way into the hut. She didn't know what else was inside with her, and was almost afraid to find out. But she couldn't stand by and do nothing. She had to find a way out before morning. Koku had made it through the operation, but he could still get an infection and die. And as he'd said, if he died, she died.

Angela pushed to her feet and felt her way around the room. The hut was made of what felt like mud bricks and sticks. The roof was thickly woven thatch, and the whole room was musty and filled with mildew. She pushed at the thatch, but it barely budged. If she had something to cut with, she might hack through the thatch and climb out that way. Making her way around the room again, she felt lower, hoping to find an old wooden box she could break up and splinter, forming a kind of wooden knife. But there were no boxes, no pieces of metal, nothing but a pile of straw and the sound of scurrying feet.

She shivered in the darkness, afraid to sit or lie on the ground. Whatever was scurrying might decide she'd make a good meal to nibble on. Rats and mice carried all kinds of disease, and sometimes plague.

No, she'd have to sleep standing up. Hopefully Buck would find her before too long. She'd give anything to lie in his arms and have him chase away all the bad guys and bad things that could happen to her.

She felt her way around to the door again, needing that little bit of spatial grounding to keep her from feeling disoriented and dizzy.

Dear Lord, she'd performed an unassisted operation on a man. She'd cleaned wounds, delivered babies, sewn cuts and even pulled a few teeth, but never had she removed someone's appendix. Her knees shook, then her hands and her entire body trembled as the enormity of what she'd done settled over her.

Though she'd been in Africa for over a year. The closest she'd come to surgery was delivering a breech baby. She hadn't had to perform a cesarean section or any other more invasive procedures. Koku could have died if his appendix had ruptured. He might still die of infection. She'd given him antibiotics just in case, but in a less than sterile environment, anything could happen.

Angela eventually squatted on the floor with her back leaning against the door. She wrapped her arms around her legs and rested her chin on her knees. She struggled to stay awake, but the dark made her feel as though her eyes were already closed, and the drama of the day had taken its toll. She yawned, closed her dry eyes and tried not to think about rodents and men with guns.

Buck would be there soon. She had to believe it. She had to.

A SOUND AT the door made her jerk awake. Angela had no idea how long she'd been asleep. A minute, an hour. She couldn't tell. The hut was just as dark as it had been—so dark she wondered if maybe she was still asleep and she'd dreamed the sound.

Then she heard it again. It sounded like metal on metal. Perhaps the scrape of a key in a lock?

She staggered to her feet and stepped to the side of the door. If someone opened it, she could potentially hide out of sight until he entered, looking for her. Then she could attack him, kick him where it hurt most, hit him over the head as he doubled up and make a run for the woods.

Angela held her breath, waiting for the moment the door opened.

The sound of a metal latch being lifted off the hasp indicated the lock had been removed and the door could be opened.

Ready to spring, Angela waited as the door swung outward.

A light shined into the hut from a flashlight. Then a man stepped through the door, his pant leg tattered and torn.

Kaleel.

He turned the beam to catch his face. He lifted his finger to his lips and jerked his head to the side, indicating she should follow.

What was he doing? Had Koku requested her presence? Should she take this opportunity to make a run for it? Why was Kaleel being so secretive?

He stepped back, looked both directions and waved

for her to come with him. Without trying to grab her as the guards had done, he allowed her to move on her own.

Angela stepped through the door, her gaze darting right and left. The camp had gotten quiet. Men were still awake, gathered around a fire pit where some kind of large animal was roasting on a spit. They had torn off strips of meat and were eating eagerly.

Angela's belly rumbled, but she didn't dare follow her hunger.

Kaleel moved into the shadow of the hut and circled around behind it. He pointed toward a stand of trees a hundred yards away from the camp's edge. "You must go, now."

She faced him, looking for weapons. Was he turning her loose so he could shoot her in the back? Or was he doing the decent thing and letting her go?

"Why?" she asked.

"You saved my leg. You are a good doctor." He nodded toward the woods. "Go."

Angela's heart contracted.

The man had risked his life to save her. If Koku found out Kaleel had released her, he'd kill him.

"Come with me," she urged. "Koku will kill you if he knows you released me."

"He will not know," Kaleel assured her. "I will place the lock on the door as if it was never unlocked."

"But someone is bound to have seen you." Angela couldn't let this man take the fall for her.

"The longer you wait, the more dangerous it becomes. Please, go, before he discovers you are gone."

"Too late," a voice said. "I already know."

Kaleel spun to face the man who'd spoken.

Angela froze, her heart stopping for a second and then racing ahead so fast it made her dizzy.

Standing on the other side of Kaleel were Koku and his two guards. He was leaning heavily on one of the men, holding a handgun in his free hand.

"I do not tolerate betrayal among my soldiers," he said.

Angela stepped forward. "Koku, don't sh—"

The warlord pulled the trigger. The shot rang out, extra loud in the quiet of the night.

Kaleel's eyes rounded. He raised a hand to his chest and crumpled to the ground.

Angela screamed and dived for Kaleel.

Koku's other guard caught her before she could reach the man on the ground. He wrapped his thick arm around her body, trapping both of her arms under one of his.

Angela kicked and fought. "Let me help him. Please." Tears streamed from her eyes as she struggled to free herself from Koku's guard.

"He's dead. And you will be, too, if you don't co-operate."

"He was only trying to help me," Angela whispered.

"That man betrayed me. He didn't deserve to live." He nodded to his guard.

The guard dragged her toward the hut again and flung open the door.

Koku followed, held up by his other guard.

The doctor in Angela wanted to tell Koku that he should be resting to allow his incision time to heal, but she couldn't.

Never had she felt such a rush of white-hot hatred for a man. And she'd saved his life. What kind of monster did that make her? She should have taken the opportunity to kill the man while she had the chance. All the children he'd kidnapped, all the men and women he'd tortured and killed. All those he would subject to his brand of terrorism still to come.

Angela hoped his stomach was full of infection and that he'd rot in hell.

Her chance to escape had passed. Not only had she blown her chance to be free, but she'd cost Kaleel his life by delaying her departure. If she hadn't hesitated, he might have gotten away with his plan.

Her heart heavy, Angela could do little against the superior strength of Koku's guard. Even if she could shake free of his grip, Koku would shoot her like he'd shot his own man, Kaleel.

The only hope she had left was that Buck would find her and free her from Koku's madness, without getting shot himself.

Chapter Thirteen

Buck had been heading for the tent when he saw a man being half led, half carried by two other, more burly men. He appeared to be injured, if the bandages around his belly were any indication. And the bandages meant someone had worked on him. Someone who might be a doctor.

His pulse quickened, and his hand tightened on the rifle he carried.

Angela had to be there. Since the man had just exited the tent, she had to be inside the structure, working on someone else or cleaning up.

His focus on the tent and getting there without being spotted, he barely noticed when the three men disappeared around the side of a thatch-roofed hut.

A gunshot rang out, diverting his attention from the tent back to the hut where the three men had gone. One shot fired. What did that mean?

Buck had been halfway across the clearing leading to the camp when the shot echoed in the night air.

"Things are about to get sticky in Camp Koku,"

Big Jake said. "Lie low until we figure out who fired that round."

Buck dropped in his position and studied the scene.

The men who'd been gathered around the fire had scattered, grabbing their rifles and rushing toward the sound of the gunfire.

"Holy hell, I think we found the doc," Pitbull said.

Buck raised his night-vision goggles and scanned the camp. A pen-like area held dozens of small heat signatures. He'd bet they were the children, corralled like cattle. He swung his head in time to see the three men reappear with another, smaller person in tow. Buck raised his goggles and narrowed his eyes, his heart pounding against his ribs.

Angela.

Buck was halfway to his feet before he realized what he was doing. If one of the men with guns looked his direction, he'd appear as a silhouette. A potential enemy threat. Koku's men didn't strike him as the type to think first, then fire. More likely, they'd shoot first and sift through the bodies later. Buck would be of no use to Angela if someone shot him.

Dropping to the prone position, he watched what was happening.

Men gathered around the two big guys, the injured one and Angela.

The man with the bandages spoke sharply to the gathering of men. They quickly dispersed, returning to the fire, where they laid down their weapons and went back to eating the roasted meat.

The guy holding Angela flung open the door to the hut and tried to throw her inside.

Angela braced her feet on the door frame and refused to go into the hut.

If the situation wasn't so dire, Buck would have chuckled at her bold determination.

That's when he noticed the man with the bandages held a gun in his hand, and he pointed it at Angela.

"We could use that diversion about now. Angela's in trouble. I'm taking the shot," he said into his microphone. He lay against the ground, sighted in on the man holding the gun and squeezed the trigger.

Just as his finger tightened on the trigger, the man holding the bandaged guy shifted, placing his body in between the guy holding the gun and Buck's bullet. The person who'd been holding up the bandaged dude jerked, let go of his charge and toppled to the ground like a felled tree.

"Damn," Buck muttered. He sighted in again, but he'd missed his opportunity to take down the man holding the gun pointed at Angela.

Before Buck could get his original target in his sights, the man grabbed Angela and held his gun to her temple. He pulled her with him toward the larger building.

Once again, the men surrounding the fire pit grabbed their weapons and raced toward the man and Angela.

The other big guy who'd originally been holding onto Angela used his body as a shield to protect the man now holding a gun to Angela's head.

Buck would bet his best rifle that the man threatening Angela was Koku.

Fiery rage ripped through Buck. He rose from his position and ran toward the camp, keeping low but hardly hiding as he raced toward Koku and Angela.

"Buck, what the heck are you doing? Get down!" Big Jake said. "T-Mac, now would be a good time to let loose that diversion."

Before Big Jake finished giving the command, an explosion lit up the night.

Out of the corner of Buck's eye, he could see T-Mac had made it to one of the trucks in the camp. Moments later, that truck exploded, sending parts flying into the air.

Men yelled and shots were fired as Koku's soldiers panicked and ran in all directions. Soon they were racing for the safety of the trees. Some even abandoned their weapons to keep from slowing down in their flight away from the destruction.

Under the cover of the explosions and resulting flames, Buck ran across the camp, hugging the shadows of the few buildings and tents until he was within a couple yards of Koku and Angela.

Buck dropped beside a pile of boards and tin, assumed a kneeling, supported position, aimed his rifle at Koku, and cursed. He couldn't take the shot for fear of hitting Angela.

Meanwhile the members of his team were closing in on those of Koku's soldiers who'd remained to fight the threat they had yet to identify. To start with, all they knew was that things were exploding around them.

The SEAL team picked them off until the last few threw down their weapons and ran for the woods.

Which left Koku, his bodyguard and Angela.

"I'll shoot her!" Koku shouted.

"The hell you will!" Angela jammed her elbow into the man's bandaged belly, ducked her head away from the handgun and twisted backward out of Koku's grip.

The bodyguard dived for her as a shot rang out. All three of them fell to the ground.

Too far away from Angela to do anything, Buck leaped to his feet and ran, his throat tight, his heart squeezing in his chest.

Had Angela been hit? He couldn't tell. All he could see was the bodyguard, piled on top of Koku and Angela. No one was moving.

As he reached them, Buck could see a hand, holding a gun, rise out of the pile.

He dived to the side as Koku fired. The bullet grazed his shoulder, but he was on his feet before Koku could aim and fire again.

Koku turned the gun toward Angela, who lay trapped beneath the big bodyguard.

Buck did the only thing he could—he threw himself onto Koku to deflect the bullet from hitting Angela.

The gun went off.

Buck held still, waiting for the pain. When it didn't come, he rolled to the side.

Koku lay still on the ground. Buck kicked the handgun from his grip, sending it flying into the darkness.

He couldn't see Angela's eyes, and he couldn't tell if she was moving. He slung his rifle over his shoulder, grabbed hold of the bodyguard and dragged his dead weight off Koku and Angela.

If Koku so much as blinked, he'd shoot the bastard.

Finally, he was able to lift Angela into his arms. "Angela? Sweetheart, tell me you're okay. Please."

She smiled up at him. "I think I passed out. I couldn't breathe with that man lying on top of me. And then I thought Koku shot you. Then everything went blank."

"You weren't hit, were you?" He silently cursed the darkness, wishing he could shine a searchlight over her body to make sure she wasn't bleeding.

"No. I'm fine now that I can breathe." She wrapped her arms around his neck and kissed his lips. "I was determined to live. I have so much I want to say to you."

He kissed her back and set her on her feet. "Hold that thought. We need to make sure you and all the kids are safe."

Angela grinned, the white of her teeth the only indication of her expression in the darkness. "I feel safer already."

There were still sounds of gunfire and people yelling. Buck couldn't relax until Angela was safely out of Koku's camp.

"Sweetheart, standing around with bullets flying

is never a good idea. We should go." He slid his rifle off his shoulder and held it in his right hand, and secured Angela's hand in his left.

ANGELA HELD ON to Buck, ready to go anywhere he wanted her to. As they stepped over Koku's bodyguard, something snagged her ankle, making her trip and fall on top of the dead man.

If not for her hold on Buck's hand, she'd have faceplanted in the dirt. A shot exploded in the darkness, so loud and so close it rang in Angela's ears.

Buck released her hand, staggered backward, steadied himself and raised his rifle.

Angela started to rise.

"Stay down!" Buck shouted.

Her heart hammering in her chest, Angela rolled off the bodyguard onto her back on the ground and looked up in time to see Koku sitting up, aiming a small handgun at Buck. He fired the weapon at the same time Buck pulled the trigger on his rifle and sent several rounds into the warlord's chest.

Koku fell back and lay still on the ground.

Angela pushed to her feet, her pulse nowhere close to returning to normal. "Is he dead? Did you kill him?"

Buck didn't answer.

Turning, Angela was just in time to see Buck drop to his knees and keel over, still holding his rifle, but also clutching a hand to his midsection.

"Buck!" Angela dropped to her knees beside him, forcing back the panic and drawing on every bit of knowledge she'd gained in school and working as a doctor. She ripped open his jacket and shirt, pushing the fabric out of the way with her fingers. "Do you still have that flashlight?"

"Inside pocket of my jacket," Buck said through clenched teeth.

She fumbled through his jacket, located the flashlight and shined it down at the wound. Even with the little bit of light, she couldn't see the damage. She needed more light and an operating room. For the moment, all she could do was stop the bleeding by applying pressure. "I need your help, so stay with me."

"Yes, ma'am," Buck said, his voice weak.

"Put your hand here." She guided him, placing his hand over the wound. "Press down."

He did as she'd told him, but she didn't know how long he'd remain alert.

Angela pulled the knife out of the scabbard on his belt and jabbed it into her shirt. Once she got the tear started, she ripped several inches off the hem, ripped it again and folded one half into a pad, the other half into a strip she could use to secure the pad to his belly.

She replaced his bloodied hand with the pad, holding it down to apply pressure. "Graham, stay with me."

He lay still, making her wonder if he'd passed out. "I'm not going anywhere," he finally muttered.

"Where's your team? I could use a little help to get you to the operating room."

"Operating room?" He chuckled. "Now I know I'm dreaming. Take my headset."

She touched his face and slid her hands over his head until she found the headset. She removed it and placed it over her ears. "Hello?"

"Who's this?"

"This is Angela. Buck was shot. We need help."

"Where are you?"

She glanced around, only then aware of where they were. To Angela, it seemed like ages ago that Koku's bodyguard had tried to lock her in her cell. "In the shadow of the small hut with the thatched roof."

"I'll be right there. The others are still mopping up what's left of the resistance."

They disconnected, and Angela returned her attention to Buck. "I don't know who was talking, but he said he'd be right here."

"Probably Big Jake." Buck tried to sit up.

"What are you doing?" She pressed her hands on his chest, keeping him down. "You could be bleeding internally. I need you to lie still so that you don't bleed to death."

"Would you miss me?"

"Damn right, I would." She glared at him, though he couldn't see her face in the darkness. "You are not leaving me again, in any way, form or fashion. I'm not letting you."

"You tell him, Doc," a voice said behind her.

Angela almost cried in relief, seeing the dark form of a man decked out in combat gear.

Keeping her voice calm, she stood. "We need to get him to the hospital tent as soon as possible."

Another man's shadowy figure appeared behind Big Jake's. "What's happening? I heard Buck was down."

"Not for long," Buck answered from the ground.

Angela recognized the newcomer by his voice as T-Mac.

"Koku had a hospital tent set up. If we could get Buck there, I can examine his wound in better lighting."

"Let's do this." T-Mac handed her his rifle. "Cover us while we're hauling this guy's sorry ass over to the tent."

Angela fumbled with the rifle. "I don't know how to operate this."

Buck chuckled briefly, the sound cut off in a moan. "Just point and shoot," he managed before going limp.

The two SEALs still standing each slid their arms beneath Buck's shoulders and legs and lifted him in a fireman's seated carry.

"Lead the way," Big Jake ordered.

Carrying the rifle with her hands on the grip, finger on the trigger, Angela led the men to the hospital tent, visible in the light from the fire pit.

Once inside, she had them deposit Buck on the operating table.

"There's a generator somewhere around here. It powers the lights," she said. "Find it and get it started. I need light."

Big Jake chuckled. "Yes, ma'am."

"T-Mac, can you put pressure on the wound with one hand and hold this flashlight with the other while I get him out of some of these clothes?"

"Yes, ma'am," T-Mac answered. He took over, pressed down on the wound and shined the light over Buck's belly, while Angela cut away his shirt and unbuttoned his pants.

"Had I known how easy it was to get a girl to undress me, I'd have shot myself in the gut a long time ago," T-Mac teased.

Any other time, Angela would have laughed, but not now. Not when Buck's life potentially hung in the balance.

The generator roared to life, and seconds later, lights filled the small tent.

Angela breathed a small sigh of relief and hurried to the cabinet with all the medical supplies and surgical instruments.

She pulled out everything she could think of that she might need to work on Buck, loaded it onto a tray and carried it to the operating table.

She didn't know how Koku had managed to steal all of the supplies, but at that moment she was glad he had. Now, she only had to draw on her limited surgical experience to do whatever it took to make certain Buck lived.

Her hand shook as she scrubbed the area around the wound with a gauze pad and Betadine solution.

A hand caught her wrist and held it.

Startled, she jerked her hand back.

"Hey, beautiful," Buck said.

"Oh, sweet heaven," she exclaimed. "You scared the bejesus out of me."

"Sorry. I just wanted to let you know I was still around, and whatever you do, I know it will be your best."

Her vision clouded as tears welled in her eyes. "I hope whatever I do is enough."

Big Jake hurried into the operating room. "The helicopters are on the way."

"Anyone else injured?" Buck asked.

"Only a few scrapes and bruises. Koku's men were so confused by the explosions, they didn't have time to react."

Buck nodded. "Good."

"We'll have a medic here in a minute to assist the doctor," Big Jake added.

Buck didn't look to Big Jake as he spoke. His gaze remained on Angela. "I have all the medical assistance I need right here." He raised her hand to his lips and pressed a kiss to her palm. "Don't look so worried, sweetheart. I'm going to be all right."

"God, I hope you're correct in that assumption." She wasn't feeling quite as confident. "I'm not a surgeon."

"No, but you were top of our class in medical school." He smiled. "You've got this."

She nodded. Whatever she found, she'd deal with and stabilize him long enough to get him back to proper medical care. "Thanks," she said. "Now shut up and let me concentrate."

Buck winked, threw up a salute and responded with a sharp, "Yes, ma'am."

The medic arrived and helped establish an IV of fluids, then assisted by handing her instruments when she asked for them.

Less than an hour later, she'd removed the bullet, ascertained that none of his vital organs had been hit and he was going to be okay. She sewed him up, applied a bandage and kissed him soundly before allowing his friends to load him onto the helicopter that would take him to Camp Lemonnier, where a surgeon would double-check her work and hopefully fix anything she might have missed.

Big Jake oversaw Buck's movement on a stretcher from the field hospital to the helicopter, walking alongside Angela as she held Buck's hand all the way.

Once they loaded Buck into the helicopter, Angela stepped in for a moment. "You know I can't go with you, don't you?"

Buck held tightly to her hand. "You're staying to help the children, aren't you?"

She nodded. "I have to. Now that I know you're going to be okay, they need someone to see to their welfare."

Buck nodded. "I don't like it, but I understand."

She pressed a kiss to his lips. "I'll see you soon. At least I hope I will."

"We'll figure it out. I promise." He gripped her hand, refusing to release it for the moment. "I'm not leaving because I want to. If they'd let me stay, you know I would."

She raised his hand to her cheek. "I know. And you know I'd go with you if others didn't need me more desperately, don't you?"

He nodded. "It's who you are. You have a heart the size of Africa. It's why I love you."

Her pulse thundered. He'd said he loved her.

"I hate to break this up, but we need to get ol' Buck here back to Djibouti," Big Jake said. "Commander's orders."

Angela kissed him once more and climbed down from the helicopter.

Big Jake exited the aircraft as well.

"Aren't you going with him?" she asked.

"Diesel and Harm will escort him all the way and make sure he doesn't pinch any nurses." Big Jake chuckled. "He'll be champing at the bit to get back here, but he needs to rest for a little while before rejoining the ranks. In the meantime, we have a bunch of kids to sort through and return to their parents. Our commander authorized me to leave a contingent of men to supervise the deconstruction of this camp and the placement of these children."

Angela's heart swelled. "Remind me to thank your commander and the US Navy for their contribution to making this a better world for these kids."

Big Jake saluted. "Yes, ma'am."

They stood for a moment in the blast of air, dust and debris kicked up by the helicopters as they lifted off the ground and flew into the graying light of dawn. Angela prayed for their swift return to civilization and proper medical care. When they'd disappeared on the horizon, Angela clapped her hands together. "Let's get to work." She wouldn't have time to dwell on what would happen between her and Buck. The children needed her undivided attention. She'd have time later to sort through her feelings and decide what to do next.

One thing was certain—she wanted to be with Buck. She still needed to have that talk with him and tell him how she felt. Preferably when he was conscious and able to understand the depth of her feelings for him.

She loved him and would take any time she could have with him.

Chapter Fourteen

Buck had to admit he wasn't the best patient. He'd given hell to the nurses who'd been assigned to see to his wound care and medications. He'd been insubordinate to the doctor who outranked him, threatening on more than one occasion to leave the small hospital before he'd been properly discharged.

When the doctor had suggested he be transported to the next level of care in Landstuhl, Germany, he'd had a conniption fit and nearly wrecked the IV stand, vital-signs monitors and everything around his bedside.

The nurses had to call in two men from security forces to hold him down while they sedated Buck.

Yeah, he'd been an ass, but all he wanted was to be released and find his way back to South Sudan, where half of his team was still assisting with the evacuation and placement of over thirty boys who'd been stolen from their families to man Koku's army.

Then there were the boys between the ages of eleven and seventeen who'd been brainwashed who had to be dealt with. They didn't know how to fend for themselves and would have gone rogue without some kind of program put in place to take the weapons and militant attitudes out of their hands and minds.

The US Army Special Forces unit would work with the South Sudanese Army and UNICEF to provide the psychological support to prepare them for return to civilian life and their families. Most of the children wanted to go home and were eager to get an education.

The navy SEALs stayed several days to ensure Koku's men didn't return to retake the camp and children. They would hand off their responsibilities once the Special Forces units were in place to provide security during the demobilization of the child soldiers.

Buck had been receiving periodic reports from T-Mac and Big Jake. Angela had done her part to treat the sick and injured and had helped set up a medical facility to take care of the children while their placement was still being determined.

Buck's belly still hurt, but not enough to keep him down. He'd argued at length with the doctor, insisting he was well enough to return to duty and South Sudan to assist with the ongoing efforts.

"Your team will return soon. If your wound is properly healing by then, we'll talk about your return to duty" was all the doctor could promise.

His commander had been by a couple times to check on his progress and to admonish him for giving the medical staff hell. "You must be feeling better to be such a pain in the ass," he declared.

"Sir, I just want to be with my team," he'd responded.

"Your team? Or the pretty doctor?" His commander hadn't bothered hiding his grin. "You'll stay here until the doctor releases you."

"Sir, at the least, I could recuperate in my quarters. I don't need to take up space that could be used on someone in worse shape than I am."

His commander glanced around at the empty beds. "We're not exactly bursting at the seams."

So Buck took to pacing the length of the ward, dragging his IV cart along until they finally unhooked the IV and gave him permission to wear his gym shorts instead of mooning the nurses.

On the third day in the hospital, Buck was ready to climb the walls. His doctor came in and declared that his wound was healing nicely.

"I'll sign your release if you promise to take it easy for the next two weeks. You can't return to duty until then."

"Well, then, what the hell good is my release?" Buck demanded.

"You can spend it moping in your quarters, or you can join your team at the All Things Wild Resort," a voice said from behind him.

Buck spun, then winced when the movement reminded him of his stitches.

Big Jake stood in the doorway, still wearing his four-day-old uniform, covered in dirt and smelling pretty ripe.

Buck couldn't stop himself from grinning. "Big Jake, you old son of a bitch." He crossed to the man, and gave him a huge bear hug, causing more pain when he again pulled at the stitches on his belly. "When did you get back?"

"Just a few minutes ago. I came straight here, because I knew you'd be champing at the bit for news and probably giving the medical staff fits."

Heat climbed up Buck's neck. "Yeah, well, they wouldn't let me get back to the action."

"The action has been turned over to other people now. I spoke to the CO, and we've been granted a pass for the next week. Like I said when I walked in, you can spend your time recuperating in your quarters, or you can join us back at All Things Wild."

Buck set his friend and teammate to arm's length. "I don't understand."

"Since our rest and relaxation was cut short, our commander is going to allow us to continue our vacation back at the resort. He even arranged for helicopter transport to get us there."

"He did?" Buck shook his head. "And he's letting me go?"

"No, he told us to take you before he court-martials you. So get dressed, pack your bag and let's go. The chopper leaves in fifteen minutes."

"What if I don't want to go?" Buck asked.

"You'd rather recuperate in your quarters?" Big Jake's brows rose. "What happened to the Buck I knew who'd rather climb a mountain than be confined to quarters?"

Buck shrugged. "I might want to go somewhere else."

Big Jake shook his head. "If you're thinking of

hopping on a plane to go to South Sudan, don't bother. The good doctor isn't there. She's not working for Doctors Without Borders anymore."

"What?" Buck frowned. "Why? Where is she? What happened down there?"

"All I know is, once they turned over the children to UNICEF, they brought in an entirely new crew of doctors and nurses. She was relieved of her duties."

"And she didn't leave a forwarding address?"

"I don't know that she has one yet." Big Jake crossed his arms over his chest. "So, what's it to be? Are you staying here and moping, or are you going to recuperate in Kenya at the resort?" He glanced over his shoulder and lowered his voice to a whisper. "If I were you, I'd go. The CO isn't too happy with you right now. He says you're a terrible patient and he's ready to send you back to the States."

Buck's chest tightened. Angela was gone from South Sudan. He didn't know how to contact her in Africa or in the States. How was he going to keep his promise to see her soon? With his commander breathing fire about his behavior, he didn't have much of a choice. He could stay and risk being sent back to the States, or go with his team to the resort and recuperate there. "I'll be ready in fifteen."

"Make that thirteen. We've been yapping that long." Big Jake spun and started for the door. "I'm jumping in the shower during that time."

"Good, you smell like a goat."

"Yeah, you would know," he called over his shoulder. "You could use a shower, too."

His nurse was there when he turned around with his discharge instructions and a big grin. "Can't say I'm sad to see you go."

His cheeks burned. "Look, I'm sorry I was such a bastard."

"No worries," she said. "We're not always at our best when we're sidelined. Just get well soon and stay out of the hospital." She handed him a T-shirt and flip-flops. "Now go. Your buddy was right—you could use a shower."

Thirteen minutes later, Buck was showered, shaved and dressed in his loosest uniform with the buttons on his pants unbuttoned to keep from rubbing his stitches. He had a gear bag with more clothes, his weapon and a pad of paper and pens. While he was laid up, he planned on writing some letters to Angela. He'd also get online and see if he could find her on social media or look up her address back in the States. There had to be a way to find her. He wouldn't give up until he did. He'd take a month of leave if he needed to and spend it all searching for the only woman he had ever loved.

T-Mac, Diesel, Harm, Big Jake and Pitbull were waiting when he reached the helicopter landing pad. They all shook hands, hugged and joked about his injury and what they wanted to do when they got back to their vacation that had been so rudely interrupted by work.

Buck strapped himself into the shoulder harness and sat back, prepared for a couple hours in the air. His injuries must have taken more out of him than he'd thought, because with the monotonous drone of the rotor blades hitting the air and the roar of the engine, he fell asleep within minutes of liftoff.

T-Mac woke him as they landed on the airstrip near the resort, where they were greeted by Talia Montclair, the owner and operator of the All Things Wild Safari and Resort.

When Buck stepped down from the helicopter, his knees buckled and he would have fallen if Diesel and T-Mac hadn't been there to hook his arms over their shoulders and help him get his feet back under him.

"I don't know what's wrong with me," he muttered. "I feel as weak as a newborn kitten."

"Could be you took a bullet to the belly."

"I've been shot before."

"But not in the gut. It tends to hit you a little harder," Harm said. "Trust me, I've been there, done that. It's not something I care to repeat anytime soon." He smiled as Talia hurried forward. "You're a sight for sore eyes."

The black-haired beauty frowned and hurried forward. "I heard one of you had been injured. That'll teach him to step in front of a bullet." She winked. "If you two could get him to the golf cart, he won't have to walk all the way."

"I can walk," Buck said. "I was just stiff from the ride." He straightened and pushed away from T-Mac and Diesel. "See? Steady as a rock." He swayed slightly and the other two men took a step toward him. "Seriously, I've got this."

"Whatever, but if you face-plant in the dirt and

tear open your stitches," Big Jake said, "you'll be on the first helicopter back to Djibouti."

"I'm not going to face-plant. Hell, I was pacing the hospital back at the base every day I was there. I got at least a couple miles a day of PT."

Big Jake shook his head. "Yeah, yeah. Put your money where your mouth is and get your carcass to the lodge. We have a surprise for you."

Buck stepped out, forcing his stiff legs to work into a rhythm that would take him along the twisting path to the main lodge. "Do I get my same cabin?" he asked.

"Yes, you do. We had a little trouble and the guests who'd been in it left early. You all have the same cabins as before." Talia had sent one of her staff ahead with the golf cart and walked with the men toward the lodge.

When the main building came into sight, Buck had to admit, if only to himself, he was glad he didn't have much farther to go. His legs were shaky, and he would give anything for a seat on a comfy sofa where he could stretch his legs and maybe have a beer.

As he neared the lodge, a large cat detached itself from the bushes and stalked toward him.

Buck ground to a stop and backed up a step, running into T-Mac and Diesel in the process. Then he realized the cat was the leopard that had been raised at the lodge since it was a kitten.

"Mr. Wiggins, you naughty boy." Talia strode up to the animal and scratched him beneath his chin. "What are you doing out of the garden?"

T-Mac clapped a hand on Buck's back. "Don't tell me you forgot about the cat."

"I did. But it's all coming back to me now. I think I'll go straight to my cabin, if it's all the same to you guys. Can the surprise wait until morning?"

"You might be able to wait, but I'm sure Pitbull won't want to."

A woman appeared, coming along the path toward them.

Buck's heart leaped until he realized the tall, lanky woman had sandy-blond hair and was grinning at Pitbull.

"Marly?" Pitbull held open his arms and she ran into them. "I thought you'd be in Nairobi still packing your apartment."

"I got done and shipped my things to the States. When I heard you were coming back to the resort, I hitched a ride with a pilot I knew. And here I am."

Pitbull wrapped his arms around her waist, lifted her off the ground and swung her around. "That's the best surprise yet." He kissed her soundly and set her back on her feet.

Buck watched, his heart sinking lower in his belly to hurt right next to his wound. Pitbull had Marly there to hug and hold. Why had he bothered to come to the resort with his teammates when he could have been just as miserable back in his quarters, where he didn't have to put on a game face?

"Hey, don't look so glum." Talia touched his arm.

"I don't feel much like being around people right now."

"Could you make it through dinner?" Talia asked.

"I had the chef prepare steaks for all of you, just the way you like them."

He was tired, but the thought of sitting among his team while they laughed and joked made him even crankier and less likely to enjoy the meal. What he wanted was to see Angela, to hold her in his arms and tell her everything he hadn't told her and needed to say before she disappeared out of his life again. "I don't think I'll make it through dinner. I'll catch you guys at breakfast."

Big Jake, a few steps ahead of Buck, turned to face him, his mouth open to say something, but was cut off by Talia, who raised her hand.

"Suit yourself," Talia said. "I'll have someone bring a tray of food to your cabin."

"That's not necessary," Buck said. "I can wait to eat until breakfast." He didn't want anyone to bother him. His brand of misery was best spent alone.

She smiled. "I insist. The chef spent a great deal of time and effort to make the meal as special as the men he's cooking for. Now, you go to your cabin and relax. The food tray will be along soon."

"Thanks," he responded with as much enthusiasm as a man heading into the dentist's office.

"I'm going with you," Big Jake said. "We can't have you passing out on the path and being mauled by tame leopards."

"I can get there by myself." He really wanted to be by himself; he suspected he was in for a big old wallow in self-pity and loneliness, and he didn't want his buddies to witness his transgression. God, he wanted to see Angela so badly, he ached in every part of his body.

"Not taking no for an answer." Big Jake walked alongside him as he split off the main path to head toward the cabins.

They walked in silence until they were out of hearing range of the others.

"You miss her, don't you?" Big Jake asked quietly.

Buck's chest hurt with a pain that had nothing to do with the wound in his gut. "Yeah. I hate that I don't know where she is and that I can't even call her."

"What would you say to her if you could find her?"

"What does it matter what I'd say? I have no idea how to find her. I'm going to ask Talia if I can use her computer tomorrow and do some searching online. Damn it!" He pounded his fist into his palm. "I have to find her. I walked out of her life once. I'm not going to do it again. I made a promise."

They'd arrived in front of the cabin he'd used the last time they'd been there. Big Jake laid a hand on his shoulder. "Whatever you do, when you see her again, don't waste time. Tell her how you feel."

"I will. But who knows when that'll be?" Buck pushed open the door and stepped through. He turned back to Big Jake. "I learned something this last mission."

"Yeah? What's that?"

"You have to grab for happiness when you can. And hold on like there might not be a tomorrow."

Big Jake nodded. "In our line of work, that's very true. Tomorrow is never guaranteed."

"And the only easy day was yesterday." Buck sighed. "Remind me of that tomorrow. Thanks for talking me into coming."

"Trust me when I say you'll be glad you did." And with that parting comment, Big Jake left Buck to settle in.

Once inside, Buck bypassed the sofa and headed for the bed, where he could stretch out and give his gut a break from being in a sitting position for two hours on a helicopter. He lay down, intending to rest, not sleep, shielding his eyes from the late-afternoon glare shining through the window. He had lots to think about, but suddenly, he couldn't think anymore.

He must have dozed off, because the next thing he knew, someone had opened the door.

"Put the tray on the table. I'll eat when I feel like it," he said without glancing up from beneath his arm still resting over his eyes. Night had settled in around the cabin, eliminating the need to shield his eyes. When he lowered his arm, he could see the silhouette of a woman in the darkness of the cabin. She set the tray on the table and straightened.

Something about the way she held herself, the way her hair lay around her head and the swell of her hips and breasts struck a chord of recognition. His breath lodged in his throat, and his heart stopped beating.

"You should eat to keep up your strength," she whispered.

"Angela?" He blinked and tried to sit up, forgetting he still had stitches across his belly. He swore and rolled to his side.

By the time he could finally sit on the side of the bed, she was there beside him, switching on the lamp by his bedside. And then she touched his shoulder, spreading fire throughout his mind, body and soul.

"Angela," he breathed as if for the first time, like a baby being born into the world. She was there. Whereas before he'd felt his life had ended, it now had begun, with Angela in it.

He wrapped his arms around her waist and pulled her between his knees, resting his cheek against her breasts. "When? How?" He laughed. "Oh, who cares. You're here now. That's all that matters."

She chuckled and lifted his face to stare into his eyes. "You ruined our surprise."

"Not from where I'm standing. Or sitting." He captured her face in his hands and pulled her down to kiss her like it might be the last kiss they would ever share. He wanted each time he kissed her to be like that. Like every kiss could be their last. He had to make it special, make her love him as much as he loved her.

Never had he been more aware of the fact that tomorrow wasn't guaranteed. He had to take full advantage of today. With this woman. The one he loved.

Chapter Fifteen

Angela had counted every minute between the time she'd watched Buck fly off in that helicopter to when she'd seen him lying in bed in the quaint little cabin at the All Things Wild Resort. Though she'd been busy caring for frightened and confused children, administering aid and comforting those who were so homesick they cried and cried, Buck was always on her mind.

And now he was here, holding her.

"I have to tell you something."

"Wait. I want to say something first." He pushed to his feet, swayed a little and straightened. Then he touched his hand to her cheek, tipping her chin upward so that he could gaze into her eyes.

At first Angela worried he'd read every emotion shining from her face. He'd know without a doubt how much she loved him without her saying a word. But she wanted him to hear it from her lips.

"Let me talk first," he said. "I've been waiting to say this since I saw you in Bentiu protesting the treatment of the refugees and women. I've wanted to tell you this since I left you in Chicago all those years ago. I love you more than any man has ever loved any woman. You are the only woman I've ever loved and ever will. I want you to be in my life. If that means giving up the navy, I'll do it. If you want me to follow you all over the world saving one child at a time, I'll do it. The truth is, I can't live without you. I'd take a bullet for you." He laughed and kissed her lips. "I already have. And I'd do it all over again. Please. Please. Please. Tell me you love me. Even if only half as much as I love you. I'll take it. I'll take anything you'll give me."

Angela's heart swelled so much it hurt her chest to breathe. "Now you shush while I talk." She pressed a finger over his lips. "Do I have your attention?"

"Undivided," he said, his lips moving against her finger, sending electrical surges throughout her body.

"When you left me in Chicago, I thought I would die. You were my first love, my only love and hopefully my last love. I can't give my heart to another when you are the one who holds it in your hands." She leaned up on her toes and kissed his lips. "Please don't walk away from me again."

"Darlin', I couldn't do it again. It nearly ripped me apart the first time. If I hadn't gone into the navy and the SEALs, I would have come completely apart. Leaving you was the hardest thing I'd ever done."

"Good. Don't do it again." She touched her hand to his chest. "My heart can't take it a second time."

"Do you want me to get out of the navy?" he asked.

She shook her head. "Not until you're good and

ready. Not a day sooner. I can survive the loneliness as long as I know you're coming home to me."

"What if I don't come home?" He gathered her closer. "Or rather, if I come home in a body bag?"

She pulled her bottom lip between her teeth, her heart squeezing hard in her chest. "I'll take whatever time I have with you. If something happens and you don't make it… I'll survive. I know I can live without you. I just prefer not to."

"What are you going to do, now that you're leaving Doctors Without Borders?"

She shrugged. "I thought about going back to the States and back to school to become a surgeon."

Buck grinned. "Liked digging around inside me that much?"

She shook her head. "No. I didn't like not knowing exactly what to do with all the parts and pieces inside. I never want to feel that helpless ever again."

"I hear there are some good medical schools in Virginia."

Angela smiled. "I was thinking the same thing. I could be there when you're home from deployment."

"I'd like that a lot."

"Me, too." She touched a finger to his lips. "Now, you need to eat and rest. I want you to be well and fit the next time we make love."

He waggled his brows. "I'm up to it if you are."

She shook her head. "No way. Not until your stitches are out and you're not in jeopardy of reopening your wound. I don't want you hurt because of me."

"I'd be willing to risk it."

"Well, I'm not." She took his arm and guided him to the table and the tray of food. "We'll start one step at a time."

"The commander felt bad about interrupting our vacation. We have all week here," Buck said.

Angela laughed. "That's not how I heard it. I heard you were a cranky patient."

He lifted his chin and grinned down at her. "I like to think that I didn't have the right doctor."

"Is that right?" She crossed her arms over her chest. "And who is the right doctor for you?"

"There's only one doctor who can work on my heart. And that's you, babe."

"Lord help me. I don't ever want to have to work on your heart." She touched his chest.

He captured her hand in his. "You have completely captured my heart." Buck pulled her into his arms. "I love you, Dr. Angela Vega, more than life itself. And I promise to always come back to you from wherever I am in the world."

"I love you, Graham Buckner. And I promise to be there, waiting for you."

* * * * *

COMING SOON!

We really hope you enjoyed reading this book. If you're looking for more romance, be sure to head to the shops when new books are available on

Thursday
9th August

To see which titles are coming soon, please visit
millsandboon.co.uk

MILLS & BOON

LET'S TALK

Romance

For exclusive extracts, competitions
and special offers, find us online:

 facebook.com/millsandboon

@millsandboonuk

@millsandboon

Or get in touch on 0844 844 1351*

For all the latest titles coming soon, visit
millsandboon.co.uk/nextmonth

*Calls cost 7p per minute plus your phone company's price per minute access charge